August 1994

Bill Helfrich:

The Summer of the
PAYMASTER

A. Nielsen

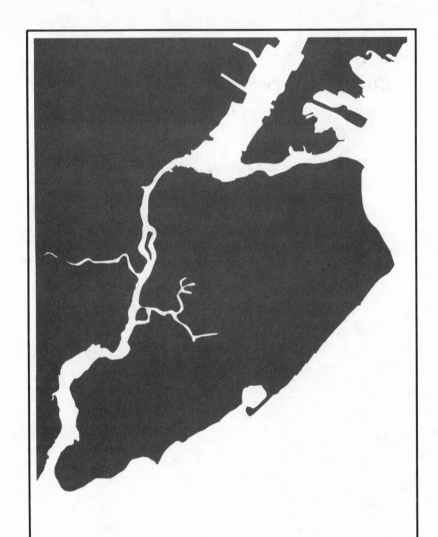

STATEN ISLAND

The SUMMER
of the
PAYMASTER

Alfred Nielsen

W. W. Norton & Company
New York · London

Lyrics on page 286 from "Fun, Fun, Fun." Lyrics and music by Brian Wilson & Mike Love. © 1964 by Irving Music, Inc. (BMI). All rights reserved. International copyright secured. Lyrics on page 160 from "Honeycomb," written by Bob Merrill. © 1954, R 1982 by Golden Bell Songs. All rights reserved. Used by permission.

Printed in the United States of America.

The text of this book is composed in Century Old Style, with the display set in Sprint. Composition and manufacturing by Haddon Craftsmen Inc.
Book design by Charlotte Staub.

First Edition

Library of Congress Cataloging-in-Publication Data

Nielsen, Alfred.
The summer of the paymaster: a novel / Alfred Nielsen.
p. cm.
I. Title.
PS3564.I348S8 1990
813'.54—dc20

ISBN 0-393-02888-7
W.W. Norton & Company, Inc., 500 Fifth Avenue, New York, N.Y. 10110
W.W. Norton & Company, Ltd., 37 Great Russell Street, London WC1B 3NU

1 2 3 4 5 6 7 8 9 0

Dedicated to Mom and Dad, with love

Alfred

The author wishes to thank
Wendy Weil and Mary Cunnane:
they put together the nuts and bolts.

The Summer of the
PAYMASTER

Part One

Go build you a log cabin
  on a mountain so high,
and hear the feathered warbird's cry
  as she goes screaming by.

—Richard Fariña,
  from *The Falcon*

Chapter 1

1

Pete's gas station was located on Staten Island alongside the world's largest garbage dump. The mountain of garbage which had come to be collected at the Fresh Kills landfill was so high that it was a topological feature on maps of the eastern seaboard. It wouldn't surprise me at all if one day I was to pick up the newspaper and learn that an airplane bound for Kennedy Airport had flown into the side of it.

This enormous collection of garbage didn't bother Pete at all. For him the rotting stench of garbage had become the sweet smell of success. A regular convoy of garbage trucks came and went all day from the dump, and when the drivers found themselves too low on fuel to make it all the way back to the city's motor pool in Red Hook, they pulled into Pete's to fill up. Throughout the long monotonous days I was to spend pumping gas at Pete's there seemed always to be at least one of these malodorous behemoths panting at the diesel pumps, and at the end of every month Pete drew up a bill for the City of New York and sat cackling over his profits.

On days when the gas station was downwind from the garbage, which seemed more often than not, Pete would breathe even more deeply, taking in exaggerated volumes of air and grinning at me because he knew that I thought he was crazy.

"You get a good snootful of that, Summerhelp?" he'd ask me. "That's money in the bank. That ole sweet roll. The more garbage, the bigger my bankroll; the smellier it is out here, the richer I get."

"Well," I told him one hot day in July when the air was fetid, "it smells to me like you're a millionaire."

"Not yet, Summerhelp. I'm still working on six figures, if you know what I mean. But give it time; give it time. There's that swim club in Great Kills didn't want me as a member five years ago. Today I'm on the board of directors."

This was the summer of 1968, which was not an especially good year, and I had returned to Staten Island because Jimmy Dietz, who had been my best friend and blood brother, would soon arrive home from Vietnam.

Jimmy had won the Silver Star, which didn't surprise those of us who knew him. He was hero material if anyone was. He'd once risked his neck just to swim after a little kid's beach ball. We'd all started out after the beach ball—me and Jimmy and Corney and the rest—because the little kid's sister was gorgeous. But long after the rest of us had given up and swum back to climb the pilings, Jimmy was still out there. We craned our necks to follow the beach ball and Jimmy's bobbing head and arms until finally the ball and Jimmy were too small to be seen. He eventually returned in a motorboat that had spotted him down in Princess Bay. He had the beach ball alongside him on the seat of the boat. He'd done all that and then didn't even try to pick up the kid's sister.

There was also this occasion when a big fire swept through the southern half of Staten Island, which at that time was mostly woods and fields, and it had been such a tremendous fire that those of us who had seen it would always call it the Big Fire. No one ever discovered how or where it had started, but by the time the smoky ashes sat cooling two days later fire companies from Manhattan and Brooklyn had been called in to control it.

I was with Jimmy the day of the Big Fire. We were out at this cabin we'd built in the woods with the rest of the guys. The air became clouded and it smelled as if everyone had decided to burn their leaves at once. I stood on the peaked roof of the cabin while Jimmy climbed the tall oak tree alongside to take a look around.

"It's a fire, all right," he said. "And it's big."

You could believe that if Jimmy described it as big, it was that and more.

"Let's go," he said excitedly, clambering out of the tree.

"Go?" I asked. "Where?"

"To see it."

We took to the paths through the woods that we knew so well and emerged on the old WPA roads. There was the fire, directly in front of us. Bright orange flames consumed the trees like kindling sticks. The old discarded tires by the side of the road burned with a black pungent soot and the fire raced across the nearby fields like waves on the ocean. I could feel the heat of it on my face and it took my breath away.

Jimmy ran toward it. I swear he did. He ran right into the damn thing. He couldn't help himself. He had to get as close to it as the heat and flames would allow. He disappeared into the smoke and I stood there indecisively for a moment and then, crazily, followed him.

There was a helicopter overhead and we could hear sirens everywhere around us. On either side of us the woods were engulfed in tall sheets of fire. The smoke burned my eyes and choked me. I thought this was it. We would die out here.

We emerged onto Drumgoole Boulevard. To our left was a ranch-style house. It was on fire. On the street in front of the house stood a woman. She was a plump woman and she wore an apron. She was weeping and clutching at her hair. We ran over and when she saw us she pointed to the house and said, "My children! My children!"

Jimmy hesitated only long enough to ask, "How many?"

"I don't know where," she cried hysterically, not understanding what Jimmy had asked. "Somewhere. Oh, God!"

"How many?" Jimmy repeated forcefully.

She understood. "Two," she wept. "Two."

Jimmy ran into the house.

I stood there, my heart pounding. My eyes watered and my lungs felt painful. I was frightened, yet in the next moment I found myself running into the house behind Jimmy. I entered the house yelling out his name. I couldn't see a thing. I coughed and thought I would vomit. In front of me the wall suddenly burst into flame and I retreated out of the house. I could smell my hair. It had singed.

I stood out front with the woman. A handful of neighbors had arrived. There was nothing anyone could do. Flames were shooting from the windows. There was an explosion in the garage and a fireball erupted, bursting the glass. It was intensely hot now and we all backed away. Up and down the street other houses caught on fire. It looked like the end of the world.

Then Jimmy appeared coming down the street carrying one of the kids and leading the other by the hand. He'd managed to find them in the house and then had found a way out. I don't know how. But I never did know how Jimmy managed to do the things he did.

When he won the Silver Star there was an article about him in *Time* magazine. I hadn't known anything about this article, and I never made a habit of reading *Time,* but it so happened that I was standing on a checkout line in a supermarket in Corvallis, Oregon, when out of boredom I plucked the current issue from the rack and opened it at random.

There was Jimmy Dietz, staring back at me.

It was the standard Marine Corps shot: dress uniform, ramrod-straight shoulders, a face that belonged on a bronze medallion.

Below the photograph was the story. Jimmy had been out with a team of forward observers when the North Vietnamese launched the Tet Offensive. He and his squad had been trapped but they took evasive action and frustrated all attempts by a company of North Vietnamese regulars to hunt them down. Meanwhile they were able to radio in vital information on the movement of troop columns toward Khe Sanh, itself under siege. The Vietnamese knew that Jimmy and his squad were out there in the hills and began a search. After three days, and with some help from Russian electronic snoop ships out in the Gulf of Tonkin, they closed in on him. Jimmy finally had no recourse but to call for an artillery strike on his own position. It was night and he and his squad burrowed into their shallow foxholes and expected not to live to see the day. But once the barrage lifted they discovered their pursuers had retreated. At daybreak a chopper appeared to haul them out—back to Khe Sanh. Jimmy earned the Silver Star and the rank of lieutenant for what *Time* called his "brave, cool-headed" leadership.

From what the article said it appeared that Jimmy would be returning home in early June. His year in Nam would be over and he would lead a gala Fourth of July parade to dedicate a new Little League field. The Little League field was to be named in memory of Cornelius

Xavier Walsh. Corney. "One of his boyhood companions who was killed in action in Vietnam," it read.

The country had needed and wanted a hero's story, and Jimmy had provided it. As I said, it came as no surprise to those of us who knew him.

When I learned that Jimmy would be returning to Staten Island I felt I should also return. I wanted to see him and tell him that I held no grudge for those few bad things that had happened between us.

That was the plan. And although I have never been one to follow through on plans, I found myself more or less pushed into this one. A day or two after having read about Jimmy, I returned from work one evening to discover that the young woman I was living with had put a new lock on the door and my belongings on the stoop. She had said during our difficult and tempestuous days together that she would never walk out on a relationship. She was true to her words. The note on my duffel bag read, "Sorry you decided to leave."

So it seemed that my karma would take me east, back to Staten Island, a place I had once loved with all my heart, to see a friend whom I had more or less lost.

I hitched rides across the country, and I was traveling somewhere in Iowa with a man who sold seed and silos when the news came across the radio about the assassination of Martin Luther King, Jr. The man told me to avoid the cities on the rest of my journey. "There's bound to be trouble," he advised. "It's not a good time."

He was right.

2

I never discovered how it was that Deluxe knew I was working at Pete's, although something tells me that Deluxe was a vital link in the grapevine that kept track of who worked at which gas station.

Deluxe may have had a real name at one time, the sort of name mothers customarily give their little boys at birth, but ever since I've known him, from the days when he played poker out behind the hard-

ware store with Sliver and Smitty and that rough bunch we called the
Purps, he's been Deluxe, plain and simple.

He turned up one night at Pete's in the middle of April after a
heavy spring rain. The air was cool and damp in the wake of the
downpour, and because Pete's place was alongside the garbage dump,
which had been situated on a marsh, the road out front was under an
inch or more of water.

I had just treated myself to a can of orange soda from the vending
machine when Deluxe sped in behind the wheel of a tooled-up 1958
Chevy. He came to an abrupt stop, not six inches from running me
over. He leaned out the window and smiled his gap-toothed smile and
asked, "Hey, Chun—what's news?"

His radio was blasting and his glass-pack muffler was grumbling
like Vesuvius. We had to shout at each other to be heard. He said he
had come by just to see me. For a moment I felt honored. God only
knows why. I had never liked Deluxe.

He sat there in the car and spat out the window through the wide
space between his front teeth and said he wanted me to stop over his
place one night. He said he'd get his old lady to cook some spaghetti or
hot dogs and we could drink beer and get all kinds of shitfaced and talk
over old times.

I was immediately suspicious. In the "old times" Deluxe hadn't
given a shit if I was dead or alive. It was Jimmy Dietz who everyone
wanted to see in those days. I just happened to be wherever Dietz
was.

"How's about tomorrow night?" asked Deluxe.

He was genuinely eager about this. I couldn't figure out why.

"Okay," I said. "Tomorrow night."

He told me the address and said, "Seven o'clock."

"Yeah," I agreed.

He pumped the gas pedal, and the mufflers growled and smoked.
Then he popped the clutch. The car fishtailed wildly across the blacktop and lurched out into the four-lane.

Pete came over to me. He wasn't working. He never worked
nights. His nights were devoted to parties at the swim club or trips to
the racetrack. He only came around at night to make sure I was working.

"You're wasting a lot of time on nonpaying customers, Summer-help," he said.

"He's a friend of mine," I explained, shocked that I had actually come to Deluxe's defense.

"Doesn't surprise me," said Pete. "Tell me—does he buy gas or just siphon it at night?"

"He wouldn't bother with the siphon. He'd just steal the car."

3

There was this tradition at the gas station, started no doubt by Pete, and the tradition held that if a guy stayed around to eat lunch, he had to eat at the front desk.

Considering that there was only a half hour for lunch, it was diffi-cult to go off somewhere else to eat, especially if, as in my case, you didn't have wheels. Forced to stay around the gas station for lunch, there was no more likely place to eat than the front desk. Every other place was greasy or smelled like garbage.

There was a problem in eating at the front desk, however. The cash register was there, as were all the account cards, and Pete was skilled at prodding the guy who was eating lunch to ring up a few sales, jot down a few charges, copy the plate numbers of the garbage trucks, stack cans of brake fluid and boxes of wiper blades. Pete would even stick a battery at your feet and ask you to juice it up with fresh sulfuric acid while you ate.

I'll admit that I had been at loggerheads with Pete from the start. The day I'd heard a stranger up at Art's Diner say that the Mobil station on Arthur Kill Road was looking for help, I finished my ham-burger and fries and wandered down there. Pete had looked me up and down, finally asking, "How old are you?"

"Twenty-one."

"Why ain't you in the service?"

"I was in the big one."

"What's that?"

"World War Two. Maybe that was the Big Two; I don't know."

"Asshole," he said. He smiled like a simpleton, mockingly. He rubbed his hands together with a mad sort of glee. "Wise guy, huh? I don't hire too many wise guys."

"How many is too many?"

He delighted in my sarcasm. "We're going to have a good old time together, ain't we? Let me tell you, Summerhelp, all's you got to do to stay on my good side is pump gas and kiss ass. You pump *my* gas into *their* cars and kiss their ass while you're doing it. If you get good at pumping gas, I'll let you fix a flat tire here and there, maybe even give you ten cents more an hour. What's more, if you get real good at kissing customers' asses—and I mean top-shelf ass-kissin', Summer-help, not that shit you picked up in college, brown-nosing—I just might let you kiss my ass."

I laughed. There was nothing else to do. I figured he must have taken some voltage under the hood of a car one day and it had re-versed the polarity of his brain. He was nuts.

"What're you doin' with all that friggin' hair?" he scoffed. "You get it caught in a belt pulley and your face comes flying off, don't be lookin' to sue me. You got no business being that close to an engine anyway. Let the mechanics fuck up the engines. You'll find plenty to fuck up on your own. Don't forget, you're here—"

"—to pump gas and kiss ass," I put in.

"My, my. What a smart little Summerhelp we got us." He raised the volume of his voice so that the mechanics could hear. "Put that hair in a ponytail or wear curlers. You got me?"

The mechanics chortled.

For the first few days I ate my lunch at the front desk, but I quickly learned that Pete intended to hound me back to work in any way he could.

I tried to find a spot out back to eat, but the smell of the dump permeated the air. The meat in my sandwich smelled . . . well, dead.

One day at noon I ducked into the compressor room. It was di-rectly off the repair bay, and inside there was an air compressor and stacks of cases of oil and other supplies. I climbed atop the cases of oil and realized I had discovered for myself the single most comfortable little cave the gas station had to offer. The sunlight barely penetrated the opaque window to my right, so that even on the hottest of days the cinder-block room was cool. Though it was dim, I had always been a

guy to eat my carrots, so I was able to read by the light of the single
fluorescent tube overhead, and in here the annoying clang of the bell
hose that summoned me to pump gas was reasonably muted. Except
for the moments when the compressor kicked on, it was a quiet,
private place.

My comfortable little kingdom didn't go unnoticed for long. Within
two or three days Pete started finding reasons to visit the compressor
room during my lunch break. It so happened that the paper towels for
the rest rooms were stored there, as were the boxes of gritty pow-
dered soap we used to scour the grease from our hands at the end of
the day. Until recently Pete had always checked on these things early
in the day. Now it seemed that noon was the best time for taking
inventory.

I was atop the stack of oil cases one noon, reading this very interesting book about Einstein's theory of relativity and how he'd proved
that we don't live in three dimensions of space and a separate dimen-
sion of time, but rather in a "four-dimensional continuum," when Pete
came in and asked, "Did you clean the ladies' room this morning?"

It was a question that didn't seem appropriately placed. I'd come
to the compressor room eager for an opportunity to read this book. Of
the few courses I'd taken in college and the fewer still I'd enjoyed,
there had been one entitled "Topics in Space and Time." It was given
by this extremely strange professor but proved to be the next-best
thing to being kidnapped by a flying saucer. The book I was reading
had been written by the same man, that odd-ball professor, and he
very clearly demonstrated how motion through time was no different
from motion through space and vice versa. And he even said that
physics was unable to prove that time moves in an arrow toward the
future. He said it could twist and turn in many directions. In light of all
that, who cared about a clean ladies' room?

"Did you hear me?" asked Pete.

"Yes."

"And?"

"Yes. I cleaned it."

"Mopped and dried, just like I showed you?"

"Yes."

"And the men's?"

"Yes."

"Just like I showed you?"

"Go look," I said. "It's clean enough to crap in—I swear it."

He hesitated. "It better be," he said.

I tried to continue reading, but Pete asked, "What about the machines? You fill up the tampons and the condoms?"

"Condom machines are illegal in this state, Pete."

"Jumpin' friggin' Jesus, I'm a felon."

He poked around, checked the fuses, eyed the gauge on the compressor. As he left, he said, "Carry a few of these boxes of 10W-40 out, Summerhelp."

"What time is it?"

"What time is it? Buy a watch."

He stood there and studied me a moment. I studied him in return. He was a thickly built man, probably quite strong. I figured he was about ten years older than my father, which would make him fifty-five. He had fleshy jowls with cindery whiskers, thinning hair that he kept hidden beneath his cap, and hands with a calloused hide thick as a four-ply tire. There were stray wisps of hair at the end of his nose that he shaved frequently, and tufts of hair extending from his ears, which gave him the appearance of *Homo sapiens ciliatus.* His teeth, I think, were his own, and they were perfect, straight and gleaming white. These flashing clean teeth, sequins in an otherwise crusty face, contributed a showman's scintillation to his repertoire of inane and sardonic smiles.

After what had seemed a long moment of studying each other, the way two sidewalk dogs study each other before sniffing rear ends, Pete placed his hands on his hips and asked, "Why don't you eat at the front desk like everyone else?"

"Because I'm not everyone else."

"Oh? What've you got—three hairy balls?"

"No. Only two. Isn't that enough?"

"What's the attraction back here? What's that stuff you're reading? You sneak back here and read smut and jerk off, don't you? You kids and all that sex makes me sick."

"Jerking off in a compressor room is sex?"

He scowled at me.

"The army must be after your ass. That's it, ain't it? You smell like draft bait a mile away. You flunked out of college or something, didn't you? You just wait till a gook mortar wakes you up in the middle of the night. That'll wipe the grin off your face."

"The army won't get me, Pete. Sorry."

"You're a draft dodger, huh? You little bastard. What're you going to try? Flat feet? Canada? Tell 'em you're queer, Summerhelp. That'll work, believe me."

I came down one tier of boxes and popped out my glass eye and held it for him to see. He backed away a half step and rocked in place. He gawked at the glass eye and then glanced at the socket in my head where it had been.

"Some fuckin' trick," he said quietly.

4

Deluxe lived in a third-floor apartment in a bad section of Staten Island. I was uneasy from the first, and walking up from the bus stop I decided to act tough. It must have worked. No one messed with me.

When I arrived I had to introduce myself to Deluxe's wife, since Deluxe hadn't bothered. Her name was Doris, and she had a bland face and small, porcine eyes. She said that she remembered me from high school days and I told her that I remembered her also, though in fact she was no more familiar to me than the Dalai Lama.

Doris was pregnant and she complained about her "condition" all night. Deluxe ignored her as much as he could. He acted as if she'd gotten pregnant just to spite him. "It ain't gonna stop me drivin' stock cars," he told me aside.

They'd already had one baby, which I didn't learn until a while later when the two of them got into a fight. They started screaming and woke the little girl up.

Doris fussed loudly about being uncomfortable. She might not have if only once Deluxe had acted concerned. When she whimpered about her ankles, saying that they were swollen and ugly, Deluxe snapped, "Of course they're ugly. What d'you expect?"

She had pouted at this and reached for a large bag of potato chips she kept handy. She made as much noise as she could, just to irritate Deluxe. She crinkled the bag and chewed mouthfuls of chips with all the grace of a cow. She looked over for Deluxe's reaction. He purposely ignored her. At that moment I knew these two hated each other and I planned a quick exit.

For the time being we sat in the front room with the windows thrown open to the noisy traffic. The radio in the kitchen was tuned to an AM music station and the television in the cramped room where we sat was tuned to a news program. There wasn't a light on in the entire place, except for the flickering light of the television screen. The spaghetti or hot dog meal never materialized. Instead there was a case of beer and a larder of potato chips and cheese twists.

Deluxe turned to me and said, "Hey—Sliver's dead. Didja know?"

"No. What happened?"

"Someone killed him," he said, as if I should have guessed. And I should have, really.

"Who did it?"

"I don't know. The cops ain't tryin' to find out, either. Sliver was into a lot of shit. Someone caught up to him and stuck him in the stomach with an ice pick. They shoved the ice pick up his ass when they was done and threw him off the old pier down in Tottenville. I'll have to show you where they pulled him out someday."

"Don't go to the trouble."

"It ain't no trouble," said Deluxe.

My boyhood days had been crowded with bullies, and Sliver had been the archetype. He had been one bad son of a bitch, and I shook to imagine how bad the character was who had "iced" him.

Doris swallowed a mouthful of chips, and I could hear her esophagus strain. She said, "I'm sick and tired of getting up to go to the bathroom every five minutes."

"So sit there and wet your pants," said Deluxe. "Andy won't care. Right, Andy?"

I said nothing.

The television was a big console unit with remote control, and whenever Doris used the remote control she aimed it at the television and thrust it forward. This annoyed the life out of Deluxe and he said, "Hey—it ain't a fuckin' gun. I told you that a thousand times. You ain't supposed to point it at the TV."

"The man in the store pointed it when he used it."

"He's a jerk."

"Not if he sells TVs he's not."

There was a news special on about Vietnam. The jungle was striking green, more green than anything I had ever seen that was green. It looked so peaceful. But of course that was the ultimate deception. It was green but far from peaceful. It was thick and menacing, bruised by black smoke and riddled with death. There were hiding places within hiding places out there, an oriental Pandora's box. I believed I could smell the mold and the jungle rot, the *cham quap* and two-step Charlie, the madness of war and the awful sweat of fear. I wondered where in that green deadly place my pal Corney had died, and where the heroic Dietz had earned his glory.

An evac chopper set down in a rice paddy. There was confusion all around. Gunfire popped and everyone lay low. The rice plants were blown back by the chopper blades. Wounded men were quickly lifted on stretchers into the chopper bay, and the crew, eager to be airborne, urged things along.

Not a movie, I repeated to myself. Life's not a movie in Vietnam.

"Dietz kicked some fuckin' ass," observed Deluxe.

There was great admiration in his voice. He felt it made us important. It made us important that we knew Dietz and Dietz had won the Silver Star.

"Dietz always kicked ass," I said.

Deluxe picked up the grudging tone in my voice and asked, "What was with yous two?"

"What do you mean?"

"You guys were so tight. Like everyone used to say—Dietz and the Chun."

"Things happen," I said evasively.

Deluxe snickered. "Yeah. Like when Dietz was going to be a priest. Some joke." Then he added, as if I wasn't there, "He said the Chun was getting too smart for his own good."

I said nothing. Maybe it had been so. Just as Dietz had been too powerful for his own good.

Meanwhile a small Vietnamese hamlet was being methodically pulverized by artillery shells. Along the road leading to the village bright red tracers sliced through a dark cloud of smoke. In the next moment appearing from the smoke was a band of Vietnamese in flight for their lives. Old men and old women and mothers with their children. The men of fighting age were conspicuously absent.

An ox wandered into the clear light and then instantly fell to the ground. The ox hadn't stumbled first. It hadn't lost its footing. It had just dropped in its tracks.

The soldiers were screaming. Their voices were pitched and anxious. A breathless radioman called in grid numbers. "Redlegs! Redlegs! HE, WP. Pour it on, you *bleep-bleep.*"

Meanwhile the terrified Vietnamese were herded together and the smoke along the hardpack road began to lift, like a stage curtain revealing a tragedy. Dozens of bodies, motionless as stones, were grotesquely strewn across the ground. Mournful wails rose from the people, who were being restrained by a squad of soldiers. The camera zoomed in on them. Their faces were twisted by sorrow and their eyes were full of grief.

Jesus, I thought, how I hate this war.

Doris asked, "What are they doin' there, them Chinese?"

"They ain't Chinese," Deluxe mocked her. "They're Vietcongs and that fuckin' village is where they got rifles and mortars and shit."

"That's bullshit," said Doris. "There's a baby there. A baby can't be no Vietcong."

"Yeah? Tell that to one of them guys got his legs blowed off because there was a grenade strapped to a baby. Them fuckin' people over there don't give two shits about babies. They got more goddam babies than they know what to do with."

Doris said, "They ain't no Vietcongs," and disappeared into the kitchen. She returned shortly with another can of soda and a jumbo bag of potato chips. She took her seat on the couch and propped her swollen ankles on an old brown hassock, asking, "Did I miss anything?"

Deluxe didn't respond. To be polite, I said, "No."

Doris ate the potato chips greedily, as if war stimulated her appetite. She stuffed one after another into her mouth and wiped her greasy fingers on her slacks. She washed the chips down with small noisy sips of soda, and when she came up for air she turned to me and saw that I had been watching her. She was embarrassed and hurriedly made an excuse about "eating for two."

The war continued on television. The villagers shuffled along the road in despair. Their village was named Binh Son, and Binh Son would henceforth not exist. HE and WP had efficiently wiped it from the face of the earth.

"I'll tell you one thing," said Doris, issuing a proclamation. She paused to brush potato-chip crumbs from her lap. "Them people was lucky to get out of there before it blew up. They'd be dead. Whyn't they go somewhere else for good? I mean, if there was a war here and someone was trying to kill my kid, I'd get out. Just try to stop me."

Deluxe told her to shut up so he could hear the TV, even though there was nothing to hear but gunfire and the wailing Vietnamese grief-song.

The American soldiers advanced in the direction of the village, passing newer bands of Vietnamese who were heading toward them. The soldiers spaced themselves cautiously and took no chances with the bodies of dead, armed Vietnamese who lay along the road. They emptied bursts of automatic gunfire fire into them. I would have done the same. There's the real tragedy. Everyone looks out for number one. Once you're on the front line, once you're out where it's kill or be killed, you kill.

A soldier emptied a burst of fire into the head of one of the bodies, and the head bounced rapidly against the ground. It fluttered like a Ping-Pong ball and was clouded by the yellow dust of the road splattered up by the gunfire. Then in a moment the head lay perfectly still. The dust drifted off and the company of soldiers continued along.

Doris started talking about something that Deluxe didn't want to deal with and once again he told her to shut up. He then leaned forward to turn up the volume on the television. It was loud enough now to be heard in the street. If I was lucky, the sounds of gunfire and mayhem would scatter any muggers who were lurking about.

Insulted, Doris pointed the remote control at the television the moment Deluxe sat back down and turned the set off, saying "You'll wake up Caroline."

Deluxe glared at her, and I could smell the smoke. I was sure he'd go over and punch her silly. Instead he reached forward and turned the TV on. I could feel him ticking like a time bomb.

Doris felt she'd won this round and tossed her head back rather regally and reached for her can of soda. She accidentally tipped the can, and the soda spilled onto the couch between her legs. She tried desperately to pull herself up before the soda soaked her pants, but with all that "eating for two" the best she could do was to raise herself a mere inch before plopping back down into the fizzing puddle.

"Shit!" she exclaimed.

Deluxe glanced over, unconcerned and a trifle amused. "Just don't get the gizmo wet," he said.

"Is that all you care about?"

She had managed to stand. She waddled off toward the kitchen, her pants dripping wet.

"You're the one who wanted the fuckin' thing," said Deluxe. He grinned at me evilly. He grabbed the remote control and tossed it out the window. "There," he said viciously. "I hope it lands in a pile of dog shit."

I wanted to leave. I'd had enough.

Deluxe turned to me and advised, "Don't never get married. Not even if she's knocked up. It ain't worth it."

Doris returned, still wearing the same slacks and holding a dish towel around her bottom. She saw that Deluxe hadn't bothered to clean up the mess. "You're a big help," she said.

"Hey, I work all day, y'know?"

"Yeah? And what do I do? Nothin'?"

She didn't bother to clean up the spill either. She moved the hassock over and sat at the other end of the couch. She said, "My ankles hurt."

"Maybe if your arm was broken you won't notice your ankles," Deluxe warned her.

"I think I'll split," I said.

Deluxe was surprised. "Stick around, Chun."

Doris had started looking for the remote control. "Where's the thing?"

"Who gives a shit?" said Deluxe.

I stood up and made my way to the door.

"Be cool a minute, Chun," said Deluxe. "Just wait, okay?"

There seemed to be something on his mind. He started to speak and then stopped. Doris had struggled to her feet to begin a search for the remote control.

"What didja do with it?" asked Doris peevishly.

"Shut the hell up a minute," snapped Deluxe. He turned to me and said, "I got to tell you something."

"Where *is* it?" Doris asked again.

"Didn't I tell you to shut up?"

The baby cried out from down the hall.

"She what you did?" said Doris.

I made my way to the hall while Deluxe, who had been trailing me, finally managed to say what was on his mind. He said he had something for me from Dietz.

"That's why I had to get you here," he said. "I'm on probation and I can't have it on the street. I was goin' to just keep it here for myself. I'll be honest with you—I was goin' to steal it. Hey, I won't lie about that, y'know? But if Dietz came back and found out I still had it . . ."

While he was explaining all of this the baby was crying frantically from the kitchen and the radio and TV were going about their business. Doris, the dish towel wrapped around herself, paced back and forth with the crying baby.

Deluxe opened the door of the hall closet and produced an object about the length of a baseball bat rolled in brown canvas.

"You know what it is?" he asked, handing it to me.

I felt the weight and the shape of it.

"Yeah," I said. "Yeah, I know what it is."

"He told me to give it to you. He said to make sure the Chun held on to it until he got back."

"He's an enigma," I said.

"What?"

"Dietz, man. He's a mystery."

Chapter 2

There was little remorse in me over Sliver's death. I didn't think it right that anyone should be murdered but—to turn a phrase—I was certain that Sliver moved in circles where murder was a way of life. He probably got what he deserved.

Yet after all these years, and even though he was dead, I found myself looking over my shoulder at merely the mention of his name. I could still feel the fear that jellied my muscles and walloped my stomach whenever Sliver approached.

When I think of Sliver I think of badland apes and dogs with mange, dinged-up and rusted nuts and bolts, a snake or two, and meat that's been left out to start a maggot farm. Those were the things that went into making him. Some of them might even have been his parents.

He had long, long arms—he could have probably tied his sneakers without bending over—and his face looked like the squashed face of a boxer on the back page of the *Daily News.* His knuckles were weapons, thick like the steel nuts used to steady girders, and his teeth were heavy and pointed and the color of gray gravel. His breath was so awful it could crack glass—even a normal person's *farts* weren't nearly as bad—and his small beaded eyes reminded me of the eyes of the boa constrictor at the zoo. You could just tell that behind those unblinking eyes there was nothing more than a small stalk of cauliflower that had passed for a brain. He was older than the rest of us by two or three years and he'd been shaving his chin and sideburns for as long as I could remember. He was the first person I'd ever seen give himself an ink tattoo by pricking himself with a pin. He mixed the blood from each pinprick with jet-black ink from an ink cartridge. When he'd finished, the tattoo read "Death" beneath a human skull. He'd checked the spelling often by comparing it with the word on the cover of *True Detective* magazine. He didn't want to make a mistake and spell it wrong, for even someone dim as Sliver knew you couldn't erase blood mixed with ink. When the tattoo was completed and he asked me how it looked, I said the skull looked like a Martian's. He grinned evilly and said, "Maybe you'd want me to use yours. I could stick my fingers in your eyes and pull your head off. How's that?"

"No. That's all right."

There had been countless days when I had tried to sneak past Sliver's den on my way home from school. The finest plaster-of-Paris Indian chieftain I had ever made at Cub Scouts was smashed to bits on the sidewalk by Sliver. He did it just to be cruel.

On Wednesdays, the public school I attended—which was where Sliver was also supposedly learning the three R's except that he played hooky almost every day—let those of us who were Catholic out of classes at one o'clock. We were supposed to travel directly to the Catholic school in the next town and report there by one-thirty for religious instruction. There were these two guys from my public school class who were supposed to go with me—Costas Spyropoulos (we called him Spyros) and crazy Corney Walsh. But they usually decided not to show up at religious instruction. They ran off instead to play basketball or drink sodas at the place we called the Shack, giving me a lot of garbage about being a faggot for going to learn about God. I tried to feel better than them and tried to look into the distant future of the final judgment and heaven and all. Sometimes it worked and I felt just; sometimes I simply felt like a faggot. In any case, I often traveled alone, back and forth, and I knew that even though Sliver could have handled me and Corney and Spyros all at once, I felt more vulnerable when I was alone and thus took precautions to avoid Sliver's territory.

For a while I became skilled at avoiding Sliver, even though this meant I had to go quite a distance out of my way. But then Sliver must have started to feel there was something missing in his nasty life and he began to make a point of trying to capture me. He soon realized that I followed a lonely and predictable route every Wednesday.

I was in fifth grade, returning home alone one afternoon from religious instruction classes, when Sliver suddenly appeared from behind a billboard and nabbed me. He accused me of having tried to give him the slip. I denied it but he twisted my arm into a hammerlock anyway and led me behind the billboard to a break in an old rusted chain-link fence. The break in the fence let out in a secluded corner of the Moravian cemetery, back where all the old wreaths and Rest-in-Peace banners were piled in a trash heap to be burned. There he tied me to a tree and told me to keep my mouth shut until he decided what to do with me.

He picked up my catechism from where I had dropped it on the ground. He glanced through it and said, "What kinda book is this? It gives you answers with the questions." He eyed me accusingly and said, "That's cheatin', Hapanowicz."

"It's a catechism," I said.

"Yeah?"

"Yeah."

"Well, what the fuck's that mean?"

"It's about religion and all. I have to memorize the answers."

"What d'you mean?"

"I have to know the answers word for word."

"Bullshit, man, you're fulla bullshit."

"No, I'm not. I swear it, Sliver."

"Why the hell you gotta do all that?"

"So I can go to heaven, I guess."

"What're you talkin' about?"

"I don't know. I mean, I didn't learn all of it yet but I think there's going to be a big test when you die."

"There'd better not be." He paused. "What's it about, this test?"

"God looks at your whole life—everything—and decides if you've been good or bad."

"Like Santa Claus," he mocked. "Shit."

I considered telling him that God was particularly hard on bullies who tied people to trees in the cemetery, but I said nothing.

"You're just a momma's boy, that's why you learn all this," he said, flipping through the catechism.

"No—" I began.

"It's because you're a momma's boy," he insisted, waving his huge bruised fist at my nose.

I reluctantly agreed.

"Heaven," he spat. "Angels and bullshit."

The catechism was the most curious thing he'd ever seen. I think this was because along with the questions there was something he hadn't known existed—answers.

He licked his ugly lips and then showed his heavy wet canines like a wolf that was about to chomp into my shinbone. He shoved his finger up his nose, hauled out a wet booger, and wiped it on my shirt. "There," he said.

"Jesus, Sliver," I moaned, looking at the booger.

"Shut the fuck up, Hapanowicz."

He tried to read some of the things in the catechism but didn't get much farther than might the missing link.

"You know all this bullshit?" he asked skeptically.

"Most of it."

"If I ask a question, you can tell me the answer without looking at the book?"

"Probably."

"Probably's what people say when they mean no."

"If I answer the questions will you let me go?"

He smiled sadistically. "Hey, Hapanowicz, you ain't never gonna see home again. Now just shut the fuck up and listen. I like this here way the questions are printed darker than the answers. Makes it easy to keep track."

He folded the soft-covered book back on itself and I heard the glue in the binding crack. I knew now that my life would be full of many troubles, for the Sisters of Charity did not approve of boys whose catechism bindings were cracked, because once the binding had cracked the pages became loose and fell out.

Sliver read a question aloud. "What are the four—' " He stumbled over the word "attributes" and allowed me to peek at it. Then he repeated with a rather strange learned air, " 'What are the four attributes of the Church?' "

" 'The Church is one, holy, catholic, and apostolic,' " I repeated immediately.

"Jesus, Hapanowicz, you can say that faster'n I can fuckin' *read* it. Did you see that answer?"

"No."

He raised the book as if it were a hand of cards and turned the pages.

" 'Name the seven deadly sins.' —What's this? Sins that kill you?"

"Worse—you go to hell forever."

" 'Name the seven deadly sins,' " he repeated.

"The first deadly sin is tying guys to trees in cemeteries."

He gave me his snarling laugh and repeated the question a third time. " 'Name the seven deadly sins.' "

"Let me see. Sloth. Envy. Pride. Gluttony. Lust. Hatred. Cupidity."

"What the hell does all that mean?"

The only words familiar to Sliver were "hatred" and, to some degree, "pride." I had to explain all the others.

"This is too easy for you, Hapanowicz," he decided after asking me a half-dozen questions. "I'm going to ask you a real long fucker and see what you know."

The dope turned to the question that asked for the Apostle's Creed. I knew that better than I knew my address and phone number.

" 'I believe in God, the Father Almighty, Creator of heaven and earth and of all things visible and invisible, and in Jesus Christ, His only Son, our Lord . . .' "

As I glided through it effortlessly, Sliver couldn't help but show his astonishment. He of course couldn't read very well, and perhaps this was why he took delight in being able to follow the words in the catechism while I rattled off one perfect answer after the next. It was, for him, the next-best thing to being able to read on his own.

The idea that anyone would bother to memorize anything at all began to intrigue him, and one day when he had tired of hearing all that religion he found a paperback book full of facts and began tying me up to quiz me on state capitals, U.S. presidents, the height of mountains, and the length of rivers.

During the years that followed, after the thrill of ambushing me and hauling me off for torture had run its course, Sliver still enjoyed coming upon me on the street or in the lobby of a movie theater or in an aisle in a grocery store and, glaring at me menacingly, demanding that I recite the seven gifts of the Holy Ghost, the capital of Colorado, the twenty-third president, the name of the highest mountain east of the Mississippi.

He flung open the door of a phone booth one wintry day when I was making a call. He cocked his heavy fist and, like a brigand demanding tribute, asked, "Who's number fourteen, Hapanowicz?"

"Franklin Pierce," I answered, fearing that if I failed to answer promptly and correctly he would carry out his threat to lock me up in the mausoleum for the night. "You wanna smell a fresh stiff all night?" was how he used to put it.

Once when I was in the fifth grade returning from altar boy practice Sliver left me tied to his torture tree and went off, saying that he wanted to see if the knots he'd used would hold me until the next day.

At first I figured that he had to be joking. This was October, and if he left me here I'd get pneumonia for sure. Even Sliver wouldn't do that.

But the time passed and Sliver didn't return. I began to worry. I looked around at the silent rows of tombstones. I shivered. What was I going to do?

After what had seemed a terribly long time I gave up trying to free myself. My wrists were chafed from having tugged and twisted against the rope. The sun had dropped lower in the sky and the shadows of the tombstones were long and ominous. It would be dark soon. I decided that I would have to scream out for help and hope there was someone near enough to hear me.

But before I could scream out this boy appeared walking along between a row of graves. He had a bow with him and a few arrows in a hip quiver. I wasn't certain that he had seen me, so I yelled over and tried not to sound too frightened.

"Hey! Over here!"

He didn't respond. He continued along his way, which would bring him steadily closer to me. I waited and watched him closely. I was prepared to scream my lungs out if it looked like he might pass me by.

The sun disappeared behind the wooded hill. Dusk quickly settled over the cemetery. The air was suddenly chilly and damp; the tombstones took on the shape of hunched shadows.

The boy was close enough now for me to see that he was my age, though, I thought, taller. I still wasn't certain if he knew I was there. My heart beat rapidly and I called out, "Hey! I'm tied up over here. There's been a mistake."

He looked my way and walked toward me. "Why are you tied up? Are you the bad guy?"

What sort of question was that? I wondered.

"No," I said. "I'm not the bad guy. I'm the good guy, mostly. The guy who tied me up—he's the bad guy."

The boy reached around and untied the knots. I felt a wonderful sense of relief.

"You shouldn't let him do it," he said.

"What?"

"You shouldn't let him tie you up."

"It was Sliver. I mean, do you know Sliver?"

"I don't know him, but you shouldn't let anyone tie you up."

"*Sliver,* but—"

"So what?"

"He's tough."

"That doesn't matter."

What was he talking about, it didn't matter?

I thanked him for helping me and he said that maybe one day I would do a favor for him.

"Just don't let him do it to you again," he advised.

Then he walked off between the tombstones toward the wooded hill, blending into the darkness. I rubbed my wrists and watched him go.

2

Two years after that incident, on a day in April when I was twelve, Woodsie and Spyros went with me to get an inner tube at the hardware store. We had taken a short cut through the woods, emerging from the path into this place behind the hardware store full of cattails and skunk cabbage. The rusted hulks of cars that Deluxe had dragged back there, supposedly to repair, were sinking slowly into the black mud. Gathered alongside an old truck body that Sliver used for a headquarters was Sliver himself, with Smitty and Deluxe—and Jimmy

Dietz, the new kid. The four of them were playing cards, using a telephone-company spool for a table and milk crates for seats.

We knew about Jimmy Dietz. His family had lived down in Princess Bay before moving here. He had gone to the parochial school in Tottenville. We knew he was going to be a priest, yet here he was, smoking cigarettes and playing cards for money. I couldn't figure that out.

Jimmy's family had moved into the big house where Mr. Mullin, the eggman, had lived for many years. I had a secret tree house in the woods from which I was able to watch Jimmy and his father, along with another man, carry the furniture and boxes into the house.

Mr. Mullin had let everything go to hell over there, leaving a lot of work to be done on the place, and several days after Jimmy had moved in I was in the tree house again and I watched him take a sledgehammer and a wrecking bar to the old chicken coops out back. I marveled at how powerfully he swung the sledgehammer and how steadily he went at the job. I could hear him grunt and I could feel the vibrations as the hefty head of the sledgehammer thumped against and splintered the old wooden posts.

I'd had the tree house for a few years, during which I had spied on Mr. Mullin and learned his habits. It was a lot more interesting to watch Jimmy, believe me.

Mr. Mullin had been a strange person. He had shuffled around town talking to himself and drooling too much for a grown man. Little kids were frightened of him, and most of the adults tried to pretend he didn't stink like hell when he was on line at the grocery store.

Mr. Mullin had sold eggs door to door for as long as I could remember, and he wasn't all that repulsive or strange until his wife died. That was when he'd started drinking heavily, according to what the adults said.

My mother took pity on Mr. Mullin and bought eggs from him even though some of the eggs were out-and-out rotten and many of the others had bits of straw and hard old chicken shit glued to them. There was guaranteed to be blood in the yolks besides, so my mother used them for cakes or cookies, or bravely ate them herself—soft-boiled. None of us kids would knowingly have eaten a Mullin egg.

Mr. Mullin used to go out back to the coops and drink with the chickens. They were the only friends he had left, I guess. He was out there drinking in the coops when he died. No one knew what had become of him for a while—not that anyone had really missed him—and even the mailman had thought that the awful smell from the coops was just the chickens. No one had figured until later that it was what was left of Mr. Mullin.

I was surprised now to see Jimmy Dietz with Sliver and the others that day behind the hardware store. A little disappointed, too. I had wanted him to be part of our group—me and Corney and Spyros and Woodsie and the rest—not one of the Purps. The Purps sucked, as far as I was concerned.

Sliver was running the poker game that day. He was the bank. His games were notoriously crooked. He all but robbed you of your money if you were stupid enough to get involved.

When the three of us appeared from the woods that day, everyone sort of said hello to everyone else, nodding to one another and that. Sliver was slow to acknowledge us, rocking his head slowly and saying with a twangy voice, "—Boys," which was how he said hello to you whether or not you were alone. "—*Boys,*" like he had wobbly springs in his voice box.

"How're we doin', boys?"

He eyed me. "What's about number—oh, twenty, Hapanowicz?"

I hesitated only briefly. "James Garfield."

Jimmy sat quietly across from Sliver. He was tall and angular. His hair was iron-brown. Just looking at him, you wouldn't think he was as strong as he actually was. In the years to come, this would fool a lot of tough guys.

Jimmy didn't know our names so he had just said "Hello" in general and gone back to the poker game.

Sliver dealt the cards. His large hands smothered the deck, making it easy for him to cheat. His knuckles were like golf balls and his fingers were thick and bony. His head was bony too, a perfect X-ray skull with a crewcut. His skin was bloodless, like a lizard's belly, and his cheekbones were ready to burst through his skin. He had a nasty wound on his elbow that was stitched up and painted with Mercurochrome.

Sliver was sixteen. The rest of us were twelve or thirteen. He'd only finished grammar school a year before, not because he knew anything but because the teachers had gotten tired of being punched around by him.

When Deluxe or Smitty was slow to ante, Sliver rapped the top of the spool with the weighty ring he'd filed from a hub nut. *Rap! Rap!* "—Boys? We in tune, boys?"

He raked in another pot and turned to us.

"What brings you boys from the hills?"

"An inner tube," I explained.

"An inner tube?" he responded as if this was a wonderful coincidence. "Don' say?" He nudged Deluxe. "Whyn't you see if we got us an inner tube these boys can buy."

Deluxe said, " 'Fwat," trying to imitate Corney and not realizing how ridiculous he sounded. No one could do the *fud'yan 'fwat* the way Corney did and no one could recall when Corney had started talking this way. He said *fud'yan* instead of "fuckin' " so he could get away with it in school and in front of adults on buses and trains, but none of us knew what the hell *'fwat* was supposed to mean. It didn't make a whole lot of difference. None of us ever really knew what the hell springs were loose in Corney's head anyhow. We knew he talked like a cartoon character. We knew he swiped warm beer from his uncle and actually drank it. He was wiry, with muscles no larger than goosebumps, but he was a great athlete. And he could always be counted on to do something to start trouble that later would make us laugh and roll on the ground.

"I'm going to buy it inside," I told Sliver, meaning the inner tube.

"What size?" asked Deluxe, poking through a muddy, cluttered pile of old inner tubes.

"Hey—they're all the same," said Sliver. "Just grab one."

"I think I'll buy a new one," I said.

Sliver didn't like the idea. He grumbled and cut the cards and then slid the deck across to Jimmy. Jimmy took the cards and dealt a hand of five-card draw.

As the cards landed in front of the players Sliver squinted at me through the rising smoke of his Lucky Strike and asked, "How much do you think old Leo's gonna charge you for an inner tube?"

I shrugged. "A buck or two."

Sliver paused to swipe up his cards. He carefully concealed them behind his knobby hands. He took his cigarette from his mouth and, for some reason, stuck the unlit end in his ear. The cigarette continued to burn and Sliver looked like something that belonged on a doorstep on Halloween.

"You know, boys, Deluxe might come up with an inner tube for a half dollar, or seventy-five cents with the guarantee. Some of them tubes ain't ever been patched. They're cherry. Got 'em off little kids' Christmas bicycles—y'know?"

"I don't think so," I said.

"You stand to save some money. Then you could sit in on our friendly little game and maybe win back every cent. What say?"

"You'll fuckin' cheat, Sliver," said Spyros.

That was pretty damn stupid of Spyros to say. Sliver was crazy, which we all knew from the time when Mr. McCutcheon, the science teacher, had shown us that five baby hamsters would fit in a table-spoon and Sliver went up and swallowed all five in one gulp. Sliver wouldn't think twice of biting Spyros's ear off or sending him home with his arms reversed.

Sliver yanked his cigarette from his ear and dragged on it. "Cheat, huh?"

He examined the faces of the players. He raised his eyebrows, and the assorted scars on his forehead wriggled. "Do any of you boys feel cheated?"

Smitty spoke up, opening his mouth to reveal his teeth, which were so ravaged by cavities that they looked rusted. "On my mother's grave," he said. "It's an honest game."

Deluxe said, " 'Fwat."

Sliver regarded Spyros and said, "Hear them? Ain't you glad you ain't that fuckin' dumb?" He looked at Smitty and Deluxe and said, "You assholes. Of course I cheat."

He put two cards facedown on the table and said, "Gimme two. The ones with pictures on 'em."

Jimmy, meanwhile, hadn't said a word. He concentrated on his cards. He didn't fan out his hand, I noticed, but kept them one behind the other in a neat stack. When he wanted to look at them he paged through the stack of five, one by one.

He dealt out the draw cards. Then he took one from the deck. "Dealer takes one," he said.

This aroused Sliver's suspicions. "Workin' on a straight? Or is it a full house, my man?"

Jimmy turned a poker face toward Sliver. He reached over and pulled the smoking cigarette from Sliver's ear and dragged on it. He spat aside immediately, saying, "That's disgusting. Don't you ever clean your ears?"

"With what?" asked Sliver. "Ain't nothin' fits in there."

"Q-tips," I suggested, immediately sorry I had.

"Oh, so's now you're a doctor, huh, Hapanowicz?"

"Just an idea."

"Whyn't you keep your ideas to yourself?"

"Sure thing."

"Unless you're looking for a bit of the old school days," he warned.

"I'm going," I said, starting in the direction of the hardware store.

But Sliver wasn't known for his ability to forgive. He jumped to his feet and grabbed hold of me. He held me in a half nelson and led me back to the poker game, snickering at my pain. "Give 'em three in a row. Start at thirty-two, Hapanowicz."

I racked my brains and tried to ignore the pain Sliver dished out. *Thirty-second president . . .*

Despite his obvious intellectual shortcomings I was convinced that Sliver was an idiot savant when it came to keeping track of presidents. God only knew what he'd do if I tried to pass off a wrong answer.

"Roosevelt," I blurted as he wrenched my arm. "Let go, dammit!"

"No bad language in school."

He kept me from straying as he picked up his cards with his free hand and looked them over. He hummed low, saying, "Hm . . . not bad. Not bad at all."

But he had nothing, not even a pair, and when I realized this I tried to signal Jimmy. I think it worked; sort of instantly, too. I think he noticed the quick shake of my head.

"C'mon, Hapanowicz, three in a row," insisted Sliver.

A museum of presidents swirled in my head. Three in a row was no problem if he'd bought Roosevelt.

"Roosevelt," I said.

"You used him," said Sliver. He yanked on my arm; my shoulder was on fire. I wished I was stronger. God, did I wish I was stronger. "Who's next?" demanded Sliver.

Piece of cake. "Truman, Ike."

"None of that Ike bullshit. Real names."

Meanwhile the betting had gotten heavy. Deluxe faded, then Smitty. It was between Jimmy and Sliver now.

"Eisenhower," I said.

"He's the one now, right?" asked Sliver.

"Man, Sliver," said Woodsie. "Don't you know?"

"Hey, asshole, you want to eat dinner in the hospital?"

Woodsie kept quiet.

"Dealer bets a dollar," said Jimmy. He laid a dollar bill on the spool. He put down his cards and waited for Sliver.

Sliver let go my arm. "Well, now. A whole dollar." His eyes widened. "Let me see." He looked at Jimmy's face but could see nothing there. He studied the money in the pot. He pondered the situation. I could hear his brain trying sluggishly to do addition.

Abruptly, he folded his cards and told Jimmy, "It's yours, man."

Jimmy reached out to take in the money. Sliver leaned forward at the same time to turn Jimmy's cards over for a look. But Jimmy's hand went out like lightning to cover his cards. He'd moved so quickly that Sliver's hand had come down atop his.

"You've got to pay to see these cards, Sliver," said Jimmy. "Those are the rules."

"I paid," said Sliver, pulling on Jimmy's wrist.

"Not enough," said Jimmy, resisting Sliver.

That annoyed Sliver. His eyes met Jimmy's across the table. "Well, fuck that, Jack. I'm takin' a look at the cards that took my dough."

With that he tried to pull Jimmy's hand away. He couldn't, though. His big knobby fingers tugged at Jimmy's wrist, but Jimmy didn't budge.

Anyone who saw it never would forget it. A look of shock and then one of respect came over Sliver. He tried to laugh it off, of course. He let go Jimmy's wrist and said, "Just jokin', boys."

Then he didn't know what to do so he turned to me and said, "Scram, Hapanowicz. You're a fuckin' jinx."

3

The pebbles dropped into my sleep, rippling its many surfaces. *Plunk.* Then another. *Ker-plunk.*

Gently, it seemed, but enough to ripple and splash, corrugating the edges of sleep, lacing together sleep and wakefulness. My dream, tingling. These waves and gentle rolls.

I wandered into the no-man's-land where sleep and wakefulness preyed upon each other, spiraling, devouring to be devoured. I was supposed to be somewhere. There was a call.

In the next moment I found myself wide awake and on my feet. I heard my name. Yes, my name.

"Who's there?" I called.

Late one night, some weeks after Jimmy had made Sliver look foolish at the poker game, I heard a few pebbles strike my bedroom window. A whispered call followed. *"Chun!"*

Chun? I wondered. What the hell was that?

I rose from bed and padded across the floor in my underwear. I looked out the window but did not open it. The night was clear. There were no clouds hiding the stars. The moon was full, rich with milky light in the sky but soft and blue down here.

"Chun!"

Down below in the blue light stood Jimmy Dietz. He seemed almost an apparition, more unreal than real. Yet he belonged there the way the moon belonged there and the woods and the owl belonged there. He was a bold and important piece of the night, and I somehow felt that if he were removed the whole scene, maybe even the world itself and me with it, would vanish forever.

"Chun," he repeated, glad to see me appear.

What was this *Chun* business? I wondered.

I opened the window and leaned out. The air was crisp and I shivered when the coolness curled about my bare skin. I watched my breath cloud the air.

"What time is it?" I asked Jimmy, realizing immediately that it was a stupid question. What could it matter, the time?

"After midnight."

"So it's tomorrow," I said, acting silly.

The moonlight had penetrated far back into my head, back beyond my eyes, and I could feel it flow freely into new spaces and fill them with wonder.

I looked out toward the woods. I noticed the doghouse at the edge of the trees, out where my father burned the leaves every fall, and I realized that I hadn't heard Champ bark. Champ was supposed to be a good watchdog. He barked whenever anyone approached the yard. Why hadn't he barked at Jimmy?

Maybe I was still asleep. Maybe that was the explanation. Maybe I was still asleep and dreaming and my dream machine had forgotten to have Champ bark at Jimmy.

"You ever been out in the woods at night?" asked Jimmy.

I knew what he meant. He meant out deep in the woods, not just a short distance. He meant out where you might find yourself alone and in darkness.

"Yeah," I lied, wanting more than anything to appear daring to him. "Yeah, I've been out there."

"It's great," he said. "Ain't it?"

"You bet. Yeah, great."

He paused. I could feel something there. "What about when there's a full moon?" he asked. And he pointed out the moon as if otherwise I could possibly have missed that grapefruit in the sky.

I knew he suspected that I'd lied about being out in the woods alone at night and now he was giving me a chance to clean the slate. Our eyes met. It was a moment deserving truth. It was a special moment in a special night. This was important. Maybe even sacred.

"No," I said. "Never. Not when there's a full moon."

"Let's go," he said, waving me down.

He jogged off smoothly toward the woods to await me. I watched him go.

I turned and looked across the room to where my little brother lay sleeping. I moved silently on the balls of my feet and closed the door to the hall. Then I quickly dressed, a thrill coursing along my legs and arms all the while. I could feel an adventure poised nearby, ready to pounce and swallow me whole.

When I returned to the window Jimmy was nowhere to be seen. I climbed onto the roof of the back porch and closed the window behind me. I crept along to the edge of the roof and sat there, my feet dangling out over the gutter. Then I pushed myself off. The air whooshed past my ears. My feet landed on the ground and my legs absorbed the jolt. I grunted.

Champ barked. What a traitor, I thought.

"Jesus, Champ!" I hissed.

He barked again and I ran across the yard to quiet him.

"Champ!"

He recognized me and started to whine and prance about in place. He swished his bushy tail. The tags on his collar jingled. I drew closer and he jumped up and braced his forepaws on my hips. I petted him and he turned his head sideways and closed his watery brown eyes with pleasure. I kneaded the stringy tendons at his throat and he reached out his pink tongue to lick my hand.

"Quiet, okay?"

I looked around for Jimmy. I called his name out low.

"Jimmy?"

Champ wanted to play. He didn't understand that there was no time for that now. I took hold of his forepaws to lower him, and for a moment it looked as if we two were dancing a minuet in the moonlight.

"Down," I told him sternly. "Down, and don't bark." He looked at me. "Good boy."

He shook himself from end to end and then walked over to his food dish. He sniffed at the food with no interest. He lay down with a sigh and rested his muzzle on his paws. He raised his eyes to me.

"Good boy," I repeated.

I glanced back at the house. It was quiet and dark. My escape had gone undetected.

I ventured a short distance into the woods. "Jimmy?"

There was no answer.

Even though the moon shed light on the woods I was hesitant to move from where I stood, at the edge, not willing to go any farther alone. I convinced myself that I wasn't afraid. I told myself it simply made no sense to go into the woods without knowing where Jimmy was.

"Jimmy?" I called, peering into the trees.

On silent feet he had come upon me from behind.

He poked me in the ribs, saying, "Chun." I jumped out of my skin. "Don't be so nervous," he said. "Let's go."

We followed the path out beyond my house and soon came to the first fork. To the left was the way to the schoolyard, to Jimmy's house, the train station, White Bridge; to the right lay the deeper woods: Weed Pond, the orphanage at Arthur Kill, Big Trees, the marshes, and Fresh Kills.

We went to the right.

The path was too narrow for us to travel abreast. Naturally, Jimmy took up the lead. He moved quickly and made very little noise. He seemed to have a particular destination in mind, though he had said nothing to me.

Sliver had ended up blaming me for his loss of face that day behind the hardware store and had sought revenge. Several days after the card game, while I was riding my bike down Benning's hill, Sliver and Smitty and Deluxe appeared on their bikes and came after me like fighter planes. Sliver and Deluxe had broomsticks and Smitty had a bola that he had made from rope and the big steel nuts that are scattered alongside the railroad tracks. Smitty twirled the bola and flung it at my chain while Sliver and Deluxe aimed the broomsticks at my spokes. They finally succeeded in busting my spokes and twisting my wheels out of shape. I had to crash through someone's hedges to escape them. My bike was absolutely useless. The wheels moved like large S's and I had to walk it home. I felt angry and frustrated. I was so tired of being bullied by the Purps.

On the way, walking my wounded bicycle, I ran into Jimmy. He was carrying his fishing rod and tackle box and he smelled like he'd been knee-deep in pond scum. He couldn't fail to notice my bike, and when I told him what had happened he decided that we should fight back. A pipe dream, I figured. Fight back against the Purps. But Jimmy instantly came up with a plan.

There was this blue bicycle that had been in the back of the Mullin place for eternity. It was a small hefty bike with fat balloon tires. It would become our weapon of war.

That night we oiled the sprockets and patched the tubes and used some bedframe angle iron to make battering rams for the front and back wheels. When we were done we could have taken Stalingrad with the thing.

We didn't want to ride around town with the *Blue Devil* and give ourselves away, so we waited until one night when the Purps showed up at the schoolyard and were harassing other bike riders the way they'd harassed me. We then ran home through the woods and grabbed two football helmets. With Jimmy driving the *Blue Devil* and me standing on the rear battering ram holding on to his shoulders, we returned to the schoolyard and one by one demolished the Purps' bikes. Our angle-iron battering rams protected our wheels and made short work of theirs.

We made a victory lap of the schoolyard and then, instead of riding off to avoid Sliver, Jimmy pulled to a stop and let the Purps envy the job we'd done on the *Blue Devil.* He must have known how they would appreciate an instrument of destruction, because they weren't one bit mad. They had laughed it off.

In front of me now in the moonlit woods Jimmy picked up the pace from a quick walk to a jog. His stride was rhythmic and begged to be imitated. He moved the way a breeze moved, hardly stirring a twig as he passed. He glided in and out of moonlight and shadow, and his reflexes were sharp. He knew precisely when to take a longer stride to avoid a root. He ducked low branches as if he had radar; he hurdled obstacles on winged feet.

It wasn't solely his ease of movement that convinced me he'd been out in the full-moon woods before tonight. There was, all around us, that special energy of Dietz. It rose from the solitude of the woods. It raised the hair on the back of my neck and thrummed my nerves excitedly. It was a creature knowledge. It was deep in the soil and fell from the sky. Life and death were wrapped in its arms. I could feel myself hungry for it, and somewhat afraid. The woods were suddenly a different place for me than they had ever been. There were new rules here now, rules that I didn't yet know, but rules for which I would nevertheless be held to account.

I tripped. I stumbled forward but I didn't fall. I cursed my clumsiness. Jimmy glanced back without a word. We continued along at the same steady pace, though now I allowed more distance between us. If I tripped again I didn't want to fall on his heels and bring him down with me.

It was too early in the spring for the trees to have leaves, and so the whole sky could be seen through the bare branches. The stars were everywhere; the Milky Way a mist. The moonlight flowed eerily between the dark lines of the trees, and the shadows were soft and seemingly alive. The night was enchanted, and the moon, joining in, played tag with us. It disappeared over our shoulders at one turn only to appear suddenly in front of us when we came to the rocky place out near Big Trees.

We finally broke from the cover of the woods where there once had been a dirt road to a farm. The farm had long since been abandoned. Everyone still called it the Conklin place though, because the Conklins had been the last people to live there.

I was tired for the moment and I welcomed the chance to catch my breath. We stood looking up and down the road. I asked Jimmy, "Where to?"

"This way," he said, indicating his left.

We started walking in the direction of the old farm.

"My father didn't like what we did to the bike," he said.

"Why?"

"He said we—I—should have asked him first."

"It was just an old junk bike. It would've been thrown out."

"He said that if I was going to put that much work into something, it shouldn't be to destroy other bikes. He said I could've spent the time and energy fixing it up for one of my brothers."

I could feel that there was more he wanted to say, and I somehow knew that the *Blue Devil* would live a short life as a battering ram on wheels.

"So I guess I'll do that," he said, looking at me.

"Fix it up for your brother?"

"Yeah."

"Do you think your father was right?"

He paused briefly.

"No," he said. "Those guys deserved to be smashed."

We continued along the road, which was overgrown with winter-browned weeds and grass. A rabbit ran off up ahead.

"What do you think?" Jimmy asked. "About the bike?"

"As long as we had a chance to get those guys I don't care what happens to the bike now."

"Good," he said.

The Conklin place came into view. All that remained of the small farmhouse was the fieldstone foundation, which was tumbling into the dirt basement one stone at a time. Scattered here and there on the ground were pieces of charred lumber. It was said that the house had burned to the ground and that Mr. Conklin had done it. Some people said it had been an accident; others said not.

Out back was a root cellar with a caved-in roof. Above and beyond it there loomed a big old barn that would collapse any day now. A large section of the roof of the barn had already fallen, and all the supporting timbers sagged and twisted under the load.

There were a few rows of fruit trees alongside the barn. Peach and apple. A few plum trees, I think. Off by itself there was a big cherry tree with many branches; it was dying and no longer gave fruit.

The trees had been planted in neat rows so that they could be taken care of properly, but over the years they'd not been pruned and now the crowded branches seemed to me like wild claws scratching at the night.

There were many stories that described the fate of the Conklins. Too many, in fact, for all of them to be true. It seemed that whatever lesson in life our parents wanted to teach, the Conklins served as a handy parable. Mr. Conklin had been lazy or stubborn or not neighborly or a spendthrift. He had left his wife because she had been a "bad woman," or maybe it was she who had left him because he was a bum and manhandled her.

Eventually Mr. Conklin had come up against hard times, and here all the stories came into agreement.

He had no food and no money. He tore the side of the barn down for firewood and then started on the house furniture. One night he set the house on fire, killing himself and his wife and their three children.

We took a path at the corner of the place and followed it out toward Weed Pond, passing near enough Iron Jud's to raise a chorus of bays from his hounds. Jud used the hounds to hunt raccoon, which he claimed was good eating. The hounds were loud and mournful, and when I saw that their sudden baying didn't surprise Jimmy I figured that even though he was the new kid, Jimmy had been out this way.

We continued along to the old WPA roads, the roads abandoned since the Depression, and there Jimmy picked up the pace. We trotted along for ten or fifteen minutes directly toward the moon and then turned to our left into the woods. Suddenly Jimmy lunged forward and dove to the ground. A rabbit squirmed past him and came in my direction. I was startled and I tripped and fell forward, landing on the rabbit. He squirmed beneath me and made a sad noise, like a squeezed baby doll.

"Don't lose him, Chun!" said Jimmy, standing above me. "Hold on to him. Just hold on."

Even though it was only a rabbit I was very nervous. I wedged my hands beneath myself and grabbed for him. He had scratched my stomach but now I had him. I stood up, holding him out for Jimmy to see. The rabbit kicked his strong hind legs frantically. He was determined to be free.

"Man, he's strong for a little rabbit," I said.

The rabbit exhausted himself and stopped kicking. He breathed heavily and rapidly and looked at us through glazed, drugged eyes. I could feel his heart and lungs through the palms of my hands. *Thuk-thuk! Thuk-thuk!*

"Let's go," said Jimmy.

I thought that he meant to let the rabbit loose and then we'd continue along through the woods, so I bent over to let go of the rabbit. But Jimmy stopped me, saying almost sternly, "No. Take him. Let's go."

We were off at a run, back the way we'd come. Jimmy was running faster than we had all night. It was a tiring pace. My side ached, and it was doubly difficult to run and hold the rabbit with both hands.

We ran all the way back to Big Trees and then Jimmy slowed the pace momentarily. He stopped for a breather and asked, "How're you doing?"

"Okay," I said. "Except the rabbit pissed on me."

"Yeah?" he asked, amused.

"Yeah."

"Want me to take him?"

If I had known what his plans were for the rabbit I might have said yes, but I didn't know then that we would sacrifice the rabbit in a blood-brother ceremony, and so I said, "I got him."

I knew we were out beyond Big Trees but I wasn't exactly sure where, nor was I certain I could find my way home very easily.

"Where are we goin' in such a hurry?" I asked.

"You'll see. There's a place out here. You'll see."

He took a deep breath and looked down the path, able to see things and places that were invisible to me. The rabbit meanwhile had started kicking again. His heart beat and my heart beat and the rhythms occasionally came together.

"You ever been blood brother with anyone?" asked Jimmy.

"No," I said.

I remembered that Corney had once cut himself with a rusted bottlecap on purpose and had wanted me to do the same so that we could be blood brothers, but I had taken one look at the bottlecap and seen how rusted and dirty it was and I told him to forget it.

Jimmy nodded approvingly at my answer. "You ready?" he asked.

I didn't know, exactly, what he was asking, but I said, "Yeah," and we were off again, running.

I wasn't sure how much time had passed before we finally came to a place far back in the woods. The moon had seeped into my brain, making me giddy. I felt sluggishly tired yet hypnotized beyond tiredness. The rabbit squirmed in my hands, and my hands were stiff from resisting him.

Jimmy lowered himself to the ground and told me to crawl behind him as he made his way under a thick stand of brambles. He went ahead on hands and knees, and I followed, inching along, using my elbows and knees. The moon stitched its way through the brambles, and eerie patches of light fell into the tunnel where we crawled. I happened once by chance to look directly into the rabbit's glazed eyes and felt a nightmarish sensation that I held a reincarnated human being who wanted to scream, "Let me out! Let me out!" It was crazy and I knew it was crazy and I knew I must never tell anyone I had even thought the crazy thought. I avoided looking into the rabbit's eyes and crawled on.

When we emerged from the tunnel below the brambles we were in

a clearing where there stood to one side a large spreading oak tree.
The moon was in its branches, sitting there, a witness to all that was
about to happen.

Thuk-thuk! Thuk-thuk!

"This is the place, Chun."

I looked around. The place. I felt that there was something oddly
familiar here. A place where spells are cast, I thought, knowing I was
being silly. I was tired. I was made dopey by the moon and my heart
pounded madly: *Thuk-thuk/lub-dub/thuk-thuk/lub-dub.*

Jimmy pulled a knife from his back pocket. It was a beautiful knife,
like a pocket knife but more than a pocket knife. The handle looked
like pearl; a red Chinese dragon with fearsome black eyes adorned it.

Jimmy flicked his wrist and the blade leaped out of the handle. The
metal of the blade glinted and the edge appeared to me sharp as a
razor.

"Ready?" asked Jimmy.

"Yeah," I said evenly.

"Hold him down."

"The rabbit?"

"Yeah. The rabbit. Hold him down—there, on the flat stone."

"Why?"

"The ceremony. We'll be blood brothers."

Jimmy knelt at the wide flat stone he'd pointed out. I joined him
and held the rabbit down on the stone on his stomach, but Jimmy said,
"No. Turn him over on his back."

I did so. The rabbit kicked wildly. But not for long.

Jimmy plunged the blade into the rabbit's chest and bared it open. I
heard the bones of its chest crack and splinter. The rabbit writhed in
agony. The warm blood spilled over my hands.

In a twinkling Jimmy had the heart out. He held it pierced on the
sharp tip of his dragon knife. It was still beating.

"We got to eat it while it's still beating, while its alive," he said.

He placed the tiny heart on the stone and sliced it in half.

"It's still beating," I gasped.

"Things don't die easy. Blood brothers don't die easy."

Jimmy stabbed one of the halves with his knife and put it in his
mouth. He chewed on it and then swallowed it.

Then he speared the other half and fed it to me, saying, "We're blood brothers now, Chun. We'll never ever give up on the other guy. Never. No matter what happens, it's me and you—like a mountain."

The heart was rubbery and chewy; it was warm and slick with blood.

I forced it down my throat and felt the moon watching while Jimmy hacked off a rabbit's foot for both of us.

We parted company at Champ's doghouse. Jimmy disappeared into the line of trees, jogging. I shuffled wearily back to the house. I climbed the wisteria trellis to the porch roof, opened the bedroom window, and pulled myself in.

I didn't bother to undress. I dragged my weary body to the bed and fell in a heap. I kissed the pillow and said nice things to it.

My muscles begged for a good long rest, and my eyes were heavy. My stomach was queasy with the tiny heart, but my mind and spirit were still out there in the woods, running—flying, yes, *soaring*—and I could still taste and smell and hear everything that had happened. My imagination burned like a sparkler. It wanted to rebuild the night, piece by piece. But the rest of my body revolted at the idea, and I lay there, twitching, caught between the two.

When finally I slept, I slept without dreaming. It made sense. I'd already dreamed without sleeping.

There were to be other midnight adventures, runs through the woods. Usually I would know when to expect Jimmy and we'd meet at a place in the trees.

The moon was full on some of those nights and everything was spooky and strange, as it had been on the night of the rabbit in the place of the *thuk-lub-dub.* But on other nights there was no moon at all. Thick clouds veiled the stars and I couldn't see my hand in front of my face. The mystery thickened then.

It didn't matter if it was winter or summer; it didn't matter if we stayed out for an hour or never returned until dawn. It was never boring and we never saw another person nor invited anyone else along.

But the first night was the night of the rabbit, the night of the vow—the night Dietz had started calling me Chun. It would never be clear to me where he'd gotten this odd name. People who heard it would ask me if I was Chinese, and when I said "Only half," they would tell me I didn't look it.

Chun. I liked it, whether it meant something or not. Dietz and the Chun, blood brothers of the forever vow: never, ever to give up on the other guy. Every run through the woods at night along the paths sealed the vow, and the paths and the woods became brother and sister to our oath.

It happened that more than once I rose from bed and went to the window looking for Jimmy when I thought I'd heard pebbles strike the glass; thought I'd heard him call, "Chun."

I would wonder, "Jimmy?"

I might even pull on my clothes and climb out the window. I'd jump from the roof and trot across to the doghouse. I'd ask Champ if he had seen Jimmy. Champ, however, would know no more than I.

"Jimmy?"

And I would creep into the woods alone—can you imagine? Into the frosty woods of late autumn and the thick humid woods of summer, into the darkness and into the moonlight, putting away my fear, thinking of nothing other than finding Jimmy, calling out his name.

"Jimmy? Jimmy? Where are you?"

Thuk-thuk, it went. *Thuk-thuk/lub-dub.*

Chapter 3

1

I first learned about this character called the Paymaster from the mechanics at Pete's. And of course once they'd set me up the way a rookie is set up to go fetch a left-handed monkey wrench, Pete corroborated every word.

"Oh, yeah, Summerhelp," Pete told me. "You just remember to do everything the way I told you, and one day the Paymaster's gonna come around and give you your reward."

Pete's Friendly Service was out on what once had been a lonely stretch of Arthur Kill Road. It hadn't always looked the same, of course, but as well as I could recall it had always been a Mobil station.

For the longest time the place hadn't been much larger than a shed, with just enough room inside for a cash register, a chair, and a desk. It didn't even have a bathroom back then, a fact which I had learned from Pete, who, for some reason, was proud of it.

Back in those days without a bathroom there had been a single pump island out front with two pumps: regular and high-test. Instead of a hydraulic lift there was a pit alongside the building where the mechanic (who back then was Pete) worked on the cars from below. There was an air pump near the pit, and above the door of the small building was a large clock.

My most distinct memory of the place as it had been was that the gas pumps and the air pump were topped by glass globes bearing the Pegasus. There was also a Pegasus in the clock above the door, and within the clock the wings of the Pegasus pointed out the hour. Yes, that was the first and strongest childhood impression of the place I'd had: the flying red horse.

I am quite surprised at the detail with which I remember the way the station had been, since my father had rarely stopped at Pete's when I was small. He bought his gas over in New Jersey because he worked there and the gas was far cheaper.

Nor did my father bring his car to Pete's for repairs. When his car wasn't running he fixed it himself—or became insanely angry at the car and made the problem far worse. Which, now that I come to think about it, is just about what Pete does.

When I was a teenager, hitchhiking back and forth along Arthur Kill Road, I occasionally wandered into Pete's to buy a soda from the vending machine and beg for rides from people who pulled in for gas. It had never entered my mind that one day I would be working there.

Pete had always owned the place, and I usually saw him there as I came and went. He was reasonably nice to me until I started pestering his customers for rides. At that point he gave me a piece of his mind and told me to leave and never return.

He hadn't changed much. To this day he was still considerate to people in direct proportion to how much of their money he figured he would get. He charmed customers, as you might expect, but treated the help like criminals. He was absolutely convinced that his employees were taking his money without justification.

Pete's Friendly Service changed over the years. The original small wooden building was taken down and there rose a much larger cinder-block building, one large enough for three repair bays and two hydraulic lifts. The old gravel-and-dirt drive was paved over and enlarged. Two pump islands were erected with overhead lights, four pumps, and a fancy oil carousel on each island.

The globes bearing the Pegasus on the gas pumps and the air pump were gone, however. There was a smaller clock in the office on the wall with a Pegasus, but the wings of this more modern icon did not move. Out front the Pegasus on the large sign atop the tall pole remained, though its days were numbered.

The first day I came to work I was wearing a pair of old blue jeans and a T-shirt. Pete took one look at me and immediately led me to a large plastic bag crammed with old gas station uniforms. I noticed that everyone else had an official oil-company uniform with the new Mobil logo and their name handily stitched over the shirt pocket, whereas the clothing in the bag consisted of hand-me-downs that had arrived here from defunct, bankrupt, or otherwise vanished gas stations. And since more than a few of these gas stations had been competitors of Mobil Oil, the logos had been removed from the shirts.

It didn't particularly bother me not to be costumed as sharply as the other guys, since by midday everyone except Pete's nephew Tom, who was incredibly vain and ran home every noon to change, looked like a grease monkey. Nor did I let it bother me that all the logos had been removed from the shirts I wore, giving me the appearance of a gas jockey who had been busted in rank. What did get to me, however, was that none of my work shirts had the same name over the pocket, and that even with the great variety of names I came across in the pile of shirts there wasn't a single Andrew or Andy.

So it came to be that people called me Roy or Frank or some other stranger's name. And the guys I worked with, including Pete, had grown so accustomed to reading names from shirts over the years that they didn't know who I was either.

The more I reminded them, rather irritably I'll admit, that I wasn't Frank or Roy, or Harry or J.J. or Rocco, the more pleasure they took in reading off whatever name was on my shirt. I considered unstitching all the names but I knew Pete would ride me for it. Let them call me whatever they want, I finally decided. I'm here a month or two, then it's "Goodbye, gas station."

That was when they decided it was easiest to stay with Summer-help.

Pete's Friendly Service was in such an ideal location that a chimpanzee family could have made a fortune there—even without the garbage trucks. What was intriguing, however, was that when Pete had chosen the location it had been populated by nothing other than mosquitoes and snapping turtles. Very few cars drove past in those days, and fewer still pulled in for gas. It had to have been the absolute poorest choice of a place to build a gas station, because most of the traffic was either headed for New Jersey or returning, and the price of gasoline in New Jersey had always been considerably cheaper than it was in New York.

But then, in 1964, the Verrazano Bridge to Brooklyn was com-

pleted, amid rumors that more than one worker had fallen into the
setting concrete of the enormous supporting pedestals and had been
buried alive. A Navajo steelrigger named Yahoo who spent all his
hard-earned pay on firewater had verified this for me and the guys one
night when we discovered him sleeping under the rapid-transit train
platform.

To serve the bridge, two new expressways crossed the island,
carrying traffic from New Jersey to Brooklyn. Once it became possible
to commute by car from Staten Island to work in other parts of the
city, housing developments sprang up rapidly on Staten Island, the
population soared, and the Department of Sanitation used the bridge
as a sort of garbage gangplank and went into the business of transport-
ing mountains of coffee grounds, disposable diapers, banana peels,
Dixie Cups, and the rest to Fresh Kills—dumping every gram of it
right alongside a Mobil station that until then had attracted barely
enough customers to remain afloat.

Pete suddenly had more business than he knew how to handle, and
certainly more than the old fart deserved. He had chosen the worst
location imaginable for a gas station and had come out of it looking like
a retailing genius.

Now the cars pulled in as if drawn by a massive electromagnet,
more in one day than Pete had seen in a month in the old days. The
numbers on the gas pumps rolled and chimed all day, from opening to
closing, and Pete grew richer by the minute.

Every sort of person came into the place. Women in station wag-
ons returning from the supermarket, husbands who gathered here on
Saturday mornings to have their oil changed, teenage boys who wandered in to fill up the gas can for the family lawnmower. And the
drivers of the garbage trucks, of course, who were New Yorkers from
the wads of gum on the soles of their shoes to their arrogant, schem-
ing brains, civil servants who played the horses and the numbers, read
the *Daily News* and did the Jumbo every day, affable, coarse, and
streetwise, with tongues that sought to destroy grammar and pronun-
ciation by way of a war of attrition headquartered in Brooklyn.

There were people on their way to Quebec who couldn't speak a
word of English (Pete told me to charge them extra for the time and
trouble I had to spend trying to understand them); people just back
from California, salesmen from Ohio who tried to sell or recruit me to

sell everything from life insurance and stockade fence to Bibles with monogrammed tooled-leather commemorative covers; great-looking girls driving flashy sports cars, wheeling in and wheeling out without me, heading for the Jersey shore, breaking my heart.

Whenever a woman wearing a skimpy summer outfit stopped for gas, Pete suddenly found the energy to come out and wash the windshield. He always made sure to offer us his opinion of every pair of tits he saw. And he could never say a word about tits without holding his hands out from his chest.

"Tits like this here—look't," he'd say. "What d'you think, Summerhelp? Like to walk over an acre of those babies barefoot?"

Even Deluxe came by occasionally to shoot the breeze, and I don't know why. Maybe I was the next-best thing to Dietz, like a relic that had been touched by a sacred personage.

Woodsie showed up one night in a prowl car. He was a rookie cop. Who would've believed it? Woodsie, a cop.

And all the while the cars came and went, hungry for gasoline, their tires rolling over the bell hose, clang-clanging for me, the Pavlov gas jockey, the gofer, the Summerhelp, demanding that I drop whatever I was doing and hustle over to pump gas into their tanks and send them on their way.

Not unlike other American twenty-one-year-olds, I had considered the summers of my life up until recently equivalent to vacation. Even when I'd had a job for the summer, it still seemed a vacation because for once I had money. I had come to accept it as a law of nature. Summer was vacation, autumn was change and newness. Not always comfortable change, not always what I might have chosen, but never malevolent and generally acceptable. Ever onward and upward.

Not so any longer.

This year brought no vacation, no autumnal promises. No guarantees. Nothing so automatic. This year, when the month of May would be a breather between the assassinations of King and Kennedy, what could be expected?

I'd not done very well with the things in life that had been expected of me and the things I'd expected of myself. For instance, I was disappointed that I'd not finished college. It was true, of course, that for a long time I'd been unable to study because of these enormous headaches I'd had, and the headaches were the result of the—well, let's say *accident* I'd had in which I'd lost my eye—but that didn't change the fact that I was disappointed.

My luck with friends and girls had not been good either. Corney was gone. I had my problems understanding Dietz. My girl in Oregon had dumped me and I don't think a girl had even looked my way since.

I didn't know what I wanted to do with myself. I wasn't sure, day by day, if life was worth living, though I certainly wasn't about to bow out. I'd never seen suicide as a viable alternative, and I didn't take myself all that seriously anyway.

I didn't know what I wanted to be when I grew up, nor if I wanted to grow up at all. From what I'd seen of mature adults in this world, their prejudices, their wars, their greed, all this brutality and lies—I wasn't sure I was willing to join their ranks.

Thus I accepted the job at Pete's and used it as an anchor, while now and again the fever of the life on the road infected me. I surely missed Oregon. I had never known how monstrously frantic New York actually was until I'd gotten away and had returned. July 5, the day after Dietz did his thing at the parade, I was out of here.

I resisted the temptation to head back west immediately; I wanted to see Jimmy. That was the plan, after all. That was why I'd traveled so far. I wanted to see his parade. I wanted to tell him that I wasn't as angry with him as he might have thought. I wanted to apologize for not having answered his letters. And I wished now that I hadn't destroyed them.

But hey—let's not forget—there was always the chance that the Paymaster might show up. That was another reason for sticking around. One day, any day, out of the blue, the next customer who drove in could be bearing gifts.

Be courteous, be helpful, be obedient and clean. Be whatever the oil company rewarded good employees for being. Wash them windshields till they squeak, rub 'em like they were Aladdin's lamp.

The way it went with this story about the Paymaster was that the oil company—Mobil Oil—supposedly supplied this man with a suitcase full of cash and sent him on his way to visit all the franchised and individually operated Mobil Oil gas stations in the free world, there to reward hardworking gas jockeys who played along.

The Paymaster drove in, or so they said, just like any other customer. Of course, he didn't identify himself, since that would destroy the whole idea. And the whole idea, as usual, was a test.

The basic concept was simple enough, really. If the gas jockey who waited on the Paymaster was neat and clean and properly attired, if he asked the Three Friendly Helpful Questions—Fill 'er up? Check the oil? Is that all today?—if he pushed TBA (tires, batteries, and accessories)—How're those tires? Is that battery going to make it? Windshield wipers, perhaps? Brake fluid? How 'bout one of these pine-scented cardboard evergreen trees to hang from the rearview mirror?—if he washed the windshield and the rear window, tipped his cap (or made some equally obsequious gesture), and smiled cheerily throughout the ritual, the Paymaster handed him a fifty-dollar bill.

Every tenth bonus or so was allegedly the Paymaster's Five Hundred: five hundred bucks and your photo in the company newsletter.

So the story went, at least, but don't hold your breath waiting.

I mean, who did they think they were kidding? It didn't take an Einstein to see what was coming down. The Paymaster was the brainchild of a clever marketing man who dwelled somewhere in the upper stratosphere of the Mobil Oil Building on Lexington and 42nd. This marketing man had gotten all he could out of puncture-proof tires and those batteries that would supposedly start your car even after a full-blown nuclear attack, and one day he struck upon the real need of the company: the Paymaster Myth.

No doubt this marketing man was generously rewarded by the oil company for making the rest of us look so stupid. The home office had been dying for some way to force those snotty little franchised operations to tow the line. The chairman of the board had always despised the idea that at the point of sale his multibillion-dollar multinational corporation was represented by ill-mannered grease monkeys who never once in their lives had clipped their nostril hairs or cleaned beneath their fingernails.

"That's what we'll do, by God!" the chairman of the board had bellowed approvingly. "We'll tell them there's a Paymaster in their future."

So now the Paymaster visited gas stations in the same mysterious way that the tooth fairy visited sleeping six-year-olds.

"Listen, Summerhelp," the guys at the gas station chorused. "You oughta be damn glad you're even getting a shot at the Paymaster."

I laughed at them.

"C'mon, Pete, tell me. When was he here last? When was the last time he gave someone fifty bucks, much less five goddam hundred?"

"Don't get smart with me," warned Peter. His bark was worse than his bite, however; I'd learned that much rather quickly.

"Who's getting smart? I just have my doubts about this Paymaster. It sounds to me like the carrot in front of the donkey."

"Well, I tell you what. If he gives you the big fat one, the Paymaster's Five Hundred, let me hear you call five hundred dollars a fuckin' carrot."

"Hey, if he gives me five hundred bucks just because I wash my face and hands and act like a prototype gas jockey, I start believing—im-mediately."

Pete laughed cynically. "You're so full of shit. You grow your hair long like the rest of them horse's asses and say you don't care about money. Hah! Five hundred bucks and you'll start believing. And you call *me* greedy."

"I never called you greedy."

"You think it."

"No I don't."

(He was the greediest bastard in the world.)

"You don't lie too good, Summerhelp. Whyn't you just say what you think?

"You're greedy."

"You're right. And do you know why? Because so is everyone else. Even you dumb hippies."

"I'm not a hippie," I said resentfully. "Don't tag me."

"No? And I ain't a greedy old fart. What d'you think of that?"

A car pulled in and I hustled out to the pump island, relieved to be freed from Pete. But he followed close behind, taunting me. "Might be him. You never know. Fifty bucks, maybe five hundred. *Five hundred,* Summerhelp. Imagine that? Why, with five hundred bucks in your pocket you could come right out and tell me everything you really think about me. Money's great that way, don't let nobody fool you. If you got a pocketful of jingle, you don't need to give a shit."

I plunged the pump nozzle into the tank.

"I doubt this is the Paymaster, Pete. This is a tan Chevy Bel Air. He'd never drive a tan Bel Air. He wouldn't be caught dead in one."

"Got an answer for everything, ain'tcha? Listen, you make sure you wipe them windshields till it looks like there ain't no glass, and sell every drop of oil and gas you can even if it means the guy won't have enough money to get buried when he dies. How's that for greedy? And you do it with a smile, Summerhelp—let me see. Ah, that's good. Just like goddam Howdy Doody. You keep smilin' like that and hum a happy tune. You might not believe in the Paymaster but you'd better believe who signs your paycheck."

The mechanics all swore to the existence of the Paymaster. They all said they had one or another friend who had met him. They even claimed that a gas jockey at Bert's Mobil on Hylan Boulevard had won the Paymaster's Five Hundred.

It was Eddie who had first brought up the Paymaster. He was a short guy, Eddie, with dense, knotted dark hair and thick forearms permanently blackened by grease. His face was always dirty, and this made his eyes appear whiter than they actually were. He smoked unfiltered cigarettes and after only a few drags the cigarette paper was about as clean as a subway platform. He looked so much like a gas-station mechanic that I finally came to the conclusion that he hadn't been born of human parents but instead had been turned out by a lathe as someone's shop project at McKee Vocational High School.

When Eddie first asked me if I knew about the Paymaster he was up to his elbows in a Chevy Nova, squatting there atop the engine block while I handed him tools. "Don't forget, if a car pulls in for gas, you gotta run. Pete wants you to be number-one gas jockey."

"Yeah," I said, without enthusiasm.

"Hey," said Eddie. "You get first dibs on the Paymaster. What the hell you gripin' about?"

"The Paymaster?"

"Yeah—the Paymaster."

"Who the hell's that?"

He stopped what he was doing and climbed from under the hood of the Nova. He turned slyly to George and Tom. He pointed at me with the wrench he was holding and informed the other two, "Hey, guys— um, Summerhelp here doesn't know about the, ahem, bonuses."

So they told me the story and expected me to believe it.

That was a day Pete had left early for the racetrack, saying as he went that he hoped there wouldn't be a thunderstorm. He had looked at the sky worriedly because his money was on a dry track.

The mechanics took advantage of the situation to lounge around the front desk. When four o'clock arrived, Tom sent George after some beer and George took the Jeep and returned with two six-packs. He had no sooner set the beer down than I was there, grabbing a cold one. I took a church key from the hook, opened the can, and sat on the corner of the front desk. Tom was sitting in the chair, his boots propped up on the desk. He relished the idea of playing boss while his Uncle Pete was gone. He probably prayed that Pete would get struck by lightning so he could take over the business.

"Did you pay for that beer?" he asked me.

"No one asked me to chip in."

"Well, I'm askin' now."

I reached into my pocket and tossed more than my share on the desk.

"There," I said. "How's that?"

We all sat there, belting down the cold beer and talking about women and engines, and since I was the youngest they told me I didn't know a thing about either subject. Then a lone car pulled up at the far pump island. I was in no great hurry to run out and pump gas. The garbage trucks had been lined up all day like camels at an oasis, and the wind had been blowing the stink of the garbage our way since noon. The beer in my fist tasted like heaven and I moaned about the driver of the car being such a stupid ass for not pulling up to the nearer island.

"Someone else do it," I complained.

Tom barked, "Hey, you're here to pump gas and kiss ass, Mac."

Meanwhile, Eddie had said to George, "Now ain't that something the Paymaster would do?"

At first George regarded Eddie quizzically, but then he caught on and chimed in, "Hell, yes. Now that you mention it I heard that's just what he'd do to see if our Summerhelp runs on down there. It's something the Paymaster would do to see if a guy deserved the big one."

"You want a big one, George?" I asked. "I'll tell you where to get one and where to stick it."

"You little prick," he said.

"You're up, Summerhelp," said Tom.

"Let me take it there, Tom," said Eddie. "Shit, I bet it's him. I heard from them in Bayonne that he's been around. Said he's drivin' a station wagon, maroon, like that one there."

"Let him," I dared Tom. "The Paymaster's a crock of shit and you know it. I don't care if there's a million bucks in it. I'd rather finish my beer."

"Listen, pal—" began Tom, raising his finger at me.

I swallowed the rest of my beer and tossed the empty can into the cardboard box in the corner. "All right," I said. "What the fuck."

I'd already kept the customer waiting too long so I hustled along the blacktop. But I had only gone a short distance when I noticed that there was a woman behind the wheel of the car. Maybe the Paymaster was a woman, I thought, laughing to myself. A reasonable ploy.

But then, abruptly, I realized I knew this woman. She was no ordinary person, either. She was Mrs. Murtagh.

Eileen Murtagh was this beautiful woman who lived in the largest, finest house in the town where Jimmy and I had grown up. Jimmy had worked regularly for the Murtaghs, mowing the lawn and raking leaves. Occasionally I had helped him, though I'd concentrated more on stealing glances at Mrs. Murtagh than I did on working.

When I came to the driver's window I saw that her two children were with her. There was a small boy in the backseat. He looked to be six years old, and I could recall quite clearly when he had been a baby.

Alongside Mrs. Murtagh on the front seat was a younger girl, who held a Dr. Seuss book in her lap. Mrs. Murtagh was pointing out pictures and repeating, "Green eggs and ham," in a lilting voice.

When she looked at me I wondered if she recognized me. I doubted she did, and for the first time in quite a while I found I was self-conscious about my glass eye.

"Fill it with regular, please," she said.

"Okay," I said.

I felt my face flush when she had looked at me. She infatuated me as strongly today as she had when I was a teenager. She was absolutely beautiful. She was Irish-looking, with lush brown hair and pale, clear violet eyes. She smiled readily, and her voice was charming. Her cheeks looked healthy, blushed and sort of plump; her eyes danced with light and made you think of flowers in a sunny field.

I had delayed there a moment, magnetized by my need to take in her beauty and the warmth of the motherliness she showed her children. I had, as a boy, fantasized marrying this woman, and I was surprised and confused that I was unable now to shake that youthful dream.

She noticed that I hadn't immediately jumped to fill her order, and she didn't know what to make of it. She glanced back over her shoulder, asking, "Am I near enough?"

"Yes. No problem."

I started the gas pumping and meanwhile cleaned her windshield thoroughly. Through the glass I watched her lead her little daughter through the book. In the backseat the boy played with a toy airplane, making jet noises. I found myself full of desire for a place in this tableau.

The gas pump clicked off. I let the nozzle sit while I cleaned the rear window. Then I pulled the handle from the tank and returned it to its slot on the pump.

"How's the oil?" I asked.

"I'm sure it's fine," she replied. "My husband takes care of that."

I nodded.

She gave me a ten for the gas and I quickly hustled inside for change.

"Je-sus, Summerhelp," whistled tall George, watching me whiz in and out of the office. "For a guy who pitched a bitch you sure are movin' now. That must be the Paymaster after all."

2

The day after I'd arrived from Oregon I rented one of the old bungalows near the Orange House beach. It was still called the Orange House beach even though the Orange House itself was gone. All that remained of the old building was the concrete floor and a pile of debris of many pieces of orange clapboard.

I knew from the first that I'd be staying on my own once I returned to Staten Island. I'd not lived at my parents' place since the weeks I'd spent recuperating from having lost my eye. Yet even though I didn't intend staying with them, I knew they'd want to know where I was and that I was in a reasonably buoyant condition. It had been for this same reason that I'd developed the habit while out west of telephoning them monthly. It was, I'd felt, like an attendance check, filing a report that said, yes, I was still on the planet and although I wasn't especially thrilled with the way things were working out, neither was I so terribly depressed.

My parents, of course, were mildly shocked to see me. They'd had no forewarning of my appearance. Mom was obviously glad, and though she neither hugged nor kissed me—we weren't a hugging kissing family—when she saw me her face lit up and she said it was a nice surprise. I'd not seen her for almost two years, since the day I'd left for Chicago with every intention of attending De Paul University. As things ended up, I wasn't at De Paul long enough to warm the seat of a chair before heading out to Oregon to smoke pot and meditate with what's-her-name.

Mom's habits were the eternal background of my memory. She pretty much looked the same and sounded the same as ever, except that she seemed shorter, coming no higher than my shoulder. Strands of gray hair coarse as yarn weaved through her reddish hair; her dark brown eyes had never seemed to have pupils.

She was tough, a real disciplinarian when it came to school or church, though her sense of humor was among the best in the world. Even when things were gloomy she could usually find a way to laugh at herself—or work so hard that she was too exhausted to ponder her difficulties. But those times when there was little to laugh at because her worries had become too burdensome, she would stay up until early in the morning, watching a Spencer Tracy movie on TV with a string of crystal rosary beads entwined in her fingers.

I didn't see my dad until later that day when he returned from work. His response to my unannounced arrival was even less animated than Mom's, though over the years of having studied his face and his brief uncommunicative gestures I'd learned to decipher his feelings fairly accurately and I knew that he felt good to see me.

I'd not failed to notice that Dad hadn't tousled my hair, which was the solitary gesture of affection he allowed himself with his children. He still tousled the hair of my brothers and sisters, but not mine. He was, I think, afraid of touching and hurting my head where I'd been hit. He couldn't hide the fact that he worried I'd become fragile; he couldn't hide the fact, though he tried, that he felt the "soft spot" of my infant skull had mysteriously returned.

My family no longer lived in the house where I'd grown up, out there where I'd been close to Dietz and the others. The house was gone now. The passing lane of one of the new highways had sliced through it. Of course, my parents had to sell the house to the state. We then moved to an apartment building at the northern end of the island right after I'd graduated high school.

I was never sure why we hadn't moved into another house, though I imagined it had something to do with money. It had so happened that this matter of the highway came at the same time that the company my dad worked for over in New Jersey was pulling up stakes and moving south. The company left him behind, and I think he took a big cut in pay when he at last found another job. Whatever the circumstances, the move had left us wounded as a family, and even though it's been said that time is a healer I wasn't sure if we would ever recover from the loss.

I stayed overnight on the living-room couch at the apartment, and the following morning, holding my youngest sister on my lap while she slobbered her cereal, I ate breakfast with my mom and gave her a sketchy account of my trip back east. I told her about the article in *Time* and she said she'd been talking to someone from the old neighborhood about Jimmy. She said that everyone was so proud of him.

Back in the days when the beaches along Staten Island had been a popular getaway for people from Manhattan and Brooklyn, which was back before I was born, there were many small summer homes and cottages and bungalow colonies up and down the shore. But eventually the beaches became polluted and the highways that were built after World War II made it convenient for people from the city to travel farther for vacations. Staten Island quickly died as a summer haven. Some of the summer places were then converted into year-round homes with basements that flooded every spring, while most of the small bungalows were abandoned and left to rot. Here and there, however, a few dilapidated bungalow courts remained, and for old time's sake I retreated to one near the beach where we'd gone as teenagers.

The landlady showed me the bungalow, calling it Number Five even though there was a number seven on it, and when she took my forty dollars for the first month's rent she told me emphatically, "Don't be thinking past Labor Day."

"I never do," I assured her.

"And don't be making no campfires indoors. They come in here, them snotty kids, and they make campfires and write filthy words on the walls. I get the cops but the cops don't catch 'em."

As she folded my four ten-dollar bills and tucked them away, she regarded my glass eye suspiciously. It wasn't uncommon for people to study me that way. They never could figure out if I was looking their way or not, and they naturally came to the conclusion that I was sneaky. It was even worse when I wore my eye patch. Then they were additionally wary of me, figuring I was Long John Silver or, worse, Moshe Dayan.

She turned this way and that to my glass eye, repeating, "No fires. Labor Day, then you're gone. Got me?"

I told her I understood the house rules and thanked her for her sage advice. Don't think past Labor Day. Don't make campfires indoors.

I had moved in with the few necessary items that had managed to tag along with me through two years of college and my travels out west, the ones I'd found on my doorstep when Betty had decided never to walk out: a sleeping bag, a duffel bag, a few select books, clothes, a pair of work boots, a pair of sneakers. I also had a few candles. Fat candles. I enjoyed doing things by candlelight, having picked up the habit from a girl in Corvallis who lived on a commune and meditated frequently. I guess I figured that if it became a habit with me I'd grow up to be Abe Lincoln or Buddha. Although I shouldn't be so grandiose; it would be enough, some days, simply to grow up.

The bungalow had a small gas stove and a bathroom with a chain-flush toilet. The water didn't work in the shower nor at the kitchen sink, so I took all my water from the bathroom sink.

There was a narrow, moldy, poorly lit bedroom in the rear, which I avoided as if it were the epicenter of plague, sleeping instead on the floor in the front room or out on the small porch. The nights were still cool, and so the mosquitoes which were commercially raised on Staten Island were still hidden by the millions as larvae.

The night I went to see Deluxe I returned to the bungalow and put the package he had given me on the kitchen table. I unwrapped the canvas.

There it was. The shotgun. It looked brand-new. That was the way Dietz had taken care of things.

I left it on the kitchen table. My head had started to ache, and so I popped out my eye, which usually helped for some reason, and put my pirate patch over the socket. I left the glass eye guarding the shotgun and went outside.

I walked among the ruins of the Orange House and smoked some grass. Then I started a tidy driftwood fire where the jetty blocked the off-shore breeze. I looked up at the night sky and thought about Corney Walsh, wondering if he was anywhere at all or if death was truly the end of all that. In either case, nothing could be done.

My attention came back to earth shortly. Alongside me, the small fire cracked and popped, the salted wood erupting in chlorine-green and sodium-yellow flares. I found some respite for long moments in the focused warmth and unpredictable flames of the fire, and then discovered myself looking across the water at the pilings where, on summer afternoons, me and the rest of the guys used to perch like seabirds. I noticed that the tide was up.

There was this Easter Sunday, one year when Easter had come early. March, not April, and for some reason Jimmy had told the guys down in Huguenot that the bunch of us would dive off Vanderbilt's pier and swim to shore on Easter Sunday morning. Jimmy had told us about this boast of his the night before it was to happen, saying that we should wear our bathing suits under our pants when we went to church the following morning. He said we'd all walk down to the beach together, including the guys who went to the Lutheran church and the guys who didn't go to church, and all of us would meet the Huguenot guys at the beach and show them that we would do what Dietz had said we would.

Corney was pissed off over the whole thing, because he didn't think Dietz should go around bragging that we'd do asinine stunts.

"That water am ice-fud'yan-cold," protested Corney.

"Of course it is," said Dietz agreeably. "If it wasn't ice-cold they wouldn't be impressed."

"Didja bet money?" asked Spyros shrewdly.

"Money's got nothing to do with it," said Dietz.

"Then why the fuck should we do it?" demanded Spyros.

"For the principle of it," I put in, knowing that this would have been Jimmy's answer.

"The Chun's right," agreed Jimmy. He paused, taking in the group with a long glance. "Those guys said no one could swim in from the end of the pier in March. They said the water would kill you. I told them they were wrong, that I could do it. They said that maybe I could, but not you guys. I couldn't let them say that, could I?"

He had us; I knew he had us.

"You should've at least bet cash," complained Spyros. "If I'm going to die, I at least want to die for money."

"That's dumb," put in Woodsie.

"Are *you* going to dive off the pier into that shit for nothin'?" Spyros answered sharply.

Woodsie looked around questioningly at the rest of us. His hair was over his eyes, because his mother gave him his haircuts and always left the bangs. He looked like a sad dog. It hadn't escaped him that no one other than Dietz had so far agreed to this suicide mission. He didn't want to be the first to say no, but he sure didn't want to say yes either.

"Maybe it ain't so cold," he stammered. "Maybe I'll do it. I don't know. I got to think about it."

"Maybe it ain't so cold," Corney mocked him. "What the fuck you got for brains? Horseshit?"

We were in Spyros's finished-off basement that night when Dietz threw down the gauntlet. We were playing this game with darts in which each guy had to take a turn holding his hand palm out on the target while everyone else took a turn throwing three darts. The idea, of course, was to come the closest without burying a dart in the guy's hand. Some guys, like Corney and Spyros, preferred having their hand on the target just to show how dumb and fearless they were.

We played games like this because there was absolutely nothing else to do on March nights. We never had any money—except for Spyros, who always did—and, being fourteen-year-olds, we wouldn't be able to drive for what seemed many years yet, so we killed time by getting together at someone's house, where we watched TV if there was anything at all worth watching, or we did stupid things like play

knuckles or destroy old plastic models of cars and battleships by dous-
ing them with lighter fluid and then putting a match to them. It was this
unending boredom that made the idea of jumping into the ocean in
March look so appealing. When it came down to it, each of us had
secretly wanted to go along with Dietz from the start. We'd only
wanted to be convinced that it wasn't as stupid an idea as it truly
appeared.

After Dietz had weaseled from us our pledge to jump in the ocean
the following morning, we found ourselves bored all over again. We
smoked cigarettes and drank Cokes and talked about girls for a while.
Then Corney came up with the idea of soaping the tracks at the train
station so the train would skid when it tried to stop. But no one wanted
to go along with the idea. We'd done it before, wasting whole bars of
soap on the tracks only to watch the train pull in and stop on a dime.

"It don't work, Corney," said Spyros.

"Then let's spill water on the conductor," suggested Corney.

"That don't work either," said Woodsie.

"We always get caught," I added. "They hear us on the roof and
we spend all night hiding from the cops. It's too fuckin' cold to hide in
the woods tonight."

"Pussy *woo-shit,*" said Corney.

"I'm ranked out, Corney," I said sarcastically. "I really feel like a
pussy *woo-shit,* y'know?"

"It am true. You am chickenshit to get on the roof."

"No I'm not."

I could feel Corney suckering me again. He'd been doing this to me
ever since first grade, when he'd persuaded me to leave my crayons
overnight on the radiator. The following morning the crayons were a
melted knobby ball of waxy colors.

He managed to sucker me day after day, and I never seemed to
learn that listening to Corney not only brought me the deepest sort of
woe, but, on more than one occasion, nearly got me killed. He led me
so far astray in public school that I was eventually sent to Catholic
school, where, I'd been assured by more than one adult, "the nuns will
fix your wagon."

Yet I liked Corney. I even liked the way he suckered me into doing
things that otherwise I wouldn't do. I probably liked him more than I
liked any of the other guys.

My feelings for Dietz were not as clear. I admired Dietz and I envied his many skills, and I wanted to learn from Dietz and become Dietz. And though I liked Dietz, it wasn't in the way that I liked Corney. With Dietz, I felt I had to measure up. With Corney, I could just be a screwball.

Corney was wiry, smaller than me (always had been), and no matter how much time he spent in the sun he never tanned. He burned. And he burned worse than anyone. All he had to do was lean out the window on a sunny day and he would burn as if he'd fallen asleep under a heat lamp. He'd get a bad sunburn and then his skin would peel, and he'd burn all over again. It wouldn't matter if he pasted himself thick with suntan oil, he still burned, blistered, peeled, and burned again. All summer long he smelled of Noxzema. If you accidentally brushed up against him from June to September—or purposely slapped his back as Spyros would—he went absolutely berserk and made you pay for it.

He had that strange *fud'yan 'fwat* speech impediment punctuated by his fits of asthma. In grade school he went to see the speech teacher every Thursday afternoon. But he never really tried to speak normally, because he enjoyed being different and was convinced that, in time, everyone would be speaking exactly like him.

It was true that we tried to imitate him. We tried to say "Fud'yan 'fwat am woo-sit," to mean, roughly, "Fucking thing is bullshit," slurring it all together as if it was a single word, even wheezing the way Corney wheezed so it would sound as if we weren't saying words at all but just expelling noxious teenage vapors that took on this sound of *fud'yan 'fwat am woo'sit.* We did this because Corney made it sound neat, and because the girls fell all over him and we figured it must have something to do with his speech. But we never quite got the *fud'yan 'fwat* down, and never had near as many girls trailing us.

Because of his asthma Corney wheezed when he ran and he wheezed when he laughed. He wheezed through his nose while he ate. He wheezed in his sleep and called you a liar when you woke him up to tell him to be quiet. He was like a balloon endlessly leaking air, but he had more energy than a flock of birds and he was one of the best athletes around. His reflexes were sharp and his hands were blindingly quick. His eye was deadly accurate and he would sooner be buried alive in hot tar than lose a game or come in second in a race. Whatever

it might be—stickball, poker, horseshoes, you name it—Corney
would sooner die than lose.

Corney was always the first one out of his house in the morning.
This habit of Corney's to rise early didn't mean he had a lot of get-up-
and-go. It just so happened that his father woke him nearly every day
at dawn and browbeat him, telling him he was lazy and didn't have
what it took to be a success in this man's world. Corney couldn't stand
to listen to this crap, basically because his father was such a hypocrite.
The only reason Mr. Walsh was up at dawn himself was that he'd been
drinking and gambling all night. He wouldn't have known success if
five solid tons of it fell on him from the top of a skyscraper.

Corney bolted from his house as quickly as he could, the morning's
first Marlboro wedged between his lips, grumbling, usually carrying
his shirt and shoes, which he would put on while sitting on the bumper
of a nearby car. He headed directly to my house, using the Carlton
Avenue path. He came in the back door, which was never locked.

It had never mattered to Corney if anyone was up and around in
the house when he arrived. My mother had once told him, "Our house
is your house," and Corney took this to heart. No sooner had he
entered the back door than he was fixing breakfast for himself. It
wasn't unusual for my father to return from the night shift to find
Corney sitting on the couch balancing a large bowl of cornflakes, the
television tuned to *Modern Farmer.* Over the years he had grown so
accustomed to seeing Corney around the house, eating at strange
hours, that when he finally sat down at the kitchen table and discovered at his elbow that poor kid from the Sandy Grounds who had been
living in the trunk in the basement, he immediately asked, "Are you
Corney's brother?"

The kid had said, "Yes," and gone on eating.

I think my father grew to like Corney enormously, even though he
thought he was from Mars, and I know that when Corney died in
Vietnam my father was deeply shaken.

The Easter Sunday we planned to go for a swim, Corney was
sitting in the kitchen at my house eating eggs and bacon well before
my sisters and brother had even started hunting for their Easter baskets. Once I finally crawled from bed he was already mopping up yolk
with a piece of toast and looking for more coffee. When he saw me he
immediately pulled me aside and unzipped his pants to show me that

he was wearing his red bathing suit. He said he hoped I'd remembered to wear mine, and I said, "Of course, what d'you think?" and then took the first opportunity I had to slip into it secretly.

We met Spyros and Woodsie at the corner, where we waited for the church bus. On the bus we took delight in daring each other aloud to pull down our pants in front of the girls. The girls said things like "Don't you dare" (except for Alice Tompkins, who said we didn't have the nerve). So we pulled down our pants to show them our bathing suits and brag how we were going swimming after church. They said, "Yeah, indoors somewhere."

"Not likely," we boasted, telling them the scheme.

When the mass was over, we met Harry the Horse and Sperm at the Shack. While waiting there for Dietz, who had served as altar boy at mass, we ate buttered rolls and crullers to screw up our courage. Dietz finally arrived. He swallowed down a cup of hot coffee and eagerly led us the half mile to Vanderbilt's beach.

We were wearing winter jackets. Sperm had heard on the radio that it was forty-eight degrees. Dietz said Sperm was wrong; he said it was at least fifty. Once Dietz had spoken we all immediately discounted what Sperm had said. We really didn't want to believe it was forty-eight degrees anyway. We were convinced that fifty was much warmer.

We'd given Sperm his nickname because he liked to draw whole armies of wriggling sperm cells on his school books. He liked the idea that sperm cells lived for nothing more than to besiege an egg cell somewhere inside the dark sexual recesses of a girl. As you might imagine, he enjoyed jerking off, and he bragged to us about how far he could ejaculate. He swore that if there were Olympics for shooting sperm, he'd be a gold medalist. After a while, at least in my mind, he actually came to resemble a sperm: a balloon-shaped head, pale reddish-blond hair shaved close to his tight, smooth skull, wispy flagellated legs, and only half the chromosomes needed to be reasonably human.

The guys from Huguenot were already at the beach when we got there. They were smoking cigarettes and drinking hot coffee. When they saw us they started laughing aloud, punching one another joyously over the treat we were about to provide.

While we were still a short distance from them, Sperm said, "They think we're going to stick our toes in and then walk home like cry-babies." He crinkled his nose and squinted, trying to see them more clearly. "They think it's a joke."

"Act like there's no big deal," said Dietz. "We'll just take off our clothes, walk to the end of the pier, dive off, and swim to shore. No big deal."

"Yeah," agreed Spyros. "Make like we do it all the time."

Spyros sounded undaunted. But you could never tell about him. He would say one thing and do another. He was sort of a spoiled kid and felt he could get away with just about anything. His father ran a con-struction outfit and owned an inboard motorboat and two Cadillacs. Spyros had every new gadget the day it appeared on a television commercial. His room was packed tighter with stuff than a Sears cata-logue: stacks of records, a punching bag, weights, baseball gloves (a fielder's mitt, a first baseman's glove, a catcher's mitt), and probably hundreds of comic books, mostly Sergeant Rock, the Flash, and Aqua-man. He usually wore brand-new clothes, and when he went to a dance his pants were creased sharp as a metal ruler and his shoes looked like they been taken from the store window that afternoon. But he was not the sort of guy to be trusted, and it was easy enough to dislike Spyros without being envious over all the stuff he had.

One thing I have to say for Spyros, though, was that he always fought his own battles. He worked out with weights and his arms and shoulders were like his father's: bulging and hard as weathered oak. He was by far the best-built guy among us, though the girls didn't like him because he flaunted the fact that he had money, and, they said, his eyes were shifty, his nose looked like a moldy turnip, and there was so much acne on his back it was like alligator hide.

I suddenly realized, now that we stood there watching the Hugue-not guys laugh at us, that we had maneuvered ourselves into a corner. We might actually have to pull off this stunt.

Standing in the sand, we unlaced and removed our shoes. Then we pulled off our socks and stood there while the Huguenot guys left the pier and came over to taunt us. They were convinced that we didn't have the balls to go through with this.

They might have been right. No sooner had we taken off our socks than Corney said, "This sand am cold as shit, Jack."

The guys from Huguenot tramped over through the brown sand and laughed at us, saying, "You assholes ain't really goin' through with this, are yous?"

They looked at Dietz and said, "Hey, Dietz, it's colder than a witch's tit. You and your guys ain't got nothin' to prove."

But they were smirking over it and getting a kick out of the fact that the goosebumps rippled our skin as we stood there undressing. We resembled plucked and bloodless chickens, just like the frozen ones in the supermarket. Our nipples were stiff and tender. Embarrassing.

"We always swim on Easter," Corney informed them, wheezing, his arms wrapped around himself. "It am part of our religion."

Spyros had meanwhile gone off to haul together some driftwood to make a big fire. Good move, I figured.

But the guys from Huguenot noticed what Spyros was doing and said mockingly, "Hey, what's the idea of a fire? You guys need a fire after you go swimming? If it's warm enough to swim, it's too warm for a fire, ain't it?"

They looked to Dietz, and the one named Carl asked, "What's with the fire?"

Dietz stood there wearing only his bathing suit. "We don't need a fire," he said.

The wind picked up and tousled his thick reddish hair. He thrust back his shoulders and refused to show how cold he was, even though there were goosebumps up and down his wildly freckled legs. "We don't need a fire," he repeated, this time to Spyros.

This was too much, we all thought. We studied one another's faces and saw that we held a common opinion. We'd like to strangle Dietz for this. Was this too fuckin' much, or what? No fire?

But Jimmy had already started across the cold sand toward the pier, and damned if we didn't all fall in line and follow him. Corney mouthed off to the Huguenot guys, "We was goin' to build the fire for yous guys. You am standin' there shiverin' your asses off."

"Yeah," said Spyros. His chest muscles flexed involuntarily in the cold and he tossed his Zippo to one of them. "Stay warm."

We marched in single file out along the old timbers of the pier. Dietz said that no one should wrap their arms around himself (as any sane person would do) but instead be real casual about it.

"We'll dive in and swim to shore," he said confidently. "Just put it in your head and do it. That's all it takes."

Jimmy, I wanted to say. Jimmy, it's freezing. Let's go home, man.

But I wouldn't be the one to surrender. Not me.

We filed behind him like a line of ducklings. Me, Corney, Spyros, Jimpie, Woodsie, Harry the Horse, and Sperm. If anyone had dared try to tell us that we would do anything as long as Dietz was leading us we would have denied it, saying that we could think for ourselves.

Well, maybe we could think for ourselves, but we would have been lying about not following Dietz.

When we had reached the end of the pier we could tell without looking back to shore that the Huguenot guys were beginning to believe we'd really do it. At the same time, we realized it was even colder out here than it had been on shore. The wind buffeted us and the horizon was gray and dismal. The surface of the water was flecked with whitecaps.

"Hey, Chun," said Spyros. "Your lips are blue."

I shivered. "So are my nuts."

Sensing that our courage had begun to flag, Jimmy said, "Remember. Nothing to it. Dive in, swim to shore. We've done it a million times before."

"Yeah, but that was in August," said Sperm.

"No, man," insisted Dietz. "That was in March. Put that right in here." He pointed to his head.

"Hey—we ain't never done this shit in March," said Sperm.

"Don't you get it?" I asked Sperm. "Tell yourself you have."

"That's all it takes," said Dietz.

He stood there at the edge of the heavy timber pier, and I looked at his shoulders and chest, which were more bone than muscle, and I followed the course of his ropy tendons. I wondered how strong Jimmy really was and how strong he had convinced himself he could be.

"I still wish there was money on the line," moaned Spyros as he regarded the cold water six feet below.

"They'll respect us for it," Jimmy guaranteed. "When we play them in football next year they'll remember that we were the crazy bastards who dove off the pier in March and they'll never be able to beat us."

Of us all, only Woodsie with his bowl-cut hair wore boxer shorts. The rest of us wore tight suits that scrunched our peckers and stopped the blood from getting past our groins. Woodsie's trunks were decorated with palm trees and looked ridiculous. He stood there miserably afraid. He started to clutch at straws, saying, "Sometimes the air is colder than the water."

"Not in March it ain't."

"Shit," moaned someone.

Jimmy calmly stepped to the edge of the pier. He pushed himself up ever so slightly on his toes. His calves knotted. Then he took a deep breath and reached up and out with his arms. He flexed his knees and pushed off into the air. Just like that. Just as he had said. Just do it.

There he was, arching across the cold gray March sky, suspended, it seemed, for our amazement, but inevitably bound for the freezing cold water. There had been something so outrageously simple about it, about the deed being done, about this lofting abandon, that no sooner was Jimmy at the apogee of his flight than I flung myself after him, sensing in the next moment that Corney, too, was airborne.

I was sailing through the air when suddenly Jimmy surfaced, and in that fraction of a second before I crashed into the ocean I could see Jimmy's face. He was terribly surprised by something; he spluttered and gasped and he yelled, "Go back, Chun! It's too—"

Cold.

Like hitting an iceberg cold. Or leaving your balls overnight in the freezer chest cold. Or being trapped naked in a meat locker with your bare ass up against the frozen walls.

For a moment, the water had been green and not at all cold. I almost laughed. Cold? This ain't cold. Jimmy had been joking, telling me in midair to go back.

And then I figured I would die. The coldness wrapped around my chest like a straitjacket and wouldn't let me breathe. I surfaced in panic, my eyeballs bulging from my head. I panted like a tired old dog. I swam frantically even though my arms and legs were numb. I swam like a beginner who was afraid of the water. The other guys, all but

Corney, had remained on the pier. They'd heard Jimmy scream. They weren't stupid enough to dive in after that.

There was no way back onto the pier. That had been the whole idea behind the challenge. Once you were in the soup, you had to swim to shore. There was no other way.

Corney was swimming madly, thrashing the water and gasping frantically. I heard him suck his lungs full and wheeze like a teapot. He yelled aloud but said nothing. He just kept yelling and wheezing, "Ye-ow!" *Wheeze.* "Ye-ow!" *Wheeze.*

I just had to get a breath. I tried to yell, knowing somehow it might help me breathe.

Dietz came alongside, paddling the water. "Chun?"

I couldn't answer. I panted and gasped and swam awkwardly, frantically. Jimmy could see the fear in my eyes. He said, "You'll make it. Believe me. I never lie, Chun. You'll make it."

He drew close and said, "I'll get you there. Don't worry."

Then he maneuvered to put me in a cross-chest carry and I managed to sputter, "No. No, I'll do it."

He said, "Good, I'm with you."

Corney yelled and splashed toward shore. I caught my breath. I would be all right. I could do it. I could put it in my mind and do it.

Corney waded onto shore. He jumped up and down and rubbed his chest and shoulders. He raced over and pulled on his clothes.

Then Jimmy and I pulled ourselves from the water. I was trembling so violently that I thought my arms and legs would shake loose. My chest heaved; my stomach ached and quivered. My skin had no feeling. My knees and elbows felt old and stiff.

"Fuckin' crazy," I stammered. "Just fuckin' crazy."

Together Jimmy and I hurried over to our clothes. Trembling and chattering, we pulled our pants on. Our hair was drenched; our shirts soaked through the moment we put them on. No one had thought to bring a towel.

"Just fuckin' crazy," I repeated.

"We did it," Jimmy pointed out. He indicated the Huguenot guys, who were approaching across the sand. "Look, Chun. Take a good look. We earned their respect. They won't ever forget what we did."

"That's good, Dietz, because I ain't ever goin' to do it again."

"Listen," advised Jimmy, "if they want to start a fire for us, turn them down. We'll run up to the pizza place on the boulevard. It's warm as toast in there."

"Hey!" one of the Huguenot guys called. "Hey, we'll start a fire for you."

"That's all right," said Dietz. "We're headin' out."

"Yeah," I said, gritting my teeth. "We're headin' out."

Carl came forward and handed Jimmy some money. Jimmy counted it out. Twenty dollars.

"We never thought you'd do it," said Carl. For some reason he looked at me and added, "Fuckin' Chun."

Spyros had come over and hadn't failed to see the money change hands.

"I thought you said there wasn't any money on it," Spyros complained.

"I didn't want anyone to do it for money," said Jimmy.

Spyros couldn't figure it, though. "But we didn't do it, man. We didn't go in."

"Not all of us," said Jimmy.

"So how'd you win the twenty bucks?" asked Spyros.

There was a pause. A small breeze passed, chilling my head. Jimmy turned to Spyros and said, "I bet on the Chun."

Chapter 4

1

On hot July mornings when we were fourteen- and fifteen-year-olds we flowed together like tributaries to the playground at Bennett Avenue. Corney Walsh came for me and then the two of us went for Woodsie. The other guys, the ones who lived down near the town circle, met up with us at the place in the woods down this dead-end street where we had our stash of cigarettes and dirty books.

We generally didn't stop to get Dietz. He had chores to do every day, and unlike the rest of us couldn't worm his way out of them. His father was too strict. And even when he didn't have chores he went off alone very early in the morning to fish or he spent time at the parish rectory talking with Father Matusiak about the priesthood.

The guys from the circle passed the deli on their way to the meeting place, and if they weren't feeling cheap they'd buy a few cans of soda and bring them along. As everyone gathered we sat there on the log or on the tamped earth, drinking soda and smoking cigarettes. We took our pornographic magazines from their hiding place and flipped through the pages, awed by the big tits on the women and disputing endlessly over whether or not it was legal to show pussy in a magazine.

"It ain't legal," insisted Spyros, who always acted like he knew more about sex than anyone else. "If it was legal, they'd show it in *Playboy.*"

"There's nipples in *Playboy.*"

"Hey—nipples ain't pussy. Twat is pussy."

"No shit, Sherlock."

"It am fud'yan legal to show twat."

"Yeah, but you got to show it from the inside."

"What the hell you talking about?"

"Walsh, you're fulla shit. It ain't legal."

"Yeah? I'll tell you what am fulla shit is your bwain, asshole."

"Hey," said Jimpie, excited. "Hey—look't this one, man. It's sick."

"Holy shit—where'd you get it?"

"Spyros got it from his old man's drawer."

"That's gross."

"Your father's a prevert, Spyros."

"*Per*vert," I said.

"You oughta know, Chun. Catholic school's full of 'em."

The photograph that Spyros had lifted from his father's drawer showed a blindfolded woman giving a donkey a blowjob. We looked at it and laughed uproariously. Harry made the mistake of saying that she was wearing a mask because she was actually Corney's mother, and Corney, without a second thought, sucked down mucus from his nose and lobbed a thick glob of lunga onto Harry's head. Harry grabbed Corney and wrestled him down. He threatened to spit in Corney's face but didn't do it.

We sat there for a while longer until Spyros, as usual, pulled out his pecker to show us what an enormous hard-on he had. Corney said, "Hey, let me see it," and when Spyros turned toward him, Corney flicked a lit cigarette at his hard-on and the cigarette hit the tip of it.

Spyros wanted to kick the shit out of Corney for it, but we all told Spyros that he had paid the price for being such a show-off over his big dick.

We finally tucked all the pornography back into the plastic bags and wedged the package under the log before heading toward the playground.

We sauntered along together. Six, eight, sometimes ten of us. That was the way to do it. Together. Like a tribe. A tribe whose costume was T-shirts, blue jeans rolled up at the cuffs, ankle-high P.F. Flyers, and flat-top haircuts thickly waxed with Butch wax. We looked somewhat like skinny hedgehogs that had defied evolution by walking upright and learning to play basketball.

It was the greatest thing of all—to be one of the guys. They teased me about my thin arms and my knobby chest and the way I gave up too quickly when we climbed ropes; they tried to get Corney to speak like a human being and quit wheezing; we were in awe of Spyros's rock-hard biceps and his father's money; we told Jimpie that his latest girlfriend went down for the Purps, just to watch him run amuck and hurl litter baskets; we needled Woodsie for being such a chickenshit and for having such a dumb bowl haircut all the time; we asked Dietz how he liked the idea of knowing he'd never get laid.

But, hell, we were together. One heart. One mind. We were a tribe and there wasn't anything we wouldn't do for one another. The sunlight drenched us and the days were generous. The summer mornings stretched into afternoon and when the sun climbed unmercifully high in the sky we quit the playground and walked down to the Orange House beach. We dove into the water—Spyros and Jimpie doing flips into the breakers—and we could hear our brains sizzle as they cooled. If someone reminded us that the water was polluted, thick with chemicals and awful diseases like polio and hepatitis, we laughed boldly and drank it, just to prove that we were beyond illness and death.

Then we raised hell up and down the beach, playing touch football and broadcasting loud disgusting jokes just to impress the girls. And if the girls ignored us we waited until they went to the refreshment stand and took the opportunity to stuff half-dead bunkers in their beach bags and horseshoe crabs under their towels. Then we sat back and waited for the screams.

"Fud'yan 'fwat it am," said Corney, expressing our sentiments squarely. "We am fud'yan together, Jack!"

2

We returned to the Bennett Avenue playground at night to play basketball or long-court stickball until it was too dark to see. And during those last hours of daylight, across the way from the playground, Mr. McDaniels sat out on his aluminum-and-nylon-web lawn chair. Occasionally his wife joined him, but only, I was convinced, if he had first twisted her arm. His three noisy kids played in the yard or splashed about in the above-ground pool alongside the unfinished patio. They seemed always to have fireworks or BB rifles, and they had a habit of running while dripping wet into the house, which made Mrs. McDaniels a maniac. Even though we were across the street, at the far end of the stickball court, when she shrieked at the kids it felt as if a knitting needle was being plunged through your brain from ear to ear.

The McDanielses' place had originally been a trailer. The trailer was this puke-green color, and the additions to the trailer that McDaniels had slapped together over the years were different shades of green, as if he was attempting to match the original color but could never quite do so.

They owned a pickup truck with a rusted bed, and a station wagon that only Mrs. McDaniels drove. They had an above-ground pool, a birdbath on the lawn, and a basketball hoop above the garage doors. Out back there was a picnic table and a barbecue grill, a stockade fence, a redwood deck, and a plastic sunflower that twirled in the wind and made a clacking noise to scare off moles and the like.

There was construction junk all over. A cement mixer. A large stack of drainage tile, a small mound of gravel, old pieces of lumber. A backhoe was off to one corner of the front lawn, and along the side of the house facing the pool there stood a scaffold from a roofing job that McDaniels had abandoned some years before. Out in the weeds in the empty lot alongside the house, parked there on what McDaniels loved to call his property ("Hey, you kids," he'd bark when we searched the weeds for a baseball that had gone foul, "get the hell off my property.") was a dump truck that hadn't budged once since any of us guys could remember.

There were always two or more additional lawn chairs set out alongside Mr. and Mrs. McDaniels to entice company over. But the additional chairs were frequently unoccupied, because McDaniels was not what you might call the perfect host. In fact, you might say he was hostile and unbalanced.

He sat there nightly, McDaniels, never too far from a can of Rheingold beer, anticipating friendly visits that never materialized. Since he felt he was a likable person, this lack of company disappointed him severely, and as his disappointment swelled he drank more beer and grew angry. It would be a tactical mistake for him to take out this anger on the neighbors, and he recognized this. So he chose instead to take it out on us.

His method was to sit there as if stalking prey, just waiting for one
of us to curse so that he could head over, an avenging angel blasted on
boilermakers. Like fulminate to dynamite, that was all it took to set
him off—a teenager cursing.

Woodsie ran. He hadn't been the one who had cursed but he knew
that McDaniels didn't always grab the guilty party and he wasn't about
to take the rap for someone else.

Spyros lit a cigarette and stood there acting tough. Big deal.
McDaniels could crush him like a bug, but Spyros could act tough in
his face because Mr. Spyropoulos was in the construction business
and hired McDaniels now and then.

McDaniels drew nearer, passing through the open gate and bending his burly frame into the incline. He was a strong man, built like a
football player. He was surly and violent and yet he probably believed
that we looked up to him. His thick arms were tanned like oiled leather
and the sun-bleached hairs on his forearms curled up through a clutter
of blue-ink tattoos that traced the entire history of the Marine Corps.
There was no doubting his mean streak. It showed right through.

On evenings when by some miracle we had managed not to curse,
not having let slip even a venial "shit" or "piss" or "your momma"
(which McDaniels considered a curse because, as he confided to us
behind a cupped hand, "You boys are really saying *motherfucker,*
right?"), he would lumber over at a casual pace to congratulate us for
finally having learned to be such upstanding young men, and to show
us that he was, basically, all heart.

"Let me see that ball," he would say, motioning for the basketball.

He then took a few shots to limber up his rusty elbows, showing us
that he hadn't yet lost the old form and bragging to us that he had been
a three-letter man back in high school, even though we knew that he
was talking about the days when anyone could have made the team,
back when people didn't even know how to take a jump shot, shooting
instead the way McDaniels still shot, pushing the ball up with both
hands like—we agreed secretly when he had gone—a girl.

He came over and stopped our game whenever he felt like it,
telling us to start again so that he could play. He would point to one of
us who wasn't very good—often me or Woodsie—and tell the guy to
take a break.

Once in the game he moved stiffly and grunted heavily. He labored for breath and purposely slowed the game down by tucking the ball under his arm and calling imaginary fouls. He muscled his way in under the boards for rebounds, taking delight in knocking one of us skinny guys on his ass.

When he'd been drinking, which was about as often as sunrise, he became intensely interested in mending our ways. He wanted us to be like him.

If he was over there in the front yard and one of us happened to say the four-letter word, three-letter McDaniels shot up and kicked his chair aside and hunkered over with fire in his eyes.

He seized hold of the guy he'd heard curse, or at least the guy he figured he'd heard curse, and if it so happened that the guy he grabbed wasn't the one who had cursed, or even if no one at all had cursed and McDaniels had hallucinated the whole thing, it didn't matter, because there was no telling McDaniels he'd made a mistake.

McDaniels didn't get free with his fists until the night he started walloping Corney. Up until then he was stupid but at least pretty generally sane. He did things like burrow his knuckles into your back or twist your arm like a pretzel, saying "You're not going to cry in front of your friends, are you?" and then wrenching your arm even harder.

Meanwhile, manhandling the one guy, he'd turn to lecture the rest of us, telling us that his wife was in tears because she had to live across the street from a schoolyard full of teenagers whose language belonged in the gutter. It was our fault that America was no longer a decent place to live. It was our fault that no one ever came over to sit with him and his wife. It was our fault that his ten-year-old son knew how to say "fuck." "Where else would he hear a word like that?" McDaniels ranted. "In school? In church?" He would twist his victim's arm until the guy said, "No. No." And McDaniels would say, "That's right. I'll tell you where he learned that word. Right over there. In his *own front yard.*"

This infuriated him so much that he just had to twist the guy's head to look him right in the eye and repeat, "His own front yard!"

He liked to bring his face close to yours when he tortured you, which meant you were treated to his foul breath. It smelled like stale beer, cheap salami, and the farts of a thousand old slugs. He spit his words and yelled close enough to your ear to set your brain ringing

and your eyeballs whirling. "Ten years old! Does it make you proud?"
And you'd better act full of shame or he would rearrange your shoulder and yell even louder. *"Does it?"*

He said we were a disgrace to our families and then recited the
first names of our fathers, a sure sign that we were in Dutch for this
one. He was shocked that Gus Spyropoulos's son cursed in front of
women and kids; he was flabbergasted that "Hap's"—Hapanowicz's—
boy hung out with this gang, this roving pack of delinquents, these
punks.

("Punks" was his favorite. And he spit with great emotion whenever he said it.)

"I killed the Japs," he boasted. "Me. That's right. I killed the Japs."

And if he'd been deep enough into the sauce, he would start calling
them "fuckin' Japs" and say that he didn't see why a man who had
killed fuckin' Japs had to come back from the war to put up with *punks.*

The lecture was never complete until he had tossed in his war
record. He'd served in the Second World War and he'd killed plenty of
Japs and he had wanted to go to Korea to kill whatever slopes might
have been left over, but he hadn't been allowed to "re-up" because he
still had a piece of shrapnel in his back from Okinawa.

"Feel that, right there," he ordered us. "You, there, Hapanowicz,
feel that there hunk of shrapnel. C'mon, you sissy, it ain't gonna bite.
Go on, press it. You won't hurt me. Burned right into me, that baby,
and ain't no one ever gonna take it out. I want to remember how it
was."

If you didn't act impressed each and every time he went through
this shrapnel show-and-tell you'd most likely be the next guy on the
rack.

"Stick a rifle in your hands and see what you can do," he would say
with great contempt for us. "Worthless punks."

It wasn't until he had finally gotten it all out of his system that he
let go the guy he had been bullying. And while that guy rubbed life
back into his arm and shoulder, proud of himself if he hadn't cried out
for mercy, McDaniels ordered the rest of us to put on our T-shirts
because, he said, it was indecent to be bare-chested.

He staggered off and tried to thrust back his shoulders, without
losing his balance. He returned to his house, where his wife, embar-

rassed, had retreated, and there he started in at her and the kids, screaming madly and breaking things.

He never grabbed Jimmy Dietz. Jimmy hardly cursed as it was, but if it had been Jimmy who had cursed and McDaniels came over and singled out the wrong guy, Jimmy owned up only to have McDaniels credit him for trying to take the blame. McDaniels knew it had been Walsh or Hapanowicz or the one with the disgusting nickname, Sperm.

He always made sure to tell Jimmy that the civics lecture didn't apply to him. He said he found it hard to believe that Jimmy would even be seen on the same side of the street as us. He said he could see how we all looked up to Jimmy and how, because of this, Jimmy was a man in his eyes.

We decided that McDaniels was afraid of Jimmy, and in our wildest dreams we pictured Jimmy kicking his ass all over the schoolyard.

3

That spring, on April 12, Yuri Gagarin had taken Vostok 1 into orbit, and when summer arrived and the locusts swarmed to biblical proportions, people who didn't know any better said it was because a Russian had gone into space. There hadn't been anything like it in people's memory—the locusts—and perhaps that was why they'd come up with vodoo explanations. From sunrise to sunset the shrill buzz of the locusts filled the air like a million miniature power saws. At night they dropped into silence but they were still there. Everywhere. Under your feet, in the car, on the windowsills, copulating on the lawns, squashed flat on driveways and roads, crawling into your bed, nesting in your hair.

"We'll finish Weaver's garage early," Jimmy told me one morning in late July, this summer of the locusts. "It'll be too hot this afternoon."

I agreed.

"I've got to see Father Matusiak later today," Jimmy added as we walked toward the Weavers' place.

As he said this he looked directly at me to be sure I'd heard. He wanted to reinforce the importance of it and didn't want me trying to persuade him to go the beach or play ball.

"For school," he said.

He said nothing more than that. It was his way of saying that his appointment with Father Matusiak had to do with becoming a priest.

He had grown a head taller than me over the winter months, and now the summer sun had brought out his freckles. We had been blood brothers for over two years, and because he had a way of coming into and going out of my life I knew very little about him. I had no idea why he wanted to be a priest. It was something he'd never chosen to explain and I'd never asked. If I was to guess, I'd guess he was doing it for his parents.

He'd spent the past year at Cathedral College, a high school in Manhattan that would prepare him for the seminary. He left for school every morning on the 7:05 train and caught an early ferry to Manhattan. From there he took the subway uptown.

He usually didn't get home on school nights until past five o'clock, and during track and basketball seasons it was more like seven. His coursework was rigorous and he used the commuting time to study. He memorized everything. Latin, Shakespeare, geometry theorems. He wrote his notes in a minuscule hand and studied until he knew them by heart.

During the school year if I saw him at all it was because I stayed around the ferry terminal at the end of the day waiting for him, or because I watched him in his room at night from my tree house.

I went to the boys' Catholic high school at the other end of Staten Island. It took me a while to travel back and forth, but my schoolwork was never as difficult as Jimmy's and I had more time on my hands. I supposed the whole point of Cathedral was to make sure there wouldn't be any dumb priests. For the most part I guess it worked.

During the early fall and then again in the spring, when once more it was reasonably warm and dry at night, I would climb to my tree house and use my binoculars to watch Jimmy in his bedroom. He sat there at his narrow desk, bent over a book which was illuminated by a small lamp.

I knew his room well. It was on the second floor. There were stairs to the second floor from the living room of his house, and the back stairs from the kitchen led directly to his bedroom. Everything in his room was neatly arranged and predictable: his Boy Scout merit badge sash on one wall, a picture of Jesus on another; his hairbrush and comb and the following day's folded handkerchief laid out on his dresser, his shined shoes tucked beneath it; basketball trophies and track medals displayed on a pine shelf over his desk; the bed always made and his shirts and pants hanging plumb-straight, clearly visible in the long closet without a door.

I would watch him through my binoculars and wonder about him. I wondered why he wanted to be a priest so badly and found myself thinking about the times when I had believed I wanted to be a priest. It was something that many guys in Catholic school went through sooner or later. But whenever a desire to be a priest had arisen in me it fled as rapidly and as inexplicably as it had arrived. The nearest I had ever come to taking it seriously was during a winter while I was still an altar boy and my only living grandfather was sick, and, as it turned out, dying. I served early mass every morning for a week, hoping that by this action my grandfather would recover.

Morning mass had been held at the old church in our parish then, the old church everyone now called the chapel. Weekday masses were still held there, but Sunday masses were now held over at the gymnasium in the new grade-school building. I recall quite clearly that the week I served early mass it was a snowy week and I had walked to mass because my father was working nights and my mother had to get my brother and sisters off to school and didn't drive a car anyway. But walking through the cold snowy mornings was not so bad; it only added to the magic. Arriving at the chapel from the brisk air and the snow during the early light of day, I would come in to the sparkling gold of the candlesticks and the colorful vestments and the close-knit warmth of the chapel, sharing the company of a handful of people who had also wandered in to lay their hopes before a mysterious God. For at least that week, and maybe even longer, I had thought that there could be no better way to live my life than to start each day in homage to the invisible Creator.

I wondered if this was how Jimmy felt about it. I wondered if there had been some special day or week in his life when something about God leaped out and took hold of his—well, took hold of his soul, I guess you'd say.

But, as I mentioned, I never asked him these things.

And I may be wrong, but I had the feeling that his God was more demanding and not nearly as warm as the one I had imagined. But I never asked him that either.

When we turned the corner and saw the Weavers' garage, we were looking at the side we had worked on the day before. Examining our work from a distance, Jimmy said, "Not bad."

The Weavers were away on vacation in the Adirondacks and Mr. Weaver had arranged for Jimmy to mow the lawn, feed the animals, collect the mail, and trim some of the shrubs. I'd been with Jimmy when he had made the arrangements. He had suggested that the garage could use a fresh coat of paint, not to insult Mr. Weaver, but saying it as an adult would give advice. "I see the paint hasn't held up on the garage," Jimmy had said. "That's too bad."

"I was just looking at that myself the other day," said Mr. Weaver. "It's been a while since it's been painted."

Jimmy had then taken out a circular from one of the hardware stores and shown Mr. Weaver a paint sale. Mr. Weaver smiled broadly, appreciating Jimmy's cleverness, and before I knew it he had given us the job.

We arrived now and took the garage key from its hiding place. We opened the overhead door and carried out the gallon cans of white paint and the small can of green paint for the trim. I gathered the paintbrushes together and then carried out the stepladder and set it in place.

Jimmy knelt and pried open a can of paint and stirred it while I stood looking out over the lawn, where the locusts crawled about like an immense but confused army attempting to organize. They continued to churn the air with their ratchet song. It was beginning to drive me crazy. They'd been at it for almost a whole month. One or two locusts, singing, charmed a summer's day; a few hundred thousand tore it to shreds.

Jimmy set to work on the green trim on the far side of the garage, the side we'd worked on yesterday. I started the first coat of white on the side facing the house.

We worked in silence, and it must have been an hour later that I had to move the stepladder around the corner to start the next side.

On that side, however, a large wasp nest hung from the eaves. Jimmy and I had noticed the nest before today but had not come up with a plan for dealing with it. The wasps had a plan, though, and they sent out a few scouts to irritate me and see if I was intelligent enough to go away.

"I'm allergic to these little bastards," I yelled so Jimmy could hear.

"No you're not," he responded.

"How do you know? Maybe I am. I could be, you know. I've never been bitten by one. If I am allergic, maybe I'll die."

I heard nothing. Jimmy had come up behind me. He stood there with his paintbrush in his hand. The brush bristles were moss-green and there were moss-green speckles on Jimmy's wrists.

"You've never been stung by a wasp?" he asked, amused.

"Never."

"Well, Chun," he informed me, gesturing at the wasp nest, "looks like you're going to do something new today."

I studied the nest uneasily.

We avoided dealing with the situation for as long as we could. We killed time mowing the lawn (chopping a legion of locusts to bits) and then trimmed the sticker bushes along the front walk. The sun grew steadily hotter throughout, and we stripped off our T-shirts. The locusts chirped on and on, and the tiny bones in my ear, trying to keep up, tapped away so wildly I waited for them to smoke from the friction.

No matter what we did to pretend it wasn't a problem, the wasps never left my mind. It was like waiting for the dentist.

"Let's smoke 'em out," I suggested.

Jimmy didn't like the idea. "We've got to get rid of the whole nest so they don't come back."

"Let's hose it."

Jimmy liked that.

The hose nozzle had a trigger, and we adjusted it so that it would send out a hard narrow jet.

"Who's going to do it?" asked Jimmy.

"I'll do it."

"Yeah?"

"Yeah."

"You're sure?"

"Yeah. Yeah, I'm sure."

"It's got to be down. You just can't spray it and run. You've got to make sure it's down."

"Hey, I'll do it. Don't worry."

We crept around the corner of the garage. I was first. I held the hose ready. Wasps came and went from the bulging nest, unaware of us.

"Closer," advised Jimmy over my shoulder. "Real easy."

We drew nearer and the wasps took notice. They began to come at us in twos and threes. One landed on my shoulder, and Jimmy skillfully flicked it away. Another landed on my nose. I smacked it and it fell. One landed in Jimmy's hair. A group buzzed me. I ducked and swatted.

"Give it to them, Chun!"

I blasted the nest with a stream of water, yahooing like a crazy man. But the nest hardly moved. I didn't know what to do. I hadn't expected it to be so strong.

More wasps emerged now. Many more. I did my best to thin them in flight with blasts of water, but they swarmed in greater numbers from the nest. One stung me, then another.

I took careful aim at the point where the nest attached at the eaves and blasted it with the water. It didn't matter. The damned nest just wouldn't budge. I couldn't believe how strong it was.

The wasps gathered their forces now for the big rebuff. They united into a dark wedge and aimed themselves at me. My only weapon was the hose.

Then Jimmy appeared from behind, racing and howling. He held a garden rake high above his head; he swung it wildly about. He clawed the nest open and yanked it to the ground. The nest was torn apart and the wasps appeared from inside like raisins spilling from a bushel basket. There had to be hundreds of them. They were not happy with us.

"Holy shit!" I yelled, dropping the hose.

"Run!"

"What the fuck you think I'm doing?"

"Faster!"

We streaked across the lawn and hurdled the sticker bushes in Olympic form. We were laughing but we didn't slow down. We just kept running down the shoulder of the road, laughing and howling.

4

I reached up for the rusted bolt on the piling. The sun reflected blindingly off the water. I tasted the salt water and then felt the throb of the places where the wasps had scored their hits. The seawater had found each tender point.

Looking down into the bottle-green water, I noticed blood. It oozed and feathered off like a marker dye. That wasn't a wasp sting there, that blood. It was a gouge from the damned barnacles that encrusted the old pilings. Their jagged shells were sharp and painful.

Jimmy was atop the highest piling. I pulled myself up to the first crosspiece, and the water shed from my shoulders in a thin curtain. I quickly examined the cut on my thigh. It didn't seem too bad.

"How're you doing?" asked Jimmy.

"I'll live."

The tide was up and so it had been a difficult swim for me, especially since we had run all the way from the Weavers'. I didn't know what had suddenly possessed Jimmy. We'd gotten away from the wasps but he had continued to run. I'd expected him to veer off onto one of the paths so we could take a break for a while in the woods, where it was cool. Instead he had stayed on the road, running. "Let's go," was all he'd said.

"Let's go?" I'd asked. "Go where?"

He had said nothing at first. He simply adjusted the pace so that we were running more slowly. Then he finally said, "The beach. The Orange House."

"All the way?" I asked. A stupid question. Of course he meant all the way. All the way at a run. This was Dietz, you understand. Jimmy Dietz.

"The wasps will be there all day," he said shortly, running at my side.

I accepted this as his reason for not returning to finish the job until later.

"We should've gotten rid of the wasps last night," he added. "We were stupid."

I didn't agree nor disagree. I was doing all I could to continue running. I didn't want to waste precious breath talking.

So we ran all the way from the Weavers' to the beach, which was a good run. Two or three miles. And somehow I had found the strength. I was surprised. And when we'd run side by side through the town circle and the Purps, who were hanging out at the phone booth, stood there and hooted at us, I knew how good the two of us must have looked, running together up Benning's hill, and this sense of pride boosted me up the steep incline. I heard the Purps hoot and felt my thigh muscles burn. I glanced over at Jimmy. His chest, lean and tightly muscled, glistened with sweat. My own chest, a sorry-looking rack of ribs, heaved like an old bellows. But I had kept up, all the way up the hill, and we left the Purps and their catcalls behind.

It was a level run almost all the rest of the way. When we came to the last rise in the road before the beach, we were out along Arbutus Avenue and the sun had turned the road tar to syrup. Jimmy picked up the pace. He was making a last dash. I struggled along and spat cottony saliva. My legs ached and my side was stabbed with pain and I could feel my face was red as fire. The sweat that ran into the places where the wasps had stung me seemed to start the stinging all over again. But I kept up with Jimmy. I was determined I would.

We crested the rise and a sudden breeze came off the water. Before us was the ocean: it bulged like a purple lens on the horizon.

We reached out our legs and ate up the last bit of road. Then we were in the sand and the sand grabbed at our ankles but we kicked our knees high and grunted as we fought the sand and raced for the surf.

Jimmy tossed off his sneakers and galloped into the waves. He dove headlong into the water and started swimming. I followed, never dreaming that I would—or could—swim out this far.

As we sat atop the pilings now, the two of us were alone out here with a big silent piece of ocean. I looked in at the distant beach and the ugly orange building for which the beach was named. The people on shore might as well have been from another land or another planet, I felt that distant from them. The jukebox music, which on shore was always loud and tinny, skipped out across the water and reached us in wordless rhythmic thumps.

To our left lay New Jersey, where the sky was yellow and green from chemical factories, or plumed with orange fire and soot from flaring oil stacks. Large tankers over there nosed up to massive storage tanks, and I recalled the time when one of those tankers, loaded with naphtha, had burst into flame and spilled its cargo. The flaming naphtha spread along the top of the water for miles and there was nothing that could douse it.

In the other direction was Brooklyn, so distant that even on a clear day it seemed to be hidden by mist.

The greater part of all was the ocean, stretching endlessly out there between Rockaway and Sandy Hook, those last fingers of land between which the world curved away into space and vast miles of water.

The pilings we had climbed were like telephone poles, held firmly to one another by bulky crosspieces, and their very existence was a mystery to us. Whenever we asked someone why they were there, we'd be told, "For the channel," nothing more.

Until today I had swum out here only when the tide was down, when the whole bunch—me and Corney and Spyros and the others— swam out and roosted here for a few hours, keeping a cautious eye on the rising tide. We made a game of diving off and going to the bottom, returning to the surface breathless but with a handful of mud to prove we'd been there.

The sun grew terrifically hot on us now, and we dove into the water to cool off. Then we climbed back up the pilings, avoiding the barnacles if we could, and sat there and dried out and watched the light splinter across the water. Schools of minnows and lazy moss bunkers swam in and out of the pilings. A band of seagulls flew close by and squawked at us for stealing their perch.

"What do you talk about with Father Matusiak when you go?" I asked, not knowing why I had. It was as close as I had ever come to asking him directly about becoming a priest.

"A lot of things," he said.

I shrugged. "Like what?"

He hesitated.

"If it's private," I said, "it's private. That's okay."

"Well, it's not that private. We talk about how I'm doing in school and how I'm getting along with my father—my parents. We talk about conscience," he added.

He paused. He stood atop the tallest of the pilings and then moved nimbly from one to the next. He continued moving while we talked.

"We talk about the difference between right and wrong, good and evil," he added, looking out at the ocean and then, slowly, at me.

The sun was directly behind him, slanting into my eyes over his shoulder. I squinted and asked, "What's the difference?"

He found this a bit amusing. "You don't know?"

"I know the Ten Commandments—thanks to Sliver, I guess. What else is there?"

"That's it, more or less."

"What else, then?"

"Good is when you're with God; evil's when you're not."

I knew what he meant. I really did. There was suddenly nothing more to say. I left it at that.

After a while a motorboat sped past and then, shortly, returned. The man at the wheel waved at us and we waved back. He slowed down and turned smoothly, coming toward us. As the boat drew closer it was obvious that he was alone. He maneuvered the boat alongside the pilings, and I could see that he wore a captain's hat atop his balding head and baggy khaki shorts that fell to his knees. He was shirtless and his sunburn had peeled a number of times, giving his skin the appearance of a glazed ham. Alongside the steering wheel he had a can of beer propped in a holder. In the stern, alongside a pair of water skis, sat a cooler chest. He looked to me like an old uncle who enjoyed drinking beer and raising all sorts of hell.

"You kids okay?" he asked over the *putta-putt* of his outboard engine.

I shrugged. Jimmy spoke up. "Yeah. We're okay."

The man looked in toward the beach and then back at us.

"Pretty far out," he said.

"We swam," I said, just busting to tell him.

The man whistled low. "That's a good swim, men."

Jimmy said, "Yeah," confidently.

There was a pause. The boat rocked gently while small waves splashed against the hull. The current brushed the boat broadside and the man steadily edged the bow around so it pointed into the waves. I could smell the pungent oil and gas as the engine alternately revved and eased down, coughing blue smoke.

The man finally said, "You're sure you're okay?"

"If we weren't, we'd say so," answered Jimmy politely.

The man regarded Jimmy with interest. "No," he said, "I don't think so. I'm not calling you a liar, of course, Red, but I don't think you'd say so. I think right now you're okay, the two of you, but if you weren't—I don't believe you'd let on." The man grinned. "Am I right or am I right?"

Jimmy laughed, and then the man laughed also. Not to be left out, I laughed along with them, though I didn't quite feel I was part of the understanding that Jimmy and the man shared.

"You kids ski?" the man asked with a new animation.

"Yeah," we chorused.

He waved us down. "C'mon. I'll take you for a spin."

I looked to Jimmy and noticed his hesitation. Was the job at the Weavers' on his mind? What about Father Matusiak? He certainly hadn't forgotten that.

Jimmy stood upright on the top of the highest perch, and I could see that he was considering things. He looked questioningly at me, but I kept a blank face. This was his choice. I knew what I wanted to do. I wanted to water-ski.

He dove smoothly through the air, cutting the water like an arrow and leaving behind only a small puckered splash. He surfaced and I waited to see what he would do. For all I knew he might have decided it was time to swim back to shore and resume our responsibilities.

The boat wasn't very fancy but it had a good strong engine, and when the man, whose name was Ed, eased it clear of the pilings and gave it full throttle, the bow nosed up and smacked across the water.

We rode south until the water pinched off at the Outerbridge Crossing to New Jersey. Then we returned north, passing the Orange House and riding the length of the island. Ed showed us how to handle the boat, and when he gave me my turn at the wheel he kept saying, "Faster. Go on, open 'er up. Faster. She'll do it."

We skied for an hour or more and then headed back. Ed cruised in close to shore for us, and when he let us off he apologized that he didn't have more time for us. "You boys are all right," he said. "I'd take you on as shipmates any day."

We thanked him for saying so.

He said, "Here, Red, let me give you something for you and your buddy." He took a five-dollar bill from his wallet and handed it to

Jimmy. "Here, buy yourselves a hamburger and a soda. Whatever you like."

Jimmy didn't want to take the money.

"Here," insisted the man. "Take it. Don't turn me down."

Jimmy took the five and thanked the man. He tucked it in his wet shorts.

We watched the man go and then headed up the beach. Fortunately, we found our sneakers. We sat in the shade of the jetty and slipped them on our feet. I was getting very hungry and thirsty, and I was grateful Jimmy had taken that five dollars.

There was a Ray Charles tune on the Orange House jukebox and the outdoor speakers rattled from the vibrations. We walked across the hot sand, wending our way through the beach blankets and the bikinis. The scent of suntan lotion lingered on the air, and my eyes devoured the girls who glistened with coconut oil in the bright sun. I couldn't believe there could be so many tempting ways to put together legs, asses, and breasts. God was a genius.

At the open door of the Orange House there stood a thick-set man with a beer gut, his arms folded across his bare hairy chest. He warned us in a gruff voice, "Don't be buying no beer."

I nodded. "We won't."

"Stay away from the bar," he added.

Coming in from the bright beach to this dim-lit place, the people and tables appeared shadowy. It was difficult to see where we were walking, and as we groped our way along the railing that separated the bar from the tables where minors were allowed, I bumped a guy's arm and his bottle of beer splashed onto the woman alongside him. He swore at me, calling me a stupid shit. The bartender had to tell him to watch his language. "Cool down, Drainpipe," the bartender warned him.

The concrete floor was cold and there was sand everywhere: on the chairs, on the tables, on the wet empty bottles, and even on the counter where we stood and greedily wolfed down our burgers.

We had a dollar fifty left after we ate. Jimmy pocketed the dollar, saying we should save it. He gave me one of the quarters and took the other to the eight-ball table. I dropped my quarter in the jukebox.

No sooner had Jimmy racked the pool balls than two older guys approached the table. They were at least twenty-five, maybe older.

They'd been drinking at the bar and they each had a bottle of beer. One of them was the guy I had bumped, the one called Drainpipe, and I was afraid there was going to be trouble. But then the other one said that the table was theirs, meaning that we would have to try to win it from them.

"We ain't lost all day," boasted Drainpipe. He was the taller of the two and seemed far more drunk than the other. I supposed he was called Drainpipe because of his height and the way his lanky arms bent sharply at the elbows.

"Lucky day," said Jimmy evenly.

"Lucky, shit," drawled Drainpipe.

Drainpipe's partner broke the rack and immediately dropped two stripes and a solid. I could tell by his form and his patience that he was a good player. He followed up with two more stripes before missing his next shot.

Jimmy looked over the table and told me to shoot first. I cleared two balls but missed the six ball.

Drainpipe was up next. He shot clumsily. He even managed to drag his cue across the table and knock some balls around. His partner told him to pay attention and he just said, "Shit," the way he had before. He took all day lining up a shot on the thirteen and then missed by a mile.

Now it was Jimmy's turn. He moved around the table like a dancer, which was interesting since he couldn't dance a step. Yet he had this incredible smoothness of movement at anything that had to do with sports. I admired and envied him as I watched his moves. Clockwise, counterclockwise. He chalked his cue, lined up a shot, and he drove it hard when he had to, or he kissed it, smooth and easy, when that was what it took.

He left only the eight ball and our three ball on the table. Drainpipe's partner had to get past the eleven and the fifteen before a shot at the eight and the game. But he was good and he made both stripes, called the eight in the near side, and made that too.

Jimmy told them, "Good game." He looked at me and then took the dollar from his pocket. He went over to the food counter for change and returned for another game.

We lost again, although this time it had come down to a shootout over the eight ball.

Jimmy dropped another quarter in the slot and racked the balls. Drainpipe made a comment about quitting before we went broke and saving our quarters for popsicles.

But we won that game, and the next one, and then all the rest. We must have played ten games in all.

Drainpipe didn't like losing. From what I'd gathered he had been shooting his mouth off all day about winning, even though his buddy had actually done all the winning. The guys at the bar ribbed him for losing to us. There was nothing he could do about it. He couldn't tell them to shut up or he would look foolish, and he couldn't win a game.

Ugliness began to creep into Drainpipe's voice, and he continued belting down the beers. He grumbled that he wouldn't mind cracking a bottle over someone's head and then spat on the floor. He even tried to provoke Jimmy by getting in Jimmy's way when Jimmy was trying to shoot.

Finally I pulled Jimmy aside and said, "Let's go. This guy's trouble."

"I'm not afraid of him."

"Neither am I," I lied, "but let's go anyway."

Jimmy gave it some thought. We finished the game and told Drainpipe and his buddy we had to leave.

On our way out back we ducked into the men's room. It smelled awful, like stale urine and spilled beer. The walls were the same loud orange as the rest of the place. There were hundreds of flies circling and buzzing, and a hundredfold more locusts. When the locusts tried to fly they crashed blindly into the walls and then dropped to the floor, where they crept about in search of sex. They were the damnedest insects. They couldn't fly, they couldn't sing, and they couldn't get enough sex.

There were broken bottles on the floor and messages on the walls about blowjobs and hot pussy and faggots. There were plenty of phone numbers and instructions about where to meet perverted or horny people.

Instead of urinals there was this long trough along one wall where the water trickled in and then flowed out a drain. Jimmy and I stood there at the trough, side by side, pissing and reading the crap on the walls.

Suddenly Drainpipe came in, banging the door into the wall. He didn't see us at first, but we heard him mutter aloud about us, calling us little motherfuckin' peckerheads. Then he made us out in his dim brain and halted. He'd already taken out his pecker to piss, and now he stood there holding it in his hand and swaying drunkenly.

"Yous little fuckin' shits," he slurred. He pointed at Jimmy. "You—I'm gonna kick your ass."

Jimmy looked at him and said nothing.

"How the fuck old are you?" demanded Drainpipe.

He hadn't let go his pecker, which made me think that maybe he wasn't the one who was actually talking, but that his pecker was a ventriloquist and he was the dummy. That would explain a lot.

He leaned against the wall to hold himself up and started pissing, right there on the floor in front of us. We backed up quickly so we wouldn't get splashed, but I felt tiny drops of it against my leg and I cringed. Down on the floor the locusts that got in the way were tossed back as if they'd been blasted by a fire hose. It didn't matter; they still wanted sex.

"Huh?" asked Drainpipe. "I said how the fuck old are you?"

"Old enough," said Jimmy.

"Oh—'sat right? Old e-fuckin'-nuf, huh?"

He let go his pecker and stepped forward and took a wild punch at Jimmy that stood no chance of connecting. Jimmy easily ducked the punch and Drainpipe couldn't stop his own momentum. He swung in a full circle and smashed his head against a board so hard that his head rocked. He stumbled back and would have fallen in a heap, but at the last moment he turned in another circle and landed in the urine trough, sitting down. He was too drunk and too stunned by the blow to his head to know where he was.

"Quick, Chun," said Jimmy. "Tie his shoelaces together."

I bent down to do as Jimmy had said. I could see what was going on here and I started snickering to myself.

Jimmy meanwhile grabbed a handful of paper towels and plugged the drain in the trough. We stood back.

"Drainpipe," I said, enjoying the irony.

The water quickly backed up and soaked Drainpipe's pants. He had gathered his wits enough to figure out that something was amiss. He looked down at his crotch and wondered dumbly, "What the—?"

He scowled at us and said, "You little shits. I'm gonna fuckin' kill yous."

He stood and lunged for us, unaware that his shoelaces were knotted together. He fell forward and flattened his face against the wall before crashing to the floor with an awful grunt.

Jimmy and I hightailed it. We raced out across the parking lot and between the bungalows. We found a break in the tall hedge that led to the private property along Arbutus Avenue and ran a short distance through the brush before we threw ourselves down and hugged the ground. We couldn't run much farther because we couldn't stop laughing. Our stomachs ached; our eyes were full of tears. We wanted to go back and do it again.

"Did you see him?" I kept asking, howling with laughter. "Did you?"

We figured that Drainpipe and his buddy would hop into a car and chase after us. So when we moved along the road we moved cautiously, hiding from cars that came from the beach. It wasn't long before a Pontiac Bonneville came roaring past. We'd heard it and had hid in time. The car was speeding recklessly. Drainpipe was behind the wheel. He was alone. The car went screaming past and we heard the tires squeal as the big Bonneville tried to take the next turn. Then we heard a crash.

We came out of hiding and ran up the road. We came around the bend and saw the Bonneville up against a telephone pole. The water from the radiator was steaming into the air. The horn was stuck. We ran up to the car and looked in the driver's side. A quick glance told us that Drainpipe had broken his nose. Other than that he was all right. He was leaning against the horn and didn't even recognize us as he looked our way and said, "I can't believe I hit the fuckin' thing."

A car approached from the opposite direction, and Jimmy flagged down the driver and said there had been an accident. The driver was on his way to the Orange House—there was nothing else down this way—and it was no surprise that he knew Drainpipe. He came over to the car and said, "What the hell you doin' with Louie's car?"

We made ourselves scarce. We knew a way through the woods on the far side of Hylan Boulevard and fifteen minutes later we emerged on Amboy Road. There we cut through Halfpenny's farm and took the

path to Benning's hill. We came down from Benning's hill to the circle—and there was Jimmy's father. He had appeared from nowhere,
pulling to the side of the road across from us. He was angry. He said
nothing to Jimmy other than "Get in the car."

I wasn't invited along. In fact, Mr. Dietz did a good job of pretending I wasn't even there. As also, suddenly, did Jimmy, who didn't say
goodbye or even look my way as he got into the car and left.

My first thought was that Mr. Dietz, blessed with that ability of all
parents to be aware of everything that you've done that you shouldn't
have done, knew all about the water-skiing and Drainpipe. But then I
realized how improbable that was and that it was serious enough that
he had discovered we had skipped out on our job and Jimmy had failed
to keep his appointment with Father Matusiak.

Mr. Dietz pulled away, lecturing Jimmy, and I walked back to the
Weavers'. I found Jimmy there, painting the garage. He told me how
Father Matusiak had called his house looking for him and how his
father had gone out in search of us.

"I've got to finish this alone," he told me, meaning the job.

"Yeah," I said. "Okay."

"Then I've got to write a letter to Father Matusiak, apologizing. I
have to bring it to him at the rectory."

I knew this was his father's demand, not Father Matusiak's.

"He must be pissed off bad, huh?"

"Yeah. But it was stupid of me. I got to admit, it was stupid."

I didn't think it had been so stupid. It wasn't right to forget to keep
an appointment, I guess. But it hadn't been all that stupid or wrong. It
had been fun.

The sun was lower in the sky. The air had cooled slightly. The
locusts shrilled on as if operated by atomic batteries.

I felt sad, standing there. It had been a great day. I could feel inside
me that I would always remember it, that I would take it out of memory often, to look at it afresh and polish it up and laugh at it heartily all
over again.

Too bad it had ended sourly.

Jimmy had been quiet. He brooded for a long moment and then
delivered the final blow.

"My father says I should stay away from you."

"Why?" I asked defensively.

"He thinks you're a bad influence."

I stopped a moment to chew on this. I knew that Jimmy had told his father everything that we'd done. I felt a little betrayed by this, but I accepted that Jimmy had to tell the truth.

"Did he think it was my fault?" I asked.

"I told him it wasn't. He still said I shouldn't see too much of you."

His father's car appeared now, coming around the corner. Mr. Dietz was checking up.

Jimmy looked from me to the car and said, "I'll see you, Chun."

"Yeah," I said. "See you."

Chapter 5

1

Someone spun to my left and then a body leaped into the sun. The basketball loomed large in my vision: both eyes back then. It loomed large and speedily eclipsed the day. Then it caught me squarely in the nose and my eyes watered heavily. A moment later blood spilled from my nostrils.

I went to the side of the court and tore a piece of my T-shirt and stuffed the piece of cloth up my nose. I glanced worriedly toward McDaniels's house. He wasn't home. I knew so because the pickup truck wasn't in the driveway. It was early in the day, besides, and he was never home until evening. I was lucky. I'd cursed like a sailor when I'd been hit in the nose and McDaniels would not have been forgiving.

The sun was white-hot and the surface of the playground melted the soles of our sneakers. The guys out on the court struggled through the heat. Their skin gleamed with sweat; their faces were cherry-red and their eyes were white and popping. They soon took a break and joined me on the side. Corney was wheezing like an old air pump, but, incredibly, he reached for a Lucky Strike and lit it. He told me I was a pussy for leaving the game for a little bloody nose. I gave him the finger and threatened to Botstein blood on his head.

"A bloody Botstein," mused Woodsie strangely. More than any of us, Woodsie was fascinated by doing the Botstein. It was the name we'd given to clearing mucus from your nose by holding one nostril and blowing the crap out the other. We called it the Botstein because one of the train conductors, a fat man named Ed Botstein, cleared his nose onto the tracks that way while he stood between the cars operating the door switches.

That was it for basketball for a while. We headed down to the circle and bought some soda and pulled up a patch of sidewalk shade. The sodas went down fast, leaving us thirsty but flat broke. Then we wandered up and down the sidewalk without direction and bounced the basketball back and forth. For a while we took shots at the litter basket, dunking the ball as if we were Wilt the Stilt. But we tired of that and headed over to the alcove at the train station and played the game of trying to hit the popsicle stick with the ball. Then the ball bounced loose and went down on the tracks and we argued over who should chase after it. Jimpie finally went after the ball, and when he returned someone said, "Let's go play stickball."

"Yeah."

"Go ahead," moaned someone else. "I ain't."

"Why not?"

"I'm tired of stickball. Besides, I suck at it."

"Yeah—fuck stickball."

"Man alive, let's do *some*thing."

"You got any bright ideas?"

There was a disappointing silence. Then Spyros said, "Hey—Dietz, man."

"Where?" I asked.

"Over at the bench."

"I thought his dickface father was still punishing him," said Jimpie.

"His old man am a pwick."

We walked over to see Jimmy and to find out if his punishment was over. He had risen to his feet at our approach, standing on the bench. He stepped up to the top board on the back of the bench and braced himself by reaching up into the maple tree above and holding a limb. His biceps muscle showed clearly. It was not a bulging muscle, the way Spyros's biceps bulged, but it was strong.

"What's up?" he asked.

"Nothing," said Spyros.

"Is your father still pissed?" I asked.

"He's getting over it."

"What about Father Matusiak?"

"We had a talk," said Jimmy, indicating that he wanted to say no more about it. "You guys play ball?" he asked me.

"Yeah."

"Who got you in the nose?"

"The ball."

"The *ball?*" he asked.

I touched my nose. It was still tender. "Yeah—the ball. It was a shitty pass, what can I tell you?"

"It wasn't no shitty pass," said Jimpie.

"You guys lookin' for something to do?" asked Jimmy.

"Why—you got some broads?" asked Spyros.

Jimmy didn't answer Spyros. "I thought maybe we'd go finish that cabin in the woods," he suggested.

We looked at one another quizzically. What was Jimmy saying?

"What cabin?"

"Out there in the woods," said Jimmy, as if we should have known all about it. He was casting out the bait. I could feel it.

"Which fuckin' cabin is it?" asked Spyros, pretending he knew of more than one cabin when he actually didn't even know about this one.

"It's not exactly a cabin," explained Dietz.

"Then what the fuck am it?" demanded Corney.

"It looks like it was going to be a cabin, but whoever was building it gave up."

"Assholes," decided someone.

"Where is it?" asked Woodsie.

"In the woods," I put in, my voice nasal because of the wad of cloth in my nostril. "Don't you listen, Woodsie?"

"And what are you, Chun? A fuckin' genius?"

"You'd never find it," said Dietz, meaning the place of the cabin.

"Bullshit," said Spyros. "We could find it."

"You can't find your dick with both hands, Spyros," said Corney.

"That's 'cause your mother's mouth is on it."

"Oh—am I wanked out?"

Spyros didn't want to bother with Corney. He turned to Dietz and repeated his claim. "I could find it."

"Never," said Dietz.

"Bullshit," answered Spyros. "I bet five bucks I could find it."

We all fell silent. This idea of a cabin somewhere in the woods that no one could find—now that would break the boredom, all right. And I could see that everyone knew it would be a cabin in a real secret place, because Jimmy had said so. We looked at one another and waited.

Jimmy told us he'd gladly show us the place and he took a long running step down from the bench. When his feet met the ground he was forced to trot to keep his balance. The dust at the edge of the grass kicked up at his heels and reflected mica in the white summer sun. He strode off casually in the direction of the railroad trestle.

None of us had moved. We looked into one another's faces. I could tell that the guys were pretending that they weren't going to allow Dietz to fool them, when in fact they were just too lazy to get up off their asses and follow him.

"He'll go over to the trestle and take a piss on the tracks and laugh at us for following him," said Sperm. "There ain't no fuckin' cabin back there. We would've seen a whole goddam cabin."

"It am *woo-sit,*" said Corney.

"Yeah," someone agreed. "It's bullshit."

I stood up and smacked the dirt from the seat of my jeans. "You fuckin' guys complain about being bored, right? Well, let's go find out about this."

"Man, Chun, you believe *everything* Dietz says," said Spyros.

Spyros was right, but he made it sound as if I were stupid for taking Dietz at his word. I turned to him and said, "He's not lyin'," and left to catch up to Jimmy.

"Fuck you, then," Spyros called out.

Corney, for some reason, joined me; the rest of them grumbled and swore until, finally, they banded together and shuffled along behind us.

Jimmy had stopped to await us at the place where the railroad service road ran tangent to the town circle. We walked along the service road for a half mile or so before it doglegged at a storage yard. There we crossed over the railroad tracks on the concrete bridge we had named White Bridge years back.

"I bet a buck it ain't there," said Spyros to Dietz. "I bet there ain't no cabin."

"I told you," Jimmy explained. "It ain't a cabin. Just the beginning. A few logs, that's all."

"There ain't nothin'," Spyros insisted. "C'mon, Dietz, bet a buck on it."

"I don't bet on a sure thing," said Dietz. "It takes the thrill out of it."

Spyros was determined to bet, though, and said, "Five to one, Dietz. Five bucks to one."

"Spyros," began Dietz, "I'm tellin' you—"

"Tell me bullshit, all right? If there's a cabin, I'll give you five bucks and take you out for blues on my father's boat."

Jimmy couldn't turn that down. Bluefishing on Mr. Spyropoulos's boat. He told Spyros, "You're on, chump."

They latched pinkies on the bet, and while their pinkies were still latched, Jimmy added, "Everyone gets to go," meaning fishing for blues.

Spyros said, "No fuckin' problem. You just lost a buck."

We continued along, Woodsie asking immediately, "How far away is it?"

"Oh, am you afwaid of the woods, fud'yan *Woods*ie?"

"Hey, man—I got to be home later. My aunt's coming over."

"Yeah, Dietz, how far we gotta walk?" asked Jimpie.

"Man," said Harry the Horse, "we could've walked to the Orange House by now."

"Shit, I don't want to go for a hike," said Corney. "Let's go get dwunk and find some mommas to pork."

"Asshole," I told Corney.

"You oughta know, Chun. That's where you eat."

"Ain't no one ever gonna let you pork 'em," Woodsie told Corney.

"Yeah, especially a girl," said Harry.

"Yeah, *Wood*sie?" asked Corney. "Your momma lets me pork her."

Woodsie took off after him. They crashed through the thick brush and disappeared. Corney emerged later, up ahead, taunting Woodsie and laughing.

Jimmy ignored them. He turned down a narrow path that the rest of us would have gone right past. We followed him down this path in single file, the seven of us, like the damn Seven Dwarfs: me, Spyros, Jimpie and Harry, Sperm, and, finally, Corney and Woodsie. We followed him into the summer woods which I had always found so magical, and still found magical despite the plague of locusts and their unending monotonous sawing song.

2

We broke from the cover of the woods along the old WPA roads, roads without houses that had been laid down out here in the middle of nowhere during the Depression. The roads were nothing more than gouges through the woods now, surfaced by fist-sized stones. Tall shafts of goldenrod and purple thistle shot up from between the ballast; the brush at the side of the road had steadily grown, encroaching the road, and in some places not even a Volkswagen could have squeezed through. In other places, where the soil was hard clay and the brush didn't grow very thick, there was still easily enough room for a Cadillac.

Unless you knew the woods to begin with, as we did, it wasn't likely you'd even know the roads were here. There were only two or three places where they joined up with the deserted back streets.

The WPA roads made it possible to drive far back into the woods, if you knew the way and if you dared. Though sooner or later all the roads narrowed, and, like rivers upstream in a jungle, they crimped off and disappeared in the undergrowth.

People came out this way in cars to drink and screw, and the places where they'd been were littered by rusted beer cans and dumped ashtrays and used condoms.

We occasionally spotted Deluxe and Smitty out here, drinking beer and Tango screwdriver mix with some girls in a stolen car that either they or someone else had abandoned. There was no telling where some of the cars had come from or what might be in them. There were stories about gangsters who had been killed and left in their car in swampy places on Staten Island. I think maybe, for mobsters, "going to Staten Island" meant they were about to be shot in the head.

More than once we were tempted to bushwhack Deluxe and Smitty—which is what we called it when we ambushed people in cars—but we decided they would know for sure it was us. Besides, Sliver might have been with them.

But we bushwhacked everyone else who was stupid enough to

drive back into the woods at night, especially people who drove back to get laid. No horny people were safe out here when we were on the prowl. We knew the places to wait, and we concealed ourselves until a car appeared creeping cautiously along the lonely bumpy road. The car would come to a stop, the headlights would go out, and we'd wait. It killed us to have to wait, but we knew we had no other choice, not if we were really going to have a good laugh.

"Whatcha think he's doin' now?" one of us would whisper in the darkness.

"Hey, guys, don't start that shit," pleaded Spyros. "My pecker goes nuts."

"I'll bet he's bullshittin' to her, tellin' her she's a real fine babe."

"I'll bet he am fud'yan porkin' her hole."

"Walsh, you're a real fuckin' jerk. You don't just come right out and pork a girl. You got to lie to her and then pork her."

"They got the radio on," said Jimpie, who was pretty suave in these matters and even claimed to have a few notches on his belt. "Some real sweet and soft music, see? Get her in the mood."

"I'd have my hand on her tit."

If we were hidden close enough to the car we could see the face of one or the other of them in the car by the glow of their cigarette ember when they took a drag and the ember brightened. And we knew we had to wait at least until the two heads disappeared from view, and sometimes that never happened and then the guy would suddenly start the car and drive off angrily. We'd call him a jerk for having a car and not being able to get laid. We all knew that once we had cars the girls would be knocking down our doors.

But when things went right and the two heads in the car dipped from view, we would rub our hands together and snicker. Boy, would this be fun!

We waited. We had learned how important it was to wait for the perfect moment.

"Every time we got to wait like this I get a hard-on," said Spyros.

"Just don't start beating your meat like you always do."

"I don't know, man—"

"You think he's got her bra off?" asked someone.

"Shit, man, I bet he don't even care about her tits. I bet he's got his fingers up her twat."

"Man alive."

"It's drivin' me nuts," said Spyros. "Look't this, man." He un-zipped his fly and maneuvered his huge erection into the night air. "It feels like a friggin' watermelon."

"I'll bet she's got a little wet twat that goes *meow.*"

"Yeah, with fur."

"Yeah."

"Don't say no more," pleaded Spyros.

"Suckin' on them nipples," said Corney, slurping.

"No he's not. I told you—he ain't a tit man."

"I fud'yan am a everything man."

Spyros began to edge away from us. We knew he'd start jerking off any minute. We heard him moan, "Oh, man—"

"You're gross, Spyros."

"Whaddya think?" asked Jimpie. "Now?"

"Yeah."

The two in the car had been out of sight for a few minutes. The adrenaline had poured through us and we had been patient, but we were ready for action now. Spyros remained off in the brush, mastur-bating noisily. He'd have to hurry it up if he didn't want to miss out.

"I'll bet he's going to put his dick in her right *now!*"

Like lunatics, we burst from the darkness, screaming and yowling. We leaped onto the trunk of the car and then onto the roof. We jumped up and down and danced on the roof, cheering and yahooing until we thought we'd wet our pants. The metal roof buckled and made an awful noise. By then the car had started up and the driver hastily threw it into gear.

We whooped and laughed and jumped on the roof until we felt the car lurch into gear. We pictured the girl, pulling on her panties and getting hysterical. Then the tires spun on the ballast stone and we leaped off the roof onto the hood or the trunk and scattered for the safety of the woods.

The car sped off and we collapsed to the ground and laughed and tried to imagine what had gone on inside the car. Our stomachs ached the way they ached after a hundred sit-ups, but still we laughed, and we might have laughed all night except for someone calling out softly, "Quiet—here comes another one," and with great effort, as the next car approached, we forced ourselves to be quiet and wait.

3

By now Jimmy had led us two or three miles. We skirted the secluded Catholic orphanage at what would have been a safe enough distance to avoid the guard dogs (one of which was an Irish wolfhound), but Spyros just had to go and creep closer and irritate the dogs. The dogs came after us and we were forced to run through the marsh. We came out of the marsh with smelly black mud on our legs and looked like a band of escaped convicts. Since it had been Spyros's fault we took a vote to see if he deserved a shot from everyone. It was unanimous. We all got to punch him in the arm. If he tried to draw his shoulder away you were allowed to punch him again. But Spyros was tough. He didn't flinch, not even when Jimmy gave him a hit. He took it silently and when we were finished he asked, "Is that the hardest you faggots can hit? I've been hit harder by houseflies."

Deeper into the woods we went. Out beyond Big Trees and then past the scrubby places where the blueberries were plentiful and nearly ripe. The anvil heat of the basketball court was elsewhere. Out here under the trees the air was cool and the earth was shaded. Except for the simmering vibrations of the locusts, it was perfect.

Since I had been out this way before with Jimmy I knew exactly where we were. But the others weren't all that familiar with this section of the woods and were feeling lost and uneasy. They began to suspect that this might be a ruse by Jimmy. They didn't say as much, but I could read it in their faces and hear it in their voices. Then, finally, when Jimmy decided to pick up the pace to a trot, they were convinced that he intended to give them the slip.

"You wait, Dietz," yelled Spyros, jogging after Jimmy. "You fuckin' scumbag, you wait."

Woodsie fell back. He complained that his side ached. He called out, "Hey—don't leave me behind," but Sperm, who was nearest him, called him a pussy and kept running.

Only Corney and I were able to keep up with Jimmy. We stayed at his heels until he proved too crafty for us. We had arrived in a wide stand of brambles. The brambles were tall and thick, climbing the trees like barbed wire, and it was in this barbed maze that Jimmy slipped away.

I knew this place. And I even knew where Jimmy had gone, but I couldn't find the way. There was a way to get down on your belly and crawl under the brambles into the clearing, the way we'd done the night we sacrificed the rabbit.

Jimmy had found the tunnel and had disappeared in a twinkling. What a great trick! I thought.

I slowed down and began searching carefully for the way beneath the brambles, while Corney, convinced that Jimmy had run on ahead, disappeared into the woods.

"Shit," I complained, looking up and down the wide stretch of brambles. I hadn't been out here since that night with the rabbit. Nothing looked familiar.

The others were catching up. They cursed out Dietz as they crashed aimlessly through the brush. From the other direction Corney was screaming, "Fud'yan wog fud'yan cabin!"

Suddenly something reached out and grabbed me by the ankle. I didn't know what the hell it was, and I jumped back. Then there was a low harsh whisper from down in the thick brambles. "Chun!"

It was Jimmy. His hand was wrapped around my ankle. He let go and I dropped to my knees, knowing exactly what to do.

Jimmy twisted himself around to crawl on his belly. I squirmed in behind him. It wasn't even a few seconds later that the guys came past. They didn't see us, but I was able to watch them. They passed so close to me that I could have reached out and grabbed any one of them by the ankle, just as Dietz had done to me.

When the guys met up with Corney, they figured something strange was going on.

"Where's the Chun?" asked Spyros.

"Yeah—where the hell's Hapanowicz?"

"Now it am both of them assholes."

"Eat shit, Hapanowicz," yelled Spyros. "Do you hear me? Eat it, Chun."

"Maybe this is like *The Twilight Zone,*" Jimpie taunted Woodsie when Woodsie had finally caught up. "Maybe a monster ate 'em."

"Monster," Woodsie tried to laugh. "Ha!"

Jimmy and I scratched along on our bellies. The earth was rich down here below the brambles. There were insect carapaces, downy feathers, scrambling big-eyed locusts, and probably, if we searched, a snake skin or two.

We quickly reached the end of the tunnel and rose to our feet. I had never been in the clearing during the day. It was the most perfectly hidden place I had ever seen. On all sides, stretching high overhead, the brambles formed impregnable walls. And in the center of the hidden clearing, below the sturdy limbs of an oak tree that was itself necklaced by green-and-brown briars, there was the very beginning of a cabin: a square of notched and nailed logs about two feet high.

"Who gives a shit, you bastards!" one of the guys yelled out.

"I think that was Jimpie," I said. "It sounds like they're moving farther away."

"Eat it waw, Chun!"

"Corney," laughed Jimmy.

The guys were lost. They circled back our way. They were still teasing Woodsie, telling him about a reckless escapee from Bellevue who roamed the woods and strangled people and then shrunk their heads and sold them to guys to hang from the rearview mirror in their car. Woodsie believed every word.

I looked over the work Jimmy had done on the cabin. The logs were somewhat thicker than fence posts. They formed a square, with three or four logs on a side. There was a rusted hatchet buried in the end of one of the logs that lay to the side. It wasn't like Dietz to leave a tool out in the weather. He must have been meaning to get back here but hadn't been able. His term of punishment might have had something to do with that.

He hadn't said a word to me about the work he'd been doing here. I wondered why. After all, we were blood brothers, and this was the place where we'd become blood brothers. I was disappointed that he hadn't told me what he'd been doing.

"They'll never find us," I said.

"We'll have to show them."

He had never intended anything else.

I wasn't sure what this meant, surrendering the secret place.

"We won't say anything about the rabbit," I said.

"Right. No one knows about that."

Deftly avoiding the brambles, Jimmy clambered up the oak tree. He yelled out to the guys. "Hey! Hey!"

They heard him and tried to follow his voice.

"Where am he?"

"Up here!" called Jimmy.

"Up where?" asked Spyros.

"In the tree. Keep coming."

"Great, man. In the tree. There's only a million fuckin' trees."

"Look into the sun," said Dietz.

There was a long moment of silence. I imagined the guys as they turned themselves like beacons, craning their necks to find Dietz.

"Right up here," called Dietz.

"There he is," said Corney. "He am in the tree."

"Where?"

"There. Look."

"Where?"

"There, asshole. In the tree."

Jimmy directed them to the spot where the tunnel came out. They dropped to their hands and knees and crawled. But they were in a big hurry and the brambles snagged them and tore their skin. They squealed like trapped pigs.

Woodsie got the worst of it. The thorns cut into his back and he started to bleed. It wasn't all that bad, but he couldn't see where he'd been cut and so he started sniveling. Corney then told him that it was a real bad cut and full of infection. He told Woodsie that the brambles were poisonous. With that, Woodsie went berserk trying to twist his head around to see his back, swearing that he could die from an infection because he had AB-negative blood.

"If I bleed too long, I'll die," he whined.

"No shit, Sherlock. That's what usually happens."

"Jesus, Woodsie," I said, "you're hardly even cut. You oughta know better than to listen to Walsh."

Corney had wandered over to the square kneewall of logs. " 'Fwat. That am a cabin? You'd get a little wet if it rained."

We gathered together and sat on the short walls. The guys began condemning whoever it was had come back here to start the cabin and then given up on it.

Someone said, "Wait a minute, man. What if you had a car and some girl to screw, you wouldn't be back here building a cabin, would you?"

"How d'you know they had cars and could get laid whenever they felt like it?"

"Well, shit, it must've been Gunch and them older guys. Crane and Granito and them."

"Those guys don't go in the woods. They wouldn't have ever found this place."

"Not no more, maybe, but they used to go into the woods and shoot Crane's twenty-two."

"I don't think it was them, and it doesn't even matter," said Jimmy.

Corney sat there blowing mucus out his nose. Spyros lit a Lucky Strike. Woodsie was asking someone to look at his back and tell him how bad it was.

I toyed with letting them in on it that it was Dietz who had done the work, to give Jimmy the credit he had coming. But I said nothing and I knew that I had made the right decision. I figured that this journey out here was Jimmy's way of asking for help.

I remembered the following moment for years. Silence fell, and with it the secret of the place draped itself over us. It was invisible, weightless, and without seam, but it was there, a special feeling and a special magic of the place of the cabin. I could see us building it and then coming back here to camp. I could see one day far into the future when we would bring our sons out here and pass on the tradition of the cabin and tell them the story of how we had built it during the summer of the locusts.

But then I saw something else. I saw that the cabin wouldn't make it that far. Something would arrive to crush it. It frightened me. It was a big empty space, suddenly opening wide in the future where the cabin belonged. It yawned wide and threatened to swallow me. I grabbed on to the log where I sat—I had been certain that otherwise I would fall into a dark bottomless pit.

"Let's build it," I said firmly, moving to the center. "We've got to build it."

They said nothing. They looked at me.

"What for?" asked Harry.

"What for? It's perfect, man."

"Perfect? Perfect what?"

"A perfect place for a cabin," I said. "Are you blind or what?"

"It's a long fuckin' way out here," said Spyros.

"Exactly. That's why it's perfect."

"How're we ever gonna build a cabin?" asked Woodsie. "Shit, remember that doghouse we tried to build? It fell apart."

"If we wanted to build it—no sweat," said Jimmy. "We could build it."

He looked around at the whole group, one by one. His eyes met theirs squarely, polling them. To me, he said, "Good idea, Chun."

The guys were undecided. They chased it around inside their heads. I couldn't believe it. They were so fuckin' lazy it irritated the hell out of me. "C'mon," I said. "Let's build the cabin. It's important."

Jimmy had pried loose the rusty hatchet. He used handfuls of dirt to scrape the rust off, and then he spat on it and rubbed it.

"Throw it away," said Spyros. "It's a piece of junk."

"C'mere," said Jimmy. "Let's see if it can chop your balls off." Then he added, "You owe us a fishing trip."

Spyros said, "Bullshit," weakly.

"And you owe Dietz five bucks," put in someone.

"Let's go do something," said Jimpie. "These friggin' locusts are driving me bats."

"Let's build the cabin," I repeated. "We can sleep out here and everything."

"Yeah. Get dwunk and screw some mommas."

"No girls, man. No girls back here."

"Why not?"

"Yeah, Chun—you gonna be a priest too?"

"Just—no girls."

"We'll have to cut down the trees far away," said Dietz. "Carry them through the woods without making an obvious trail. Then slide them in here through the tunnel."

Spyros said, "Let's just burn the brambles. They suck."

"Sure, Spyros," I said sarcastically. "If we burn down the brambles, anyone would be able to find the cabin. Is that what you want?"

"Take a hike, Chun. No one comes this far back in the woods. Just us."

"What about the guys who did this?" I pointed out, knowing that it had been Dietz and no one else. "What about them?"

"They'll know where it is anyway."

"Maybe not," I said. "The woods change."

"These woods ain't ever gonna change."

"Hey—them guys don't come out here. They got cars and girls, remember?"

"We oughta find a place no one knows," suggested Woodsie.

"Jesus H. Christ, man—nobody knows *this* place."

"Let's just do it," said Jimmy. "If you're in, stick here. If you're not, you got to leave now and swear never to tell anyone about it."

No one chose to leave. The idea of the cabin had finally taken root in their heads and now they wanted to build it.

"We've got to plan it out," said Jimmy.

Suddenly the line was crossed. We began to piece together the way the cabin should look. We drew out ideas in the dirt and stretched our minds forward. We needed hammers and hatchets and bucksaws and spike nails and a big mother crowbar. We could borrow all these things from our fathers. Spyros could get the nails and the crowbar. Jimpie had a bucksaw in the basement at home that his father never used.

It was all to be on the sly. Not a word to anyone. The cabin was a secret oath. It was blood. Yeah, we'd cut out the tongue of the first pussy motherfucker who said a word.

"Don't tell *anyone.*"

We swore to it.

Part Two

At some point in the 1960s . . . though he overlooked the connection, he was annoyed because the attendant at his favorite filling station no longer checked his oil and cleaned his windshield unless asked. He switched filling stations; it was the same there.

—William Manchester,
from *The Glory and the Dream*

Chapter 6

1

"Let's say, Summerhelp, you pump two dollars of regular and the guy gives you a five. You run inside, ring it up, and run back out with the change. Simple, right?"

"Yeah. Nothin' to it."

"Are you lookin' at me?" demanded Pete. "I can't stand it when I don't know if you're lookin' at me or not."

I'd heard this lecture before. It was his favorite, and the example never changed. It was always a five and three singles.

"I'm looking," I said. "I'm listening, too."

"Good," said Pete. "Now suppose that the same thing happens—a guy gives you a five for two dollars' worth of regular except it so happens that the guy across from him is getting three bucks' worth and he's already handed you three singles. What do you do now?"

Before I could answer, he rattled on.

"You might figure you'll be efficient and take the three singles from over here and use them to make change for the five over there. Then all's you got to do is stroll in and ring up the five, right?"

"Wrong."

"You bet your ass it's wrong. It don't work that way at my place. You take those three dollars and you run your ass in here and ring up a three-dollar sale. Then you hustle back out there, get that five, get back in here, ring up another sale—a two-dollar sale—and then get out there with the man's change. Take your efficiency and stuff it. You do it my way—know why?"

"Because it's your money," I droned. "And your money doesn't belong in my hand or in my pocket. *Your* money is only happy in *your* cash register. And the sooner it gets there, the happier it is, and, for all I know, the sooner we'll have peace on earth."

The crusty lines of Pete's oil-browned face cracked and he grinned, mocking me. He reached out with his horned and greasy hand to pat my face. "Well, that's a little more than I needed to hear, but my, my, that college education didn't go to waste on our little Summerhelp, did it?"

"Straight A's in gas-station management."

"Clever. So fuckin' clever. Let me explain something to you, Summerhelp, in hopes I can change your attitude, maybe get that chip off your shoulder."

"Not again, huh?"

"I'm paying you, right? If I want to pay you to fix flat tires, you fix them. If I want to pay you to go out front and pick your nose, then you pick your nose. If I want to pay you to stand still and listen to someone older and more experienced, you stand still and listen. You ought to be more grateful. I don't do this for everyone, you know."

"I'd really rather work. The time goes faster."

"I'll try not to talk too slow."

"I quit. There's no reason I should put up with this. What you're telling me is that you don't think I can make change out at the pumps without screwing up."

"It makes sense to do it my way."

"Of course, it's your business. Anything that doesn't make sense goes. Just like evolution."

"You know what I think, Summerhelp? I don't think your hair grows long for no good reason. I think it's trying to get as far away from your brain as it can. You talk nonsense. Let me tell you why it makes sense to do it my way and see if you can agree.

"You get busy out there one day and a customer gives you the exact amount for a sale and you decide it doesn't make sense to run in to the register with all these other cars pulling in, so you fold up the two or three dollars you've got and stick them in your top pocket.

"Well, it just so happens that you forget to ring that sale up, being that you're so busy, and before you know it the same thing happens, but now it's a five-dollar sale and you fold up the five and stick it in your pocket. Which means you've got eight bucks in your pocket, only it's *my* eight bucks.

"You go on home and your wife does the laundry and if she's got half a brain—although I can't see how she could if she married you— she checks your pockets and, guess what? There's the eight bucks! 'My, my!' she says. 'Look't here—found money.' "

"I'm not married."

"I'll get around to that, don't worry. A guy with pimples like you got can't expect broads to be falling over themselves for you. And just close your trap a second. I'm getting pissed off enough just thinking about this without figuring that you're tuning me out.

"I mean, think about it, Summerhelp. Look at it from my point of view. I'm what the government calls the small businessman. Do you know what that means? It means I ain't got a chance. It means when the shit hits the fan I'm on the receiving end.

"If eight bucks of my money ends up in your pocket every day, I suddenly got eight bucks less than I should—and you got eight bucks more. That's a sixteen-dollar difference between us. At six days a week, that's, let me see—"

"Ninety-six dollars."

Pete smiled craftily. "Funny, how you come right up with that figure."

"It doesn't make sense anyway. Jumping from eight dollars to sixteen like that."

"Ah—that's because you don't understand money, Summerhelp. I could see that from the first day you walked in here looking like a stoned-out hippie pirate. I said to myself, 'Here comes a kid who believes the world runs on love and peace. Poor bastard.' " He looked at me. "That's why I hired you. I knew you needed help."

"I don't know how to begin to express my gratitude."

"Try listening close. If you have eight dollars of mine, I'm short eight dollars that day. Right?"

"Right."

"Okay. So tomorrow I got to do at least eight dollars of business to break even. Which means no profit. Right?"

"Right," I said, though I knew he was skewing the numbers.

"But that means I had to make eight dollars twice—which is six-teen bucks—just to break even. After six days of that shit, I'm in the hole—what was that number you came up with?"

"Ninety-six dollars."

"A considerable sum."

"What I want to know is how you figure I'm walking out of here with close to a hundred bucks a week from some scam that doesn't even exist."

He narrowed his eyes. He scratched his whiskered chin. (He only shaved when he had a date with one of the widows who were in constant pursuit of him.) Then, in harmony with the clatter of the power tools and the tapping valves of an old Ford, he hummed a few bars of a dumb tune, a sure sign that his temper was approaching the red zone. "Tra-dee-la-di-dum, Summerhelp. Tra-lala-dee-do. I'd like to fire your ass just for mentioning that."

"Mentioning what?"

"Stealing a hundred bucks."

"How'd we go from three dollars here, five dollars there, to a hundred a week?"

"Exactly my point," he said triumphantly.

"This is crazy, Pete."

"You know, Summerhelp, top-pocket money is interesting stuff. I mean, it's only human nature for a person to think that the money in their pocket is theirs. It's a habit we've fallen into.

"Now take a person like yourself. You're not married, so it's not your loving wife who finds the money. *My* money. What happens in your case is this. You stop on the way home from work for a cold beer or a nice gin and tonic. You reach into your pocket for your smokes and you *find* eight dollars there instead. Next thing you know, you're saying to yourself, 'Hell, I know whose money this is, that old son of a bitch. He don't pay me worth a damn and eight lousy dollars isn't going to bust him.'

"Next thing you know, there's my eight dollars out on the bar, buying drinks for you and all your barroom buddies, maybe even a broad or two. They all decide that you're the most generous big shot since Diamond Jim.

"Don't do it, Summerhelp. No money in your top pocket. Ring up one sale at a time. I don't want you to have money in your pocket ever. And don't keep it in your hand any longer than you'd hold your pecker in the middle of Yankee Stadium."

I acted bored. Pete smirked and warned me. "You'll see," he said. "It happens every fuckin' time. You'll see."

A week or so later, just before Pete was about to leave for a swim at the club, he called me aside in the shop and asked if I recalled the lecture about top-pocket money.

"Word for word," I assured him.

His face was in the shadows, and when he smiled his teeth gleamed carnivorously. The wind happened to be carrying the odor of garbage our way. It settled in around us like a fog.

"Now don't get all-fired pissed off at me, Summerhelp. All's I want to do is teach you a little lesson."

"How long is this going to go on?" I protested. "I mean, you tell me this bullshit every other day."

He took out a crisp five-dollar bill and popped it between his fingers. He displayed it for me as if I'd never seen one.

"I guess you might say it's put up or shut up, Summerhelp."

He laid the five on the workbench and said, "That's coming out of your pay. After taxes, of course."

"What for?"

"In exchange for the money in your top pocket."

I stood there motionless, resisting the impulse to check my pocket.

"Or—we can make a little wager," suggested Pete.

"Such as?"

"If you don't have any money in your top pocket, I'll double this and give it to you right here and now. Cash."

"And if there is money in my pocket?"

"We double it and it comes out of your pay."

I knew I was probably better off letting him take the five dollars out of my pay. I probably had money in my top pocket. I hated to admit it, but he was right. I'd stopped at a deli during lunch the other day and "found" three dollars in my pocket and used it to buy lunch.

I reached into my pocket now and, sure enough, there was money there. I tossed the folded bills onto the workbench and didn't even bother to look at them.

"I didn't steal it, Pete. I forgot, that's all."

He looked at the money and said, "Don't try it again, Summerhelp, or you walk. You can't get away with it, and I'll tell you why."

He paused and drew my attention to the folded bills on the bench. "Hear them?" he asked.

"What?"

"You can't hear them? Crying like orphans because they ain't in my cash register?"

He picked up the bills, saying, "There, there. There, there."

I couldn't believe it. "You're nuts."

"Yeah, could be. But I ain't broke."

2

At Pete's Friendly Service, every customer was to be treated with equal respect, for any one of them could be bearing the reward, any one of them could be the Paymaster.

Yes, I'd come to believe it. The mechanics weren't simply pulling my leg. I'd seen a photo of a gas jockey in the company newsletter. He was smiling. He was holding five one-hundred-dollar bills. With such irrefutable evidence, the game had changed.

Mind you, I surely wasn't about to become the company's darling lickspittle, but if I had to wash windshields and sell oil and TBA for Pete anyway, I had nothing to lose by staying on my toes for the Paymaster.

Be sure to pose the three magic questions. Be sure to perform the highly symbolic washing of the windshield and rear window. That was all it took. For a shot at fifty dollars could anything be easier? For a shot at *five hundred?* For that, three questions and clean windows? Gents—it was in the bag.

"Wipe all the time," explained Pete.

The two of us hovered by the pumps. It was obvious that there was a master and his boy here: Pete in his clean, starched blue uniform, a leather cap pushed back on his balding head, that greedy glint in his eyes powerful as a pair of klieg lights. Beside him, there I stood, in my also-known-as clothes, taking instructions.

A car pulled up. I smiled wanly at the driver.

"Fill 'er up?"

"No," said the man. "No, I don't need gas at all, to tell you the truth. If you could, though, would you check the oil? I never could figure out how."

Pete popped the latch and yanked open the hood. We ducked beneath it, and in the semidarkness and rising pungency of the engine, Frank's calculating smile shone like the plot of the devil.

"What you do with this kind," he began, "is poke around under the hood while the oil's going in. Feel the play on that fan belt. Check the water in the radiator. Then tell him one thing or another's getting old. Some bottom-shelf item. A belt or a hose or a wiper blade; somethin' we got on sale so he thinks he saved money by spending money. We don't want to sell him the Brooklyn Bridge, y'know. Two bucks here, three there. It adds up. The guy might not listen to you. He might not buy a damn thing. But that fan belt he's got might snap in two next month, or that radiator hose might bust wide open tomorrow. If he finds himself stranded on the Pulaski Skyway one night with a fuckin' fan belt good for nothin' but hangin' himself, you can bet your sweet ass he's goin' to remember that little Summerhelp who wanted to sell him a new one. He'll come back here, don't worry, and when he does—that's when we sell him the Brooklyn Bridge."

Pete closed the hood and approached the driver solemnly.

"The oil's fine," he told the driver. "But you'd better get yourself a new fan belt soon."

"Oh, really? How soon?"

Pete shrugged. "Who knows? It might break today, it might not break for a month. I'll tell you this—you sure don't want it to break during rush hour on the BQE."

Fifteen minutes later, the man had a new fan belt and Pete's cash register had gobbled down another tasty treat.

Pete never stopped the lessons. I really believe he had some strange idea that I wanted to learn the gas-station business.

"Yeah, wipe all the time," he droned. "Keep a dirty rag in your left back pocket for checking dip sticks, and a clean rag in your other back pocket for cleaning door handles and chrome."

The hot sun and the offensive gases from the dump must have been too much for him today. He wore a loony smile and his face was flushed; his jowls were the color and texture of corned beef. He pretended there was a car in front of us and he mimed the ritual and then told me to mime it. I felt very foolish but I played along.

"Nope, nope," said Pete immediately. "Wipe that door handle, Summerhelp. Don't be touching it with your grimy fingers." He grinned at the imaginary customer. He even tipped his cap. *"Excuse the boy—he went to college."*

I pretended to wipe the door handle that wasn't there. It was the wisest decision. It always made the afternoon pass more smoothly when I humored Pete.

"There, sir," sang Pete, pointing out my work on the door handle to the invisible customer. *"How's that? Dandy day, isn't it? Fill it, did you say?"*

He turned to me. "Summerhelp, you listening? Wipe that door handle and don't be poking your face in my customer's nose."

"But, Pete—I did wipe it."

He ignored me. *"Oil, sir? Been hard to start, ma'am?"*

He tipped his cap and ogled the imaginary woman.

"Let the customer see you wipe that door handle and hood ornament," he went on. "If he says to fill it up and it takes more than ten gallons, why, you wipe his ass if he asks. Clean the windshield and the back window too. Use that blue crap in the squeegee and don't streak it up. Don't spill gas on the blacktop. Ring up each sale separate. Don't forget them paper towels cost ten for a cent. You can get three cars, front and back windows, with one friggin' towel if you use it like I showed you and not the way you've come up with on your own. Do every last thing the way I showed you. And, dammit, Summerhelp, one other thing—put a Band-Aid on that big pimple on your chin. It looks like a volcano. I don't want my customers seeing white pus first thing they pull in here. And I'd tell you to cut your ugly hair before bats start flying out of it, but you'd probably raise holy jumpin' Jesus."

He walked away, checked the tally on the cash register, strolled out to the Jeep, and got in. He fished around in his pockets for the keys and couldn't find them.

"Summerhelp!" he bellowed. "Get me them keys from the hook."

I retrieved the keys for him and he sped off somewhere. I returned to my work.

Five or six flats stood in need of patching. Thankfully, there was a lull at the pumps. I mounted the next tire to be repaired and thought about Pete's screwball lessons. I wondered about the Paymaster, too, and whether it was necessarily true that he would pull in for gas. He might only need oil, or a wiper blade, or water for his battery. He might need nothing at all for his car. Maybe he'd just pull in and ask directions.

I was a little suspicious now, wondering if perhaps Pete and the mechanics knew far more about the Paymaster's techniques than they were letting on. It wouldn't strike me as fair for one of them to score the fifty or five hundred dollars when I was the one hustling in and out to the pumps. I began to be a little more alert.

Thursday of the following week, I was repairing a tire in the shop when I heard the bell hose clang. I looked up to see a shiny Packard at the nearest pump island. I recognized the car immediately as belonging to Monsignor Riordan, the pastor at St. Anne's. He had two Packards, in fact. Both of them were classics and he kept them in mint condition. Pete predicted that one day the monsignor would sell the Packards, steal the money from the poor box, and run off with a woman to Barbados.

It used to be that whenever I was in the middle of a job and the bell hose rang, I would complain that it was always me who had to drop what he was doing and run to the pumps. I had tried to use this excuse because it was the same excuse the mechanics always used, even when they were lounging around. But lately I had decided that since between them they only pumped gas for one out of a hundred cars, nothing would make me angrier than for one of them to get to the Paymaster.

I put aside the tire I was repairing and even though I knew the monsignor wasn't the Paymaster in disguise I hurried out to the pumps because I aimed to establish the pump islands as my little fiefdom. The mechanics were to stay away. I wanted to stick that fifty-dollar bill in their faces. I wanted to pull five one-hundred-dollar bills from my top pocket and, right in front of Pete, say, "Look't here, look't here. My, my, found money and all that folderol."

On my way out to the big shiny Packard I was surprised to see Father Lusenkas emerge from the door on the driver's side. I'd had no idea he was now at St. Anne's. The last I'd heard he was teaching up at

Cathedral again. I wondered if this assignment to Staten Island was a
disciplinary action by Cardinal Spellman, which it had been the last
time Father Lusenkas had found himself here.

"Hello, Father," I said, wondering if he would remember me. He
had taught up at Cathedral when Jimmy was there. He was a tall and
lean man. Handsome, I guess you would say. He'd always been a very
popular priest, and I recalled when he'd been in hot water with the
cardinal for getting arrested in Alabama during the civil rights demon-
strations.

For a while he had been the confessor at the Catholic high school
I'd attended, which meant that you confessed eyeball to eyeball without the screen between the two of you. Confession in those days was
generally held in the biology lab, where Father Lusenkas sat in a chair
across the table from you, his thin purple stole draped over his shoulders, while you knelt on a portable kneeler. It took some getting used
to, confessing that way, but after a while I didn't mind it at all. I learned
how to admit to my transgressions and put them right out on the table,
so to speak. I mean, in the dim confessional in church, where the
priest was nothing but a shadow and a voice, you really felt you had
done wrong. But at school it was far different. Father Lusenkas would
have you kneel to patter, "Bless me, Father, for I have sinned," and
the rest, just as if you were in the confessional box, but then he'd have
you sit across the table from him and he'd talk to you like you were a
human being who wanted someone to say that it was all right to have
screwed up. And throughout it all, confessing your sins and receiving
advice and penance, you could see his face and he could see yours and
there was no need to hide anything. I had always come away feeling
good.

"Fill 'er up, Father?" I asked.

"Yes," he said. "Thank you."

He stood there and stretched his arms as if he'd taken a long drive.
He was wearing his collar and a short-sleeved black shirt. The shirt
was stained by perspiration.

Waving his hand at the hood as does a person who has no comprehension of engines and wishes not to learn, he asked, "You'll check
underneath there?"

"No problem."

He paused.

"How's the bus doing?" he inquired, indicating the church bus at the far end of the lot.

"Eddie's been working on it," I said. Then, to show I knew something about these things, I added, "He thinks it's the valves."

"Oh? That's serious, isn't it?"

I didn't have a chance to answer. Pete had appeared, tipping his cap in greeting to the priest. "Hello, Father. How are you today?"

"Just fine, thank you. And you, Pete?"

Pete had taken his clean rag from his back pocket. He folded it over as if searching for the cleanest part and then used it to wipe the door handle, which already gleamed immaculately anyway.

"I can't complain, Father," said Pete, buffing the handle.

"I presume that means business is good."

"Well—" began Pete. He grinned. "It can always be better, Father."

I popped open the hood and exposed the cleanest engine I'd ever set my eyes on outside a showroom floor. Pete came around to admire the engine, and while Father Lusenkas left to talk with Eddie about the bus, he made a few nasty comments about how the Catholics had money to burn.

"I mean, look at this car. And the old buzzard's got two of them. It beats hell out of me," he said, wiping the impeccably clean valve cover. "They wear funny hats and black dresses and drive around in fancy cars. You ever seen a skinny priest or a priest who drives a Volkswagen? Not on your life, Summerhelp."

I wanted to say that Father Lusenkas was skinny, but Pete rambled on.

"Some racket they got. Three square meals, a roof over your head, nice car, pocket money, vacations in Italy, and all you got to do is once in a while splash water on babies and say, 'Dominick's got all the biscuits,' or something like that. Some racket." Then he added with a nasty laugh, "Of course, you can't never get laid. Not if you don't want to piss off the man upstairs."

The pump handle clicked off when the tank had filled and Pete told me to get back to what I'd been doing. "I'll finish with the padre," he said. "Make sure he gets charged every cent. There's no charity here. Hell, it's good I ain't Catholic. I'd probably be damned."

I returned to the tire machine, where I mounted the next flat,

removed the stem from the valve, and popped the rim seal with the
tire tool. I was pulling the inner tube free when I looked up and saw
Father Lusenkas in front of me. The sun was over his shoulder and his
features were shadowed. And because he wore black, he appeared
indistinct. He was a dark outline against the bright outdoor light. It
gave me a start, because for a moment I thought it was Jimmy. I had
never before realized how similarly the two were built.

"You're pretty good at that," he said.

"I get lots of practice."

He paused. I could tell that he remembered me.

"Are you still in school?" he asked. "You were at NYU, right?"

"I was. I dropped out. I went to De Paul for a semester. Well, not
even a semester. It wasn't in the cards."

"How are you feeling?" he asked, and I knew then that he remembered the whole story and how I'd lost the eye.

"Good."

I continued to work on the flat. Father Lusenkas followed me over
to the workbench, where I roughed up the tire at the site of the leak
with some sandpaper and then brushed the sticky acrid glue on it.

"I'm at a loss," he said. "I forget your name."

"Hapanowicz."

"Yes—Andrew. St. Peter's." Then he said something in Polish.

"I don't understand it," I said. "Neither does my father anymore.
Just my grandmother, but she doesn't understand English too well."

He was amused.

"What's the word on Jim?" he asked.

He was the only person I ever knew who called Dietz Jim.

"He'll be home in three weeks."

"I've said mass for him."

I nodded. "I'll tell him."

"I'll look forward to seeing him."

"So will I."

He said goodbye and returned to the big shiny Packard, where
Pete awaited with the charge account slip. I watched while the two
carried out the transaction and talked for a few minutes. Then I saw
Father Lusenkas point my way.

I was busy with another flat tire and didn't see Father Lusenkas
leave. Pete disappeared into the office and then went over to the

church bus to ream out Eddie. A few cars came in and I went out to the
pumps, and then when the pumps were quiet again I returned to the
shop and started cleaning the tools in the corner where the solvent
bucket was kept.

I thought about my conversation with Father Lusenkas. I appreciated that he hadn't immediately asked about Jimmy, or that when
he was trying to recall my name he hadn't first recalled me as Jimmy's
friend. Because I'm sure that although both of those ideas had passed
through his mind, he had been considerate enough not to approach me
that way.

Yet I also could have understood if he hadn't done it that way.
Because I understood just how wide a shadow Jimmy cast; I understood this better than anyone.

Pete wandered in to watch George pull the water pump from a
Fairlane and then came over to see what I was doing. I was at the
workbench farthest from the office and farthest from the mechanics. I
had finished cleaning the tools and was now pulling old batteries from
beneath the bench and stacking them in the short hall just inside the
rear door.

"Settin' them up and knockin' them down, eh, Summerhelp? Slip,
slap, thank you, ma'am."

"What's that?"

"Small talk. Relax."

A car pulled in for gas. The bell hose rang. I stacked the battery
that was cradled in my arms and started out for the pumps.

"Hold on," said Pete.

"There's a car—"

"What am I? Blind? I can see the damn car." He hollered over to
Tom. "You're up, Tom."

Tom was up to his ass in an engine job and called back, "What the
hell's wrong with Summerhelp?"

"I must be going crazy," yelled Pete. "But I think I'm the boss. I
think I *own* this goddam place."

"Jesus, Uncle Pete."

"Uncle Pete, bullshit. Go on, pump gas for once. I got something
to say to Summerhelp."

Pete turned to me, and his face was about as sympathetic as I'd
ever expect to see it. You would think he was about to tell me that he

had only a month to live and wanted to make restitution for all the snide things he'd said not only to me but to everyone else who had ever worked for him.

"I was talking to the padre over there, y'know? And he happened to say he knew you and that you were a decent enough kid. And he said you were like this—" he showed me his crossed fingers—"with the kid who won the Silver Star."

I nodded. "Yeah. Dietz."

"Right. Dietz."

Pete paused. "He'll be home soon."

"A couple weeks."

"Good."

Pete hesitated. I started working on the batteries again, and when Pete said to take it easy I just continued what I was doing. I sensed where he was heading with this uncharacteristic concern of his and I wanted to keep myself busy.

"Then he said something about . . ." He pointed at my eye, the missing eye. "And I started remembering about how it was in the newspapers."

"Front page," I said, not looking at Pete. I was working hard. Harder than was called for. A few drops of sweat fell from my nose onto the thickly greased surface of one of the batteries. One drop dissolved in the granulated greenish lead-sulfate salt. The others simply sat there, refusing to evaporate or dissolve.

"Yeah," said Pete. "That's right. Front page. I remember people coming in here and talkin' about it. No one ever got the whole story, I guess, but it had something to do with this football game down in Midland Beach. There was a big slugfest after the game. Some asshole drove his car onto the field and tried to run kids over. Three or four kids were hurt bad, some broken bones and that, right?"

"Right."

There were no more batteries to stack. I felt wedged into the short hall between Pete and the back door. I stood there. I could feel and hear my heart pulsing in my one ear.

"The padre helped me with my memory," Pete continued. "He remembers it like it was yesterday. One night a couple weeks after the fight at the football game—around Thanksgiving—there was this bunch hanging out down there in Midland Beach, and the next thing you know this car comes speeding around the corner with a shotgun pointing out the window. Both barrels were emptied and it was done just right. A little birdshot in their asses, but nobody was killed."

"That's what I've heard," I said. I turned to examine the stacked batteries and used my booted foot to nudge one tighter to the wall.

"A few months later a bunch of guys—and everyone figured they were from Midland Beach—jumped this kid down on the beach and beat the livin' shit outta him. Smacked him with a baseball bat and might as well left him for dead. The kid was in a coma for a few days, but he finally snapped out of it."

Pete paused to see how I would react. I hated being reminded of all this. I could still see the never-ending dreamscape of that coma, a worrisome and colorless banishment with a small voice which said that things weren't as they ought to be. I could feel the danger of it again, of sliding off into vast spaces that would dilute me. Nevertheless I somehow kept a poker face as Pete continued to piece things together.

"I got this friend, see? He's a detective down at the St. George precinct, and he told me, back a few months when this friend of yours got the Silver Star, that it was probably him blasted the kids on the corner, only no one could prove a thing at the time."

That's who it was, all right, I thought. I should know. I was in the car.

"And now that the padre refreshed my memory," said Pete, "I recall it was a little Polack kid got the shit kicked outta him."

I stood there with nowhere to go, and Pete looked at me squarely. "How am I doing?"

I felt my stomach do flips, as if I'd gone through all of it again. "Interesting story."

I attempted to walk away, saying, "I got things to do."

Pete took a step to the side and blocked my way. He held me momentarily by the shoulder, saying, "The Polack kid lost his eye but never said shit or Shinola to the cops about the whole thing. This other guy, meanwhile, goes off and gets the Silver Star."

"Yeah," I said. "Yeah. I know the story, Pete. I got work to do."

"Well, go ahead," he said, stepping aside. "Go ahead. But let me tell you one thing, Summerhelp, if I was that little Polack kid, I'd be mighty fuckin' pissed off."

Chapter 7

1

Jimmy wanted to be alone now and then, just like anyone else. He enjoyed going fishing, which was something I didn't much care for, and he liked to go off into the woods at dawn with his bow to hunt.

For his fifteenth birthday he bought himself an old rowboat, which he always called a pram, and he spent hours patching it and giving it a fresh coat of marine paint. When he had finished, the boat looked brand-new.

I tried to help Jimmy with the boat, but I really didn't know what I was doing or how Jimmy wanted it done. Yet even though Jimmy was very particular about the way things should be done, I think he would have put up with my mistakes. The real problem was his father, who would criticize my work the moment I appeared and wouldn't let me do anything without stepping in to show me the right way to do it. It wasn't long before I saw that it made more sense not to come around to see Jimmy until the pram was finished.

I saw more of Jimmy than any of the other guys did and yet I never knew from day to day when I'd see him next. He was always busy. He mowed lawns and trimmed hedges for people. He painted porches and cleaned windows and watched over houses for families who were on vacation. He must have earned enough money by the time we were sophomores to buy a yacht instead of that little pram. But he saved the money to help pay his tuition at Cathedral.

At home he had a long list of chores, not just the easy ones like taking out the garbage, but also washing floors and weeding the vegetable garden and helping his father change the oil in the car.

It was remarkable that he'd been able to work on the cabin with us every day until it was finally done. I never learned how he'd managed that but I knew it was a good thing he had. I don't know if we would have finished the cabin without him, or if it would have come out as well.

He went to confession on Wednesdays at school and then went again every Saturday afternoon. I couldn't understand why. He couldn't have sinned *that* much. He hardly ever cursed. He would never steal. He didn't have a girlfriend and didn't seem to want one. He ignored all our dirty books but didn't make a big deal of it when we sat there drooling over them. He thought we were stupid for jerking off. He said it was a waste of time.

I figured he went to confession twice a week to make sure he hadn't slipped up and committed a sin without knowing it. There were an awful lot of ways to sin if you were Catholic, and mortal sin frightened Jimmy. It was the only thing I'd ever heard him say he feared. He couldn't imagine anything more horrible than to die in the state of mortal sin and go to hell forever.

I told him that there wasn't any such place as hell. I told him it was something they'd come up with to scare us into behaving. He told me in return that I was absolutely wrong and "thinking dangerously."

He liked to repeat words like that, just the way he'd picked them up from one or another priest. We had a handy relationship that way. He imitated the priests he respected and I was a good sinner for him to practice on.

Jimmy and I killed many weekend nights together during the winter after we'd built the cabin. We usually played cards or chess, or just sat around talking. We persuaded the guys to camp out with us one night in late November. It was chilly, and although all we seemed to do was cut wood and huddle around the fire, it wasn't so cold that anyone backed out and headed home. While we were returning to our comfortable houses the next day, we decided that camping in the winter had only one advantage: no mosquitoes.

We had our first disciplinary action during the winter. Spyros had bragged about the cabin to the Purps and we'd learned that Sliver and Smitty and Deluxe had tried to find it. Of course they'd failed. Not even old Daniel Boone could have found the cabin.

Our punishment for Spyros was fifty push-ups—which probably only Spyros and Dietz could have accomplished anyway—and we each got to punch him in the shoulder ten times. He had to show us his shoulder the following day, and if it wasn't black-and-blue we planned to punch him that day and every day until his shoulder was obviously bruised. Spyros was lucky. His shoulder resembled a piece of gray-and-blue steak the day after the punishment.

It had always been understood that Jimmy would be a priest. You could see it in him and no one could recall when that hadn't been so. It had made Jimmy different and somewhat mysterious from the start.

Each week he served as an altar boy at nine-o'clock mass on Sunday and occasionally returned for a later mass with his parents. There were eight children in his family. He was the oldest. When his parents and his brothers and sisters marched into church together they took up most of the first pew.

Jimmy's father was stern in church, which was nothing unusual for him. He was also stern at birthday parties and picnics and most of life's other joyous occasions. He had once given my younger sister a lecture when she'd tried to help blow out the candles on his daughter's birthday cake. I know this happened, because I was there. I'd walked my sister over to the house for the party, and when Mr. Dietz made her cry I took her by the hand and started to leave. Jimmy's mother, however, came over and said something about "His bark is worse than his bite" and led my sister back to the party. Mr. Dietz hadn't found it necessary to apologize to my sister himself. He just stood there like some fabled birthday-party troll, probably wishing he *could* bite someone.

When in church Mr. Dietz shuffled up to receive communion his brow was furrowed and he seemed to have very little patience with the people who had gotten ahead of him in line. He acted as if there was only so much of God to go around. When he closed his eyes and threw back his head to receive the host, he hardly extended his tongue for fear that everyone would see it was indelibly marked with all the nasty words a person could say. As he returned to the pew with the host in his mouth he looked like a bear who had captured a choice morsel he didn't intend to share, and later, at the prayers at the end of the mass, the ones said in English, his voice rose loudly above everyone else's. He was determined that God notice he was there.

Mr. Dietz was such a dyed-in-the-wool Catholic that when the pope declared that St. Christopher wasn't really a saint he immediately removed the ex-saint's statue from his dashboard, trashed all the medals as if they had betrayed him, and then hurried to a lawyer to have his son Christopher renamed Bartholomew. Afterward, if you happened to call Bart "Chris," Mr. Dietz snapped at you and said that if you couldn't keep his children's names straight you weren't welcome in his house.

Sunday mass was celebrated—another expression I picked up from Jimmy, that mass was "celebrated"—over in the gymnasium at the grammar school. The little church—the chapel—where we had gone for many years was too small now. More and more houses had been built every year. Open fields became developments overnight. Long stretches of woods were leveled in a twinkling. New roads criss-crossed where there had been none. The parish grew explosively. There was much talk about building a new church, but the monsignor added new classrooms to the school instead. Everyone winked and called him shrewd for this.

At the nine-o'clock mass on Sunday mornings, the mass they called "the young people's mass," Jimmy's partner on the altar was Charles Goudis, a tall and sickly guy who was skinny as a broomstick and weighed less than a postage stamp. He was two years older than Jimmy and he also went to Cathedral. In another year he would be in the seminary at Dunwoodie.

My mother was very strict about my attending Sunday mass and there was no sense trying to argue with her over it, because that would do nothing more than bring down my father's wrath. Even though he wasn't Catholic himself, my father wouldn't let any of us miss mass. His reasoning was plain and simple. "You're going," he would say. "That's final!"

So every Sunday I played this game. I rose from bed and washed up, grumbling just enough for everyone to see I was doing something I disliked, dressed in the clothes my mother had ironed and left hanging in the doorway, asked my father for money for the collection, turned down breakfast so they would think I was receiving communion, and then left the house pretending that I was on my way to mass.

Corney and Spyros and Woodsie were Catholic too and the group
of us gathered at the corner and waited there for the rickety blue-and-
white church bus to come laboring up the hill. Blue and white, I had
learned, were the colors of the Virgin Mary. The parish was named for
her. Our Lady, Star of the Sea. She was also known under other
circumstances as the Seat of Wisdom, the Tower of David, the Mirror
of Justice, and so on—more titles than the New York Yankees and the
Boston Celtics combined.

We kept a stash of cigarettes and a recent copy of *True Detective*
magazine in a plastic bag by the telephone pole in the brush so that we
had some way to kill the time.

From where we stood we could see down to Jimmy's house. In the
days when Mr. Mullin had lived there, Corney used to sneak down to
the house to steal a bottle or two of beer from the back porch. He'd
drink it before the bus arrived, even if it meant guzzling it. "Bourbon
on ice," he'd say as he hurriedly downed the beer. Afterward, he
always belched loudly.

Like clockwork, at a quarter past eight every Sunday, Jimmy appeared at the door of his house carrying his surplice and cassock on a
hanger. The way the surplice and cassock hung down it looked as if
Jimmy was carrying a scarecrow designed to ward off old Beelzebub
himself. He brought the clothes home for his mother to launder and
press. She felt it wasn't proper to ask the women of the Altar Society
to do her son's garments when she was perfectly capable of doing
them herself. Which didn't make a whole lot of sense to me, because I
was certain that Jimmy's mother was in the Altar Society anyway.

Jimmy knew we were at the corner watching him but he never
looked our way. He simply crossed from the front door through the
opening in the tall hedge to the driveway and got in his father's car.
Then his father came out of the house, taking the same route from the
door to the car. He got in the car, started it, and backed out of the
driveway. The car came up the street toward us, and when Mr. Dietz
made the turn at the corner he looked right through us. Jimmy, sitting
alongside his father on the front seat, appeared solemn. He barely
nodded hello to us.

It had always seemed to me, as I witnessed this same scene Sunday after Sunday, that Jimmy was like a handcuffed prisoner in the
front seat of that old Plymouth, kidnapped by the world's biggest

grouch. He certainly didn't look like a person who was on his way to "celebrate."

The girls we were interested in didn't want to be seen on the same corner with us on Sundays. They knew we'd be an embarrassment to them. Instead they waited at an earlier stop and were on the bus when we climbed aboard. They always looked great on Sunday, dolled up in bright colors: yellows and pinks, lavender and white lace, their faces rosy, the scent of their perfume lifting us off the ground. They wisely waited until after mass, when we all walked together to Carol Dante's for doughnuts and rolls, to daub on their lipstick and pencil mascara on their eyes. They were allowed to wear makeup except at mass, and if word ever reached home that they'd been seen in church wearing lipstick or mascara they'd be put under lock and key in the dungeon for a week.

Whenever we got on the church bus, Jimpie was already sitting with Toni DiSogra. He went to her house every Sunday morning to walk her to the bus stop, and they held hands during their walk and the whole time while they waited for the bus and then sat side by side on the bus, still holding hands. They let go of each other's hand only long enough to let some sweat evaporate into the air from their palms. They held hands until they entered the church, where there was an unwritten law that prohibited teenagers holding hands, but once the mass was over and they were outside, their hands were glued together again. The two of them had exchanged "friendship rings"—whatever the hell that meant—and Jimpie was stocking shelves at Shop-Rite and saving his money for an engagement ring. I think they'd secretly picked out their wedding day while the rest of us had been napping after snack in kindergarten.

It was awful. I mean, I liked Margaret Stampf, and since she was the first girl who'd ever let me feel her up and tongue-kiss, I could feel myself get hot just looking her way. But I sure as hell wasn't about to go through this silly thing with friendship rings. I bought her birthday presents and I once even got her a corsage for the sophomore dance at my mother's insistence, but I just couldn't spend all day with her the way Jimpie was held by suction to Toni.

The prettiest girls liked Woodsie. None of us ever figured that out. All he did was turn red and giggle when they talked to him. He claimed he never even tried to kiss with an open mouth, much less use his

tongue or weasel his hands under a blouse. For a while we had this
theory that all the pretty girls liked Woodsie because he showed them
so much respect. But then we figured they actually didn't know the
difference between respect and dumbness, and we resigned ourselves
to the fact that Woodsie had boring evenings with pretty girls and
didn't know any better.

Of course, no one else had as many girls chasing after him as
Corney. Many of the pretty ones who eventually gave up on Woodsie
and hadn't had their more intimate desires met ended up wriggling
lustily on basement couches or on the rug in the TV room with Corney
while their parents slept. The girls had reached some sort of secret
accord to share Corney until he was dead from sexual exhaustion.
Poor Corney.

The girls knew that we guys skipped mass whenever—well,
whenever the spirit moved us, you might say, and depending upon the
vigilance of Father Matusiak. If Father happened not to be there in the
parking lot to direct our steps in the straight and narrow when the bus
arrived, we sauntered off to a nearby luncheonette, where we played
pinball until mass was over.

The girls, of course, enjoyed lecturing us about this, saying that it
was a mortal sin to miss mass, and we responded sharply, asking them
if they intended receiving holy communion on those tongues that had
done all that tongue-kissing.

But when they suggested that maybe they ought to stop all that
tongue-kissing, we became a bit sheepish and changed our tactics.

One Sunday, the summer after we'd built the cabin, the church bus
pulled into the parking lot and Father Matusiak wasn't at his post. It
would be nothing for us to slip off to the pinball machines. But I'd been
having other thoughts lately. I'd seen Jimmy serve mass on several
occasions, and had found that with him up there it wasn't all that
unbearable a thing to go through. The other guys had already started
on their way across the lot when they realized that I wasn't going
along.

"Yo, Chun! Whatcha doin'?"

"Goin' in."

"What for?"

I shrugged. "Mass."

They laughed. They figured I was joking.

"What am with you, Chunnie? You afwaid of goin' to hell?"

I knew why I wanted to go. I wanted to figure out what it was about Jimmy and the mass that was so appealing, but I wouldn't say this to the guys. So I simply told them it was none of their business and went inside.

It got under their skin. They must have thought I had some kind of scheme going on, or that there was a new foxy girl in town who got turned on by guys who went to mass and received communion. They followed along and slid into the back row with me.

The girls noticed us and wondered what sort of funny business we were up to. Carol Dante left her seat, genuflected in the aisle, and came back to grill us.

"What're you guys doin' here?"

Corney made three quick hand farts and said, "Makin' farts."

"I should have known."

Mr. Lewis, one of the ushers, came over and told Corney, "Be still, young man."

Carol, quite ladylike, returned to her seat. Mr. Lewis kept his eye on us.

"This sucks already," said Spyros. "And it ain't even started yet."

"Yeah, Chun, what're we doin' here?" asked Woodsie.

"Andy, man—let's go."

"Go on, if you want. I'm staying."

"Shit, what's this? You gonna be a priest too?"

"Not the Chun, man. He likes feeling up Maggie too much."

"Yeah. Who'd give up them tits to be a priest?"

"You guys shouldn't talk like that in church," I said.

"Cut the shit," said Corney.

"Yeah, Chun," said Spyros. "What's with you?"

The bell struck the initial note and everyone stood. There was something there from the first, from the moment that Jimmy and Charles Goudis appeared leading the way for the priest across the altar.

"Who am he?" asked Corney, meaning the priest.

"I don't know," I said, although I reasoned that it was the priest who excited Jimmy so much. He taught at Cathedral and was a friend of the Murtaghs. "I can't remember his name," I added in a whisper.

Jimmy drew my attention. It was obvious that he approached his duty seriously. This gymnasium with the cold, polished stone floor, the metal folding chairs and padded kneelers, the winched-up basketball backboards, the glazed cinder-block walls and the plain glass-and-steel windows might be for many others the place where they endured the weary habit of the mass, but for Jimmy it was the Holy of Holies. As far as he was concerned, God was here.

He was reverent throughout the service and yet moved with the same ease and grace as he did when he played basketball or swam or drew a bow. He commanded attention without wanting it. If there had existed a magazine for altar boys, he would have been on the cover.

There was magic in him, I decided. And it was a magic I didn't find completely alien. It was that sort of magic I had felt when I had gone to serve mass on those wintry mornings while my grandfather lay dying. It was the magic I'd felt this past year, back in October, when my class was taken for sophomore retreat to a Jesuit retreat house out on Long Island. The retreat house was a large stone building with long quiet hallways and private rooms. There was a wide white-marble staircase just as you entered, and other small hidden staircases throughout the building. A massive but approachable silence had filled the halls and the small chapel. For the first two days of the four-day retreat I had felt that . . . that I was *this close* to discovering something extraordinary about the world, about God, about existing. But on the third day, this very strange priest gave us a scathing lecture and showed us slides of the Shroud of Turin. We came to call him simply "Feel-the-Pain," because he went through Christ's Agony and Crucifixion in minute detail, recounting each lash of the whip, each thorn of the crown, every step of the way to Calvary. He demanded at every breath that we feel the pain. "Feel the pain of that scourging at the pillar, guys. Feel those nails being driven through the bones of your hands. Feel that pain, suffer that humiliation."

While he lectured us he salivated noisily and his large head wobbled as if it would fall off his shoulders. He finally told us how we were responsible for all this pain and for crucifying Christ. At that, the silence I had enjoyed was frightened off, and the magic of the place crumbled.

But I could find this magic again, or allow it to find me. On days when I would be out in the woods alone or sitting atop the peaked roof of our cabin, I would drift off and suddenly realize that there was something else here, something just beyond my reach, something peering over my shoulder, something I could chase but never, it seemed, catch. It would send shivers up my arms and legs.

. . . From the rear of the gymnasium the large standing fans circulated the air but failed to cool the parishioners. The humidity was overwhelming. People fanned themselves with the church bulletins. Babies fussed and were jounced to no avail.

Corney and Spyros and Woodsie were bored stiff. They weren't even bothering to stand or kneel any longer. Corney sat there smelling the nicotine stains on his fingers. Spyros busied himself using a ballpoint pen to draw a pair of dice showing a seven on his forearm. Woodsie sat daydreaming until Corney got him to play rock-breaks-scissors. Mr. Lewis finally came over and put a stop to it.

When the communion line formed, Corney and Woodsie and Spyros promptly stood and took places at the end. It was only a ruse. As soon as they drew abreast of the side entrance they were gone out the door. They had signaled for me to join them but I continued up to the communion rail. There I knelt, awaiting the approach of Jimmy and this new priest.

I knew I shouldn't have been receiving communion. I hadn't confessed my sins. I hadn't fasted, either: I'd eaten a banana I'd smuggled from the kitchen at home.

But at the arrival of the priest I boldly tilted my head back and extended my tongue to receive the host. Despite everything I had learned to the contrary, I knew it wasn't true that this was a sacrilege for which I could burn in hell. For the moment at least, there was that magic of knowing what God knew.

2

Toward the end of July that year, a week or so before broomstick Charles Goudis left for a month to work as a counselor at a summer camp in Pennsylvania, Jimmy asked me if I remembered enough Latin to serve mass.

"I don't think so," I told him, knowing that there was no sense in lying about it. He would have tested me on the spot. I admired that put-up-or-shut-up attitude of his.

"How long will it take you to learn again?"

"What for?"

"We can serve the seven-o'clock mass together."

He meant the weekday mass that Goudis had been serving with him.

"I'm rusty. But I can be ready in a week."

"Good," he said. "Great. I'll tell Father."

During the week that followed, if anyone came upon us in the woods or out on the pilings or snipping the hedges at the Murtaghs' and overheard us, they might have thought they'd slipped into a foreign land as Jimmy and I swapped the Latin phrases of the mass.

We would be partners now in everything. We worked together on Saturday mornings down at the auction, which was this place that sold mostly secondhand goods from stalls set up in the old airplane hangars at the abandoned airfield. We mowed lawns in the afternoon. We walked to the beach together; we showed up at the schoolyard like Siamese twins; we were together so often that when one of us showed up without the other, the guys would ask right away, "Where's Dietz?" or "Where's the Chun?"

We hunted together for hours. Bow hunting.

Jimmy taught me how to fashion my own bowstring and how to keep my fiberglass bow free of frays by nicking it clean with a razor.

Our bows were identical. Green fiberglass with a gentle recurve. Jimmy had bought his first. He'd had it a full year before I bought mine. I had seen mine at the auction in one of the booths. The man wanted eight dollars for it. I had five. Jimmy told me to haggle for it, the way he had done with the old Italian man who had sold him the pram. He said that if the man didn't take the five dollars, I should turn and walk away. The trick, he said, was to forget how badly I wanted the bow. "Just tell him, 'Forget it,' and walk away."

I did as Jimmy had instructed. The man insisted on getting no less than seven dollars for the bow. He was stone deaf to my attempts to haggle.

I said, "Forget it," and turned to go.

"G'wan," he called behind me. "What d'you think? You think I can't get *ten* dollars for this bow?"

I continued walking. I had wanted the bow so badly I would have readily paid the seven dollars. Jimmy must have known this. He had searched my pockets to make sure I had only the five.

I had started to turn the corner to the book aisle when the man called, "Hey, kid! C'mere!"

I looked back at him and said aloud, "All's I got is five."

"C'mere. Just c'mere."

I approached him warily.

"Listen," he said. "I've seen you. You work at the baker's there, unloading the truck, right?"

"Yeah."

"So you're a working stiff, like me. You know money don't come easy, right?"

"Yeah. But all's I got—"

"I know what you got. Tell me this: a man's word is his bond; you've heard that, right?"

"Yeah."

"I'll tell you what. You give me five dollars today and two dollars next Saturday. I trust you. Here."

He handed me the bow. I took it in my hand and I knew I'd never let go of it now, not even if he wanted a million dollars and I had to work unloading the baker's truck until I was five thousand years old. He had me.

"Six dollars," I managed to say. "Five now. One dollar next Saturday."

I handed him the five.

"You won't screw me?" he asked. "You're good for the dollar?"

"I swear to God."

"Don't do that. He might hear you. If you got to swear, swear on someone in your family."

"I swear on my dog."

"That's better."

I met up with Jimmy and showed him the bow. He nodded approvingly and said, "Five?"

I said, "Five," figuring I was close enough to the truth.

The following week I paid the man. He took the dollar and nodded. He said, "You got off without interest, y'know."

With what I earned from the jobs Jimmy arranged for us, I soon had enough money to buy a half-dozen arrows, a finger guard, and an extra bowstring. Instead of buying expensive leather arm guards we made them from old bicycle inner tubes. We made hip quivers from a pair of little kid's corduroy pant legs. We chipped in to buy a kit to repair our broken arrows and experimented with the best ways to replace nocks and worn feathers and to glue splintered shafts. The best arrows were put aside for rabbit hunting. The others were used for target practice.

At night, whenever we could, the two of us headed back to the cabin. We had finished it a year ago and no one used it as much as me and Jimmy. It was about as large as a one-car garage, and we had built an upper and a lower floor. There was a peaked roof, and the only entrance was by way of an opening below one end of the peak. The roof was of logs covered by plywood, tarpaper, and shingles, and it was a sore spot with Jimmy since the rest of us had voted to go steal the materials from the developers who had built houses all over Benning's hill.

We sat outside the cabin at night, Jimmy and I, and started a fire to boil a pot of water for instant coffee. We drank the coffee by the fire and played a few hands of knock rummy or spit in the ocean. We casually flipped through the pages of the outdoor magazines and the catalogues from Herter's and L.L. Bean, and I never ceased to marvel at Jimmy's breadth of knowledge about the hunting and fishing equipment. He always had something to say about the bows and rifles and fishing gear that sounded reasonable and accurate.

Of course, it could have been nothing but talk. I had no way of determining if what he said about the equipment was necessarily true. But his words had that ring of truth, and he had never, in all our days together, tried to bullshit me. Even when things happened later and his life became sort of a lie, he still didn't try to bullshit me. Between the two of us he always dealt straight up.

And I knew that whenever someone chose to challenge Jimmy's words, Jimmy always rose to the occasion. Later, when the time came that we had turned sixteen and were in the habit of sneaking into Dilly's Tavern by the back door to drink beer and shoot pool, there was a night when we were watching a game of eight ball and Jimmy said something about a bank shot on the table. The man who was shooting at the moment turned to Jimmy and said that he wished Jimmy would keep his remarks to himself. Jimmy said, "You're right. I'm sorry."

At this, the man added that Jimmy wouldn't know the difference between a bank shot and a stiff dick anyway. Jimmy took exception to the comment and said, "It's a dead shot, whether you see it or not."

The man had finished the game and had won. He turned to Jimmy and said, "Your turn, junior."

"Do you want to play for money or just the table?" asked Jimmy.

"I don't take money from strangers."

Jimmy grinned. "I do."

By the end of the night the man owed Jimmy fifteen dollars. He paid up without a squabble. He was very impressed with Jimmy's game and even while he was losing he had started slapping him on the back and calling him Dietz.

It happened often that way with Jimmy. He had all the skill and charm in the world. He probably could have been anything he wanted to be.

When we left together on weekday mornings for mass, Jimmy always asked first thing, "Did you eat?"

"No. 'Course not."

"Great," he said, punching my arm lightly.

We had an agreement to receive communion every morning, which meant skipping breakfast. Later, if we could, we went back to the cabin after mass to fry up some eggs and bacon.

The first path we followed on our way to church led us a short distance through the woods before we emerged at the back of the Murtaghs' house. We stayed as far from the house as we could, not because the Murtaghs would complain—they were extremely friendly and generous people—but to respect the fact that they allowed us to cut through their property.

The sun spilled from the east across the wide lawn. It reflected in broken rainbows from the beads of dew and the hundreds of small spiderwebs sewn everywhere between blades of grass. The dew wet our sneakers as we shuffled past. A mockingbird song rose from behind us. A plump squirrel scrambled off at our approach, clawing its way up the trunk of a wide tree before spiraling around to the far side. Then the sun slipped quietly behind a low puffy cloud and flared the edges of the cloud with golden light while the scattered jewels of dew lost their luster and the pocket rainbows momentarily faded.

Crossing the street to enter the woods once again I grabbed for a few loose stones. Good-sized ones, rounded and perfect for throwing. I was on the lookout for that dog that usually chose this spot to start tagging along with us. He was a smart dog and I generally liked him. But he was sneaky and undisciplined, and when he tracked us through the woods he scared up the rabbits before we could get a shot off. It didn't help to call to him. He didn't respond. All that worked was to pelt him with the stones. Not so much to hurt him, just to get his attention.

Jimmy stopped for a moment and drew back his bow without nocking an arrow. He held the bow drawn while the tension traveled through his rigid forearm into his shoulders and back. He didn't flinch. He held that perfect form steady. Then he smoothly eased off and said something, approving the feel of it.

We continued along the path in silence. The locusts chirred. They were only a handful now. The millions of last summer had gone wherever it was last summer had gone. It was said that in seven and seventeen-years, the locusts would return. In seven years I would be twenty-two. That was a long way off.

The dog that tracked us appeared skulking through the trees to our right. I let loose a warning salvo across his snout and he made himself scarce.

We came to a clearing and drifted abreast, our arrows nocked, ready. The grass was knee-high and damp. The air was warm. Thin ribbons of mist rose from the low wet place where skunk cabbage grew. Mosquitoes, shaken from sleep, landed on my bare arms and neck. I disciplined myself not to slap at them.

The path entered the trees again and then eventually let out on the WPA roads. Jimmy kept a quick pace. At random moments, sensing game nearby, he slowed the pace and lowered himself to a crouch. He scanned the brush, alert for the slightest motion. Then in a flash he was upright, his bow drawn, an arrow slicing the air: *zzzuupth!*

"Missed!" he scolded himself. "C'mon, Jimmy. Concentrate."

Often it wasn't until Jimmy's arrow had frightened off the game that I would see the animal. Rabbit, squirrel, maybe a raccoon that was wandering in the unaccustomed light of day, maybe a cock pheasant. We had seen deer, but never close enough for a shot. And we knew it was illegal to shoot deer on Staten Island. No deer hunting in city limits.

We veered back into the trees for the final path to the chapel. A pair of yellow warblers crossed in front of us, appearing suddenly from a gap in the trees and then swooping and gliding away, the pair riding the air as if the air had smooth curves and exhilarating bumps that we wingless creatures knew nothing about. A crow cawed from high atop a plumb-straight poplar; boasting, it seemed. Then it lifted away on easy pulses of its strong black wings, cawing noisily at the sun.

We kept that good pace, quick, but careful not to work up a sweat. We would soon be on the altar and didn't want to smell like we'd come from a basketball game.

The land swept uphill gradually, following outcroppings of shale and clay, and then descended into a hollow where the sun slanted through a glen of bright green ferns and orange mushrooms. We saw an animal disappear over a distant log and didn't know what it had been. When we came to the spot, Jimmy searched the ground for prints. There were none.

As we approached the end of the route I realized just how much I loved the woods. I loved the air of them in my lungs and the way they set my heart thumping. I looked forward to taking up the lead now and again, the unseen strands of spiderweb breaking across my face and chest as if I'd broken the tape at the end of a great and important race. There simply was nothing better than to run the woods with Jimmy. The dawn woods, the full-moon woods; the woods throbbing with wisdom and mystery and that ultimate knowledge that dwelled just past my skin, just outside my brain, just beyond my soul.

It would be exciting to bag a squirrel or a rabbit. We had yet to do so even though we both were excellent shots. But I wouldn't be disappointed if we never did. Running the woods was enough for me. It was the best part of life.

Jimmy felt somewhat different. He was intent on the hunt. To run the paths was not enough. He was out after prey. He was taut and

ready, like the bowstring. His gait was that of a born hunter. His
reflexes were poised on a hair trigger. He was strong in the arms and
hands and legs. On a hunt he was crafty and patient—and, I imagined,
ruthless. He often threw back his shoulders and thrust his chest forward, as if daring the prey to confront him. He wanted the next
meadow to conceal a rabbit or fox, or, better yet, a man-eater. The
larger the foe, the more fierce the prey, the more eager he was for a
confrontation. He was here for no other reason but to flush the beast
from hiding and slay it.

3

There had been a well out beyond the chapel some years
ago, and now in its place there was a spring encircled by stones. It was
alongside the spring that Jimmy and I emerged from the woods, and it
was there, beneath the boughs of a large blue spruce, that we hid our
bows and arrows.

It pleased us when we managed to arrive before the sacristan had
unlocked the tall pointed-arch doors, because the sacristan didn't try
to hide the fact that he respected us for showing up so early. He would
always have a few simple words of praise, saying something like "Not
much moss grows under your feet, does it, boys?"

His name was Ed Garrity and he was a man who had lived his life
by schedules. For many years he had been a deckhand on the Staten
Island ferry, and now, retired, he built wooden ships in bottles and
maintained the chapel and its grounds. He took water for home from
the spring out back, advising us that it the best water in all of New
York.

Mr. Garrity was a short and stocky man who walked like a pendu-
lum. He wore bifocals that made his eyes large and wobbling. The first
thing he did every morning, after unlocking the doors to let us inside,
was to walk over to the small altar on the Epistle side of the main altar
and kneel there (in the silence we could hear his bones crack as he
lowered himself to his knees) to repeat his daily prayers for the soul of
his departed wife.

Early in the day like this, the church hushed and empty, it wasn't
possible to escape the feeling that we were rustling from sleep spirits

of a bygone era, friendly and pious souls who assembled as the front line of the day's homage to Christ.

We crept up the aisle as if this were so, as if we were not alone. We passed behind Mr. Garrity and disappeared into the sacristy, and, as usual, I didn't fail to notice the mole on Mr. Garrity's bald pate. This mole of Mr. Garrity's, I felt sure, would be my undoing.

Like all the others who attended early mass, Mr. Garrity received communion every day. And it so happened that whenever Mr. Garrity knelt to receive communion and I stood there holding the gold communion plate beneath his grizzled, unevenly shaved jowls, the mole on his head captured my attention. It was attached there by the barest pedestal of browned skin, and I was strongly tempted to painlessly separate Mr. Garrity from this unsightly growth by giving it a quick, inconspicuous fillip.

It was not an easy temptation to resist, and I managed to prevent myself from doing it only because I'd become entangled in strange questions. For instance, what if the mole sailed through the air and landed in the ciborium with all those consecrated hosts? I mean, what if the next communicant were to receive not only the Body and Blood of Christ, but a little brown piece of Mr. Garrity to boot?

I had taken the precaution of preparing excuses for my action should I go through with the deed one day. Of course I would apologize. I'd say I was sorry, that I hadn't realized it was a mole. I'd say I had mistaken it for a dead fly or a windblown raisin or something that had fallen from a tree: a globule of sap or a caterpillar dropping.

No doubt I would be asked the battery of questions you were invariably asked when you were caught doing something untoward in church. At the top of the list was the question of how I thought Jesus would feel about this flicking of moles into a communion vessel.

I would have to admit that even though it hadn't been mentioned in either the Old or the New Testament, it was likely that Jesus would not like it one bit.

(Who knew, though? Maybe he approved, maybe he didn't. Maybe he found it funny. But I knew by the questions they would ask what answers they'd want, so that's what I would give them. It would satisfy them and get me out from under the gun.)

Worst of all, however, would be to confess the strange event. I was certain someone would decide it was a sin. I tried to imagine how it would be to say, "Bless me, Father, for they tell me I've sinned. I flicked Mr. Garrity's mole from his head during communion and it landed in with the hosts."

I'd be in trouble all over again for having made a mockery of the confessional. And *what,* they would demand, what would Jesus think of *that?*

Again, I would give them the answer they wanted: There isn't a single thing on earth that Jesus finds funny.

I got to recognize all the rest of the people who attended mass and received communion daily. There were these two old women who helped each other up the aisle; there was a man in clean coveralls and a clean work shirt who always smelled of fresh after-shave and old roofing tar; a thin mousy girl who wore the same green kerchief every morning; a policeman in uniform; a man whom I recognized as a conductor on the rapid transit; a woman who was my mother's age and who always waited to be the last to receive communion. There were others also, and none of them were especially distinctive and would not have been memorable at all except for the unexpected relation I formed with them. For even though I served the morning mass with Jimmy for only two weeks that summer I have yet to forget the faces of those people who dutifully knelt at the communion rail each and every morning. Nor have they forgotten me. That was the unexpected thing. I didn't know even one of them by name, except for Mr. Garrity, and I presumed that they didn't know me. Yet for years afterward if I saw one of them riding past on a bus or walking along the sidewalk or shopping for produce or sitting in a prowl car or collecting fares on the train or unloading roofing supplies from a truck, our eyes met, we would nod hello, smile, and go along our separate ways until the next chance meeting brought us together.

The chapel had been built on the grounds of a home for sailors. Old sailors who had no home of their own, sailors down on their luck, sailors waiting for their ship to come in.

The building which had housed the sailors burned to the ground before I was born, but I knew it had been a large wooden building, because my grandfather Hapanowicz had a framed photograph of it. It was where he had stayed when he first came to this country, and he'd always called it "the bethel."

The chapel sat on an abrupt rise of land, in a location where you might expect a lighthouse, and when the windows on the ocean side were opened you could look out and see the shipping channel and the purple curve where sky and sea dissolved.

At the rear of the chapel the ceiling was low, with a narrow aisle separating the pews. Toward the front the ceiling rose considerably higher, though not nearly as high as that of most churches, and here the aisle widened as did the chapel itself.

There was a choir loft in the chapel that held no more than five or six people. Tucked beneath the choir loft, on either side of the aisle, stood the curtained confessionals, and along the walls, carved in polished wood, the stations of the cross marched along from betrayal to agony to death.

There was craftsmanship everywhere: the wrought-iron spiral stairs leading to the choir loft, the stained-glass windows, the ceiling trusses, the wood-carved borders, the filigreed arch above the altar.

The floorboards creaked but still shined. There was no foam rubber on the hard wooden kneelers. There was no air conditioning, and in winter the heat banged through the pipes. It was small and intimate, touched softly by candlelight and the eastern sun as it rose from the sea. And when you served mass here you felt that the small congregation of the faithful could reach forward and scratch your back. I could hear them turn the pages of their missals, thin as insect wings, and I could make out their whispered English as if it were a susurrant echo, mystically translated, of the Latin I pattered at the altar.

As soon as Jimmy and I entered the sacristy, having tiptoed behind Mr. Garrity, we donned our red cassocks and exchanged our dew-dampened sneakers for the polished shoes we kept in the altar boys' closet. We didn't yet slip into our lace-edged white surplices, and so as we moved about the preparations for mass wearing only our cassocks we looked like absurdly young cardinals.

We had been entrusted with the key for the wine cabinet. Few altar boys were. In the days when the wine hadn't been locked it was not unusual for altar boys to be caught with alcohol on their breath. Spyros and Corney had both been canned for getting into the wine and then eating the hosts like they were Ritz crackers.

We filled the water and wine cruets and then I carried the cruets out to the altar and placed them side by side on the small linen-draped table on the epistle side alongside the neatly folded finger towel and gold finger bowl. The priest's Latin of the moment of the washing of the hands crossed my mind. *Lavabo inter innocentes manus mea . . .* I wash my hands in innocence.

We donned our surplices and made a careful inspection of the altar: the clean white altar cloths and fresh flowers (placed there daily by the women of the Altar Society, who, like clever elves, were never seen going about their work), the shiny gold tabernacle gate, the tall candlesticks, the hidden saintly relics, the sad crucifix.

One by one, except for the two elderly women, the congregation had wandered in. All was ready.

Jimmy lit the six tall candlesticks on the marble altar and returned to the sacristy, where he asked me, "Do you want book or bell?"

I hated taking bells. I was afraid I'd forget when to ring them. The most important and sacred passages of the mass were signaled by the sounding of the bells. If I daydreamed and missed one of the cues, as I had the day before, I'd feel foolish.

It had served me right when I had failed to hear the cue for the Sanctus yesterday. I'd always had trouble keeping my mind tethered during mass, and yesterday, while kneeling during the Offertory, I had found myself thinking about the fact that there were relics of one or another saint buried in the marble slab of the altar. I couldn't recall if the nuns had told us this in grammar school, and so I couldn't decide whether it was true or if maybe I had made the whole thing up on my own. But whatever the truth of the matter, I started wondering what these relics might be. Was there a piece of the person in the marble? And was that legal? Or was there a piece of their clothing or something the blessed personage had touched?

It wasn't long before that Jimmy Rogers's tune "Honeycomb" was lilting through my head and I was singing softly to myself—Got a hank of hair and a piece of bone/ Made a walkin', talkin' St. Jerome—and I completely missed the cue for the Sanctus and Jimmy had to hiss, "Chun!"

Ring! Ring! Ring!
Sanctus! Sanctus! Sanctus!
"Book, Jimmy," I insisted today. "Book."
He frowned.
"You've got bells."

Shit. "Why'd you even ask?"

"Just curious."

Father Joseph appeared in the sacristy, entering by the side door. We called him Speedy because he tore through the prayers like a chain saw, fast and loud and growling, and he expected your responses to be the same.

"Good morning, men."

"Good morning, Father."

"Good morning, Father."

"How are we set?" he asked.

"We're ready," said Jimmy.

"Up early again today. Very good, men. Very good."

Father Joseph was big. He was taller than Jimmy and he was so portly that the chasuble he wore for mass was the size of a Scout pup tent. His hair was salt-and-pepper and his large hands seemed always to be chafed. He was demanding on the altar and he was tough in confession. If you happened to go to confession and discover that he was on the other side of the screen you seriously considered lying.

The garments the priest wore during mass were kept in the long narrow drawers of a wide flat table. The vestments were always laid out by the time we arrived. Altar Society elves.

While Father Joseph dressed for mass he repeated some prayers in Latin, quietly, kissing the silk maniple as he pinned it on the left sleeve of the long white alb he wore. He then took up the stole, kissed it also, and prayed for immortality. He draped the garment over his shoulders like a long scarf. Finally, the chasuble completed the costume.

He then bowed to kiss his prayer book and bowed to the crucifix above the changing table. The pressed silk of his garments meanwhile caught the light and reflected it in wavy patterns. He turned to face me and Jimmy, the pair of us having stood dutifully in place, watching.

Jimmy dropped to his knees. He couldn't wait for this blessing. I knelt also, but with much less enthusiasm. I'd always felt a little foolish about being blessed by a priest.

Father made the sign of the cross over us, saying, *"Benedicat vos omnipotens Deus, Pater, et Filius, et Spiritus Sanctus—"*

"Amen."

"Amen."

We rose from our knees. Father Joseph took up the chalice and turned toward the door to the altar. His chasuble swished the air, reminding me of Zorro's cape.

He must have read my mind; he must have figured I was daydreaming. "Look sharp, there, Hapanowicz," he told me. "Father Gormley tells me you nearly missed the Sanctus bells yesterday."

"Yes, Father."

"Let's keep those hands up while we walk. Prayerful, not like the bow of a ship."

We came to the door.

"Have a look, Hapanowicz," said Father Joseph.

I peeped around the edge of the door. Scattered throughout the quiet chapel, dimly lit by the light through the windows and the candles, were the faithful: the girl in the green kerchief; the old women; the roofer who wore Old Spice; the woman who insisted on being last; Mr. Garrity and the tenuous mole.

"Well?" asked Father Joseph. "Is the chapel still there?"

"Yes, Father."

"Then let's not keep the Lord waiting any longer."

I reached for the bell cord and pulled on it. A clear note struck the air. The congregation rose to their feet.

Jimmy and I led the way. At the foot of the altar we genuflected simultaneously and then moved apart to allow Father Joseph to step up and place the chalice before the tabernacle. He then returned to the foot of the altar, where he stood while Jimmy and I knelt at his feet. He made the sign of the cross, saying, *"In nomine Patris, et Filii, et Spiritus Sancti. Amen."*

"Amen."

"Amen."

"Introibo ad altare Dei," Father Joseph began with a growl.

(I will go in to the altar of God.)

"Ad Deum qui laetificat juventutem meam," Jimmy and I responded.

(To God who gives joy to my youth.)

"Judica me, Deus, et discerne . . ." continued Father Joseph, rapid and noisy as a Gatling gun, shattering, it seemed, the peace of the chapel.

We plunged forward into the strange two-thousand-year-old ritual, changing common wine and bread into God's Son. How strange. How very strange. . . .

Jimmy was riveted to every word and gesture, while I became this wandering balloon, straining once again at the guy wires, growing skyward.

I was off in the verdant woods of spring, the midnight runs of winter, the humid air and insect call of summer, the smoky crispness of autumn. I was the campfire and the briny marsh. I was Weed Pond and Big Trees. I was the old Conklin place and Iron Jud's. I was the *thuk-lub-dub* of rabbit heart and the forever vow. I was the paths, and the paths ran through me like blood vessels and nerves. There was a power here, a power of the cabin and the woods, a power of me and Jimmy Dietz.

Chapter 8

1

When there was nothing else to do, I watched the garbage next door grow. It grew steadily into the sky across the four-lane from Pete's. It grew on either side of us. It grew malodorously and it grew exponentially. It grew not necessarily because the number of people grew, but because the number of things which all those people felt they couldn't live without grew.

In things lay happiness, they believed, yet every thing had become disposable. The Madison Avenue gang had cleverly turned it into a virtue. Disposable razors, disposable cigarette lighters, disposable diapers, disposable pens, disposable people. Small wonder the word for "kill" in Vietnam had become "waste."

All of New York City's trash traveled out here to Staten Island. This could have meant that our politicians had pull or, conversely, were fall guys, depending upon how you felt about being known as the host for the world's largest garbage dump.

Whenever there was a ballgame up at Yankee Stadium or Madison Square Garden, the waxed cups and popcorn boxes, the half-eaten hot dogs, the beer cans and ice-cream wrappers that the fans threw on the floor and, occasionally, in a trash container had to go somewhere.

A small portion found its way to the dump at Rockaway, in Queens, and a still smaller portion was taken to a landfill in Brooklyn. But the bulk of it—all grade-A, they'd assured us in placating tones—was carted over to Staten Island.

Whenever the litter baskets on the city streets in Manhattan and the Bronx, Queens, and Brooklyn were spilling over with rubbish, the litter baskets were dumped into a fleet of large trucks and the trucks came to Staten Island.

The dumpsters at twenty-six thousand restaurants were unloaded out here; the garbage bags from millions of kitchens; tons of street sweepings and sewer skimmings; old phone books; canceled checks; miles of ticker tape and Wall Street confetti; dreary office memos; Fulton Fish Market bones; enough cigarette butts to bury the dead; enough popsicle sticks to build a 1:1 scale model of the Sixth Fleet; uneaten food, bottles, bags; newspapers; magazines that hadn't made their way to the old-magazine nirvana in a dentist's waiting room; and, of course, many many unmentionables.

Dumped on Staten Island. Dumped on what had been a very pretty, quiet marsh.

How thoughtful of the rest of the city.

I stood out front at Pete's and looked at the mess over there at the dump. I wondered if maybe the Paymaster could do something about all this madness.

Of course I'm not speaking about a Paymaster who was a machine that pumped out fifty-dollar bills. That Paymaster, with his thick wad of money and his oil-company mission to keep employees in line, wouldn't understand what I was feeling.

I'm speaking of an entirely different sort of Paymaster. One whose gifts were far more meaningful than money, one who traveled at will beyond ordinary space and time, one who knew how to glide along a continuum where space and time were at his beck and call. A Paymaster who carefully chose apprentices to whom he revealed his masterful technique.

I didn't believe that such a Paymaster would subscribe to any of this philosophy of waste. In that omniscient way of his he'd tell me that this superdump out here on Staten Island would rank with Angkor Wat and the Tomb of Tutankhamen as an archaeological find of the first order.

Perhaps, taking advantage of the way he could do a soft-shoe and dodge the more common restraints of space and time, we two will join an expedition of thirty-fifth-century archaeologists on a dig at Arthuir Kille, Statenisland.

"They'll reconstruct the psyche and culture of the post-WWII American to a T," the Paymaster predicted.

(I don't recall where we were that night, the Paymaster and I. Perhaps we had gone for a ride into the future to watch Corney's son pitch a no-hit ballgame, just as Corney had done twice.)

"They'll be speechless over our craving for newness," said the Paymaster, speaking of the thirty-fifth-century archaeologists. "They'll write one treatise after another about our need to buy a new gadget just to hope it would grow old as quickly as possible so that we could buy the next newest gadget that did the same thing as the old one, only the new one did it faster or slower or quieter or louder or was pretty or colorful or plastic or Bakelite or ceramic or stainless or 'darling' or 'super' or 'neat' or was the one used by a movie star or sports hero or a sexually appealing person we wanted or wanted to be—all of which really came down to 'new.' "

The Paymaster then rummaged through his stack of old and future newspapers and books and belles-lettres and scientific journals in an attempt to find the one entitled *Twentieth-Century Ultramaterialism as Elucidated and Documented by the Arthuir Kille (c.1970) Super-dump.*

"The spelling of Arthur Kill was screwed up by a bureaucrat back in 2445 and never corrected," explained the Paymaster as he continued to search for the document.

He was unable to come up with it and dismissed it with a wave of his hand. He told me that I could sift through the papers and books at my leisure.

"This ultramaterialism was a mode of life destined to doom," he went on. "When the basis of reality is change, nothing stays 'new.' Especially all the items you buy on whim. They start becoming old the moment the cashier puts them in a bag. And if you get caught up in this newness game you find yourself growing tired of the thing you thought was so new—like your two-year-old children. You find yourself driven to go after the real new thing and get rid of this other new thing that has very sneakily become an old thing—just the way your eighty-year-old mother did.

"The whole point was to buy, buy, buy. Not to keep and cherish. That's it in a nutshell. Buy something new, get rid of it as soon as possible. Planned obsolescence, they called it. According to the government, not even a hospital or a school had cash value after twenty years.

"It's a handy way to keep the dumps filled, and without the dumps, all those acres and acres of old new things, there wouldn't be any way to appreciate just how really fast the new stuff grew old and how damn quick you'd better unload the old and jump on the new. I mean, God forbid someone else would realize styles had changed before you.

"The Throwaway Society. The Era of Waste. That's what they'll call these times."

He practiced what he preached, the Paymaster. (I never knew his name, never thought to ask. It seemed unimportant. I never had to call his name to get his attention—he was latched onto me like a radar beam.) He disliked throwing anything away that might still have some usefulness. Piled in the back of his Country Squire station wagon there were old toasters, radios, lamps, automobile parts, aquarium pumps, deflated basketballs, you name it, all of which he intended one day to repair.

Sadly, he was inept at tinkering—or quite skilled at tinkering and a complete failure at repairing, depending upon your point of view. For try as he might he couldn't wire a lamp or replace a simple switch or patch an inner tube. He tried awfully hard, even though it frustrated the life out of him.

"I'll tell you, Sport," he admitted, "hand me a screwdriver or a wrench and you're looking to make the bad worse and the broken unfixable."

2

There was no telling when it might happen, but rest assured it always did. Just when it appeared that Pete and I could come to some sort of a compromise and work together without wanting to strangle each other, he grew long ogre teeth and snapped at me hungrily, and I used the only defense I had—sarcasm.

He couldn't stand the idea that I wasn't in the army. He said my glass eye was no excuse because it only took one good eye to sight a rifle anyway. He was certain that if I'd had two good eyes, I'd be a draft dodger. I told him he was right, which hardly helped matters.

He hated my long hair and he figured that my sexual habits must therefore be strange.

"Who's on top when you get laid, Summerhelp?" he asked.

"The sheep."

He had fired me twice. Once in late April, once in May. This was June and he was overdue.

Both times he had fired me I had obligingly walked off. Before I could reach the end of the blacktop, however, he had called me back for a final lecture.

"You'd just up and walk off a job, wouldn't you?" he asked.

"What are you talking about? You *fired* me."

"Didn't put up much of a fight, did you?"

"Why should I? You're the boss. If you say I'm fired, I'm fired."

"You damn kid," he said. He looked about as if for a heavy tool to whack my head. "You don't do anything else that quick when I tell you."

"Am I fired or not, Pete?"

"Let me tell you a little something. I built this business up on sweat and aching bones, Summerhelp. I came back from Korea and I went to the bank and got what they called a 'veteran's preferred loan,' which was just more banker's malarkey. You see where that half of the building is? That's where I dug a pit by hand so's I could change oil and do lubes and repairs from below without shelling out for a lift. And it was *outside,* Summerhelp. Freezin' cold, rain and snow, with a little silly-ass kerosene stove in here didn't do squat to keep you warm. In and out, in and out, all frickin' day and night. Alone. Just me."

I didn't know what to say. I was sure he had worked hard. He had the money and the thriving business to show for it. He had hydraulic lifts and heat in the winter; a roof over his head when it rained. Workers, too. He was in grease-monkey heaven.

He wanted me to realize how difficult it had been. He wanted me to realize that he'd seen hard times. I guess, not unlike everyone else, he simply wanted people to recognize and approve his efforts.

But then he had to go and bring up things about World War II and Korea, trying to compare those to Vietnam. I tried to tell him that there was no comparison at all between World War II and Vietnam, and very little between Korea and Vietnam. But he had been in World War II and Korea both, and he couldn't understand why the U.S.

hadn't bombed the living daylights out of China.

"What the fuck's the sense in having a goddam atom bomb if you don't use it?" he argued.

"Oh—you'd like to blow up the whole world, I suppose?"

"No. Not the whole world. Just them fuckin' commies."

It wasn't the political differences between us that really angered him. I think other things angered him and he needed a good spirited argument with me to vent his spleen.

His wife had died a few years ago. They'd had a daughter, an only child, who was married and raising two children in Indiana, leaving Pete to live by himself in a style that would have better suited a much younger man. Which is to say that he had plenty of spending cash and no responsibilities at home.

He usually took his meals out and was frequently at the track or the swim club or one of the cocktail lounges, his arm flung over the shoulders of a woman who was as lonely as he.

He dated several women, mostly widows it seemed, though there was one he had begun to see more or less regularly. She drove a new LTD and he called her Honey Bee. She and Pete seemed to enjoy each other, although occasionally she got under his skin and then he was surly and about as comfortable to have around as a hair shirt for the next few days. The only other things that annoyed him as much as a lovers' misunderstanding with his Honey Bee was when one of us screwed up at the pumps—like the day he decapitated Eddie with words alone when Eddie happened to short-change a customer—or when he dropped a bundle on a bad tip at the track.

And then there was the business. The old adage was true: you don't own the business, the business owns you. Pete was never satisfied that there was enough cash coming in, and he hated the idea that he would probably leave half the business in Tom's hands. I don't think he liked the idea of having worked so hard toward the future only to find the future not there when he arrived.

Tom was his nephew through the family of his deceased wife, and from what I'd gathered, Tom's father had been dead ever since Tom was an infant. Pete had assumed somewhat of a fatherly role toward Tom, but for some reason also found him basically irritating. I know he occasionally bawled out Tom for his gambling habits—Tom loved the back-room poker games at Hanson's and couldn't resist long shots at the track—which seemed awfully hypocritical to me, considering that Pete went to the track every chance he had. They frequently got into heated arguments, and I suspected that the only thing that prevented Pete from telling Tom to take a hike was Pete's devotion to the memory of his wife and brother-in-law.

All in all he was a curious man. I'd learned from people who had known him—like Art at the diner and an old-timer named Slim who came in to do repairs at night when we were backed up and the two of us were there alone—that Pete's wife had been quite an attractive woman to whom he had been absolutely devoted, even though they frequently had arguments that popped the roofing nails and flapped the shingles on the house. Slim said that her death was sudden. She passed on in her sleep one night, and although Pete never spoke a word of it to anyone Slim felt certain that he was angry with himself for having slept there alongside her without having known she would never awake. Slim figured that Pete believed he could have done something. "But she'd had one of those bubbles in her blood vessels," said Slim. "No one could've done a thing. Hell, there wasn't even time to pray, I'd bet."

The death of his wife had crushed Pete. Only the business and the routine of work had kept him going. Slim said that it had taken a few years for him to bounce back, though I wondered if he had really. I wondered if he'd been so crazy and angry before his wife's death.

3

I was surprised when I saw Father Lusenkas and Eileen Murtagh together. I mean, I realized that they knew each other, and I'd even once been at the Murtaghs' while Father Lusenkas was visiting them, but it still came as a surprise to see them together.

Father Lusenkas had dropped off the monsignor's Packard for an oil change and a lube. I'd thought he might wait around for it, but then Eileen Murtagh appeared. When she arrived she called, "Chris," across the lot to get his attention. Moments later, as she pulled away with him in the car, Pete chose to mimic her, singing a high-pitched "Chris. Oh, Chris." He laughed devilishly. "What do you think, Summerhelp? His place or hers?"

Seeing how I squirmed at the innuendo, he cackled delightedly and said the priest sure knew how to avoid "prostrate" problems.

"Pros*tate,*" I said, unable to restrain myself.

"Well, yeah," said Pete. "That too, that too."

When the Packard was finished and Father Lusenkas still hadn't returned, Pete looked at me and said, "Chris is gonna need some oxygen when he gets back here."

"Jesus, Pete," I said. "He's a priest."

"Look't here," George said, "Summerhelp's got thin skin."

"Yeah, so don't say nothing about his weird eyeball," Tom relished adding.

"Or that fuckin' ponytail," George scoffed.

They were right. I surely was sensitive. Not so much about my hair or my eye, but about Eileen Murtagh and Chris Lusenkas. Even though I knew there was probably nothing unusual about the two of them being together, I guess I wondered if they were—well, involved.

There had been this one particular day when Father Lusenkas visited the Murtaghs, and it was a few years back, in early November—November 1962, to be exact, when Jimmy and I were sophomores in high school. I remembered the date because of the missiles in Cuba.

Jimmy and I had raked leaves over at the Murtaghs', and since there was a very large lawn over there the job had taken us all of two consecutive Saturdays. Those two weeks were the weeks during which Kennedy and Khrushchev went eyeball to eyeball.

Jimmy was customarily paid once a month for the work he did, and on the Saturday after the missiles were supposedly gone from Cuba we went over to pick up our pay.

The Murtaghs' house was on a gentle rise of land, a white colonial surrounded by that large green lawn and a handful of tall trees. On one side a row of hedges divided the property from the Wilsons, and on the other side, separating it from the woods, stood tall lilac bushes that each May blossomed wild and fragrant. Jimmy had figured that the lawn was at least a half acre and he said that the land also included two more acres in the woods. He had learned this from Mr. Murtagh himself.

Jimmy had various jobs he did for the Murtaghs. Throughout the year he cut the long hedge and mowed the lawn; he pried weeds from between the cracks in the slate walk and the flagstone patio. When the work backed up, as it did when the leaves fell or the snow was heavy, Jimmy brought me along to help.

Mr. Murtagh was quite particular about the place. He never let anything get out of hand, and it showed. The house could have been in *Better Homes and Gardens* or the set in a Hollywood movie. At Halloween there was always a straw man leaning against the lamp post out front and a jack-o'-lantern on the brick steps. At Christmas there were bright incandescent bulbs in the windows and pinpoint white lights in the lower branches of the walnut tree, as if a net in the tree had caught minuscule wayward stars. And when it snowed, Mr. Murtagh was out there first thing to make a snowman and dress it with a sporty cap and an old scarf.

During the spring and summer the Murtaghs hosted backyard barbecues and fancy dinner parties. They held the parties outside, where they had a patio and an in-ground pool. Chinese lanterns were hung out and the cars of the guests lined the circular drive and spilled out onto the street. Mr. Murtagh often used caterers for the parties—which I knew because one of my mother's friends worked for the caterer—and on the occasion of Mrs. Murtagh's birthday in August there was always a live dance band.

Mr. Murtagh worked up on Wall Street, and people around town said he was sharp, a man who knew how to get ahead in this world. He always dressed in smart-looking business suits and carried a leather briefcase. Whenever I happened to see him on the train he was absorbed in the *Wall Street Journal* or engaged in a conversation about stocks and bonds—or politics. He left early in the morning to take the rapid transit to the ferry, and when he returned home at the end of evening rush hour, Mrs. Murtagh was waiting at the train station for him in their car. I didn't know how the other guys saw it but I thought Mr. Murtagh had a pretty good life.

One of the paths Jimmy and I frequently used ended at the Murtaghs' backyard, and we either had to go through the Wilsons' yard, which Mr. Wilson didn't allow, or pass through the Murtaghs' and pick up the path once again on the far side of the road. Mr. Murtagh had never disallowed us the use of his property as a shortcut, and in appreciation we made certain to stay close to the hedge and remain as quiet and inconspicuous as possible. Occasionally, however, Mr. or

Mrs. Murtagh would see us as we crept past and would wave hello. If we had our bows Mr. Murtagh would call over, "What did you bag today, boys?"

When we passed the house at night we might by chance make out the motion of people inside. I must confess that when I happened to be alone I would stop and watch briefly from the shadows, curious about the life Mr. and Mrs. Murtagh lived together. Sure, I felt I was spying, but not doing anything terribly wrong. For instance, I never crept close to the windows, and I never tried to watch Mrs. Murtagh undress or anything like that. I caught glimpses of them and tried their life on for size, nothing more.

When Jimmy and I arrived at the Murtaghs' that Saturday in November, it was a clear day with an Indian-summer sky. Mr. Murtagh answered the door, wearing white knee-length shorts and a gray Fordham T-shirt. He was a tall man, with sandy-brown hair cut close to his head. He said hello and asked us to step inside. We entered the house and stood in the foyer.

Mr. Murtagh said, "Wonderful day, isn't it?"

Stupidly, I didn't know what to say, so I stood there nodding my head. Jimmy said, "Yes."

I think that Mr. Murtagh must have forgotten why we'd come. He must have thought we'd stopped by to talk about the weather, because he repeated, "Wonderful day."

After a moment he said, "I just finished a tennis match down at Clove Lakes." He looked directly at Jimmy. "I've been thinking about constructing a court here. That side lawn would be a perfect place— and there would be a lot less grass to cut."

He walked over to the window and looked out at the place he had indicated, imagining, I supposed, how the tennis court would look. Then he turned to look back over his shoulder at us and said, "Of course, that would cut into your profit, wouldn't it?"

"It's a good spot," said Jimmy agreeably.

"Maybe come spring," said Mr. Murtagh.

Then he recalled why we were there and snapped his fingers and said, "I have your money inside. I'll be right with you."

We stood there and waited. We could see through the foyer into the living room. The curtains were open, and the brightness of the autumn day streaming in showed things distinctly and with a clean luster. The house smelled fresh and the furniture looked comfortable and new. The brass andirons at the hearth were buffed, and above the mantel hung a portrait of Mr. and Mrs. Murtagh. The two of them were posed sitting together, with Mr. Murtagh just behind his wife. His arms appeared around her waist and his hands rested with hers on her lap. It was impossible to see what they were sitting on; the artist had not included it. So they seemed to be on the air, effortlessly lifted by the afternoon light.

Voices rose from the back of the house. I distinctly heard Mrs. Murtagh. Eileen. The only woman I knew who could be called lovely. I'd found myself dreaming about her at night. She wasn't old enough to be my mother, but she was too old to be my sister. If only this hadn't happened, this difference in our ages. She would have been the sweetest and prettiest wife I could ever have imagined.

During the day I occasionally watched Mrs. Murtagh from the cover of the woods, as I had watched Jimmy from my tree house, wanting to see how these people who were important to me acted when they were alone. I felt there was something vital about them, something that was absent in most other people, and I wanted to see if they surrendered their secret more readily when they thought they were by themselves.

I would watch Mrs. Murtagh at her kitchen window while she stood there washing the dishes or when she came out to hang the laundry. When she worked in the yard she wore her work gloves and dug with a spade in the flower garden. In the summer she took the long pole with the stiff net and skimmed the water in the pool. When she filled the bird feeders she stood on tiptoe and stretched her arms. Her blouse rode up then, revealing her trim body, and I would blush. She clucked aloud to the birds and scolded the squirrels for stealing birdseed, and as I watched her it was all I could do to keep my heart from flying out of my chest.

She laughed gaily from the back of the house now, and my stomach went into excited little jumps.

I knew she was almost thirty. I'd heard her say as much to Mr. Murtagh just the week before, telling him for some reason with a laugh, "Ed, I'll be thirty soon enough, thank you."

I'll admit, I felt strangely embarrassed at being so—I guess they say infatuated—over a woman that much older than me. Something about it seemed wrong, though I didn't know why it should.

I wished there was some sort of time machine that could unite the two of us. I guess it wouldn't do to have her become younger. I didn't think that I could ever shake the idea that she'd once been older. I would always feel that I was too young for her. Instead of the machine making Mrs. Murtagh younger, it would have to accelerate my age. Besides, that made more sense, for then I'd be moving in the right direction, whereas she would have had to go backward. It struck me as much more probable, my acceleration.

There was another voice from the back of the house other than Mr. or Mrs. Murtagh's. A man's voice.

"Have you been in here before?" I asked Jimmy.

"A few times," he answered.

He was somewhat abrupt, acting as if I'd interrupted him.

"You like it?" I asked.

"What do you mean?"

"The house. In here. What do you think?"

He looked around. "It's nice. Yeah, it's nice." Then he snickered at me. "What're you going to do, Chun, buy it?"

His attention was on the people in the back room and I knew he would ignore me, so I said, "Maybe."

Mr. Murtagh returned with a white envelope that contained our money. Jimmy's name was written on it.

"Here you are, boys," said Mr. Murtagh. "I want to tell you that I was very pleased with the work you did." He looked at me. "Both of you."

"Thanks," I said.

Jimmy took the envelope and said, "Thank you."

We could still hear the voices, though the words were not distinguishable. Eileen's voice, then the man's. There followed a quiet clicking of coffee cups being placed down, a spoon stirring sugar.

Mr. Murtagh noticed how both Jimmy and I hesitated. He turned his head toward the voices and then looked back at us.

"Oh," he said to Jimmy, coming to a sudden realization. "I forgot. You know Chris—Father Lusenkas."

"He taught at Cathedral last year," said Jimmy.

"Of course," said Mr. Murtagh. "And you served mass for him here on occasion, if I recall. He always speaks so highly of you. He's up at Fordham now, I guess you know."

Jimmy nodded.

"Well, come along," said Mr. Murtagh, beckoning us to the back of the house.

We followed him through the kitchen to the sunporch, where Father Lusenkas, wearing a tan sport shirt and black pants, sat at a glass-topped table alongside Eileen Murtagh. It was strange to see him without his collar.

I felt awkward, as if we'd interrupted a private talk.

"Here we go," said Mr. Murtagh.

Father Lusenkas was already on his feet, shaking hands with Dietz and calling him "Jim," and saying how very good it was to see him again.

Mr. Murtagh then introduced me, and I immediately recognized Father Lusenkas from the occasions when he'd offered mass at our parish. I also realized that he was the priest who held a basketball record from his student days at a high school in the Bronx. Jimmy had told me how good he was.

I shook his hand. When I felt the strength of his grip I tightened mine in return. He gave me a smile at this, in a way that only I would know its meaning, saying, it seemed, that he saw I was no weakling. I was grateful for this secret exchange, all the more since I knew I was hardly strong in comparison and because now that I stood there with Mr. Murtagh and Father Lusenkas and Jimmy, all three of whom were tall, I felt even shorter than I was and quite insignificant. I was certain that Mrs. Murtagh noticed this, and I shifted uncomfortably when she looked my way. God, she was pretty.

We all took seats around the table. Mrs. Murtagh offered us a plate on which there was a stack of small triangular sandwiches. Jimmy declined the food but I took one of the sandwiches—it was egg salad—having recalled that my mother said it was polite to do so. There was a bowl of fruit and a pitcher of apple cider on the table. At Mrs. Murtagh's elbow, on a serving table, stood a steaming electric coffee pot. She told us, "Please. Help yourselves."

I nodded and chewed the sandwich.

The sunporch was filled with light. The sugar maple which had shaded it all summer long now stood without a solitary leaf. House-plants in macramé cradles hung from the white beams, and Mrs. Murtagh didn't take two steps without stopping to examine a plant, moving leaves aside and testing the soil with her fingertips. I decided there and then that this was something that my wife would do. She would make sure the plants in the house thrived.

Jimmy and Father Lusenkas made small talk about Cathedral, sharing a joke about some faculty member who taught geometry, and then discussed basketball. Meanwhile Mr. Murtagh was up and down, excusing himself as he went to another room and then came back. He did this again, returning the second time pushing a bassinet. Mrs. Murtagh scolded him lightly, but he defended himself easily, saying, "He's sleeping yet. Look." He drew Father's attention to the baby, saying proudly, "He could sleep through an earthquake."

I recalled immediately one day the past spring, in April, when I was passing by the house and saw Mrs. Murtagh walk to the lawn swing and sit down. I realized then that she was going to have a baby.

Mrs. Murtagh stood now and checked the baby, reaching into the bassinet and gently touching his blanket. She told Father Lusenkas, "He's terrible," meaning Mr. Murtagh, though she was obviously tickled by the whole thing.

The volume of everyone's voice had dropped a notch. The adults talked about the baby's upcoming baptism, and I was beginning to wonder if Jimmy and I should leave. Never wear out your welcome. Another lesson from Mom.

"Ed," Mrs. Murtagh said, "I really do think he'll wake up too soon here."

Mr. Murtagh teased her, saying, "Mother knows best," and carefully pushed the bassinet from the sunporch. He returned but didn't sit. He grabbed an apple and started eating it as he stood by the windows surveying his big yard. "How about a tennis court, Ei?" he asked.

She asked, "Don't you have enough projects already?"

Then, out of the blue I guess you could say, Father Lusenkas looked directly at me and asked how I felt about the missiles in Cuba.

I was at a loss.

Just about everyone had feared the world would end in a nuclear war because of the missiles the Russians had in Cuba. President

Kennedy had appeared on television, telling everyone the bad news, and that's when it began. People walked around looking numb and pale, and the lines for confession came out the church doors and wrapped around the block. Some people, I heard, committed suicide. My mom never once let go her rosary beads. I'd been shooting pool in the back room at Dilly's with Sperm and Corney the night the president was on television, and a few of the men at the bar said Kennedy was a horse's ass and others said we ought to bomb the hell out of the Russians right now. They said George Patton was right, we should've taken Berlin—whatever the hell that meant. But I didn't want to repeat to a priest what I'd heard those men say, and I couldn't remember very well what Brother Denis, who read the *New York Times* to us in class, had said about it.

"Were you frightened?" Father prompted me.

What could I say? Mrs. Murtagh was sitting there, waiting to hear how I would answer. I didn't want to appear cowardly, but I didn't want to pretend to be braver than I really was. Jimmy was there, after all, and he would call me on it later if I pretended.

"I wasn't afraid," I spoke up, feeling closer the truth than not.

Mr. Murtagh asked of us, "Is Phil Amodeo really building a fallout shelter over there at his place?"

"I'm not sure," I said. "He's dug a hole."

"He's ready to pour the footings," said Jimmy. "He's been working from blueprints he sent for."

"That's a clever idea," said Mr. Murtagh. "A good fallout shelter could mean survival. After this business in Cuba, there's no telling."

"Oh, Ed, that's not the answer," said Mrs. Murtagh. Her sudden firm disagreement with her husband surprised me. I was concerned that she might have started an argument. I knew how it could be between my parents when they disagreed. There was simply no easy end to it.

"Honey, I know how you feel," said Mr. Murtagh. "It's not a pleasant thing to consider. But if it happens—what then? We have to survive, don't we?"

If *it* happens, I thought, scared for a moment.

"There won't be anything to survive *for*," said Mrs. Murtagh. "And if we start thinking about surviving, we'll give up on finding peace."

"There's nothing wrong with doing both," answered Mr. Murtagh. There was a sharp edge to his words. Though polite and respectful, he seemed to demand an end to the discussion.

"But we're not doing both," said Mrs. Murtagh, coming forward in her seat. "Ed, really. What genuine effort is anyone making to find peace?"

"Look. You can't talk to the Russians. Everybody knows that. They only understand power. Khrushchev has promised to bury us. Does that sound like a man who wants peace?"

"It sounds to me like a man who's afraid," said Mrs. Murtagh.

"Well, let's hope so. And if he is, I'm for keeping him that way."

Mrs. Murtagh said nothing for a moment. She looked down into her teacup. She seemed to know that her husband wanted the final word, but she wasn't finished speaking her mind.

"We seem to be fighting everywhere," she said. "We send the marines to Central America. We have military advisers in Asia. We have troops in Europe."

"Someone has to keep the peace," said Mr. Murtagh.

"It doesn't appear to be working, though, does it?"

"Of course it's working."

"We'll be in a war in Vietnam soon if we're not careful," said Mrs. Murtagh.

Mr. Murtagh discounted this with a shrug and a laugh. "Oh, come on, Ei. You can't believe that."

"Yes, Ed. I do believe it."

For a moment things felt uncomfortable, the way it feels after someone's said something they shouldn't have. Then Mr. Murtagh turned his attention to me and Jimmy, saying, "There was a plan for a fallout shelter in one of the magazines recently. *Popular Science* or *Popular Mechanics.* One of those, I think. Let me show you."

He left the sunporch and disappeared into the house. After a moment I heard a closet door open and then he called out, "Honey, where are those magazines?"

"They should be there, Ed—no, wait, I moved them to the basement last week."

I heard the closet door close and then I heard the hollow sound of Mr. Murtagh on the basement stairs.

Mrs. Murtagh smiled faintly at Father Lusenkas and said, "I think

Ed feels I don't understand politics. He'll listen to me, but he doesn't hear what I'm saying."

Father Lusenkas chose to be diplomatic. "You're both after the same thing. Ed's point of view is different, that's all. He feels a responsibility to protect the family. I think men look at it from that angle."

"What do you think, Father?" I asked, fearing I might be interrupting but not wanting to hear about the differences between Mr. and Mrs. Murtagh. I wanted things between them to be perfect. "About the missiles?"

"Well, they have other missiles that can reach us anyway. Just as we have missiles that can reach them. There's really been no solution. But in getting the missiles out of Cuba we went to the brink of destruction. For the time being, people feel a great sense of relief. The politicians have scored a large victory. Kennedy was strong. He went the distance with Khrushchev and looks like a hero. Yet it remains to be seen what will be done with the rest of the weapons. I don't have high hopes, I'll tell you that."

Mrs. Murtagh leaned forward, and her fingers seemed to walk across the glass to Father Lusenkas's hand. She touched his hand, which I noticed was faintly freckled, and then gently withdrew her touch. She said to me and Jimmy, "Chris has an idea that gets him in hot water. He wants to do away with all the missiles."

I couldn't quite understand why such a sensible idea could get him in trouble.

"It sounds like a good idea to me," I said naively.

"It's a wonderful idea," explained Father. "And you would think that everyone would agree with it—at least in principle. But it proves to be rather controversial. There are people who argue strongly against the elimination of nuclear weapons."

"Why?" I asked.

"They feel that nuclear weapons give us the edge over the Russians we need. They feel that nuclear weapons have prevented the Russians from starting the Third World War in Europe."

I frowned. It was the sort of adult logic that left me confused and annoyed. "But—" I began. "But does that make sense? I mean, they have atomic bombs too."

"And we live in fear of the day when something goes wrong," said

Mrs. Murtagh. "It won't matter who fires the first shot. War has changed forever."

Father Lusenkas turned to Jimmy and said, "If you recall, Jim, I wasn't permitted to speak about the issue in class at Cathedral. It was considered far too political. My arguments that Jesus himself had been killed as a result of politics never went over well."

He paused at that point as if to allow the conversation to drift elsewhere—to babies or basketball or the leaves we'd raked. Eileen Murtagh, however, wanted him to say more. "Tell the boys, Chris. I'm sure they're interested."

He hesitated for a moment. He wanted to find the words. His hands came together as if he intended to pray. I hoped he wouldn't. I couldn't stand prayers and praying. But he didn't pray (unless, maybe, he had used that moment to say a quick prayer in his head), and now he opened out his hands as if he had something there to show us.

Eileen Murtagh had come closer, as had Father Lusenkas. Jimmy and I also bent close, looking at the priest's hands, hanging on his words. The four of us must have resembled treasure hunters who had crowded together to examine our find.

"It's all very simple, really," explained Father Lusenkas. "And of course it's not original. It's all there in Matthew. The Sermon on the Mount."

At that moment Mr. Murtagh returned and placed the magazine he'd been looking for on the table. A fallout shelter appeared before us. It was an artist's conception of the family fallout unit. There was an air stack for "filtered air" and a stack for "exhaust air." Inside a cutaway view there was a large water barrel labeled "drinking water." And gathered around a card table, playing Monopoly and apparently very comfortable with waiting out the radioactive fallout, was a family of four.

"Ed," said Mrs. Murtagh, slightly scolding her husband, "Peter was telling the boys about his ideas."

"Oh," said Mr. Murtagh, picking up the magazine. He looked at Father Lusenkas and said, "Are these the ideas I think they are?"

"Ed," repeated Mrs. Murtagh lightly.

"Yes," said Father. "Yes, they are. Those radical notions you dislike so much."

"I think I'll do a little planning, Chris," said Mr. Murtagh good-naturedly. "Just in case the good Lord doesn't quite see things your way."

Mr. Murtagh left the sunporch through the door to the yard, and I could tell by the way he paced back and forth out there that he was looking for the perfect place to build the fallout shelter. Perhaps there would be no tennis court after all.

Meanwhile Father Lusenkas went on to tell us this incredible idea. And even though it wasn't just a single idea but a whole series of ideas, I would always come to think of it that way—the incredible idea.

He mentioned how Jesus had taught us to turn the other cheek and "resist not evil." He pointed out how weapons and bombs were instruments of evil, since their only purpose was to kill millions and millions of people: people whom God loved. He said that if we were really to follow what Jesus had taught, we should do away with all our weapons. "We should disarm totally," he said. "We should show the world that what we stand for is peace, that we are not willing to harbor weapons that can slaughter millions. We should turn the other cheek. It would take a great deal of courage, but isn't that what Jesus did? Wasn't he willing to surrender his life to do what was right? Isn't that the whole message?"

"The Russians would attack us," I suggested, feeling stupid for having done so. Feeling, even, a traitor to the noble ideas Father Lusenkas had sketched for us.

"Perhaps they would," he said. "Or perhaps the power of such an act of faith would be unassailable. If it's to kill or be killed, you're called to lay down your life."

"What about self-defense?" I asked. "It's all right to kill someone in self-defense, isn't it?"

"Even then it's not the *right* thing. It's perhaps, at best, the necessary thing. Andrew, don't you think Jesus could have defended himself if he'd chosen? Don't you recall when he instructed Peter to put away his sword?"

"So even if you can defend yourself, you shouldn't?"

"That's the message we get, isn't it?"

It was impossible, I figured. Who could do that?

Mr. Murtagh had come back inside, and we could hear him down the hall. "Guess what I came across while I was looking for that magazine?" he asked as he entered the sunporch. He held up a green book with a gold seal and the year 1948 printed on the cover. "The *Oracle.*"

It was a high school yearbook, and Mr. Murtagh laid the book on the table and opened it to a page where he'd held his finger. He pointed out the varsity basketball squad for me and Jimmy, showing us himself and Chris Lusenkas. Then he flipped the pages and showed us Eileen. Unlike Mr. Murtagh and Father Lusenkas, who had looked so skinny and boyish, sort of out of date, Eileen had been simply gorgeous.

Then Mr. Murtagh turned to the candid shots at the end of the book, where there was a photo of the three of them. Mr. Murtagh said, "Look at these two handsome and popular seniors just begging for the attention of a cute sophomore."

In the photo, Eileen was seated on a stone wall. On her left was Mr. Murtagh, kneeling as if proposing marriage, and on her right, also proposing, was Chris Lusenkas. The caption beneath the photo read: "Eenie, meanie, minie, mo . . ."

They continued talking about their high school days, and no one mentioned war or atomic bombs or missiles, for which I was grateful. There were some ideas that got me awfully confused, and mixing war and religion was one of them.

We soon left the Murtaghs'. Since it was Saturday, Jimmy, who had been strangely quiet while we'd been with Father Lusenkas, wanted as usual to go to confession. We traveled together along the paths until we reached a fork. Jimmy continued on toward church and I decided to go back to the cabin.

There were few leaves remaining on the trees, but those which remained and even the ones on the ground had kept their color. In the dry bright sunlight the reds were like rusted flames and the oranges and yellows were tissue-thin gold.

I walked alone through the woods and tried my best to figure out what it was that people could possibly disagree over strongly enough to be willing to destroy the entire world. I couldn't answer this, and because I couldn't I began to see a bit more clearly what Father Lusenkas had tried to explain. There simply wasn't any other way to stop wars than to turn the other cheek, to refuse to take a life.

Impossible.

I continued along the path, deep in thought and afraid. I was angry at God for having been so stupid and unfeeling as to have made the world this way.

The wall of brambles hid the cabin well despite the way in which autumn had stripped the trees. I crawled through the tunnel and climbed to the roof of the cabin. From the surface of the roof I picked up a leaf that was the color of pumpkin skin and looked through it at the sun.

The world was beautiful, I decided, but there were insane people running it and maybe that wasn't God's fault. Maybe He'd done the best he could. Maybe it was the first time He'd made a world and needed more practice. Who knows?

Only the cabin and the woods and the paths and doing things with Jimmy made sense. Everything else was crazy.

I vowed to protect the things that were important. The cabin, the woods, the paths. And Jimmy.

Chapter 9

1

The first weeks of June came and went, and Jimmy hadn't yet arrived home. There was nothing in the newspaper about him either, but since bad news always traveled faster than good I took this absence of news to be a favorable sign.

I wondered if the parade would be held without him, and I imagined that it would. It was necessary for them to go through with the opening ceremonies, because the new field was a showcase for the All-Star competition.

It made sense that the field be named for Cornelius Xavier Walsh. He was the very best baseball player among us, far better than whoever was next-best. If he hadn't gotten so screwed up they say he might even have had a career in baseball.

I felt somehow that Jimmy wouldn't miss the parade and the ceremony. And even though I disliked parades and speeches and that sort of hoopla, this was one parade I intended to see. But when there was no word on Jimmy, I finally called his house, hoping that his father wouldn't answer. The two of us had never resolved the fact that we didn't care for each other.

But my luck was poor when I called and Mr. Dietz picked up the phone.

"We don't know when to expect him," Mr. Dietz told me when I asked about Jimmy. His voice was rather gruff. "They tell us it's classified information."

"But I thought he was finished. I thought—"

"Andrew," Mr. Dietz interrupted sharply, "whether you know it
or not, there's a war going on over there."

"Yeah, but—"

"He'll be home when he gets here."

He'll be home when he gets here, I thought.

"Oh," I said flatly. "Thanks for clearing that up for me."

We were about as inclined as two bricks to talk after that exchange. Neither of us said goodbye. We simply cut the connection
without another word.

2

Pete came into the shop early in the afternoon one day in
the middle of June and called me over. He had spent an hour or so that
morning with his Honey Bee and now was considerably mellowed.

"Get in the Jeep," he said. "We've got a road call."

"Me?" I asked. "A road call?"

"Are your ears stuffed with shit?"

"I'm surprised, that's all. Honored, in fact."

He told me nothing about the nature of the road call. I hoped we'd
find a gorgeous nineteen-year-old girl out there with a car that
wouldn't run. I wanted to pull up in the Jeep like a modern Lancelot
and rescue her from the woes of the breakdown lane.

"Let's go," he said, handing me the keys. "You drive."

We hopped into the Jeep and immediately Pete told me to take a
left onto the four-lane. "You know where the swim club is?" he asked.

"Yeah."

"Well, let's go there first. I intend to give that little snot-nosed
manager a piece of my mind. Then we'll pick up some hamburgers and
something to drink." He leaned his head out the side window and said,
"Look't that sky, Summerhelp. It's a great day, ain't it?"

I peeked out at the sky and said offhandedly, "Yeah."

"You don't care, do you? I mean, you don't really know what it
means to have a good day instead of a bad day."

"Right now it's beginning to feel like a bad day."

He raised his hands to show he meant no harm.

"We'll get us something to eat," he continued, "and then do a little research into the oil business. You'll thank me for this, wait and see. You'll look back on today as—what do they call it?—a turning point in your life."

"I thought this was a road call," I said.

"It is."

"I thought there was a car stalled or something."

"If we're lucky, there will be. Some poor bastard who's all thumbs and stuck somewhere by the side of the road will end up paying for our lunch and then some. You see people like that all the time, their car broke down and not knowing what to do. Don't you ever wonder what happens to them?" He folded his arms across his chest and grinned, pleased over the prospect. "Yessir, Summerhelp. Always remember—get laid in the A.M. and get someone to pay your way in the P.M. That way you don't feel rushed or cheated. You don't lose sleep over your bills and you don't have to go prowlin' around at night hoping to find a place to oil your tool." He leaned forward and looked up at the sky again, this time through the windshield. "A wonderful day, just wonderful." Then, without pause, he told me sharply, "Turn here, turn here. It's a shortcut."

He was in such a hurry for me to make the turn that he was ready to reach over and do it himself. I hit the brakes and threw in the clutch pedal; I jammed the gearshift lever down into third and spun the Jeep into the turn. From behind came the screech of tires and the blat of a horn.

"Asshole," said Pete, looking back. Then, as we turned, he yelled out as if the other driver could possibly hear him, "Stay awake!"

When Pete had mentioned this imaginary person who was stuck by the side of the road with no other purpose in life than to pay Pete's bills, I was tempted to say something about the Paymaster, not the one that the oil company used to get people to do what they wanted them to do, but rather a Paymaster who was genuinely worth admiring: the sort of person who never passed by anyone in need without offering to help, one who never considered the cost, understanding as he did that the good deed was reward enough itself. And although he might himself be all thumbs and maybe not have all the answers, he'd do everything he could for people in distress. It wasn't so important that he know how to start a stalled car or change a flat tire. And maybe he couldn't bring home your buddy from Vietnam. The important thing was his role as the ultimate Good Samaritan. The important thing was that he be more substantial than the hollow image of hype and money created by the oil company. The important thing was that he would go out of his way to help people.

Pete went on about the manager at the swim club, saying how he was mighty angry with the little squirt and intended to ream him out but good. Apparently the manager had neglected to take care of a leaking seal on a pump in the pool's filtering system and the Health Department had meanwhile pulled a surprise inspection.

"The goddam Health Department sends *me* a letter because I'm on the board, threatening to close the place down for a week—even if I do fix the pump." He looked over at me. "That's their way of punishing me for being bad, and it might have worked except for the fact that I'm connected with city hall these days. Garbage pays in more ways than one. Remember that, Summerhelp."

He continued to chew over the situation with the club manager and the Health Department. As he did so he rubbed his chin, which happened for the moment to be so clean-shaven it shined. He squinted as if peering into a sneaky plot that was slowly becoming visible. "I see what's going on here with that surprise inspection. I wasn't born yesterday. It's that fuckin' Bert."

Pete insisted that when we arrived at the swim club I accompany him to give the manager a piece of his mind. I didn't want to go, particularly. I didn't want to have to witness someone getting a verbal scourging from Pete. But Pete reminded me that this was a road call and a turning point in my life. He said he was giving me a golden opportunity to observe good management technique firsthand.

We pulled into the parking lot at the swim club, and I parked the Jeep. We could see the three pools through the slatted fence. The water was sparkling blue and inviting. I could hear kids at play as they splashed and yelled, and I could see them one by one as they climbed the ladder to the slide and took a swift and joyful ride down into the blue pool. There was something so wonderfully simple about the fun the kids were having that as I sat there in the Jeep and Pete jabbered on, I suddenly recalled with unusual vividness the weekend Jimmy and I took a bus upstate with Corney to see Harry at a camp where he was working as a counselor. We spent the afternoon of the first day swinging on this thick rope into a cold stream of water that tumbled down the mountainside. The current was swift and strong, and when we dropped into it from the rope we were dragged along and cast onto a sandbar a hundred feet downstream. If the sandbar hadn't been there we would have been washed away into the next county. The only person all day who could swim against the current was this skinny dark-haired girl. Not even Dietz could do it.

Sitting there in the parking lot of the swim club, and having recalled that weekend upstate with Dietz and Corney, I realized it was time for a vacation. I decided that once Jimmy arrived and had fulfilled his duties as the hometown hero I'd take him for a few beers and suggest that we leave the very next day for a canoe trip upstate, maybe even cruise down that same mountain stream and find that rope swing.

"You know what that means, don't you?" asked Pete. "Good management technique?"

"I suppose, yeah."

"No—no you don't," Pete said. "Not any more than you even know it's a good day today.

"I'll tell you what good management technique is," he continued. "It's getting other people to see that since you're the boss they ought to keep their trap shut until you ask for their two cents. Simple, see?"

He got out of the Jeep and told me to come along. I didn't want to be part of this but figured that if I didn't cooperate he'd make me walk back to work. Besides, I so enjoyed the idea of being out on this phony road call while the mechanics were back at the station I didn't want to do anything to irritate Pete. So after only a moment's delay I followed him to the club office.

Pete found the manager and interrupted his conversation about a lifeguard who had called in sick, telling him he had some questions about the pump seal. Together the three of us disappeared down into a subsurface room that smelled pungently of chlorine. The pumps and circulation equipment provided enough noise for Pete to jump on the man with both feet and even yell a bit without being heard by the club members.

It wasn't very pleasant, of course. It felt like a visit to a torture chamber. The manager was a nice person. A quiet and well-meaning man, I imagined, and I felt bad for him when Pete blamed him for much of what had happened. Pete told him bluntly that if there was ever any more trouble with the Health Department he'd be given his walking papers.

"If this place closes for even one hour," Pete warned him, "you're gone."

It was embarrassing to stand there while someone was forced to submit to one of Pete's tirades. And Pete was a lot nastier with the club manager than he'd ever been with me. It was as if he personally disliked the man. In fact, he seemed to be taking the whole incident personally, and I think this was because he relished his position at the swim club and didn't want to lose it.

While Pete read him the riot act the manager smoothly avoided acknowledging my presence. I was relieved at this, having felt uncomfortable from the first. But then when Pete turned to leave, the man shot me a glance that made me feel small, and I knew the man was right in thinking little of me. I knew I'd have to say something to Pete about having brought me along.

When we ascended from the filter room Pete flitted about at poolside for a few minutes like a politician, talking with one person after another about the beauty and convenience of the club.

Then we returned to the Jeep, where we sat for a while longer and watched the female flesh on parade until Pete had had enough—which was indicated by the fact that his tongue was lolling down around his knees.

"Now, there, Summerhelp," he informed me once we were on the road, "a lesson more in life and business and then, seeing as we haven't come across any emergency roadside repairs, you'd better get back to work so's I can stay solvent.

"Slow down," he ordered. "Slow down. Pull into Hanson's here. Time to belly up and eat."

I turned the Jeep onto the graveled lot of Hanson's Tavern. Hanson's was known for its thick juicy hamburgers. When we went inside Pete said, "This is on me," and without asking me how I would like mine he ordered two hamburgers to go, with raw onion, salt and pepper, ketchup, and pickles on the side.

We returned to the Jeep with the food, and Pete directed me to drive along Hylan Boulevard. At the first red light we caught he told me to pull over so he could use the pay phone at the corner. He jumped out, dialed a number, and growled into the receiver, "Who's this? . . . George? Yeah, well listen, you tell Tom that I just drove past on my way to Haverty's for a distributor cap and I was gonna pull in but me and Summerhelp are up to our eyeballs out here, so you tell him I seen three cars at the pumps and there wasn't anyone out there washing windshields and kissing ass. I'm on my way back right now. Tell him to shape up."

He returned to the Jeep cackling.

"What're you lookin' at?" he asked me. "Drive. Go on, drive."

"Where to?"

"The fuckin' hereafter. Where do you think? Straight ahead on our side of the road. Drive."

We continued along Hylan Boulevard for a few minutes before Pete directed me to turn into the parking lot of a deli.

"Keep it running," he told me.

He went inside the deli and returned with a six-pack of Piel's beer. We continued down the road, driving into Dongan Hills before he told me to turn right. I did so. Then a left and another left, which brought us up a small street where Pete had me park. We were looking across Hylan Boulevard now at the island's largest service station. Bert's. Four pump islands, four pumps on each island, and at least a half-dozen gas jockeys scurrying about like a trained dog show.

Pete handed me a hamburger and a bottle of beer. I unwrapped the hamburger and then reached over past Pete and fished around in the glove compartment for the bottle opener. I popped open the beer and handed the opener to Pete. I drank down half the beer before I had even tasted the food.

Pete ate noisily and sloppily, not saying a word. His attention, as you might expect, was on the gas station across the way. He narrowed his eyes suspiciously at the place. Meanwhile a soupy mixture of meat juices and ketchup oozed from his bun and plopped onto the floor of the Jeep, grazing his crotch as it fell.

"Listen," I said, surprising myself. "I didn't think it was a good idea to bring me along when you gave Mr. What's-his-name that ration of shit."

"You didn't complain at the moment," said Pete evenly, studying the gas station.

"I didn't expect you to be so rough on him."

He paused, still watching the cars as they steadily pulled in and out at Bert's. Then he took a swallow of beer and belched grossly. "He was out to screw me, Summerhelp. He still is. Him and that bastard." He indicated the gas station. "They'd each give their right nut to get me off the board. The pricks."

I didn't understand what was going on here.

"I needed a witness, that's all," said Pete. "If push comes to shove, you were there when I put him on notice. Was all that equipment in that room working when we was there?"

"As far as I know," I said.

"There weren't any leaks, right?"

"None that I could see."

He bit into his hamburger, breathing through his nostrils. He grumbled to himself. "What's with you?" he asked, his tongue heavy with food. "Why is it you can give me lip over everything but can't take a stand?"

"What's this about?"

"Let me tell you a little something about swim clubs and that shit, and then I want to tell you about the oil business and why you'll be poor all your life. And then I'm goin' to tell you why you've got only one good eye while the bastard who slugged you with that baseball bat still has two."

I swallowed a mouthful of beer and leaned back against the door. "You're right, Pete. It is a wonderful day. How could I not have noticed?"

He mimed my yapping mouth with his hand as if he were a deaf-mute, and then said, "See? With the mouth."

He shoved the last wedge of his hamburger into his mouth and slurped. His cheek on one side bulged like a chipmunk's. He chewed and swallowed, then licked his fingers noisily. He indicated the gas station across the boulevard and said, "That's the bastard who turned me in to the health inspector. I wouldn't be surprised if he sabotaged the pump seal. He'd know how to do it, the prick."

I didn't quite get the connection, and when I tried to put the two ends together I nearly lost it all, unable to comprehend how a pump seal at a goddam swim club could matter a hill of beans while there was a bloody war going on that was killing thousands and thousands of people, a war that had taken one of my friends and was now refusing to surrender home another. Sitting there in the Jeep, my back pressed against the door, the bottle of beer raised to my lips, I thought I might fall into that same endless dark that had yawned open below me the day Jimmy had led us to the place of the cabin and I had glimpsed its future. But I was able to decide not to be swallowed, to bring instead Pete and this absurdity back into focus, knowing that had I fallen into that darkness only the Paymaster could have saved me, for only he knew the territory.

"He belongs to the club," said Pete. "He can't stand the idea that I'm on the board and he's not. Sure, he fucked up the pump seal. You can take book on it."

"Why, though? Why him?"

"The bastard's my brother," said Pete, as if this were reason enough to sabotage a pump seal.

I looked at the busy gas station. "Bert? He's your brother? Really?"

"*Really?*" he mocked. "*Really?*"

As if by way of explanation, Pete said, "Do you think I'd sit here and call my own brother a bastard if he wasn't my brother?"

I didn't fully understand his logic, though of course it wasn't the first instance of that.

"Busiest service station on Staten Island," continued Pete. "Only place in the whole damn city that's got him beat is a station over in Brooklyn. But that ain't a Mobil station. Bert here, he's Mobil—"

"Like us."

"Like *who?*"

"Like you."

"Maybe you ought to go into cahoots with Bert and that nephew of mine. They'll have my place lock, stock, and barrel before the dirt hits my coffin."

"You're paranoid."

"Oh, am I?"

He pointed out the gas station and said, "When I came home from Korea, Bert was already in business for seven or eight years and making money hand over fist. I'd worked for him for a few years after the world war—cut my teeth, as they say. Then I went into the service and fought them lousy slopes and when I came out I figured it was time for good old Pete himself to share a little of the wealth." He looked at me to make his point. "A guy who goes off and gets his ass shot at for his country deserves a little consideration—wouldn't you say?"

"In some cases," I hedged.

He shook his head. "There's a word for guys like you. It escapes me right now, so let's just settle on piss clam."

"Fine."

The cars continued to pull into Bert's. There hadn't yet been a moment when there weren't at least two or three at the pumps. I watched the gas jockeys hustle, and I told Pete, "There isn't anyone over there as good as me. They're slow."

Surprisingly, Pete agreed, saying, "I'll give you that, Summerhelp. You're quick on your feet."

He went on with his story about Bert, telling me that when he returned from Korea he approached Bert for a loan so he could go into business for himself.

"Not one red cent," rued Pete. "He said I didn't have a head for business. He said I'd go under in a month. 'What's wrong with the banks?' he asked me. 'They got money to burn—go see them.'

"He was kind enough to explain that if the business went sour— which he said was an eight-to-five shot—and the bank came after me, well, that was good business. But if it was him who had to come after me for the dough and force me into bankruptcy, he'd be a greedy prick in everyone's eyes."

"So that's what you did, right? You borrowed the money and now you've got a good business, so what's the problem?"

"Hey—this ain't been no picnic, Summerhelp."

"I think if we're discussing business man to man you ought to call me Andy."

"You've had too much beer."

I swallowed down the one I was working on and took another.

"The bank rates weren't so bad. They gave me some sort of vet-eran's discount—a big come-on, I figure—but I'd depended on Bert charging me next to nothing for using his dough." He turned to face me. "It wasn't like he didn't have it."

"You're still mad, after all this time?"

"I just want to beat him at this game, that's all. But he's like a ferret. He just won't let go." He drank some beer and burped loudly and wiped his mouth with the back of his hand. "He wouldn't even cosign the loan for me, the hump. He said that he sure wasn't goin' to put his business or house on the line for me. He said he wasn't going to pay for anyone's mistakes but his own.

"The only choice I had was to buy that little piece of swampland in the middle of nowhere and hang on by my teeth, which I ain't got no more anyway. There were some mighty rough times, let me tell you. I think I might've thrown in the towel if I wasn't so pissed off at Bert.

"But then the bridge was built and the new expressway—and then lo and behold, like an angel of the Lord, Summerhelp, that sweet, sweet pile of garbage gets dumped on my doorstep.

"Everything changed after that. There were even offers to buy the place. And one of them offers, through an agent of course, was from Bert himself.

"You wait and see, Summerhelp. Of course, I hope you croak before me—nothin' personal—but you wait and see when my toes turn up if Bert and that nephew of mine don't try to buy out my daughter. I just smell it, and it makes me sick."

"I don't understand it. I mean, you're in business and making good money. Why stay pissed off?"

"That's because you don't give two shits about getting even and staying even."

"Which brings us to Aesop's fable of the boy with the glass eye?"

He said nothing. He was steamed about all that had happened over the years between him and Bert. There must have been more to the story, things he wasn't telling me. Maybe they'd been forced to share a bed when they were boys and Bert had pissed the sheets every night. Or maybe Pete was the bed-wetter and hated Bert for knowing it. It just seemed to me awfully senseless for the two to hate one another to the extent that Bert would actually sabotage a pump at the swim club.

"Bert does over four hundred thousand gallons a month," Pete informed me. "The oil company gives him a penny a gallon. You know what that means?"

I moved the decimal point in my head and came up with the number. "Four thousand dollars a month," I said with some surprise.

"And that's just gasoline," said Pete. "Makes you think, eh, Summerhelp? You figured crazy Pete wasn't nothing but a dumb old grease monkey, right?"

I didn't answer because I didn't want to lie.

"You notice that sign up there?" asked Pete, pointing out the tall steel pole where the large Mobil sign rotated. The letters were all blue, except for the *o,* which was red. It was the new company logo.

"What about it?" I asked.

"Do you know why the *o* is red?"

"No. Why?"

"It's the ass of that stupid red horse flying away."

"The Pegasus," I said.

"Which is what I got on my frickin' sign pole. It pisses the hell out of me."

"Why? I think the Pegasus beats this thing."

"Why? Why the hell you think?" He was exasperated with me. "You ain't ever goin' to be a businessman," he predicted. "People look at my sign and decide I'm old-fashioned. They look at Bert's sign and they figure his place is modern and all that. Shit, it's got to be costing me two thousand bucks a month just because I got that flying horse."

He reached into the bag at his feet and pulled out two more bottles of beer. He handed one to me and opened the other for himself. I took the opener from the seat when he had placed it down and popped the cap off my bottle. The beer fizzed up through the neck and I sucked on the froth.

"I've been on the phone with the head of marketing every goddam week for a year. Some fancy-ass VP probably got his name on the door and all that phony baloney, doesn't know shit from Shinola about running a gas station, but he tells me that I got to score with the Paymaster before I get a new sign. That's their latest game.

"I told him that if I don't get a new sign soon, Paymaster or no Paymaster, I'm going with Esso or Texaco. I told him to fuck himself if he don't like it. Fuck him and that red horse. It's bad enough Bert does twice the volume I do—garbage trucks included—but I won't put up with that old sign for much longer."

"I like the Pegasus."

"Yeah, and you like long hair and noisy music and you think it's goin' to be great to be poor. The only pot you'll have to piss in is that shit you smoke, Summerhelp—and for Christ's sake don't look at me with that funny eye that way."

"It doesn't look, Pete."

"That's what I mean."

We sat in the Jeep and drank the beers and watched the gas jockeys. They washed every windshield, checked under every hood. I imagined I could hear their droning litany:

Fill 'er?-Oil?-Hear-about-this-month's-special?-How-about-a-credit-card-application?-Is-that-all?-Come-back-soon.

"The Paymaster drops a fifty every month or so in Bert's lap. The company newsletter put him on the front page. Highest-volume Mobil Oil station in New York City. *Bert Scores Again with the Paymaster.*" Pete shook his head. "I hate the son of a bitch."

"Jesus, Pete, there's more to life than pumping gas."

"You'll never learn. I might as well give up on you right now." He breathed deeply. "Listen, Summerhelp—I think you're a real dumbass for wearing your hair in a ponytail—"

"Hey—" I began.

"Let me finish," said Pete. "I'm warming up to say something decent, and that don't happen every day." He swallowed down some beer. "Like I say," he went on, "you oughta cut your hair, for one, and I'd like to strangle you for takin' the side of them slopes in this war—"

"That's not exactly true."

He pointed his bottle of beer at me. "Pipe down."

I started the engine.

"Where are we goin'?" he demanded.

"I'd like to get back to work."

He waved me on. "All right. Let's go."

I pulled onto Hylan Boulevard and Pete said, "Lay on the horn a minute."

I said, "What for?"

"Because it's *my* fuckin' horn."

I blasted the horn as we passed Bert's and a man in coveralls at the door of the office looked our way. I presumed this was Bert, because once the horn had grabbed his attention Pete leaned out the window and gave him the finger.

As we drove along, Pete finished his beer and dropped the empty on the floor, where it rolled around and banged into the bare metal of the doors and seat frames. It was his third beer, and it was the alcohol that had made him talkative.

"What I was goin' to tell you is that I used to fight all of his fights.

Bert's I mean. Guys were even lined up to kick the shit outta him just
to have someone to beat up. They'd pick a fight with him for anything,
even his name. But that didn't go on very long, because word got
around that if anyone laid a finger on Bert, they'd have to deal with me.
Of course, he was older than me and didn't like the idea that his little
brother had to fight his fights.

"Now, I've done some thinkin' about you and this buddy of
yours—this hero?—and I remember reading about you in the newspapers after those bastards tried to kill you. I figured you were a gutsy
kid for not dying.

"I don't know the rest, but I'm sure that you never went back and
got those bastards. And I figure it's because this buddy of yours fought
all your fights and you never learned how to get your own licks in. And
even if he didn't come right out and fight for you, there probably
wasn't anyone goin' to mess with you because they knew who was
backing you up.

"And you won't agree with me, Summerhelp, but take it from
someone who's seen the big guys fall, you can't let anyone do you like
that and not go back and hurt them. It just ain't the way the world
works. Believe me.

"You ought to do that. You ought to go back and get them bastards
and get them good and dirty, just like they got you. But you won't. You
got guts, but not those kind of guts, and so's it's a good thing you ain't
over in the jungles or they'd've made monkey meat outta you by now.

"Sure as God made the green apples, even though you work hard,
I would've canned your ass by now just for your hair and that shit you
smoke, but I figured you were a gutsy kid for not dying and I got to
give you credit."

"He didn't fight all my fights," I said.

Pete looked at me. His eyes were a bit bloodshot from the beer.
"He did."

"He didn't. I'm telling you, he didn't. I mean, most of what you said
is true. The bad guys left me alone, generally."

A silence fell between us now, the way it does between people
who have suddenly found themselves being more personal and sin-
cere with one another than they had thought or imagined they would
be.

Pete directed me to turn on Giffords Lane, which would take us farther from work. He didn't say where we were going and I didn't ask. I was too involved in mulling things over.

We turned a corner onto a street shaded by sycamores where the houses were small and the lawns were neat. I pulled to the curb and popped out my eye and put on my patch. Pete said nothing, which I found unusual. I said, "My head hurts."

I then continued down the street until Pete told me to pull over in front of a small brick house. He opened the door on his side and said, "Little Honey Bee needs someone to rub on the suntan lotion in the afternoon. You get on back and get to work." He got out of the Jeep and leaned down to look in at me. "No more road calls, either. From now on, you toe the mark."

"Got it."

I pulled away from the curb and drove slowly down the street.

Chapter 10

1

Along the lonely stretch of four-lane road that separated the salt marshes of Arthur Kill from solid land, there rose a steel-grate bridge over the Fresh Kill that allowed traffic to pass above the tidal water that streamed in and out of the marshes twice daily. Just south of this small steel-grate bridge stood a locally famous eatery with great birch-beer soda and a penny arcade. The eatery was called Al Deppe's and the house specialty was a long hot dog with a tight skin that popped open between your teeth and squirted fatty meat juices into your mouth. Deppe's served hamburgers, too—what place doesn't have hamburgers?—and the birch beer came in tall, frothy mugs made of thick glass. The popcorn at Deppe's tasted different from popcorn everywhere else in the world. It was better than movie-theater popcorn, better than amusement-park popcorn or even circus popcorn. It was the best popcorn anywhere, and if I ever taste it again I'll know, for it will immediately remind me of frothy birch beer and grilled hot dogs and those few but precious nights—my First Holy Communion (I was dressed in a smart navy-blue suit with a fragrant carnation in my lapel); my sister's grammar-school graduation; an Easter or two; a visit from my Polish grandfather or my Irish grandfather and the uncle who lived with him—those occasions when we all piled into one or two cars, me and my brother and sisters, our mother carefully reviewing our manners before we arrived to eat at Deppe's, and then, after hot dogs and birch beer and popcorn, heading off down the road in the old Dodge with ice cream in hand to the drive-in theater.

My grandfather or my father often gave me a few dimes to play the arcade games—Pokerino and bowling were my favorites—but I was too small to have any skill at the games and I never earned even one of those precious coupons that, when added up, could be exchanged for prizes.

When I grew older and went to the arcade with the guys, I had enough skill and knowledge to manage from time to time to walk off with a prize worth almost as much as the money I'd spent to win it.

There was always the same junk in the display cases: sets of cocktail napkins with stupid jokes printed on them. Chinese handcuffs, rubber alligators, cheap magnetic compasses, plastic pencil cases, two-headed coins, handshake buzzers, smoke snakes.

Occasionally one of the guys would win enough coupons to get a plastic cigarette case that had a slot in front for the matches and a cartoon of a character with a big mouth saying, *Go ahead and take one, you cheap bastard!*

To win the decent things, though, like a Zippo lighter or a genuine leather wallet, we had to pool our coupons and then do the odd-finger to see who got them all. Whenever the short man with the canteloupe head who ran the arcade saw us doing this, however, he tried to tell us it was illegal.

"Illegal, my fud'yan ass," Corney told him.

We knew the man was lying and we pestered him to death and made fun of the shape of his head and his bent nose until he finally gave in and handed over the prize we were after.

I happened to mention Deppe's to my dad when he appeared at Pete's one night with a flat tire. It was only the second or third time I'd seen him since I'd arrived from Oregon. He'd shown up one previous night to change his antifreeze and to remind me that my mom's birthday was the following week. I'd told him not to bother with the antifreeze, that Pete's prices were exorbitant, but for once in his life he seemed unworried about the extra dollar. He had to get to work and so he'd stayed only long enough to take care of the antifreeze. When he pulled away into traffic that night I said half-aloud to myself, "No one changes their antifreeze in May," realizing that there had been other reasons for his visit.

I hadn't shown myself too frequently at home, turning up only when I had laundry to do, and later for my mom's birthday to give her a porcelain figurine. My dad worked shift work at a refinery in New Jersey and often took on work with a house painter during the day, so we rarely crossed each other's path during my brief visits at home. And even when we did see each other there seemed so little to talk about. We could have talked baseball, but baseball had become unimportant to me and I hadn't followed the teams for years. Not a one of the players' names registered with me. So we did a brief dance around the words "hello" and "how're-you-doing?" and "fine" and "that's good," and continued undisturbed in the directions we'd been headed.

The night he brought the flat to be fixed I happened to mention it was a real shame that Al Deppe's would be leveled for the highway, hoping this wouldn't recall how our house had likewise been sacrificed for the highway, but realizing the connection was unavoidable.

"Yeah," he said. "I remember going out to Deppe's with your mother, back before the war."

The war. That was how they spoke about it, my dad's generation. There was no need to explain further. There was no need to be specific and say "World War Two." Even with your grandfather there was no need to be explicit. My Irish grandfather had gone to what he called "the 1914 war." My Polish grandfather had been in both wars, so he had to say "the first war," or, optimistically blind to Korea, "the last war."

I remembered growing up and hearing about "the war." It was an early word in life. It was taken as natural, a part of the world. You grew up, you learned childhood games; when what had once been the far distant future ultimately arrived you went to high school; you—impossibly it had seemed—became old enough to shave and maybe even drive a car, and then you waited for the war to come get you.

"Do you remember it when it was new?" I asked my dad, adding, "Deppe's?"

I'd taken his flat tire and had mounted it on the tire machine. I broke down the tire and removed the inner tube.

"You ought to get tubeless," I advised, experienced tire man that I'd become.

He made a face. He habitually resisted change.

"Deppe's was opened in 1921," he said offhandedly. "That was the year before I was born. I remember a 1921 Dodge that used to ride around with the advertisement on the roof."

He seemed distracted from his memory of Deppe's. His attention was on the tire. I could see he wanted to reach over and help. That was his way. He liked to give people a hand. I recalled when the men from the local Lutheran church had learned that he was a Lutheran who had drifted from the fold. A group of three of them came over one day, when we still lived out there where the woods had once stood, and they tried to talk him into going to church. I didn't know exactly what they'd said to try to convince him, though I knew they would fail. I recalled how he returned to the house after the men had gone. He stood at the sink, washing his hands, because, ironically enough, he'd been changing a flat tire during their talk, and while he stood there at the sink he said aloud, "No one offered to help. If even one of them had handed me a lug nut or rolled up his sleeves and said he'd give me a hand, I might have shown up at their church."

I was beginning to speculate that God sent flat tires purposefully to my dad to get him to say things he might not otherwise say and thus reveal the shaded, quiet portions of himself.

Dad moved closer now, his hands just itching to reach inside the tire and help me extract the tube. But he could see there simply wasn't room enough for two pair of hands and he reluctantly stood and watched. I liked it. I liked, for once, being able to do something for him other than buy him razors and after-shave or a new flashlight for Christmas (he never wore ties) and polo shirts and leather belts for his birthday.

"So when did you first go to Deppe's?" I asked.

"Hm . . . I don't know. One of the neighbors took us when we were kids. My father didn't drive."

This surprised me. "He didn't? He drives now."

Dad laughed a short laugh. "We couldn't afford a car."

I frowned with disbelief. "You didn't have a *car?*"

"Things were different then. Money didn't come easy, and the Depression, of course. . . ."

I pulled the inner tube from the tire as if extracting a rubbery length of intestine. Then I ran my hand around the inside of the tire, feeling for a sharp object. I found nothing the first time around but I continued the search. Meanwhile, Dad had taken the inner tube from where I'd draped it over a hook on the wall. He replaced the valve stem and filled the tube with air. It swelled like a bloated black sausage.

"Where's the water?" he asked.

"I'll do that," I said.

"No—it's okay."

"It's my job. Pete'll have a piss fit if he sees a customer lift a finger."

But he'd already found the water trough with the curved bottom we used to test for leaks, and he submerged the inflated tube in it. He began looking for the rising stream of air bubbles that would indicate a leak. "This is the same guy, all these years, isn't it?" he asked.

"Pete?"

"Yeah."

"Same guy," I said.

"I remember when this place wasn't any bigger than a one-car garage. He used to work from a pit outside. I'd drive past on winter mornings on my way to work when it was too damn cold to move your fingers and I'd see him out there under a car. I don't know how he did it. He's one tough bastard, I'll tell you that."

"Yeah," I said, as if proud of Pete and proud I worked for him.

A car pulled in for gas, and I hustled out to the pumps. Two others arrived while I was wiping the windshield of the first and I jumped from one car to the other, hoping Dad wouldn't decide to come out and help, yet feeling that if he did it would only be just if he, a man who never showed greed, scored for five hundred from the Paymaster.

When I returned to the repair bay, Dad was holding his finger over the leak. The surface of the tube was still filmed by water, and when he removed his finger to show me the leak the escaping air spluttered in small, quick-to-burst bubbles.

I wiped the tube dry and waited for a moment to make sure there wasn't a trace of water to spoil the seal of the patch. Then I draped the deflated tube over an anvil tongue on the workbench. It responded listlessly, like an atrophied flatworm. I applied the thick, clear glue with its brush, and while waiting for it to dry I found myself in a vivid déjà vu that I treated carefully, not wishing it to fade or crumble, seeing myself kneeling on the sidewalk while Dad—who knew absolutely everything—showed me how to patch a bicycle inner tube, way back when . . . when he loomed so much larger than life and, unknown to me, I was merely passing time as a little boy on my way to now.

In all that time I don't recall that Dad ever changed. It didn't seem to me that he had aged or become in any way different from the person I saw in various snapshots archived in my memory: a man of average height, trimly built, with thin hair, strong forearms, and hands that were regularly scarred by a burn or a rash from the chemicals out at the plant in New Jersey.

When I finished the tire, he tried to pay me. I refused the money, telling him I'd take care of it. He was about to protest further, his hand digging for his wallet, but then he stopped himself and realized he should allow me this gift and said, "Okay. Thanks."

He opened the trunk of his car and I jockeyed the tire into the well where the spare belonged, tightening it down with the big wing nut. and the jack base.

We stood there together and he asked, "So—how're you doing?" and he waved his hand at his own eye and head.

"Not too bad," I said. "Not like it was."

"Good," he said, nodding.

"There's no longer a soft spot in my head," I joked.

He regarded me quizzically.

A truck pulled in at the diesel pump, and I told him, "Got to go."

As I was standing alongside the truck, pumping the smelly diesel fuel, Dad drove alongside and said, "I'll see you. I'll bring some burgers over one night."

"Yeah. Thanks."

"See you."

2

The old airfield was a few miles from Deppe's, along Richmond Avenue, and there, in two of the hangars that were no longer used for airplanes, was a loosely organized and generally maligned market called "the auction."

At one time the airfield had been used regularly, but during the years while we were teenagers few planes came and went from it. We did see a two-seater land one day, though it didn't land on the runway. In fact, it didn't land anywhere near the runway. It had landed instead on the road—Richmond Avenue—and then taxied up the driveway of the drive-in theater that had been there in those days. We thought it was one of the craziest things we'd ever seen. We were out there in the tall weeds in the field between the drive-in and the airfield when it happened—me and Corney and Spyros. The three of us were hiding in the weeds gobbling down a chocolate layer cake we'd stolen from the baker at the auction. The plane appeared from the sky, buzzing close enough to our heads to trim our flattops. At first we thought the baker knew about the stolen cake and had sent for a police plane, but then we realized how ridiculous that was.

The plane landed on the road in front of us and, as I said, taxied up into the drive-in. No one ever believed us when we told the story.

How the place out there that sold things had come to be called "the auction" was a mystery. I'd never seen anything auctioned there, nor did I know anyone who had. When I asked one of the old-timers, like the man who cleaned bluefish out back or the woman who sold lamp-shades, I was told the place was called the auction because that's what it was.

"But nothin's ever *auctioned* here," I pointed out.

This didn't matter to them. The place had always been the auction and it would always remain the auction. Case closed.

Since the place was open only on weekends, the merchants arrived very early every Saturday morning to set up their stalls. They sold baked goods, fish, meat, candy, clothing, used books, linens and tow-els, cheap jewelry, rebuilt appliances, "factory seconds" (whatever *they* were), furniture, footwear, cosmetics, wigs, toys—you name it, they had it or could get it.

There was an arcade at the auction in the spacious plywood room between the big hangars, but the machines there were rigged. They swallowed your loose change like a sewer grate and it was impossible to win even a single coupon.

The girls who came around and stood by the arcade machines wore thick makeup and tight skirts with dark stockings. They smoked menthol cigarettes and their language was foul—which interested the life out of us, since the rumor was that you could take one of them into the unlit storage rooms and feel her up for free. Though if you wanted to fuck or get a blowjob it would cost ten dollars, so the advice was not to get too horny over the free feels.

Jimmy worked at the auction every Saturday from early morning to noon, sometimes later. He unloaded the baker's truck first thing, then the butcher'. Afterward, he worked at the counter for the butcher. He sliced cold cuts and wrapped steaks and chops, wearing one of those long aprons with a bib that was always streaked with beef blood.

Those days in late autumn when Jimmy first started working at the auction were the days of his hibernation. At least that's what I call them. I saw more of the far side of the moon than I saw of Jimmy that fall and winter. I knew he was busy and all, commuting up to Manhattan for school, playing basketball, serving mass, working. But there was something more to it. He'd been busy since the first day I'd known him, yet he had generally found time for us to hunt squirrels or play cards back at the cabin. That no longer happened. We didn't see each other except in passing. And when we did spend a half hour together, usually because I waited for him in the ferry terminal long past the hour my train had left—get this—he would call me *Andrew* the whole time.

This change in him had to do with Father Lusenkas. Jimmy had been very quiet and pensive the day Father Lusenkas told us how the Sermon on the Mount was the way to bring peace to the world. In the days that followed he started to submerge himself even more deeply in religion and his future role as a priest and a peacemaker. It seemed strange to me, but what I saw him doing, I think, was lose himself. He was strangling out the old Jimmy. I mean, think about it, why else would he stop calling me Chun?

He had copied out every single word of the Sermon on the Mount in that tight hand of his, and then memorized it. He studied all his subjects even more intently than in the past. On the train in the morning he read *Plutarch's Lives,* and the guys who went to Brooklyn Tech and took the ferry with him said he no longer went below deck to have a smoke and a cup of coffee, but stayed alone on an upper deck, his nose in a book.

He read the New Testament over and over again. He pored over his geometry and trigonometry, Latin and Spanish, pulling straight A's.

It was senseless to try to get in touch with him for a movie on Saturday night. He just wouldn't go. Nor would he go to neighborhood parties or dances at the church.

I had taught him to dance just that past summer. Slow dancing. I didn't know how to teach him to dance fast, and he had great difficulty in learning on his own because, strangely, although he had rhythm in basketball and running, he couldn't keep a beat. But I'd managed to teach him slow dancing one night when he'd shown up at my house and said point-blank, "Teach me to dance, okay?"

"Me?"

"Yeah. You."

We went up to my room, where my brother was trading baseball cards with his friend. I kicked them out and closed the door. Then I stood there and didn't know what to do.

"Put a record on," said Dietz, indicating the record player in the corner.

I quickly thumbed through my small collection of records, looking for a slow song. I soon realized that most of the slow songs were about falling in love or falling out of love and that I might actually have to dance with Dietz to one of them. It made me uncomfortable enough to think that we'd dance together, let alone to a love song.

Fortunately, I found Santo and Johnny's "Sleepwalk," which was an instrumental, and as far as I knew didn't have anything at all to do with love. I played the record and danced around by myself, telling Dietz that there weren't any steps to it. "You just sort of shuffle and make circles, y'know?"

"There's got to be steps, Chun," he'd insisted, watching me dance with the air.

"There's not."

He took a small paperback book from his back pocket. It was an Arthur Murray instruction book for beginners. He opened to the section on "Waltzes and Fox Trots" and showed me the pictures of numbered feet.

I took the book away from him and said, "You can't learn to dance from a book. Believe me."

"All right," he agreed. He looked so damned sheepish I could hardly believe it was Dietz.

"Then we've got to dance," he pointed out. "Right?"

"Yeah," I said, feeling I'd cornered myself.

He put his arms out from his sides and said, "Okay. How do you hold a girl?"

"It depends, I guess. Some of them don't like you to wrap both arms around them. They want you to hold one of their hands, like old people dancing at weddings."

"Put on 'A Thousand Stars,' " said Dietz.

"Jesus, Jimmy, that's a love song."

"Don't worry, Chun. It's a good song."

So I put on "A Thousand Stars" and we danced around to it a half-dozen times before my little brother burst into the room and saw us and I refused to dance any longer.

We went outside afterward and walked to the town circle to see the guys. On the way, Jimmy asked, "What do you do if you're dancing with a girl and you get hard?"

"Press it into her," I said. "That's what it's there for."

He had started to come along with me to a few parties during the summer, bringing his own copy of "A Thousand Stars."

Late in the summer he started seeing a girl named Karen Wazewski, just to experiment, I think. He took her to a few parties and dances, and brought her along with me and Margaret Stampf to the movies. But then, in October, a week or two after we'd had that talk with Father Lusenkas at the Murtaghs', Jimmy abruptly told Karen it was over between them. I remember her crying on Carol Dante's shoulder at a party the night she took the phone call from Dietz. For the next few weeks Karen gave me letters to hand to Jimmy, ignoring me when I told her that I hadn't seen much of him lately. She thought I was lying. The other girls thought so too. But I wasn't lying. Jimmy had started to travel to hear Father Lusenkas, who spoke in churches and clubs all over the city and up in Westchester and Rockland. He stood alongside Father on the streetcorners and in bus terminals, helping him hand out pamphlets that praised civil disobedience and nonviolence. They gave people a small booklet with the sayings of Mahatma Gandhi, a copy of which Jimmy habitually carried in his suit jacket pocket. He was fired up by these new ideas, and I began to have this vision of Jimmy becoming a sort of second Jesus, a Jesus who would rid the world of war and those damned bombs and missiles once and for all.

Father Lusenkas spoke occasionally on Staten Island, and one night I happened to be at a Holy Name Society dinner when he addressed the meeting. I was not exactly a guest at the dinner. I was there because the dinner was being held in the church hall of my high school parish. I'd gotten in trouble at school for flinging a banana peel across the lunchroom, and Brother Charles Edward, after trying unsuccessfully to choke me to death, offered me a choice: to sit in jug every afternoon for a week copying definitions from the dictionary, or to report to the Holy Name dinner Friday night to wash the dishes and mop floors. I chose the dishes and the dirty floors.

They served roast beef with gravy, mashed potatoes, and limp, stringy green beans at the dinner. When the meal was over the dishes were stacked higher than my head in the kitchen. Oozing from between the thick white plates were leftover pieces of meat and fat, potatoes soaked dark with gravy, and matted green beans like seaweed abandoned at low tide. It was quite a mess, and I was alone. I would never in my life throw another banana peel.

There was an automatic dishwasher machine at my side but it was noisy and made the whole place shudder, and I wasn't allowed to use it until after Father Lusenkas had spoken. For the time being I had nothing to do, so I peeked out the service window at the dining room.

The members and guests of the Holy Name Society, having just finished dessert, stirred sugar into their coffee and lighted cigarettes and cigars. They sat back in their chairs and some patted their full bellies and gazed up at the ceiling, while others went around shaking hands and jabbering, the way insurance salesmen and politicians do. Soon the president of the group tapped on his water glass with a spoon, and when the murmur subsided and the men had found their seats, he announced Father Lusenkas. Tucking away a few index cards in the open fold of his cassock, Father stepped up to the podium.

Jimmy and Mr. and Mrs. Murtagh sat close to the head table, which was where the Holy Name officers and the bishop were seated. The chair alongside Jimmy was empty. Father Lusenkas had been sitting there.

Jimmy was dressed like a seminarian. Black suit, black shoes, white shirt, and a thin black tie. In the lapel of his suit jacket there was a small gold pin. I could see it shine in the light. He sat and took notes throughout Father's address even though he must have heard the words a hundred times by now.

Mrs. Murtagh wore a gray-and-blue dress with a white corsage and a string of pearls. She wore rouge on her cheeks; her eyes, with mascara and shadow, seemed large and penetrating. Her long hair fell onto her shoulders like a soft wool shawl. I had never seen her dressed for an evening. She was pretty enough to stop you in your tracks. She was what men called stunning, I imagined.

She was the only woman at the dinner, which made her stand out even more. For some reason, as the evening wore on, I became convinced that women were not generally allowed at these dinners and I concluded that it was only because she was so pretty that the men had allowed her to stay.

I'd thought for quite a while that Mrs. Murtagh showed up when Father Lusenkas was speaking only because she had nothing else to do with her time. I was wrong, of course. And I had no idea that her strong belief in peace and civil rights was slowly but steadily driving a wedge between her and her husband. I wasn't aware enough to pick up the small cues.

Father Lusenkas was quite impressive. He was tall and trim and commanded your attention. His feelings seemed honest. He spoke without reading from notes, and from the first word his firm tone seemed to put people on notice, which isn't something most people enjoy.

Father Lusenkas related the question of peace to his experiences as a freedom rider. I hadn't known about this side of him. My admiration for him swelled considerably. I knew it took a brave person to do what he had done.

He explained that at this very minute the situation in the South was desperate. Colored men and colored women were being denied their rights as citizens, and even being denied basic human respect, merely on the basis of the color of their skin, while other men and women, those whose rights were not being threatened, failed to rally to their support. He pointed out how wrong this was in God's eyes, and said that it was the duty of every person here tonight to right this wrong.

He went on to talk about the demands of conscience. He said sins of omission were no different from sins of commission. I wasn't quite clear on this until he added that to ignore evil, to allow it to grow, was a sure way to cooperate with it. He said it was impossible to ignore evil and pursue goodness at the same time. "Goodness must be continually cultivated," I recall him saying. "For evil grows like a weed."

He concluded his talk by saying that men and women of justice must always be vigilant and not be lulled into inaction. He said that since the pursuit of goodness is not always enjoyable and the submission to evil is not always difficult, it is far too easy in this world to become a lazy accomplice to wrongdoing. "Not to stand for someone else's human rights is to deny your own humanity," he added firmly. "And to deny your humanity is to deny your kinship with Jesus Christ."

The audience paused and then clapped politely. They had been made uneasy by certain things he had said, shifting in their seats and raising their eyebrows at one another. A man within earshot of me had leaned across during the talk to ask another, "What's this crap? Is he supposed to be talking politics?"

Yet two or three people at various places in the room couldn't resist rising to their feet to clap.

"Well said!" exclaimed a wiry man who wore thick glasses and a corduroy suit jacket. He couldn't understand why the majority of people were still sitting. He looked around as if wondering what speech they had heard.

A priest on the far side of the room had also chosen to stand to applaud.

Jimmy had remained seated, appearing rather humble, but he clapped approvingly.

Mrs. Murtagh had sat, clapping, and then risen to her feet. She was enthusiastic and tried to summon the rest of the audience to its feet. But Father Lusenkas had thrown out a moral challenge, and the last response the audience was about to give was a standing ovation.

It was difficult for me to figure out Mr. Murtagh's reaction to the speech. He seemed mostly concerned about his wife's reaction. He had risen from his seat to lean across the table. He wanted to reach over and take her by the elbow and direct her to sit down before she carried her cheerleading too far. But she had already moved away, having engaged herself in conversation with the bespectacled man in the corduroy jacket. Mr. Murtagh then sat down and stirred his coffee and said nothing until Father Lusenkas returned and patted him on the back. They exchanged a few words and Mr. Murtagh even smiled and nodded, as if in approval of Father's speech.

At that moment Brother Charles Edward came over to the service window and told me to get to work on the dishes.

3

Father Lusenkas returned to the South on a number of occasions to demonstrate in bus terminals and attend rallies in churches. He was at a church that was firebombed the following week, and he was taken to jail at least twice. A car in which he was traveling was run off the road at night in the middle of nowhere. For a while, at school, we were told to pray for his safety.

It wasn't long before he made himself unpopular with Cardinal Spellman. Perhaps the cardinal and the other church authorities had grown tired of using parishioners' money to bail him out of Southern jails. Early the following spring he was relieved of his teaching duties at Cathedral and sent to Staten Island to assist a parish priest and hear the confessions of Catholic schoolboys. He eventually must have heard enough about masturbation and petting and fornication to figure out that the reason people didn't line up to go to jail for someone else's civil rights was that they were more interested in getting their rocks off.

Jimmy was eager to follow in Father Lusenkas's footsteps. He tried to take extra courses at school in order to enter the seminary all the sooner, but his request was turned down.

He planned to join Father Lusenkas and Mrs. Murtagh on a trip to Alabama in February, but his father wouldn't allow it. The decision angered Jimmy, and he and his father argued fiercely over it. Finally Father Lusenkas came over to arbitrate the dispute, which embarrassed Jimmy. It was all such a disappointment for him that he suddenly remembered I was alive and that once upon a time I had even been his best friend and blood brother. He came to my house late the same night that Father Lusenkas and Mrs. Murtagh had departed for Alabama. He tossed a few loose snowballs at the window and called, "Chun—"

I'd somehow known that he would be calling. I'd known nothing about the argument with his father or that Father Lusenkas had come over to settle it. I'd known nothing about Father Lusenkas and Mrs. Murtagh leaving for Alabama. I'd been in the dark about all that. But I'd not been able sleep and I could feel those odd waves of energy—very nearly see their colors—and I knew surely as I knew the night was waiting beyond my window that Jimmy was on his way over.

When the snowballs thumped against the window glass, I jumped to my feet. I crossed the room but didn't want to fiddle with the storm window, so I waved to Jimmy through the frost ferns on the glass and hoped he saw me.

The weather had been frigid every day for the past week. It was no different tonight. I'd heard my father say that the furnace was doing all it could, but still the house was chilly.

I dressed hurriedly in the cold. By the end of the long night that lay ahead I was to wish over and over that I had dressed more warmly, for the cold night would bring Jimmy and me close to death.

The ice on the back-porch roof was too treacherous to risk, so I crept down the stairs and sneaked out the back door. I moved carefully, soft on my feet, exiting the house without stirring as much as a mote of dust.

Jimmy and I joined up and walked briskly into the woods. The snow was dry and crusty and squeaked beneath our sneakered feet. The air was stinging cold; our breath clouded our faces. We wore jackets, no hats or gloves. We were in trouble this night but hadn't yet figured that out.

We walked quickly toward the cabin, and we'd worked up a sweat by the time we arrived there. As soon as we came to a halt, we were chilled. It hurt to do anything at all with our hands, but we managed to throw together a fire. We curled up to it and pushed our cold sneakered feet near enough the embers to turn the rubber soles gummy.

Jimmy had brought along a pint of brandy that had already been opened. We drank from the bottle and shivered while we talked. Jimmy told me that Father Lusenkas and Mrs. Murtagh had left earlier in the day for Alabama. They were planning to meet with other people in Philadelphia, where a group of twenty or so would head by bus for Alabama. He told me how his father had been arguing with him for days over allowing him to go, and, finally, how Father Lusenkas himself had arrived to settle the dispute.

"I asked Father about how Jesus had said He had arrived to set a son against his father," said Jimmy.

"What did he say?"

"He said that it was true, and that this was an example of it. But he said that I was misinterpreting the lesson. He said I was assuming that standing up for someone's civil rights was more important than obeying my father, which is not necessarily correct. He said my father was not asking me to ignore the situation, but rather to submit to his judgment."

"He means that your father's not asking you to do something that's wrong? Is that it?"

"Yeah. But I think it's wrong. Look at everything that Father says about it. Look at how he says that you can't ignore wrongdoing without being wrong yourself. God wants people to do things like this, right?"

I shrugged. I didn't know. All I knew was that a conflict raged inside Jimmy. He was wild with a need to conquer badness, to set the balance of justice, to be good in the eyes of God. He needed an enemy large enough to test his mettle; he needed Goliath.

It hadn't taken long for the brandy to set my head swimming, and now Jimmy's dilemma had me dizzy besides. When he passed me the bottle I drank from it even though I felt queasy and numb. I was convinced that the burning of it in my throat would warm me throughout. So I drank and shuddered and forced my belly to hold the brandy down.

Jimmy reached for another log and laid it on the fire. He must have sensed my tiredness and the way the brandy had me swooning, for he said, "You can go back home if you want, Chun. There's no sense both of us being cold and mixed up."

"That's all right," I said. "I'll stay."

The fire wasn't able to keep us warm. It didn't warm our backs, for one thing, and whenever I tried to edge closer to the flames I was pushed back by the smoke or, crazily, the very heat of the pulsing embers.

"This is nuts," I said. "I'm cold and I can't get close enough to stay warm."

"Yeah—yeah, it's cold as a bitch," said Jimmy.

He had been drinking earlier; I could tell.

The sky was crowded with wintry stars. They gathered above and around us as if we sat inside a glittered dome. I thought fleetingly of the night we'd gone back to the Conklin place, the night of the rabbit, and even though that had been only two or three years ago I felt so much older and even wiser.

"Why didn't Mr. Murtagh go with them?" I suddenly asked.

Jimmy shrugged. "I don't know. Maybe he has to work."

"I don't think he feels the same."

"Maybe," said Jimmy, his voice vague.

I then wondered about Father Lusenkas and Mrs. Murtagh and how close they were, and then felt wrong about my thoughts and tried to banish them.

"Did they argue?" I asked Jimmy.

"Who?"

"Mr. and Mrs. Murtagh."

"I don't know."

He pulled out a cigarette and leaned close to the fire to light it. He kept the pint of brandy close to his chest, taking greedy swallows and then washing his mouth with more. He spit a mouthful into the fire once and watched it flare and smiled.

"I don't understand why all of this has you so crazy," I said, hoping he wouldn't be angry.

He sat with his feet drawn up under his butt, rocking.

"Yeah? All of what?"

"All of what? This stuff with Father Lusenkas, what d'you think?"

"Well?"

He was drunk.

"Do you think that you're supposed to go down there and go to jail or something?"

"Yeah," he said. "Yeah, that's what you're supposed to do. That's what it means to have a living faith."

"Well, sure, I know that they tell us things like that in school, but—well, shit, Jimmy, that's not for sixteen-year-old guys like us. I mean, what if you go down there and some big sheriff clobbers you with a billy club? That would hurt. You could be killed."

"That's the whole idea, Chun. Of course it would hurt, of course you could die. If it was all so easy and didn't hurt, everyone would be doing it."

Still hunched, he suddenly growled angrily and wheeled. He flung himself toward the cabin, unleashing a solid blow into one of the hard, frozen logs. He busted open the skin on his knuckles. He looked at the torn skin and it seemed to anger him further, so he punched the log once again as if determined to teach his fist a lesson.

He sat back up close to the fire and said, as much to himself as to me, "I should be there."

"So—" I began.

The words fled me for a moment. The brandy had shellacked my brain. "I mean, what's right, then?"

"I'll tell you what's right is what you tell yourself is right. Nothing else makes any sense. Even if someone tells you different, you still believe what you believe. You might do what they tell you to do, but you don't ever change."

The fire was dying down. There were no logs left and it would be useless to try to chop more because all the wood was frozen hard as stone.

The branches of the bared winter trees clacked against one another like dry old bones. Their large limbs creaked and groaned in the wind. They had seen many nights like this, cold and alone, but couldn't figure us out and saw in our fire their distant fate.

An ember suddenly popped and sizzled, disturbing the bed of ash the way a meteor disturbs the moon.

"I'm goin'," said Jimmy decisively.

I knew what he meant. He meant Alabama.

"I know what's right and what's wrong, and I'm goin'."

He had finished the brandy and his eyes were watery and distant. He stared into the fire, where the fading embers had kept the shape of a log. "You turn the other cheek," he said, seeming to look back into a dream for its meaning. "If you can."

He paused. The embered log collapsed and there was not another to burn.

"Who could do that, Chun? Turn the other cheek? It doesn't mean anything if you're weak to begin with; it only means something when you're strong."

He didn't understand that there were many ways to turn the other cheek. He thought it all had to do with physical strength. He didn't understand how difficult it was to be weaker than others and have them bully you and then try to forgive them. He didn't understand that unless it was important to God that the weak forgive the strong, then the weak themselves were unimportant, and God had put them here to be abandoned, nothing more. But if God cared at all about the weak of the earth, then forgiveness was of great importance.

Even though the fire had burned steadily, we'd never really gotten warm. And now that only a few twinkling embers remained we began to feel the terrible biting cold. Nevertheless, we didn't leave. We'd become lazy and tired and sort of uncaring. We seemed stubbornly inclined to sit there under the wintry sky and watch the embers die, no matter how cold we were. It was too bad we had finished the brandy. It had made me light-headed but I felt now I could use it.

I wasn't going to be the one to suggest that we get up and leave, no matter how cold and tired I was. I could stick it out as long as Jimmy could. I convinced myself of this even though for years I had not been able to outdo or even match him in anything. He was stronger and faster, smarter, more determined, and in many ways had reached manhood while I was still struggling to shed my adolescence.

I looked at him. He sat with his feet drawn up, rocking ever so slightly, the empty pint in one hand, the other hand drawn musingly to his chin. I could feel the debate rage on in him, and I was surprised that he hadn't stood up and, in a show of supreme frustration, lifted the cabin above his shoulders and heaved it a country mile. Feeling his frustration, I suddenly realized that his anger and his drunkenness was not so much because of his argument with his father but because of an argument within himself. He needed to face this challenge of turning the other cheek. He didn't know if he could do such a thing. Of all the gifts God had given him, this one he wanted most desperately might be out of his reach. Though I could hardly believe that. I could hardly believe anything was out of his reach.

I abruptly realized that he really wasn't certain if he could be a priest—and I also realized that he had yet to face this. He still thought it was inevitable. There would be an explosion when he discovered otherwise. Out here in the cold and unforgiving night I could see the tamped charge and I could smell the sizzling fuse.

4

—Wake up, Mouse, or die. Wake up or die.

I heard Iron Jud's voice. I dreamed he was giving me a massage, warming me up after that foolhardy plunge into the ocean back in the year when Easter was early. . . .

—C'mon, Chun, said Jimmy. Wake up.

—Where are you, Mouse? Come back here. Leave the other place.

Iron Jud, humming, shifting talismans and humming, rubbing me ruba-dub-dub/thuk-lub-dub . . .

—Chun, said Dietz, his voice on edge, his hands up under my shirt, rubbing me furiously. —Chun!

Jimmy, I wanted to say. Jimmy, let's go home. I'm freezing. I've had enough.

But I could say nothing. I was asleep and freezing to death. I walked nimbly along the edge of that pit that had opened here the day we'd all decided to build the cabin. And even though I knew it wasn't real, I also knew there was no escape.

Iron Jud and Jimmy brought me around and forced me to move my arms and legs. They forced me to stand and pump my muscles. My feet and hands had no feeling; my face was like a brick.

We crawled under the brambles. Once we were beyond them and on our feet, Iron Jud directed us to keep moving. My knees ached and I couldn't stop shivering. Jud turned to me continually, showing me how I must move my arms to stir my blood. But I ached so and wanted to cry. I was confused, but then, as my confusion left, I saw the danger and I feared I would lose my fingers and toes.

"Move or die," Iron Jud commanded, picking up the pace.

Then he ran ahead. He would meet us at his place. It was closer at hand than any other warm haven. Besides, Iron Jud knew what had to be done to thaw us.

Iron Jud added a few logs to the fire in the wood stove and set out a pan of steaming water. The cast-iron stove was cherry-red now, generously pumping out heat. Jud's pair of hounds, neither of whom had a name, appreciated the extra heat as much as we did. They crowded close to us and licked our bare feet and I realized I had no feeling down there at all.

Jud raised an army blanket for a makeshift tent near the stove and instructed me and Jimmy to strip down to our underwear and huddle in the steamed heat. We did so and it wasn't long before I felt my blood begin to flow and my joints loosen. Gradually and with some pain the feeling returned to my fingers and toes. My face was frostbitten, as were my ears, and when sensation returned to them they throbbed as if burned. Jimmy's knuckles, the skin torn and purple from the angry blows he had given the log, bled afresh in the steamed warmth.

Jud's place was small, a two-room house raised off the ground on pillars of cinder block. It was constructed of planks, plywood, and corrugated sheets of metal. It wasn't the best-looking of places, but it wasn't a shack either. He kept it in good repair without ever spending a dime on materials.

There was no electricity in the place, and Jud cooked on his wood stove. He ate squirrel and raccoon, fish (bass and carp), turtle, and woodchuck. He said he had a special recipe for woodchuck, because it was impossible to eat woodchuck if you didn't first soak the meat in vinegar for five days.

Out back he had a garden and a handful of fruit trees and berry bushes. He toted all his water from Weed Pond, a half mile away.

He raised a few rabbits in a hutch alongside the house, and when it came time to eat one he lifted it by its scruff and *crack!* killed it in an instant by breaking its neck between his viselike hands.

It was to be considered a special event that Iron Jud had brought us to his place. He wasn't what you would call hospitable, though neither was he mean-tempered. He certainly had never given us any reason to be afraid of him. We understood he was a hermit, possibly a half-breed Iroquois, and that he liked to be left alone. We also knew how he'd earned his nickname. His muscles were hard as an ironwood tree.

He sometimes encountered us in the woods and went on past without uttering a single word. And we presumed that there were other occasions when we were out in the woods and he watched us without our knowing it.

When he wanted company, which was not often, he would appear at one or another bend in the path or stand in the middle of a clearing, silent as an old volcanic stone. He would stand there with the sun slanting yellow across his leathery face and he wouldn't break his silence, waiting to see if we'd notice him. I always noticed him before Dietz, which surprised me, and it was always shocking to see him; he appeared as if from nowhere.

Once we had seen him, though, and if he wanted company, he

would wave for us to follow him. Sometimes he would lead us to his place to have us help him lift a large timber or lend a hand with some other chore that needed more than one person. Other times he would bring us to his place to show us a litter of raccoons or lead us to Weed Pond to show us how strangely the turtles acted in early spring.

He didn't say how it was that he had happened to be out near the cabin that cold night at such an odd hour, but I believed that he had secret and magical powers—which, of course, Jimmy did not. Jimmy would claim later that Jud had smelled our fire. Nothing more mysterious than that had occurred.

Jud kept the wood stove hot and replenished the basin of water regularly. He gave us tea with sugar and told us how it was not wise to mix cold weather and alcohol. He said we ought never do it again, that next time he might not be there.

Once we had warmed up and put on our clothes it was still dark outside and I was very tired. Jud directed us to sit at his small wooden table. He carefully indicated that Jimmy was to sit in the chair to his left; I was shown the chair on his right. He lit a candle and stood it atop an upturned coffee can in the middle of the table. He was very ceremonious about this, and we watched him with great curiosity.

From a rough pine shelf above the table he took down a leather pouch. He untied and loosened the drawstring, spilling the contents on the table. Our eyes widened. Before us was a collection of all the small and valuable objects Iron Jud had seen fit to save throughout his long solitary life.

Talismans, I thought, fascinated by the objects and the reverence Jud paid them.

The candlelight danced freely over the talismans: a beautiful quartz arrowhead; a ragged hunk of jade; an eagle's claw; a pin from the St. Louis Exhibition; a whalebone awl; a lens; an 1892 double-eagle gold piece (which, we later decided, had been the year of his birth); a few polished stones; balls of amber; a collection of colorful feathers; a braided leather thong; a pitted piece of meteorite.

Across from us, Iron Jud's sharp features were shadowed from below by the candle flame. His face seemed godly and fearsome, as if it had fallen through the clouds from a totem pole.

There was something in his manner that told us we weren't to touch any of the talismans laid out on the table. He began to hum, and the vibration began in his chest and throat but soon could be felt through the table. His dogs rose up from their warm places by the stove when he began this humming. They whined a bit and looked at him with their sad hound eyes. Then, slowly wagging their heavy tails, they lumbered over and nuzzled Jud's knee. He ignored them and they soon turned away and settled back to rest.

The three of us were gathered around the circle of light cast by the candle. Jimmy and I watched Iron Jud's thick fingers reach out and rearrange the positions of the talismans. He pushed the jade here, the arrowhead there, the eagle claw close to the gold piece. He put the piece of meteorite in his mouth, wet it with his saliva, and then placed it back on the table.

Throughout it all, he continued to hum.

The old man seemed to have put himself into a trance. He studied the pieces of bone, metal, leather, stone, claw, and feather, and then shifted them from place to place.

I could see no meaning in any of this, and when my eyes managed to meet Jimmy's I could see that he was equally puzzled.

At long last the pieces fell into place for Iron Jud. He ceased humming and I felt as if a machine beneath the ground had finally come to rest. It was deadly quiet now. The wick of the candle spluttered. Iron Jud's eyes, deep and solemn and thick with prophecy, took in our faces. The candlelight chiseled his brow and Iroquois cheekbones. His right hand came up slowly. He pointed directly at Jimmy, witnessing, "Eagle who flies above."

Then he turned his hand toward me, his index finger quavering slightly. "You," he predicted. "Mouse who sees in all directions."

I was suddenly disappointed. I hadn't liked to be called a mouse. And in the years that followed I would find it ironic that I was fated to wear a glass eye. Too bad about the mouse thing. I had otherwise liked the idea of seeing in all directions.

Shortly after Jud had finished reading the talismans the first light of day lifted away the night. The candle flame on the coffee tin rapidly grew weaker. The hounds, who had been asleep and motionless as thick rugs, now raised their bones and stretched their knobby joints and pawed at the door.

We thanked Jud once again for saving us and departed. The hounds followed us a short distance before they detected a fresh spoor and followed it.

It was still cold as hell, and Jimmy and I walked quickly all the way. We knew how damned lucky we were not to have died. And we knew we'd catch hell for this stunt when we returned home.

5

No one came out of those days unscathed. Father Lusenkas was arrested in Alabama, and I'd overheard a few of the brothers at school mention that he'd finally gotten himself in deep trouble with the chancery. He suddenly was giving fewer speeches.

Mrs. Murtagh had also been arrested, but Mr. Murtagh had flown down to have her released. The story was in the local papers, which was something Mr. Murtagh apparently didn't appreciate. I'd learned this by listening to my mother comment to friends on how Mr. and Mrs. Murtagh were now doing things separately that they had always done together.

Jimmy's father had been certain that Jimmy had left for Alabama that night against his wishes. When he called my parents and found out I was missing from my warm bed, he alerted the police, who then sent out our descriptions to the state police from New Jersey to Alabama.

Our parents of course knew about the cabin, but before they thought of getting Spyros or Corney to lead the police back there it was dawn and Jimmy and I had returned. My parents weren't quite sure if they should beat me or welcome me home. But my mother took one look at me and Jimmy and had my father rush us to the hospital, where we spent most of the day, because this Filipino doctor who had never seen frostbite became very interested in poking our ears with pins.

The night out there in the freezing cold created a new bond between me and Jimmy. Or maybe it was the old bond grown stronger, the way they say a broken bone grows stronger when it heals.

Jimmy seemed to have come to some compromise with himself over this business of turning the other cheek. I didn't think he had found a way to resolve it altogether. There would always be a conflict raging deep within him, for, of all the people I've known, Jimmy Dietz possessed both the strength to turn the other cheek and the strength to bust a jaw.

After that night I think he slowly began to realize he would never be a priest. He didn't come out and say as much, closing the doors to his thoughts as quickly as he had opened them. But he did say that he didn't think he'd finish high school at Cathedral, which was a strong hint. Whatever it was about the priesthood that had held him charmed was slowly becoming less appealing. I think that for the first time in his life he realized how angry and confused he was. He was facing things larger than himself.

The next few weeks passed quickly. Winter departed; the ground began to thaw and soften. It wasn't long before we returned to running the wet paths and hunting rabbit. Only rarely did Jimmy dress up in his black suit to go listen to Father Lusenkas or follow the stations of the cross. He still served mass on Sunday, but ever since that big argument with his father he began to join me and the guys at the diner for coffee and a smoke instead of going to church with his family. He didn't think it was necessary any longer to go to confession every Saturday. He started seeing Karen Wazewski again, and one night at a party at Carol Dante's I saw him with his hand up Karen's blouse.

He worked at the auction every Saturday even while he was being punished, and toward the end of March, when one of the guys who helped unload the trucks was fired for stealing, Jimmy brought me along and told the baker and the butcher that I was a hard worker, and honest too.

We started out for the auction early those Saturdays in the spring. The trucks arrived at seven and the auction opened for business at nine. Traveling along the paths, it took us no longer than forty minutes to get there.

We met at this place in the woods halfway between our houses where a stand of birch trees laden with yellow catkins arched over a small field of fiddlehead ferns and wild violets. There was a boulder beneath the birches, and whoever arrived first could be found sitting there, waiting for the other guy.

Once we had joined up we scooted along the path that took us through Big Trees and to Arthur Kill Road. We continued along the road for a short distance before plunging into the tall reeds on the far side. Here there was no longer solid ground beneath our feet. We moved on a springy platform of hummock and woven cattail roots. It was like running on a surface of matted rope, and at the places where the weave disappeared our feet sank through into black muck.

Occasionally a board appeared to bridge the watery hollows. Jimmy said the boards had been placed there by duck hunters and this professor from Princeton who studied the birds and muskrats and wrote about them for magazines.

Certain days the boards were high and dry; other days they would be on the surface of the brackish water and they bowed under our weight. We splashed ankle-deep into the dark water then. Our sneakers would be wet and smelly by the time we climbed the sandy hill where the marsh disappeared and the farthest runway of the old airfield cut a straight line to the auction.

At work I followed Jimmy's instructions to the letter. He had been at this routine for months and had learned the best way to unload the vans and stack the goods and maneuver the hand trucks. Inside, at the counter and display cases, he knew where to store each cake box and sausage package, and how to appease the butcher's wife, who insisted on examining everything no matter where we stored it, and the baker's wife, who screamed if she saw a loose human hair.

When the doors opened at nine, the customers trickled in and Jimmy donned his apron and went to work behind the counter. He looked up to the hook where the next number was queued and called it out loud. He answered customers' questions about salami and baloney and sweet and hot sausage as if he'd been born to the trade.

Meanwhile I continued to unload the last few items from the vans, after which I collected five dollars and a hero sandwich from the butcher, and an additional five dollars and a piece of pastry from the baker. Then I wandered around the stalls, losing myself between the tall shelves of old books and used comics, killing the time until noon.

It happened that the second or third week I was there, the guy who had been fired for stealing came around and found me at his old job. He arrived with a friend, and at first I had no idea who they were or what they wanted. They simply planted themselves at the rear of the butcher's van and wouldn't let me past. Jimmy was inside by then, working the counter, and I think they knew that.

The guy who had been fired was the smaller of the two. He was my height but built like a slab of concrete. I was hoping to find a way out of this without having to fight him. I'd have my ass kicked for sure.

"Why are you giving me a hard time?" I asked them as they blocked my way.

"You took my frickin' job," said the shorter guy.

"There was nobody doing it when I came."

"Hey," the big guy warned me—he had a scar on his lip fixed as a sneer. "Shut the fuck up."

"It's a free country," I said, relying on a worn old line that had never carried any weight with bullies.

The other guy poked me in the chest, saying, "You took my fuckin' job."

I said nothing for a moment. Then, trying not to sound too afraid, I said, "I don't want any trouble."

"I think you're a fuckin' faggot."

I lifted a box of pigs' feet and tried to carry it past them. They pushed me back and the big guy reached over and grabbed the back of my neck and squeezed until I put the box down.

"Hey, listen—" I began to say.

But the other one, the one called Vic, reached out and punched me hard in the stomach. My breath went out of me and I doubled over. My eyes watered and I thought I would black out.

"Cut it out," I managed to say, still bent over.

Vic said, "Fuck you," and I heard him spit and imagined it had landed on me. At that I straightened up and called him a scumbag and tried to run between them. The big guy grabbed me, though, and whipped me back against the inside of the van.

Vic dared me to repeat what I had called him, so I told him I had called him a fuckin' scumbag.

He punched me again. At least twice, I think, in the ribs and in the side of my face. Then he stepped back and the big guy said, "Shit, let's go. He's a pussy."

They took a few jars of pigs' feet and smashed them on the ground and then walked off down the line of trucks. As they left I heard the guy who had punched me call his friend Ivers, and I suddenly realized that the two were Ralph Ivers and L'il Vic Gigliotti. They both had a reputation larger than life at the public high school where Corney and Spyros and the others went. They didn't come any tougher or meaner.

I'd heard from Spyros that Ivers had made short work of Sliver one night after a dance down in Tottenville. "Wiped the fud'yan sidewalk with him," Corney had added.

My ribs and stomach hurt, but I knew I was lucky to have gotten off without a broken jaw. The pigs' feet, spilled open on the ground, looked and smelled ugly. I knew I'd have to pay for them. I'd tell the butcher I'd dropped them. I wasn't going to say a word about Ivers and L'il Vic. I didn't want Jimmy to feel he'd brought it on me by getting the job, and I didn't want him to ask why I hadn't fought back. The only explanation I could give wouldn't make sense to him. He wouldn't understand that it didn't make any difference—that I couldn't fight my way out of a paper bag and never had been much good at it, that trying to fight always ended up being more frustrating than simply taking my lumps and licking my wounds.

For a few weeks after the incident with Ivers and L'il Vic we were able to get a ride to the auction on Saturday mornings with Spyros and his father, who was doing some work out that way. Mr. Spyropoulos had made it clear that we were to be waiting on the corner on time for him. He said if we weren't there he wouldn't wait. As it turned out we never missed the connection, and by the end of April, when Mr. Spyropoulos had finished his work, we returned to the paths.

The first Saturday after Mr. Spyropoulos had stopped driving us, we met at the birches and followed the same route we'd used before, heading out at a fast pace beyond Big Trees to the road, where we crossed over and parted the winter-browned reeds to the trail through the marsh. Toward the end of the trail we noticed that there were a few beer cans and small piles of rubbish. We couldn't imagine who had dumped the stuff there.

Farther along, there was more garbage—and an awful stench. We figured some ignorant slob had dumped a load of it out here. We hoped he'd drowned in it.

Suddenly we heard heavy equipment and men's voices. Then, at the sandy hill where the marsh gave way to solid land, we ran into an embankment of garbage that rose over our heads. We found ourselves knee-deep in a foul stew of old food and soggy cardboard, pieces of banana skin, bottles, and chicken bones. We slogged along, our noses turned up, until we found a way out.

We rose up from the miserable trough, discovering that the break in the embankment was a narrow cut between two immense piles of garbage. We couldn't figure out why it was here, though we suspected it had something to do with the heavy equipment we'd heard.

Above us, a scavenging flock of gulls screeched wildly. We were sure there were whole colonies of rats burrowed below the filth. The stench had made me sick to my stomach. I felt myself turn green.

Before us, on a road of packed earth and gravel, there stood a collection of garbage trucks and bulldozers. We walked over toward a dump truck that had just unloaded a pile of dirt. We stood there and watched the operation, about as surprised by all this as we would have been if they were building a launch pad for Mars.

At first, the men ignored us, the way men who are working make a practice of ignoring curious boys who wander nearby. But when we remained glued to the spot for some minutes we must have shown the defiance and dismay we felt, for the men found a reason to take a break and say something to us.

They were friendly, especially the one man, calling good morning over the noise and vibrations of his bulldozer. He brought the machine to a halt and stepped down. "You kids want to be careful standing there. When we start up 'dozin' again"—he pointed out the bull-dozer—"you'll have to move along."

"When are you going to be finished?" Jimmy asked, not moving an inch from the ground he held. "How far are you going?" he added, sweeping his arm as if in a gesture to lay protection on the marsh.

The man didn't answer. He had taken off his canvas work gloves and now folded them and held them in his hand. He pursed his lips and seemed to be considering the breadth of Jimmy's question. He knew Jimmy didn't want even a small corner of the marsh to be covered by garbage. He knew that what Jimmy really wanted was to tell him and the others to leave for good.

When he drew near to us he stopped and turned toward the flat marsh. The wind was running through the reeds, turning them in the sun and showing where they were green with spring growth. The random pools of water lying here and there among the reeds formed jigsaw shapes and were silvered over by the long rays of morning light. The man took a moment to look closely at the marsh and the Arthur Kill beyond, taking careful measure of the place before turning to us. He looked us up and down, amused by our wet dungarees and muddied sneakers. His lips pursed again and he sighed, but still, he said nothing.

A younger man who had heard Jimmy's question had meanwhile walked over. He held a thermos cup of steaming coffee in his hand and answered sarcastically, "We're goin' till we're outta garbage. By then we ought to fill everything from here to frickin' Jersey."

He laughed at his own remark, but the man from the bulldozer and the two or three others who had also wandered over by now found nothing amusing in it. They looked us over with puzzled and sympathetic eyes. We must have appeared as opposites to them. Jimmy was tall and angry and had spoken his piece; I was smaller, quiet, studying every move and gesture. We were opposites but we were twins: tossed up by the marsh where these men had been sent to make space for more garbage than God had ever intended should exist.

Except for the one named Dan with the sharp tongue, they seemed momentarily to feel bad about their chore. They looked out over the pretty marsh and brooded. Their shoulders sagged, and I could feel a sense of helplessness begin to bury us, the way the marsh was senselessly being buried.

Then Dan, who felt none of this, stepped forward and poured the rest of his coffee on the ground in a purposely wasteful gesture. He'd felt insulted that no one had laughed with him, and he stood in front of us and put his hands on his hips and demanded, "What the hell you little fuckin' hayseeds doin' in this swamp? This is off-limits to the public."

Jimmy eyed him and then looked away as if he couldn't be bothered. He asked the older man, the one from the bulldozer, the question that no one had yet answered. "How far?" asked Jimmy. "How far are you going?"

"All of it," said the bulldozer man. He had pulled a bandanna from his pocket; he used it to wipe his brow. He looked over the land and echoed his words. "Yeah. All of it."

"What's that mean?" asked Jimmy, who knew exactly what it meant. He wanted to hear it from the men who would do it.

But Dan wasn't finished with us. He hadn't taken kindly to the way Jimmy had looked at him as if he were a dung beetle. He stepped between us and the bulldozer man and said, "It means *all of it.* It means no more mosquitoes, no more skunk cabbage, no more To-bacco Road—understand?"

"I wasn't asking you," said Jimmy evenly.

"Yeah? Yeah? Well, you little fuckin' wise-ass, I'm tellin' you, whether you like it or not."

Jimmy was ready to hit him, and I knew this even though I had never seen Jimmy ready to hit anyone. It didn't matter to Jimmy that the guy was ten years older and broader and possibly stronger. Jimmy wasn't one bit afraid. He wasn't afraid to hit him, and he wasn't afraid to be hit in return.

The older man intervened, saying, "Calm down, Dan. What the hell you want to go and pick on a kid for? Can't you see this place is important to them?"

Dan told Dietz nastily, "I just want to tell you, *Red,* watch out you don't get run over out here. You ain't supposed to be here. This all belongs to the city now."

Dan stomped off and climbed aboard his truck.

The older man said, "Listen, boys." He raised his hands to soothe the impact his words were sure to have on us. "There's no future for this land other than what city hall's got planned. I ain't been out this way in years. I remember it back when you could hunt ducks in the winter and run off to the beaches in summer. Hell, it was like the country out here then, and some places still are. You boys must love it. But nothing around here will stay for long. And that's that."

He pulled up his ample belly and tucked his shirt down his pants. "Now, I'll tell you," he went on. "The whole marsh is going to be filled in with garbage, compacted, covered over with earth, and then black-topped. There's goin' to be a big shopping mall out here in years to come. It's going to have a Macy's and a Gimbels and even a Bam-berger's for all I know, all indoors with fountains and plants and that shit."

"What for?" I asked. "There aren't even any houses here."

These were the first words I'd said, and the man seemed surprised that I'd found my tongue.

He shook his head. *"What for?* Ain't you boys heard?"

We didn't know what he was driving at.

"It's been in the papers," he said.

"We don't read the papers," I said philosophically. "It's always bad news."

"Look, enjoy this while you can. I mean, it's a life out here that boys and dogs love, you know? But boys and dogs don't carry clout."

"So it will all be gone?" asked Jimmy, frowning. "When?"

"A few years. Four or five, I imagine. The marsh will be gone, then the woods will go next."

I couldn't believe this. "The *woods?*"

"The bridge to Brooklyn's going up," he explained. "You wait and see what that does out here. It'll be like an invasion. There's a six-lane highway going to run east-west, and another four-lane going to run into it. They'll meet over there at Al Deppe's. In ten years, you won't recognize this place. There's going to be houses everywhere and cars zipping along between Jersey and the city—that is, when there ain't traffic jams ten miles long. It won't be nothing at all like it is now. Nothin'."

Jimmy took in this information and said not a word. He turned to look over the marsh and the distant early-spring woods where the buds had emerged like buttons on the branches.

Ten years, I thought, believing this was a long, long time and that maybe things wouldn't come to pass the way the man had described them.

"It's stupid," I said. "Whose idea is it?"

The man opened his palms and shrugged. "It's not anyone's idea. It's just progress."

 # *Part Three*

The researchers' most impressive
accomplishment, however, is in using
aerial black-and-white photographs to
detect half-meter-wide buried
footpaths, some of which have been
traced for a few kilometers. . . . grass
growing above the paths is slightly
greener. . . .

Science News, Vol. 130, No. 21

Chapter 11

1

Since many fewer cars stopped for gas at night than during the day, I started to think that if the Paymaster wanted genuinely to test a gas jockey he would not arrive at night, when business tended to be slack, but rather in the middle of the day, when the demand was heavy and a gas jockey's patience ran thin, when instead of smiling and asking, "Fill it up?" the gas jockey simply asked, "What'll it be?"—no way to sell volumes of gasoline—and instead of "Check the oil?" it was "Thanks," as if selling a few dollars' worth of gasoline was all there was to it. What about that oil? What about tires? Batteries? Fan belts and hoses?

If the Paymaster came, he would come when the action at the pumps was hot and heavy. And if he came during my watch he'd see me zip from car to car, good-natured and efficient, and wonder why I was here, at the gas station by the superdump, instead of top jock at Bert's. He'd hand me five hundred dollars and wish he had more to give. "Sorry," he'd say. "That's all the dough the rules allow."

I'd treat Dietz with some of that money. Rent a canoe for our trip upstate. The rest would be for Oregon. Maybe I could convince Dietz to grow his hair long and the two of us would team up and head west. Maybe build another cabin.

This was the way Pete and the mechanics had painted the Paymaster, even though I knew there were other dimensions to this epic character. They could have purposely hidden the arcane dimensions of the Paymaster, although I find it unlikely. I think the Paymaster whom

I was coming to know was thoroughly unknown to them. He dwelled in their blind spots.

I was sure that Pete and the mechanics and the marketing pooh-bahs of Mobile Oil and all the others who were waiting for the Paymaster to drive into their lives had not even begun to fathom the depths of this mystery. For them, it was the dough. But I ask you, what's a fifty-dollar bill or five hundreds compared to a ride with the Paymaster? A ride along the continuum?

Take, for instance, that car of his. Everyone figured he would drive in here behind the wheel of an automobile no different from any other. Let me tell you, it's far more than a car the Paymaster drives.

It might appear to be a Country Squire station wagon, circa 1953, with a cargo of broken appliances and pieces of scrap wood, a copy of *The Way Things Work,* Volume II, on the front seat, a vise bolted to the rear bumper so he would set up shop wherever he stopped. But it was much more than that. It was a chariot souped up to light speed, a clever time machine that never needed lubrication or adjustment, a lint-free magic carpet, a mathematical joyride on the continuum.

It was fun, fun, fun.

"C'mere," he once told me. "I'll show you where I hide the extra key for Peggy"—he had named the car Peggy in honor of the Pegasus and had labored over the job of attaching a winged horse from an old weather vane to the place where the hood ornament belonged. "You might need it one of these days."

"What for?" I asked, not having presumed that I'd ever be skilled enough to navigate the continuum alone, even though it should have been obvious to me that this was why he had arrived, to take on a worthy apprentice.

We were in the desert then. The heat was a heavy weight and the air was dry as lizard's skin. Mirage ribbons rose, snaking the horizon. The sky was thin and lusterless, tired of the fierce sun, and the distant mesas showed the color-coded lines where they'd been strapped and stacked by ancient thrusts of Mother Earth.

The Paymaster—I never knew his name or even if he had one—was latched on to me by a strange hybrid force: part radar, part telepathy, part humorous instinct. He had gone around to yank open the hood to show me the extra key. I had been sitting on the ground in the small shade case by Peggy and now stood and slapped the dirt from the seat of my pants. I came around to help him with the hood. I could see how the strain of pulling on the hood had reddened his face. Half-moons of sweat stained the armpits of his seersucker suit.

Together we managed to pull up the hood and he showed me a key dangling by a loop of coat-hanger wire on the fuel line.

"There she blows," he said. "Don't forget."

"Roger."

He smiled. He had a good smile, perhaps the best. Top-shelf. It went with his broad sense of humor, a shining light on a dismal horizon.

He liked yard sales and flea markets and secondhand shops, for he claimed that these places represented mail drops along the continuum. He liked popcorn and movies—especially matinees—and he loved parades and ribbon-cuttings, children riding ponies, Stetson fedoras, fixing anything broken (which was a grand achievement, for he was all thumbs), 78-rpm records, and pilsner beer. And he loved the Pegasus. Yeah, he sure loved that flying horse.

We rode along for a while and gave Peggy her head. Time and space did their knit-one purl-two while I paged through the old newspapers the Paymaster had picked up from a little boy who was selling them on a corner. He had bought up the whole lot, dumping whatever change he'd had into the little boy's hand. The boy's eyes had widened at this unexpected sale and the Paymaster had smiled.

The papers offered an interesting assortment of news. The box scores from Corney's two no-hitters; the letter to the newspaper from the mother of the two children Dietz had saved during the Big Fire; the headline about my cracked skull; Dietz's Silver Star heroics; Father Lusenkas's arrest in Alabama.

I was still a tenderfoot along the continuum and I had quite a lot to learn. But the Paymaster was a patient and thorough teacher.

We stopped one evening for something to eat, back when I wasn't quite convinced if he was the Paymaster of the continuum. He preferred diners and claimed to have an unerring ability to choose the best within a hundred-mile radius—curious language for a man who generally pooh-poohed tangible measure—and we had no sooner stepped from the car to go into this particular diner than he was raving about the food. Such high praise even though he had never before eaten here.

He was already on his way across the lot when I mentioned that he'd left his door unlocked. He stopped walking and looked back, regarding me with mild surprise.

"Let me tell you, Sport, if you want to navigate the continuum and use those fancy techniques been making your eyeballs pop and your stomach flop, you've got to begin with trust. You savvy?"

I didn't know what to say. "I just—someone might steal something. I mean, I try to trust, but—"

He led me back to Peggy and directed my attention to the collection of odds and ends cluttering the rear cargo area. He put his hands on his hips and asked me, "Would you steal anything you see there?"

"I might not," I answered, not at all insulted by the question. After all, I had been a thief. Not on the grand scale of Deluxe and Smitty, but a thief nonetheless. I'd filched loose change, shoplifted a few items. I suspected the Paymaster knew this; he wasn't expecting a saint. "I might not steal anything," I repeated. "But someone else just might."

"For the moment, let's concern ourselves with you, no one else. That's the most we can expect from anyone—on either end of the continuum. You can't answer for the population of the world, can you? There's philosophers and politicians enough for that. Let's consider what's right and wrong for you and see where that takes us."

He bent down to examine more closely the items in the car and he pointed to the broken radio and the deflated basketball, the one-armed doll, a tennis racquet with sprung strings, his leather suitcase on the back seat, Volume II of *The Way Things Work,* a spare suit (blue serge, frayed at the cuffs and sleeves), his tool kit, and a Dutch Masters cigar box.

"So tell me—honestly, Sport—is there anything in there you'd steal?"

I looked over the items one by one, determined to search my heart. If I felt there was anything I'd steal, I'd tell him.

He followed my eyes and when it seemed I had carefully considered the situation, he asked, "What about the cigar box? Would you steal that?"

I hesitated. "What's in it?"

"Would it matter?" he asked pointedly.

A good question. I gave it some thought. I wondered what could be in the box and what I would do if I knew it contained something of extraordinary value. I could feel myself auctioning off my honesty. I felt my heart erode and didn't like the feeling.

"No," I answered. "It wouldn't matter. I wouldn't steal it."

He smiled that great smile of his. "That's an honest answer." He clapped my back.

"How do you know?" I asked. "That it's an honest answer?"

He indicated the space around us: the parking lot, the small town set neatly on a nearby hill, the water tower against the sky with the word DIXON painted in large even letters across it, the highway overpass, the blackbirds in sudden torn calligraphy across the sunset—all of which appeared commonplace to the ordinary traveler, yet every detail of which nevertheless pulsed with the unmistakable harmony and peacefulness of the continuum.

"You don't stick around the continuum if you're dishonest," he said. "You'll find yourself back in the everyday world in a flash." He snapped his fingers. "Guaranteed."

Then he indicated the diner. "Seeing as we're both still denizens of this place, let's eat. I'm famished."

We went inside and sat in a booth. The special was corned beef and cabbage and the Paymaster advised me to order it. I followed his advice and when the meals arrived we ate in silence until the Paymaster looked me in the eye and said, "Oh. By the bye. It's stuffed full of brand-new fifty-dollar bills."

I didn't quite get his drift. "What's that?"

"The Rembrandt."

I laughed. "The Rembrandt?"

"Dutch Masters. Where's your culture?"

I looked through the window at Peggy and mused, "The Dutch Masters box."

"Yeah," he said. "You couldn't get another fifty in there with a shoehorn. There's a lot of gas jockeys expecting to be rewarded. Can't let them down."

I looked from the car to him. He was eating a large flaccid leaf of cabbage. I looked back at Peggy. She was still dusty from our jaunt through the badlands and needed a serious washing, but the Pegasus on the hood glinted proudly in the rosy, waning light.

"So, then," I said, amused and impressed. "You really are the Paymaster."

He glanced up from his meal and wiped a dollop of yellow mustard from the corner of his mouth. He grinned and said, "Funny, even with a top-shelf apprentice like yourself, the way a box full of money will make a believer of a person."

2

By the end of June I was running the place alone at night, under certain restrictions. No repairs, no tires, unless it was an emergency. Otherwise just pump gas, and, "Summerhelp, try not to get held up."

Every night when I went solo, Pete handed me the same instructions.

"Don't try to fix anything except what you know how to fix," he began one evening. "Which ain't a lot. You know how to fix a flat—"

"Blindfolded."

He looked at my glass eye. "Is that a joke? I don't know if it's a joke."

"It's a joke."

He said, "Oh." He paused before continuing his standard list of dos and don'ts. "You know how to change hoses, install headlights and bulbs—just don't fuck with the headlight alignment or people will be driving outta here cockeyed—and you can charge up batteries; you know how to do that, or at least you ought to, I showed you enough times. Make sure you always attach the clamps to the battery posts before you switch on the juice. Got it?"

"Got it."

"But don't fix nothin'—even if you know how to fix it—unless it's an emergency or the world stops driving on gasoline."

"Because the pumps come first," I parroted.

"You learn good."

"I'm sure the Paymaster will reward me."

Pete grinned. "If a guy expects you to fix a flat or some other bullshit, you explain how you're here by yourself until the other guy gets back from his break."

"What guy?" I puzzled.

"The other guy."

"I thought I was alone."

Pete shook his head at me.

"What d'you have for brains? You don't ever admit you're alone at night. The next thing you know, there's a stickup. Some crazy bastard walks in and pokes a gun barrel between your ribs and robs me blind."

Pete noticed that I didn't speak right up and applaud his strategy for avoiding holdups. "What the hell's your problem, Summerhelp?" he asked. "Don't you understand English?"

"What I don't get is why it matters so much that I pretend there's two of us here if the guy who's sticking me up has a gun. What the hell would it matter if someone else was here? Do you think we'd rush the guy or something?"

"You'd just better hope you get a stickup man who's a flappin' queerbait. Maybe he'll leave the money and settle for a blowjob."

"I'd rather give him your money, personally."

"Anyone leaves here with my money, you better have a bullet hole to show for it."

It was his practice to come around for a look-see and check the day's tallies before leaving me on my own. Like a man at a slot machine, he stood at the cash register and rang up the numbers, holding a piece of cardboard over the small window where the totals showed so I couldn't see how much money he was making. He must have thought that with this information I would strike for higher wages or somehow be able to embezzle his business. As each of the day's totals for gas, oil, and the rest appeared, he peeked behind the cardboard and never once failed to grumble at the amount of business he'd done.

He had driven in minutes earlier with Honey Bee—her real name was Madeleine—and they were on their way over to Monmouth to see the trotters run. He was dressed in a checked sport jacket and bright red golf pants, and his cordovan loafers boasted little tassled items on the uppers. He had shown himself surprisingly adept at scrubbing the grease and dirt from the cracks in his deeply furrowed hands, and he had lent a rakish touch to his outfit by tucking a paisley silk handkerchief in the breast pocket of his sport jacket. He then cleverly used a wrinkled cotton handkerchief from his back pocket to wipe his brow and blow his nose. It reminded me of the two-rag method he insisted I follow at the pumps. One for dipsticks, one for chrome.

Tonight there was a sporting cap atop his head that had somehow remained fixed at a jaunty angle despite the windy ride over in his big Chrysler convertible. When he'd parked the car and strode across the lot in his evening get-up, he'd looked like a big old bullfrog that had been kissed by a desperate princess.

He always took his time ringing out the totals. It was one of the few occasions when he concentrated. He stood there so long, in fact, that I was still able to smell his after-shave an hour after he'd left.

After he'd seen all the totals he made sure to wind out the cash register tape and take it along with him. He reset the register so that in the morning he would be able to see exactly how much business I had done.

"To the penny, Summerhelp," he said, trying to convince me that the figures always came out. I knew this wasn't true, because I'd more than once seen the accountant duck behind the accessories rack with his arms full of cash-register tapes, credit-card receipts, vouchers, and the Pete's Friendly Service checkbook, trying desperately to make it all come out "to the penny" while Pete brandished a crescent wrench inches from his sweaty brow.

Madeleine always waited in the Chrysler while Pete rang out the tallies and gave me his final instructions. She tried not to be impatient and busied herself by using the rearview mirror to check her hair and make-up. Her hair was teased and tinted. Her cheeks were rouged. She wore carmine lipstick and green eye shadow and never tried to conceal the fact that she was pleased with having landed Pete. Her man had money and could repair cars—that solved two of life's most pressing problems in one stroke.

Standing alongside me at the cash register in his evening getup, Pete asked if I remembered everything he had told me.

"Hey, Pete, I know what to do. It's a gas station, right?"

"What's that? Do you see *gas station* written on that window?"

"Okay. *Service* station. I can handle it. I mean, the point is, it's not the Manhattan Project."

"Oh, pardon me, I forgot—you almost were an engineer. A minor little problem of finishing school is all that stands between you and genius."

He fumbled with a stack of receipts he'd taken from a locked drawer. "Listen, that priest who knows you said you were good with figures. Or something like that. The way he talked you'd think you had a good head on your shoulders. Imagine that—you fooled someone." He cackled. "C'mere, let me see you write a number."

I thought he was being sarcastic. "Is this a test for the job? To write a number?"

Pete craned his neck to see how his date was doing. He waved to her and called out, "Business, business. You pick yourself a horsey from the paper."

He turned to me. "Yeah, it's a fuckin' test, if that's what you want. Just write a number, Summerhelp."

"Any old number?"

"Yes, any old goddam number."

I wrote the date. "How'd I do?"

Pete looked at it carefully. "Not bad. Not bad at all."

He then showed me the stack of receipts. They were credit-card carbons. There was a master list attached to the stack, with every single credit sale listed by dollar amount, gallons of gas, quarts of oil, and so on.

"Look't this mess," he said, showing me the master list. "That dumb fuckin' nephew of mine was lucky to get out of second grade, the way he writes numbers. Look't this here, Summerhelp." He showed me a number on the master sheet. "Now what's that supposed to be? Is that a five or a six?"

"It's a two. Put your glasses on."

"Glasses my ass," he protested. "No wonder he loses his shirt playing cards and betting," he said, referring again to Tom. "He can't read what he writes." He pointed a finger at me and said, "Don't never gamble, Summerhelp. You'll lose."

"This is advice you give me on your way to the racetrack?"

"Hey—Tom's stupid, that's why he loses. And you—I hate to break this to you—you're plain unlucky."

Madeleine called from the car, "Pete? Pete, honey?"

"Jesus," he moaned. He poked his head out the door and chirped, "One minute more, sweetheart."

He put his hand to his pecker and said quietly, "Down, boy. Down." He regarded me with a mad, gleeful eye.

"You're going to miss the first race," I advised him.

He turned his attention to the master list, telling me that if nothing else was going on I should recopy the numbers from the receipts onto the master list. "Just like you see it here, but so's someone can read the friggin' numbers."

Outside, Madeleine adjusted the sheer kerchief that had protected her coiffure during the windy ride in the convertible. She tied it carefully at her throat and admired herself in the rearview mirror. Then she pouted her lips and tapped the horn lightly, singing out Pete's name. Pete looked up and slurped. "Just what the doctor ordered."

He regarded his reflection in the plate-glass window. He adjusted his cap and shifted his pants at the waist. His last words to me were "Don't let anyone steal my money, Summerhelp. Take a round if you have to. I can always get part-time help, but money's hard to come by."

His date was thrilled to see him. You'd think they were twenty-year-olds and Pete had been overseas for three years. She cuddled up to him in the front seat and Pete smiled and gave her a kiss. He patted her on the cheek and then reached down and patted her where I couldn't see. He was grinning widely as he started the car. Then he leaned back his head laughing and raced the Chrysler convertible across the lot and into traffic.

3

Once all the sweeping and cleaning and putting away of things was behind me, once the bathrooms were replenished with legal and illegal items, the tires stacked and the phony sales banner posted for everyone to see, I copied down all the information from the sales receipts that Frank wanted on the master list and then sat out front with a can of soda and watched the traffic flow past.

Now and again a car or two, perhaps even four at a time, pulled in for gas. I hopped to it then, scampering from one to the next and chattering amiably, "Fill 'er up? Check the oil? Anything else?" I cleaned windshields and rear windows until they vanished beneath my touch, leaving behind nothing but the squeak.

There was a radio in the office, and I cranked it up and sang aloud and used the rhythm to keep me going at the pumps. I stood beneath the Pegasus rapping the beat of "(I Can't Get No) Satisfaction" on the metal hood of the pumps in the humid summer air. There was no wind, but I could smell the garbage. The vapors crawled this way at night, on their way to infiltrate the city and make people even filthier and more violent than they already were. I could hear the men who poked around over there at the dump each night taking potshots at the rats. I remembered when Dietz and I had first seen the garbage.

Above the growing mountains of garbage I could see across to New Jersey where the gas flares burned high and bright in the towers, where the refineries and chemical plants brewed yellow and green and brown gases to hide the stars and stain the dawn and spread cancer like dust. And while I stood there, singing, beating time on the lid of the high-test pump or hustling from car to car, I knew I was in a holding pattern in a place where I would rather not have been. I'd lost my love for the island and I was really here doing nothing other than waiting for word on Jimmy. Then it was *adios*.

I must admit that I was occasionally afraid for Jimmy. He should have been home by now, but as far as I could figure he was still in Vietnam. I had tried to learn his whereabouts from the Marine Corps. It took a half-dozen phone calls before I was pointedly told that I couldn't be told. It would have been enormously frustrating, all that telephoning, but having scoped out ahead of time that I was on a wild-goose chase I made sure, especially when I called the Pentagon, that I was good and stoned on the last bit of Mexican gold I had.

Lately at the bungalow I had found myself awakened by bad dreams. I usually wasn't able to fall asleep afterward; my head pounded and my body trembled. This had happened to me in the past for a few months after I'd lost my eye, but before then I'd not had bad dreams since I was a little kid and had latched on to this unshakable fear that beyond my window there lurked an evil prowler who was just waiting to spring into my bedroom and viciously stab me the moment I closed my eyes. On those childhood nights, I went into my parents' bedroom and crawled into the cozy and secure valley between their bodies. But the nights I awoke from bad dreams out at Bungalow number five (seven) I could do nothing but get up and dress and walk along the beach.

The Fourth of July parade and Little League field dedication went on as planned, as I figured they would. It was a perfect summer's day. Warm but not humid, the sky a deep undiluted blue; the air was fragrant and somehow buoyant, the way the air can be when you first meet a pretty girl. A Broadway musical would have been hard pressed to come up with a more wholesome, picture-perfect Fourth.

I was confused for a while on my way over to the field for the dedication. There were new streets everywhere and nothing looked familiar. I finally homed in on the distant beat of the marching band and arrived at the field as the teams and coaches and women's auxiliary paraded onto the outfield. I looked over the pint-sized baseball players in their clean uniforms and brand-new caps. Their gloves were larger than their heads and they lined up on what seemed to me a scale model of a baseball field.

I could smell the hot dogs and hamburgers cooking in the Quonset-hut refreshment stand and I recalled how it had been after a game at the old Little League field, when me and Corney and the rest of the team, wearing oversized caps and our baggy Weisglass Gold Seal Giants uniforms, crowded up to the counter at the small refreshment stand. Corney and I ate our hot dogs and ice cream and drank our sodas before bicycling home. We talked about the game, of course, and Corney always had a lot more to brag about than me. Envious of his skill at baseball, which was the beginning and end of my existence then, I often wished in those days that I could have been Corney.

A podium had been set up for the dedication between home plate and the pitcher's mound. The president of the South Shore Little League stood there and introduced the chaplain from Fort Wadsworth, who opened the ceremonies by praying for God to bless the field and the youngsters who would play here, and to remember in His mercy the soul of Private Cornelius Xavier Walsh, the brave soldier to whom this place was dedicated.

The borough president was on hand, and he gave the first speech. He was an Italian man with thinning hair and a bristled salt-and-pepper mustache. He was short and dumpy and when he had some difficulty bending the microphone down to his mouth one of the men from the league had to run out and set it for him. He started to speak, but then there was a piercing screech of feedback from the loudspeakers and he couldn't be heard. He tapped the microphone and looked around helplessly while several men scrambled up into the "press box" behind home plate and performed some electrical voodoo to correct the problem.

Meanwhile the silent crowd stood patiently in the stands on this breezeless day; the teams and coaches and women's auxiliary were assembled in a grid on the outfield grass. Finally, the borough president spoke. He told us, predictably, that baseball builds character in young men and prepares them for the future. He said that baseball, since it represents all the best things in the American spirit, is far more than a game. He said that Private Walsh had provided us with a clear demonstration of this marvelous power of the game of baseball to build strong and virtuous young men who would carry on the tradition of a great nation. He went on and on like this. Obviously he hadn't known Corney.

It was impossible for me to stand there and not recall the Fourth of July when Corney persuaded me to twist together the fuses of two cherry bombs and toss them into his neighbor's mailbox. He'd always had the ability and charm to do this to me, ever since that thing with the crayons on the hot radiator in kindergarten, suckering me into stunts that promised nothing but trouble.

The mailbox was one of those rural-type mailboxes; it sat on its own post and boasted a little red flag that seemed to have no real purpose. Once we had decided upon the deed, we wasted no time. I twisted the fuses of the cherry bombs together and Corney lit them. The fuses sizzled and sparkled and Corney hurriedly opened the mailbox door. I tossed the cherry bombs inside and then Corney quickly slammed the door closed and we ran.

We'd imagined that the mailbox would give a superior echo when the cherry bombs exploded. We'd never figured the mailbox would be launched. When we saw it shoot into the air, higher than a basketball hoop, and then land on the street, we fell down laughing. We were laughing so hard that we couldn't even run away from the irate man who owned the mailbox and came storming out of his house. He was going to call the cops, but then, looking at Corney, he said, "Oh—it's you," and hauled us over to Corney's yard, where Mr. Walsh was hosting a barbecue. There he made us confess our deed while Mr. Walsh's friends were tossing cherry bombs into the swimming pool and watching the water gush.

The girls around town ignored Corney until he was fifteen or so. Then he became a flagrant alcoholic and all of them, simultaneously, fell deliriously in love with him. They loved him in the way that the girls back then seemed to love any guy bent on self-destruction.

I couldn't figure it out. Several of the girls, except for the fact that they adored Corney and might even have wanted to have his babies, were actually intelligent, besides being attractive. But they weren't as interested in fine manners or boxes of candy or birthday cards as much as they were in saving a guy from certain doom. Hence the reason for many of the stupid things we guys did. We'd go get our faces banged up and our bones broken to bits, we'd run along the wooden cover of the third rail and swing from trees, we'd dive headfirst into shallow water where people dumped shopping carts—just to get the attention of a girl, who, the very next day, might not even remember your name.

There was one gorgeous girl in particular who dated Corney. Her name was Julie Digilio. She was what people called petite. We called her "boss-looking." She dressed in tight slacks or skirts (with foxy dark stockings), and she moved smoothly and danced hot. Her small voice was husky—breathless—and her hair was long and thick. She had large dark eyes that one of the girls who was angry because she couldn't turn Corney's head called "bedroom eyes," as if this made Julie a slut, which she wasn't, though the description of her eyes as "bedroom eyes" made all of the guys even more intensely interested in her. In our opinion she had bedroom breasts and bedroom legs and bedroom ears and even bedroom toes to go along with those beautiful bedroom eyes. I'd seen her once in a tiger-skin bikini down at the Orange House and I had to race into the water to hide the instant erection that bulged my Jantzen's. The water sizzled and smoked around me, and the erection didn't go down for three days. Honest.

Julie had moved to our end of Staten Island from Brooklyn, and she'd made no secret of the fact that she felt she'd been banished to Siberia. She would act very, very bored with us and our town, and whenever she talked about trees or woods or places without concrete and noise, she sneered. Yet we all put up with her. Gladly. The girls even came to like her, imitating her boredom and disdain.

Julie fell for Corney, even though—or because—he was the only one of us not tripping over his feet to get next to her. They started what might be called dating, which in Corney's case meant that he had chosen Julie as the girl he gave the most grief.

There was an incident at one of Carol Dante's parties when Corney got rough with Julie. Carol's parents were wary about her going out at night, and so they allowed her to have fifteen or twenty of us over there in the finished-off basement every Saturday night. We played loud music and danced and made out on the couch until our lips were numb and our tongues permanently knotted together. We smoked cigarettes and secretly drank beer in the adjoining garage, while Carol's parents remained upstairs, blithely unaware of everything we did.

Corney and I drank together on our way to the parties at Carol's house. We drank pints of whiskey or blackberry brandy. We even mixed the two, expecting to survive the ordeal. Corney could do it. Corney could drink creosote. And no matter what he was drinking, he always said, "Bourbon and water, easy on the ice."

I usually couldn't drink a whole lot without feeling sick or dizzy, and when I was stupid enough to drink with Corney I drank too heavily and the world spun out of control. I collapsed and vomited painfully, while Corney maintained his posture and, incredibly, started on another pint, opening it to the tune "Bourbon and water, easy on the ice."

One night in April, when we were seventeen, Corney started to get mean with Julie at one of Carol's parties. He finally pushed her into a wall, and I went over and took him aside and persuaded him to go for a walk. He was drunk, of course, and I'd hoped that the cool night air would sober him a bit. Fat chance. Instead of me walking him, he led the way, and I soon discovered that he had cans of beer and pints of vodka stashed at every conceivable location along the lonely stretch between Carol's house and the train station.

I was angry at him for having pushed Julie, and now that I saw that he couldn't drag himself away from booze I realized he was hopeless and I began not to like him. We stopped beneath the light of a streetlamp, and while he guzzled down a beer I told him that he shouldn't be so rough with girls. He said that I ought to mind my own fud'yan business and told me to leave him alone. So I did.

When I returned to the party I gathered that Julie had been worried about Corney since the moment we'd left. She was actually crying. It didn't make sense. She was the one who had been humiliated and mistreated, yet she was so concerned for Corney that she couldn't be comforted.

Seeing me, she came running across the room and threw her arms around my waist, sobbing, "Oh, Andy, what can I do? I love him so much."

I felt embarrassed, but I managed to put my arms around her trembling shoulders. Her tears dampened the front of my shirt.

"Take me home," she asked, her voice weepy.

We left the party arm in arm. It was wonderful to have her so close, and yet it was also odd and uncomfortable. I found myself feeling sorry for her, even though I couldn't understand her reaction to this guy who had only an hour before shoved her into a wall, and with her so close to me, I was filled with a maddening sexual desire for her.

We walked along the same route I'd taken just a half hour before with Corney, and Julie said, "Corney's really not like this." She wiped tears from her eyes and attempted to explain herself to me. "If people could only see him the way I see him," she said, repeating, "He's really not like this."

I wanted to tell her that I'd known Corney almost as long as I'd known my own mother and father, and that as much as I hated to admit it, Corney really was what he appeared to be. He was a seventeen-year-old drunk hell-bent on destroying himself and anyone else who wandered within his range of fire. But I didn't tell her this because it wasn't what she wanted to hear and she wouldn't have believed a word of it anyway. Besides, even though I could see the truth of the matter, it would hurt me to have to open my mouth and condemn Corney to his fate. To actually speak the words appeared for the moment to have too great a prophetic power.

Throughout the walk to her house, which took a half hour, Julie stayed close to me. The night air had grown colder, and she found me to be warm and comfortable. We walked on and she cuddled into my body and occasionally wrapped both of her small, thin arms around my waist. I certainly had no objections.

"It's so much darker and quieter here than Brooklyn," she said. "And sometimes it's so boring I cry all night."

Her Bay Ridge accent sounded foreign to my ears. It gave her voice a rough edge, a streetwise toughness. Her hair was teased and stiffened by hair spray; she wore mascara and pale pink lipstick. She was like an imperfect diamond: sparkling but slightly clouded by a grit that turned away the light. Almost everything about her excited me, and whatever didn't excite me intrigued me.

She lived in a two-story brick house near the town circle. It was almost midnight when we arrived, but this didn't seem to concern her. She invited me inside and asked me to wait on the front porch, adding, "I'll tell my parents I'm home."

The porch was enclosed, and it was furnished with a couch and two wicker chairs. There was a fish tank at one end and a shelf with plants. Julie hadn't turned on the lights and the porch was only dimly illuminated through the windows by the streetlamps.

I wandered over to the couch and sat down. I listened intently to the quiet interior of the house and, not hearing voices, presumed that Julie's parents were in bed.

Julie returned to the porch and joined me on the couch. She lit a cigarette and smoked pensively. She asked, "Where do you think he's gone?"

"Probably to Dilly's."

"That's the bar?"

"Uh-huh."

"What do you think he's doing there?"

"Drinking beer and shooting pool, I suppose."

"Are there girls there?"

"No. Not even old baggy ladies."

This information seemed to relieve her. She took a series of deep, final drags on her cigarette, and the ember tip glowed like a soldering iron in the shadowy light. She then confessed that she had started the trouble with Corney tonight, implying that he'd been justified in pushing her into the wall. She said she'd given him a hard time because she knew he had been seeing other girls. From the way in which she'd said "seeing" I concluded that Corney was laying all these girls, Julie included, and I grew more than a little envious of him—not to mention angry that these girls not only put up with his bullshit, but treated him kindly in return.

Ironically, Julie chose that moment to move close to me and ask, "Are you his best friend?"

"Sort of," I said, knowing I was closer to Corney than anyone else was.

"Are you pissed at him or what?"

"I think I gave up getting pissed at him," I lied, hoping to appear reasonable.

"Don't give up on him, Andy," she pleaded. "He really doesn't have anyone but us."

With that, she pressed herself into me and stroked my thigh. She stretched her head up and kissed the underside of my chin. I turned my face to meet hers and kissed her. It was delicious.

She snuggled into me and I felt and heard the lacquer in her hair crinkle. I detected a perfume that had escaped me earlier and wondered if she had daubed it on fresh when she'd gone inside. She worked her fingers through my hair and started kissing my earlobe. We exchanged nice sloppy wet kisses and began grinding into each other. I tried to get her to lie down but she pushed herself gently away, whispering, "I'll be right back."

She disappeared into the house, leaving me so immensely hungry for her I was actually trembling. I had such a hard, pulsing erection I was sure it would burst like a foamy fire extinguisher and drench my pants and then dry up and weld my legs together at the crotch before Julie returned. I reached into my back pocket and took out my wallet. I checked to see if the one and only condom I owned was still there, knowing damn well it would be. It had been there so long that it had pressed a circle into the wallet leather. I took the condom out and said, "Tonight's your big night," and slipped it into my pants pocket for convenience.

Julie returned wearing a long red robe that trailed on the floor. Judging by its smoothness and the way in which it played with the stray light and crackled with static electricity it must have been silk or satin. She sat down the couch alongside me and the robe parted, revealing her sweet bare thigh. Then the robe closed and her leg disappeared smoothly behind the soft folds of the garment. It had been only a glimpse, but I realized in that moment that she was wearing only panties. I responded to this tantalizing moment with the most stupid reaction of my life. I stood up and said, "Well, you look ready for bed. I guess I'll be going."

She furrowed her brows. *"Going?"*

"Well, I thought . . . I figured you, er . . . y'know, were ready for bed."

She paused. "Ain't you ever been with a girl before?"

I didn't know what, exactly, she meant by this, and I didn't know how to ask what she meant without appearing stupid, so I said, "Yeah. I've been with girls."

"So?"

I sat back down alongside her. I patted the condom in my pocket and wondered how I'd go about getting it on, wishing I'd done it while she'd been inside.

In the next moment, we flung ourselves together. She wrapped both her legs around my one leg and clung to me like a vine. She darted her snake-like tongue into my mouth and searched for my missing tonsils. Then she nibbled my ear with her sharp teeth and called me "Baby" while rubbing and humping my body to a waxed shine.

I tried to turn her over so I could get atop her, but she didn't want that. She unzipped my fly and pulled out my pecker, stroking it and speaking of it in glowing terms. I tried to tell her I had a bag and why don't I take a moment here and slip into something a little less comfortable so's we could—

There was this crash. I didn't know what to think. Julie, who was delirious for me, hadn't heard a thing. She moaned delightedly, yanking on my dick like it was a prize toy.

Then there was another crash. Broken glass.

I ejaculated. Semen spit into the air. I was coming all over her hand just as another window was broken. We were under attack. I suddenly put it all together. Someone was outside, pelting the porch windows with rocks. And it didn't take a genius to figure out who.

That little shithead! That *fud'yan* shithead!

A rock that had sailed through a window struck the fish tank and bounced off. Water began to trickle from the tank onto the floor.

There was noise from within the house. A rumbling, door-crashing noise. Mr. Digilio, a burly New York City fireman who had reportedly punched his car and dented it one winter morning when it wouldn't start, came barreling down the stairs. He hit the light switch and the porch was bright as an interrogation room. He stood there, breathing hard, wearing only a strap undershirt and boxer shorts, looking hairy and mean as a werewolf.

A stone crashed through a window, struck the opposite wall, rolled back across the floor.

"What the hell's going on?" he demanded. "I'm gonna kill some son of a bitch."

Mr. Digilio, seeing me, of course immediately associated me with this madness and growled, "Who are you? What are you doing here?"

I'd had just enough time to shove my dick back into my pants, hiding this now-little piece of evidence, but I'd not been quick enough to also zipper up my fly, and I was certain that Mr. Digilio would see this and then, surely, I'd be the son of a bitch who would be killed. There would be no questions asked. The cops and the firemen had a pact. Any son of a bitch found with his fly open in the presence of one of their daughters was to die.

Extending my hand to shake his, I said, "I'm a friend of Julie's. My name is Andrew Hapanowicz."

He was so unprepared for my response that he might have acceded to this peace proposal, except that another stone came sailing through the air, breaking yet another porch window on its way to breaking a window in the wall before landing in the living room.

We all ducked into the front hall. Mrs. Digilio had appeared at the foot of the stairs. Her husband told her to phone the cops. Then he stared outside and said, "I can't even see him. Where the hell is he?"

"Probably over in the woods there," I answered, pointing.

"He's throwing from *there?*" asked Mr. Digilio with great doubt in his voice.

Stupidly, I pointed out, "He's good. He threw two no-hitters."

Mr. Digilio suddenly recalled that I didn't belong in his house. He glowered at me and pointed to the front door. "You," he said. "Don't let me see your face around here no more."

"Daddy," began Julie.

"And you," he said firmly. "Go to your room."

He led me to the porch, and right there on the floor, in the path of exit, was the packaged condom. Mr. Digilio noticed it and said, "What's this?"

"Hmm . . . must've fallen out of someone's pocket."

Mr. Digilio squeezed my arm and it gave way like a thin balloon.

"Take that fuckin' thing with you," he whispered harshly in my ear. "You come around again with this bullshit, your cock's gonna fall outta your pocket."

I nodded in firm agreement. I wanted there to be no misunderstandings.

As I left the house, a prowl car appeared, cruising the street with its sirens mute and its bubble-gum dome twirling blades of red light. I heard Mr. Digilio call out to the cops, telling them that some kid in the woods was throwing stones at his house. The cops didn't get very excited. They knew how useless it was to chase kids through the woods. When Mr. Digilio noticed that the cops weren't in a hurry, he said, "Yo, I'm on the job too," which is a code between cops and firemen. The cops said, "Hey, it's like chasin' Robin Hood, y'know?" But they drove close to the woods anyway and scanned the darkness with their spotlight.

I slipped down someone's driveway, climbed a rail fence, and entered the woods. I started home, and it wasn't long before Corney emerged from the brush. He cackled at me and asked, "Didja fuck her, Chun?"

"I would have if it wasn't for you, you prick."

"That am woo-fud'yan-shit. She am a cock-teaser. I bet she played with your dick and told you it was the best one in town."

"Got to hell, Corney," I said, trying to lose him.

He pulled a pint of Tango screwdriver from his back pocket and drank from it, saying, "Bourbon and water. Easy on the ice."

He never seemed to get enough. "Bourbon and water," he'd say, though he never, as far as I knew, drank bourbon.

He soon started bringing booze to school. He swiped a syringe from a diabetic aunt and filled oranges with vodka. He spiked cans of Coke with rum. He soaked his Twinkies in brandy.

He was finally kicked out of school for drunkenness and then tried to work construction with Mr. Spyropoulos, but he couldn't show up on time and was never sober.

For some reason, his wheezing faded and then disappeared. His luck at winning ran out also. The army drafted him. Either they didn't notice he was an alcoholic or didn't care. They needed cannon fodder.

He was five days short in Nam when a grenade from a launcher busted him open. Five days.

Everyone applauded when the borough president finished his speech. Then the league president stepped up to the podium and read a telegram from the local congressman, who had sent his apologies for not being able to attend the ceremony. I was certain that the congressman would have shown if Dietz had been there. He wouldn't have missed the opportunity to have his picture taken with a hero.

Finally the color guard prepared to raise the flag. They were the genuine article: four spit-and-polish soldiers from Fort Wadsworth who must have practiced this routine in their sleep. The soldiers on the outside each carried a rifle. One soldier of the inside pair carried the U.S. flag, and the other of this pair carried what I presumed to be the colors of Corney's regiment. This flag was eventually folded and presented to Mr. and Mrs. Walsh, just as the triangularly folded American flag had been presented to them at Corney's funeral. Mrs. Walsh was wearing sunglasses today because she'd been crying. Mr. Walsh was wearing sunglasses because the sun burned his bloodshot eyes.

With much ceremony and perfectly coordinated movements, the color guard marched to the flagpole in centerfield. There, above the scoreboard, a big sign identified this place as the Pvt. Cornelius X. Walsh Memorial Little League Field. The soldiers halted and stood like stone figures at present arms, while the flag was raised and "The Star Spangled Banner" escaped in loud wobbled phrases from the shaky public address system. When the flag reached the top of the pole the two soldiers on the wings raised their rifles and fired into the air. The crowd cheered but the flag drooped listlessly in the becalmed air.

Everyone marched off the field. The podium was lifted away, the foul lines were limed, and the batting orders were exchanged. The umpires conferred. The home team took the field to rousing cheers. They warmed up: grounders in the infield, soft-tossed flies in the outfield. The pitcher used a brand-new white ball as he wound up and showed the catcher his stuff.

Then the warm-ups were over. The batter stepped to the plate, settling himself in the geometrically perfect still-white outlines of the box. The umpire lowered his mask and pointed to the pitcher, calling out, "Play ball!"

I had noticed that Father Lusenkas was just outside the entrance to the field with a small group of people, some of whom identified themselves as Quakers, and others who were nondenominational conscientious objectors and pacifists. Mrs. Murtagh stood there with this group, and as usual she looked simply beautiful, though today, seeing her assembled with this group of protesters, I seemed to be able to look more deeply into her. I suddenly realized that she was probably a strong person, committed enough to her beliefs to expose them to the light of day for others to see—and perhaps condemn. I began to have feelings for her that were different and somehow more firm and basic than my infatuation over her violet eyes and thick brown hair. It surprised me. Not her presence or her dedication to her ideals. It surprised me whenever my feelings changed. Sometimes it was a pleasant change, like the first breeze of spring after a biting cold winter, and other times it was shocking and unpleasant, like the ocean water in March that Easter—or like learning things about Dietz and Corney that had made being buddies not so simple.

The group that Eileen Murtagh and Father Lusenkas were with had choosen this occasion to hand out antiwar leaflets. This angered many people. They felt that the Fourth of July was sacrosanct and that to protest a war on this day was unpatriotic. A broad-shouldered man who wore a baseball cap with the name and logo of a local fuel-oil company demanded that they leave. He had made his demand of the crowd in general, but it was he and Eileen who ended up nose to nose, arguing. I'd never expected to see her so angry. She refused to be backed down, even though the man was taller than her by a foot and wide enough to throw a full shadow over her.

"You got some nerve coming here and handing out this crap!" the man protested. "It's the Fourth of July and this kid died fighting for his country. You and the rest of these traitors say that we oughta turn tail and run. Don't it mean anything that this kid died?"

Eileen said, "We're here because we care about wasted lives. We're here because we care about the living. We don't want more and more young boys to die for a meaningless cause."

"Let me tell you something." The man leveled his finger at her. "I fought in World War Two. If you'd tried this bullshit back then, you'd've been hung. Whyn't you go defend your country instead of knocking it? Whyn't you leave decent people to honor the memory of the boys who died for us?"

"Because if I do, others will die."

During the course of this argument, I noticed how Father Lusenkas continually glanced over at Eileen. I thought he was preparing to
step in, should the argument become too heated. But soon enough I
realized that he was only keeping track of the situation out of curiosity. Eileen Murtagh was on her own, as I suspected she wanted to be.

The man finally stomped off, grumbling and looking back over his
shoulder.

Then Eileen saw me. Before she had even said hello she thrust a
stack of leaflets into my hands. I felt trapped. I really didn't want to be
involved with this, but I wasn't very good at turning her down.

"We got his attention, didn't we?" she asked, meaning the angry
man.

"Yeah."

"That's what we're here for," she added.

I stood there, uncomfortably, and handed out the leaflets, hoping
Eileen and Father Lusenkas and the others would take most of the
heat from the crowd.

I watched people take the leaflets from me and then watched as
they threw them to the ground. Many of them turned to glare at me. I
could see that they hated and feared me. I wondered what it was that
bothered them so. I supposed I threatened them. I supposed I represented something they didn't want to deal with. They probably had
sons fighting over there. Or sons buried over here. Or missing sons.
And here I was, long hair and all, telling them it was wrong.

But it *was* wrong, the war, and I asked myself if these people really
thought the war was right, or if they were simply afraid to admit it was
wrong, afraid to admit their own powerlessness over war and peace
and the lives of the ones they loved.

I felt the controversy sharply, and I didn't enjoy it. I was confused
enough about the war without telling others what was right and what
was wrong. I didn't feel I could be very vocal about peace when one
friend had died and another was missing. I felt I was betraying them.
Yet I couldn't agree with the fighting. I couldn't say it was right. And
because of my missing eye, I'd never be forced to decide. I'd never be
pushed to the wall, I'd never have to make a stand.

As soon as my small batch of leaflets was gone, feeling lost and
confused on a perfect Fourth of July day at a Little League field in a
hometown that had been transmogrified, I slipped away.

4

I double-checked all the doors and made sure that the compressor was off; I stuffed the cash from the register into the canvas money roll and slid the roll into the safe behind the accessories rack. The safe was shaped like a big pipe, and the weighty lock that went on from below capped it and closed with a distinctive click. The business day was over. Pete would make no more money until tomorrow.

I made certain to leave the cash register drawer open, the way Pete had insisted, so that anyone who came poking around could look in the plate-glass window and see for himself that there was no cash to be had.

Then Pete arrived, just after the cash was stowed away and before I was ready to hit the circuit breaker and douse the big lights out front. As usual I was prepared to disobey him by leaving the light above the Pegasus burning. He would bawl me out for it and tell me never to do it again, but I would do it again tomorrow. I wanted this votive light to brighten the night.

Madeleine wasn't with him, and I thought the two might have had a fight and that Pete had returned to slip into his coveralls and relieve his frustrations by taking a hammer to a perfectly good muffler.

I noticed that there was a heaviness to his walk, and it was this that convinced me he'd had a disagreement with Madeleine—or had lost his business at the trotters. His feisty manner had abandoned him. He was not the same man who, earlier, had confidently streamed out of here behind the wheel of that big Chrysler. Even the clothes, which had seemed so bold and outlandish, now appeared wrinkled and worn, lacking in color. He was a bullfrog again; a would-be dandy in hand-me-downs.

I waited for him at the door. He didn't raise his head as he came through the shadows. I had never seen him so quiet and solemn. I had never seen him so emptied of anger.

He finally looked up at me and grunted, saying, "Open late."

"A couple minutes. Yeah."

"Make a few extra pennies for me, did you?"

"Yeah—a few."

"Good," he said distractedly. "Good."

He walked into the office, and I followed him. He glanced around and then looked out at the illuminated Pegasus. He said nothing. There was a newspaper under his arm, which at first I had mistaken for a racing sheet. He tossed the paper onto the desk and said, "Left the track early. I just dropped Madeleine off."

I nodded. I'd never heard him call her Madeleine. I wondered what the problem was, and I imagined how strange it would be for him to ask me for romantic advice. I knew that was absurd, though. There was something he wanted to tell me. I could see it when he forced himself to look at me directly. He glanced at the newspaper and then looked at me again, and what I could gather from that gesture made me nervous. I began to feel weak behind the knees. I knew what was coming now. I just knew it, and I fervently wished that the little boy along the continuum who had been selling yesterday's and tomorrow's newspapers to the Paymaster could have sold one to Pete. Anything other than today's news was bearable. But it was today's newspaper that Pete had brought with him when he returned early from the track, and it was today's news I'd have to bear.

"Page three," he said. "Maybe you'd better read it."

Chapter 12

1

Jimmy had led a patrol into a Vietcong sanctuary in the Iron Triangle. The objective of the mission and its precise location were classified. The only solid information was that the patrol, which had been in the field for two weeks, had been out of contact for the past five days. They were now "feared missing in combat."

I didn't know how to take the news. It didn't say he was dead. It didn't even really say the patrol was missing. *Feared* missing wasn't missing. And since I had always been confident in Jimmy's ability to overcome adversity, to conquer circumstance, it seemed traitorous of me to think he was lost and helpless.

When I'd first read the news I should have thrown out my chest and cast the newspaper into the trash and said, "Who are they kidding? They're talking about Dietz. Jimmy fuckin' Dietz! *Missing,* they say? Missing? Not unless he wants to be."

After Pete left me alone in the office and I read the news I should have locked the door on my way out and strode confidently across the lot, coming to Pete to punch his arm and boast, "Looks like Jimmy's got them guessing again, eh?"

Instead, having turned out the office light and closed the door, I took a long moment to tug on the handle to make sure it was locked. Then I walked numbly across the lot and returned the newspaper to Pete, saying, "Here you go. Thanks."

He said nothing.

"Wait and see, I guess," I said.

"Yeah."

The light above the Pegasus flickered as if to go out. It sparked again, but one of the bank of bulbs went dark.

"You left it on," said Pete, noticing the light.

"Yeah."

"You ain't supposed to do that."

"I know."

Missing, I repeated in my head, trying to get it to mean something else. Missing, missing, missing, missing—it could mean anything.

"Want a lift?" asked Pete. "Maybe get a drink at Hanson's?"

"Yeah," I said. "Yeah. Good idea."

We climbed into the Chrysler and drove silently to Hanson's. We went inside for a few beers. There was a baseball game on the television. I had no idea who was playing and couldn't have cared less. Alongside me the bowling-pin game clanged and the lights rolled and flashed; there were conversations up and down the bar. The cigarette smoke was so thick it began to turn solid. I had to get away. I had to leave.

"I'm going," I soon told Pete. "See you in the morning. Maybe."

"You okay?"

"I might go," I said. "Back west."

Pete hesitated, then said, "You've got money comin' to you. Don't leave without it."

I walked along Amboy Road and then followed Arbutus Avenue toward the old Orange House. Hanson's was a mile or two from the bungalow, and it was a good night for a walk. There was a cool breeze off the water and the sky was overcast. The moon was visible, and at three-quarters appeared like a ball that had become stuck in the sky above the ocean. The stars were hidden in the haze. Missing.

I reached the bungalow and decided I was through with waiting around for Jimmy, through with waiting for the Paymaster—what a scam, really—through with Staten Island. I should never have returned. What a mistake that had been!

I wanted out. Pete owed me two or three days' pay but I didn't want to wait around for it. I had two work outfits I would keep, one bearing the name "Louie" and the other, ironically, "Pete." That was a fair exchange. And even if it wasn't, I didn't care. I just wanted to go.

I stuffed my clothes into my duffel and rolled tight my sleeping bag. I took a handful of books and left the others behind. I had to adopt a pioneer's philosophy of sparseness. I would take only what I could carry. It wasn't as bad a proposition as it seemed. We all entered the world with nothing more than little naked bodies, and I'd always found these belongings that we gathered along the way to be burdensome. People held up banks to get money for this shit and then used it to fill superdumps. What a waste. What a goddam waste.

I didn't know what to do with the shotgun. I wished now I had never taken it from Deluxe, for by doing so I'd more or less vowed to wait through hell and high water for Dietz.

I held the shotgun in my hand and thought, Well, where the fuck was Dietz the night those bastards bashed my fuckin' eyeball? I mean, goddam Dietz, the mighty fuckin' Jimmy Dietz, king of the barroom brawl, undefeated champion of the street fight. Dietz the Merciless. Dietz the Powerful. Dietz the Avenger. Where the fuck was he when they did my ass in? It was him they were after, not me. It was the guy with the shotgun they'd wanted, and Ivers had set me up nicely to take the fall for Dietz.

I started to hate Dietz all over again. It was his fault I'd lost my eye. He just hadn't known when to stop kicking ass.

Carrying the shotgun and my stuffed sleeping bag in one arm, I dragged my duffel behind me and went down onto the beach.

I could see the pilings. They appeared as sticks in the shimmering swath of light cast by the moon. I thought of swimming out there and throwing the shotgun into the ocean. A fitting burial for all weapons.

Instead I sat down on the edge of a block of concrete that had once been the floor of the Orange House and felt, suddenly, that I would cry. But I could find no tears, only a wrenching sense of sadness and betrayal.

You don't aim a shotgun, Chun. You point it. It's not a rifle.

I pointed the shotgun at the moon.

Blam! I imagined.

The moon fell from the sky and hit the water without a splash. Illusions are that way.

I needed only to dispose of the shotgun and I could leave for Oregon. I would catch some sleep on the ferry and then take a subway to the Port Authority Terminal. From there I'd take a bus to Jersey and start hitching rides.

But I had no idea what to do with the damned shotgun, and I was suddenly angry that it had this power to hold me here when otherwise I had made up my mind to shake the dust of this place. I wasn't willing to swim with it out to the pilings. Even if I could overcome my fear of being alone in the water at night, I was so protective of the shotgun I couldn't bear the thought of getting a drop of water on it. I wouldn't even lay it down on the beach in front of me, imagining that it could be wounded by a grain of sand. So I sat with it cradled in my lap and admired how the moon buffed the barrel with a waxen light, while I tried to figure out what to do with this burden of Dietz's.

Silent now, the snorting fiery barrel had exploded angrily that night when Deluxe, behind the wheel of a stolen 1957 Mercury, took the corner with the tires squealing. Ivers was at his side. Dietz was in the backseat with me, and he pulled the shotgun from beneath an old blanket and pointed it out the rear window.

Hey, that's the shotgun, Dietz!

We were down in Midland Beach and there were a bunch of guys on the corner in front of a magazine store. Dietz and Ivers had been talking about getting revenge for the fight at the football game, and I could see what was going to happen.

"What the hell are you guys doing?" I blurted. "Dietz—what the fuck's the idea?"

Ivers snarled and pointed his finger at me like a gun. "Not a fuckin' word—*Chun.*"

Just then the shotgun shattered the air and rang the car like a bell. Ivers grinned with satisfaction. Deluxe yahoo'd and floored the gas pedal; the car lurched, speeding away. The acrid odor of gunpowder peppered the air and made it unbreathable.

I craned my neck to see what had happened on the corner. Two of the guys were on the ground. The plate-glass window of the store was shattered.

Dietz glanced at me and said, "No one's dead, not at this range with the choke open. Just a little birdshot. You can't let them do you shit, Chun, and get away with it—understand?"

"No. No, I don't understand. You suckered me into this. Why? Why the fuck did you do that?"

Deluxe jammed on the brakes. I had to brace my arm against the back of the front seat to stop myself from falling forward.

"You want to get out, Chun?" asked Deluxe.

"Yeah, Chun," said Ivers. "Whyn't you get out and walk? I'm sure if you get lost those guys will help you."

Dietz told Deluxe, "Let's go." Then he turned to me and said, "Relax. They started it, not us."

Beneath this near-full moon at the old Orange House beach the small waves broke onto the shore weakly. Even the sound of their arrival was weak, a faint purling. If the sea instead was enraged and the waves crashed the shore, if the winds were whipped and twisted by a hurricane, tossing up stinging grains of sand and driving sprays of sea, I might have been able to cast the shotgun into the water. But I had no desire to hurl the shotgun into these weak waves and soft breezes, knowing they would be unable to absorb its power.

The shotgun had actually been mine, I suppose you could say, before it had been Jimmy's. There had been this terrifically hot Saturday in August, the second summer after we'd built the cabin, when Jimmy arranged a job for us at the rod and gun club picnic. We rose early that day and double-timed to the cabin, even taking the WPA roads to cut the distance. We carried our bows unstrung, which was unusual. Jimmy generally preferred to be ready to let an arrow fly.

At the cabin we lifted back the wide flat stone that covered our food cache. We took out six eggs and a jar of instant coffee. There was a hunk of cheese that we decided was edible even though it had a fuzzed fringe of whitish mold.

We threw together a cooking fire and boiled water for coffee. We drank the coffee black and sugary and tossed the eggs and cheese into a big cast-iron frying pan and then ate this omelette while the eggs were still drippy. When we finished we wiped our chins and drank more coffee. We each smoked a cigarette and then hid our bows and returned the instant coffee to the cache. We left water in the frying pan to soak loose the now crusty eggs, and when we drowned the fire the bed of embers hissed and smoked thickly.

We crawled out through the brambles, and once on the outside we turned, as we always seemed to turn, to look back at the wall of brambles. It was impossible to see the cabin. There was no better-kept secret. Until the winter night Iron Jud had happened upon Jimmy and me out here, the only people ever to see the cabin were the guys who had built it.

We took off for the rod and gun club at a jog. The cabin path to Big Trees; Big Trees to the lonely store on Woodrow Road; then over the golf course path—across the fairway at the fifteenth hole, then to the green at the seventh hole to leave sneaker prints on its moist crewcut surface. A new path followed—when had Jimmy found this one?— through the Sandy Grounds, where sad and miserably poor colored people raised hogs and tended withered gardens in the grainy soil; then to the flat land near Fresh Kills—the dump.

We walked from there, emerging at the landfill gates onto Arthur Kill Road, where we managed to grab a quick ride from one of the older guys we knew. He drove us a short distance and then we walked at Jimmy's fast pace, arriving at the picnic grounds just before nine o'clock. It was already hot and unbearably humid.

Jimmy made sure to remind me that he would do the talking, which meant that I should refrain from saying certain things, such as that we had never bagged game with our bows; that Jimmy was going to be a priest (which was no longer really true that I could see anyway); that he could quote Shakespeare; that he had won a math contest.

Jimmy asked around for someone named Ray, whom we eventually found at the food tent. Ray was a hefty man with ears as big as cabbage leaves and a wrestler's chest. His neck was thick and sturdy as a steer's. He told us that three hundred people were expected today. There was no time to waste, he added, and he put us to work right away unloading bags of charcoal, cases of soda, and boxes of frozen hamburgers and hot dogs. We worked steadily, and when we finished Ray sat us in a corner of the tent and showed us a mountain of corn that had to be shucked.

We were still at the corn when the picnickers began trickling onto the grounds. Ray fired up the large charcoal grill and told me and Jimmy that we would be in charge of the counter.

"It's all you can eat for the price of admission," he said, as if warning us. "You know how people are when it comes to food they think they don't pay for. They'll eat till they're sick."

He remarked that in another hour, when the people would be three-deep at the counter, Jimmy and I would have to fling food at them if we expected to avoid a riot.

"And it's goin' to get hotter'n the boiler of a battleship in this tent today. Don't go passin' out on me. If you need salt tablets, speak up."

He grinned devilishly at this, then added, "I wouldn't be surprised if we didn't make our own thunderstorm," pointing up at the inside roof of the tent where the steam from the big corn kettle had condensed and was dripping back down. "Pretty soon here you two won't have enough time to bend down and tie your shoes." He slapped a half-dozen hamburgers on the grill. "So grab a couple of sodas and some burgers and eat while you can. Then brace your balls for the crowd."

For the next hour or so it wasn't anywhere near as wild as Ray had predicted. He cooked the food while Jimmy and I served it. We had the opportunity to lounge a bit and wipe the counter and watch the pretty girls drift past. The public address system came to life and scratchy music emerged, mostly the songs that older people enjoyed and could be heard to sing off-key after a few beers. There was a horseshoe pit nearby, and although I could hear the ring of the horseshoes all I could see of them was the occasional arc of one against the fuzzy humid sky. Down at the corner of the counter a clutch of men had gathered to drink beer in large plastic cups and swap lively tales about hunting and fishing. Jimmy listened closely.

People came through the gates in steadily increasing numbers. The picnic tables, which had seemed so plentiful this morning, were soon all taken. Newcomers were forced to lay a blanket or tablecloth on the grassy spots under the trees. Later, when these locations disappeared, there was no recourse for people but to stake out a patch of ground at the edge of the dry and dusty ballfield.

The food tent was the hottest place on earth that afternoon. Ray stood at the grill with ranks and files of hot dogs and hamburgers sizzling before him. His face was red; sweat beaded his forehead and oozed from his thick flabby neck. His T-shirt was soaked clear through, and it pressed against his chest and showed his hairs like soaked steel wool. When the fat of the hamburgers dripped into the charcoal bed and suddenly caught on fire, the flames leaped at him and singed his forearm hairs. He quickly doused them with water from a milk bottle he kept close at hand. "There, you nasty bastard," he said, "drink that." Then he looked over at us and said, "This place is hotter'n a camel driver's business end."

We agreed, for all we knew about a camel driver's business end.

The pace quickened. The crowd was larger and hungrier. The day was hotter and the grill pulsed at our backs.

When things were in full swing it was all we could do to keep up. The people were three-deep and hungry. When a person in the back pushed too hard to get up front or hollered out of turn, Ray took quick action. He brandished the long double-prong fork he used to spear the hot dogs, advising the crowd sternly that there was plenty of food to go around. "No one's going to leave here hungry. If you do, I'll take you to my house and feed you myself."

People marveled at how quick and smooth Jimmy and I could work with hardly a word passing between us. When the pace was at its peak we didn't even need eye contact to know what the other was doing or where he was or what he needed. When someone in the crowd shouted an order, I didn't have to repeat it to Jimmy. I merely turned, and Jimmy, who had snatched the food from the grill, handed me a paper plate with exactly what I needed. I took the plate and turned smoothly and handed it across the counter. Then I grabbed the next order or one by one caught the wet, chilled cans of soda that Jimmy tossed from the large Coca-Cola cooler. The two of us moved like dancers who practiced together endlessly, not missing a beat, always synchronous.

Meanwhile the knot of men at the corner dealt hands of blackjack, and when they became loud or their language was raw, Ray reminded them that this was a family picnic.

They rambled on good-naturedly about the Beaver Kill—a trout stream upstate somewhere—and they compared various rifles and fishing techniques and canoes. They talked about outboard motors and knuckle cuts of venison, shotguns and drinking bouts, and they guffawed in unison over a loose woman named Bluebird.

They bantered with Jimmy, calling him Red, until he asked them not to, telling them his name was Jimmy. They did what he asked, because even though some of these men were old enough to be his father they strove for his approval. I had seen other men do this, many times. It was remarkable how eager they were to have Jimmy look up to them. They felt it was important. I recall how a man came up to us out of the crowd at the beach one day and told Jimmy about his son who had died in the Korean War. The man talked on and on about his dead son, telling Jimmy how much he reminded him of his son. He said that he still had his son's car in the garage—a 1949 DeSoto— and it was in mint condition. He told Jimmy he was welcome to come to his house for a look at the car anytime he wanted.

The men at the corner of the counter gambled not only at cards but also at horseshoes, the three-legged race, the egg toss, and just about everything else. They set odds on the turkey shoot, and I heard them bet that Jimmy wouldn't drop a can of soda all day long, but that the little fart would drop at least three. Bastards.

"C'mere," one of the men said, motioning to Jimmy.

Jimmy glanced at me. I nodded, saying, "I can handle it," meaning the counter.

"See this here?" the man asked Jimmy, producing a dark-blue numbered raffle ticket. "You know what that's for, don't you?"

Jimmy nodded and said, "The shotgun."

The man seemed not to hear and continued talking, asking Jimmy, "You know what the grand prize is, don't you?"

The man indicated the words on the ticket as if Jimmy needed help reading English.

Jimmy didn't need to see the words. He knew what the grand prize was. He had been dreaming about it for weeks.

"An Ithaca Model 37 slide-action with a variable choke," said Jimmy. "Twenty-gauge."

"You bet," replied the man. "And she's a beauty, a real beauty. They got her down there on the trophy table. She shines like a new baby's ass."

The man turned the raffle ticket in his hands. It was obvious that he intended to give it to Jimmy. He delighted in Jimmy's knowledge of the value of the shotgun and knew that Jimmy would appreciate this prize.

Finally the man pushed the ticket across the counter to Jimmy, but Jimmy was reluctant to take it. He was never easy about taking something he hadn't earned.

The man laughed kindly. "It's yours," he told Jimmy.

"I can't pay for it until later."

"You don't have to pay—it's a gift."

Jimmy took the ticket and thanked the man, asking his name.

"Phil Cooper," said the man.

"Thank you, Mr. Cooper."

Jimmy studied the raffle ticket, and then looked up at the man and thanked him again.

Immediately a new competition arose among the men at the corner. They'd been drinking and gambling for hours, and when they saw what Pete Cooper had done they didn't want to appear to be pikers, so they too purchased raffle tickets for Jimmy. To assure that there would be no mistaking the winning ticket, each of them wrote his name on the back of the ticket he bought.

They bet on which ticket would win—each man backing his own, of course—and told Jimmy that the pot was his no matter who won.

"You'll have a new shotgun and money to buy shells," one of the men predicted.

Then another man, up to his eyeballs in beer, slurred something about knowing the chairman of the raffle committee, and he staggered out into the bright sun bragging he would go fix the contest for Jimmy.

Jimmy and I had a chance to grab a few hamburgers and some corn on the cob. We sat on the ground and leaned back against the refrigerator. Jimmy took a big bite from his burger and fanned out the raffle tickets. He chewed and swallowed his food, studying the tickets.

"Wouldn't it be great, Chun?"

He felt closer and closer to that shotgun. The men at the corner had succeeded in convincing him of his luck. He had become certain he would win it.

"Yeah," I answered. "It would be something, all right."

He pointed out the tickets, asking, "Which one do you think will win?"

I looked at the tickets and I had this strange feeling that I could actually see a short distance into the future. I could see enough to know that none of these tickets would win. The winning ticket had yet to be bought.

"I don't know," I observed diplomatically. "I'm not sure."

"Take a guess, Chun. If you guess right, I'll split the pot with you."

He had become absolutely sure he would win the Ithaca. In his mind no one else stood a chance.

"I don't know," I repeated.

He frowned at me. "What's with you?"

"What d'you mean?"

"I think you're envious."

"Hey—I don't want the shotgun. What would I do with a shot-gun?"

"Maybe you don't want it, maybe you do. No one bought a ticket for you. That's bothering you."

"Not so much."

"Then pick one."

I could see he wouldn't let me rest until I did what he wanted. "That one," I said. "The one with the three sevens." (It didn't stand a chance.)

Jimmy took the ticket I had chosen and put it aside as if I had actually charmed it.

The men continued to drink beer and play cards. Even though Ray had warned them earlier about putting their blackjack money on the counter, there were coins slung in every direction and dollar bills drenched in shallow pools of spilled beer.

The demand for food slackened, and Jimmy ran off on an errand for Ray. The man on the PA announced the final opportunity to buy raffle tickets. I was still convinced that the winning ticket had not yet been purchased, and I was even more convinced that I was the one destined to buy it. I was as certain of this as I was that I was standing on the earth.

I reached into my pocket and pulled out my money. I had fifty-five cents. Not enough. I needed a dollar for a ticket.

"Sale of raffle tickets will end in five minutes," squawked the loud-speaker. "Get on down to the shooting range for your ticket and come watch the lucky winner walk off with this fine shotgun."

My heart was pounding heavily. I knew Jimmy wouldn't approve my plan, but it was the only way to win that shotgun for him. He had this hard and fast rule that we never asked for an advance on our pay. If we thought we would need money during a job, to buy lunch or cigarettes, we should bring the money along—or do without.

I looked over at Ray. He was drenched with sweat. His white apron was stained by old brown blood. His red-jowled face hung tiredly on his thick neck and heavy shoulders. A token few hot dogs and hamburgers sizzled lazily on the fire. The charcoal bed glowed weakly. Ray leaned back and looked around casually. He had, at long last, an opportunity to relax. He raised a large glass of beer to his mouth, and it disappeared down his throat like water down a drain.

"Ray," I called over. "I need a dollar."

He just looked at me. For a moment I thought that maybe, with Jimmy gone, he had no idea who I was or why I was here.

"From my pay," I went on. "If you could."

He balked. "What for?"

"A raffle ticket." No lie.

I could have clarified matters; I could have explained that it was a raffle ticket for Jimmy, knowing that to take such an approach would have been a clever way to get the dollar. But I wanted to get the ticket on my own. I wanted it to be my ticket.

Ray considered the situation. I couldn't understand why he just didn't give me the dollar. According to what Jimmy had arranged, I would be earning ten dollars today, maybe more. What was the big deal over a dollar?

Even though Ray hadn't bought a ticket for Jimmy, maybe he didn't want anyone other than Jimmy to win the shotgun. It wouldn't surprise me. Obviously the others were willing to go to the wall to see to it that Jimmy walked out of here with that shotgun. What they didn't realize was that they were on a hopeless quest. I would buy the winning ticket, no one else.

"Not even a dollar, Ray," I explained, showing him my two quarters and nickel. "Just forty-five cents."

Phil Cooper had been listening, and he told me. "Hey, don't get all excited, kid. The tickets are gone by now. Besides, you don't want to hurt your friend's chances, do you?"

"They're not all sold," I answered. I looked at Ray. "Well?"

"I guess—" began Ray.

"I deserve a chance to win, don't I?"

"All right," agreed Ray. He reached into his pocket and took out a roll of bills. "Here's a dollar."

I grabbed the dollar and immediately ducked under the counter and hurried off. Ray called after me, "Where are you going? Hey! Come back here!"

Where did he *think* I was going?

I turned around as I ran, calling back, "To buy a ticket."

I had no choice in this. The winning ticket beckoned. I raced head-long between the picnic tables in the direction of the shooting range, the dollar in hand, streaking past the picknickers and stepping on at least a few plates of food. I felt I could run at light speed and disappear into tomorrow, but I knew I had to be here today, buying the shotgun ticket. I arrived at the trophy table just in time. The drawing was about to take place. Quickly I borrowed a ballpoint pen from a man who sat at the raffle drum. I wrote "Chun" on the back of my ticket and hurried back to Ray's stand.

Jimmy had also returned. When he saw me he asked, "Where'd you go?"

"Into the future a bit."

He looked at me the way he always looked at me when he thought I was being screwy, brushing aside my remark.

The PA man announced the big moment. I edged close to Jimmy, who stood over near his benefactors. He had taken out his tickets, holding them in one hand. His other hand hung at his side, and from behind I pressed my ticket into his palm as the man on the PA read off the winning number.

2

I wrapped the Ithaca Model 37 slide-action in the canvas and stuffed it in my duffel. The mosquitoes had suddenly come to life on the beach and were sucking me pale and bloodless.

I would leave for Port Authority at this ungodly hour, packing a shotgun, and woe betide the crazy bastard who tried to mug me. As if—even if I had shells—I'd use the shotgun. I hated the noise and the feel of the weapon. I hated having it with me.

I left the beach and waited for a bus on Hylan Boulevard, knowing how infrequently they traveled this late at night. But I was in no hurry. Oregon wasn't going anywhere.

Few cars came along. I could hear them long before they appeared and passed me. The four-lane road was bordered by woods, and I could see the headlights of approaching cars strike high up the trees. The cops rarely patrolled out here and the cars that came past speeded recklessly.

Between the cars there stood stretches of loneliness, and during the loneliness I thought deeply about Dietz and Corney. I prayed that the Paymaster might appear in his Country Squire wagon and transport me to Oregon the quick way—via the continuum.

Missing, missing, missing—didn't mean shit, really.

I guess I knew I would be gone for at least a few years and by the time I returned—if ever—this place would have changed even more. I might not recognize it at all then. I might be an old man wandering up and down streets, asking for directions to places no one knew, being treated as if I were daft.

I'd avoided the old neighborhood since I'd returned. I hadn't thought I would like what I found. I knew the woods were being leveled; I knew there were three or four times as many houses as there had been. I knew it had changed into something foreign, something uncomfortable, a new place that gluttonously chewed and swallowed memories.

Suddenly, more than anything tonight, I wished I could see where we'd grown up, me and the guys. I wanted to see those places where life had been charmed and simple and full of adventure, out where I'd dodged Sliver and followed Jimmy through the woods. Out where we'd built that wonderful cabin; out where Corney had been alive. I knew it wasn't likely there was much left, but I wanted to see what I could. Even a morsel would be satisfying.

I decided to walk. It would give me time to think. Maybe I was being hasty or just plain nuts, bolting like this for Oregon.

Missing, it had said. No need to hit the panic button. He'd been missing, supposedly, the night we'd nearly frozen to death back at the cabin.

I began to walk back along the same route we'd followed, Dietz and I, that day we ran from the wasps and swam out to the pilings. Back when there were the million locusts. Back before the cabin.

I hoofed it along Arbutus Avenue, and now and again a car passed. I would have hitched a ride but I wasn't particularly interested. The walking settled my head, made it feel cool and clear.

A car that had been traveling fast pulled to a stop on the road ahead and backed up. The guy on the passenger side leaned his head out the window and asked, "Want a ride?"

"Yeah," I said. What the hell.

I opened the back door and shoved my duffel bag in, following behind it. I settled into the backseat as the guy behind the wheel put the car in drive and took off, heavy on the gas pedal.

"Want a brew?" the guy on the passenger side asked me.

"Yeah. Sure."

He grabbed a can of beer and opened it with a church key and passed it back to me, the head foaming up and spilling.

"Hey—I know you," said the guy who had handed me the beer. "You're Chun, ain'tcha? Dietz's buddy, right?"

"Yeah," I said, sort of pleased. "Andy Hapanowicz."

"You know my brother. Eddie Jimpie."

Jimpie's brother, I thought, studying the guy's face. "Bobbie? Is that your name?"

"Yeah. Bobbie Jimpie."

He reached back to shake my hand, saying, "Man, my brother told me lots of shit about yous guys. He told me you used to jump outta the woods and climb onto cars when people was screwing in 'em. He told me about Dietz and the time those pricks down in Midland Beach jumped you and beat the shit outta you. Dietz went AWOL from the marines and came back and kicked their fuckin' asses for it, too."

I'd found myself nodding at everything he said, and when he came to the part about Dietz going AWOL I continued nodding. It wasn't true, of course, but if that was how the legend had grown, who was I to deny it?

We spun through the town circle and I saw how everything had changed for the worse. It all looked shabby and desperate. The storefronts were barricaded behind heavy metal curtains, drawn and locked with padlocks large as footballs. There was graffiti on the brick walls, which I couldn't wholly condemn because among the scribbled names and rock group insignia there were also peace signs.

A group of guys were gathered over at the bench, resembling vegetative cuttings of the Purps. A squad car sat idling alongside the phone booth, and the glass in the phone booth was shattered, as if a bomb had gone off. The streetlights and the light over the train station were dismally weak. The darkness was winning.

It was no longer a town circle. It was a sad and abused place, not a place to be proud of. Many of the people who lived here now had arrived from elsewhere and had no idea of how precious a place it had been. They had no idea what had been destroyed.

For a while we passed familiar places: Woodsie's house, Weaver's garage, the schoolyard—where two trailers had been towed in and set down as portable classrooms. We drove past Julie Digilio's and then the Murtaghs'. The large side yard at the Murtaghs' wasn't so large any longer. There was a house there now.

As we passed the Murtaghs' I thought of the incredible idea. Trash the missiles. Simple. Melt them into plowshares that glow in the night.

It never happened and probably never would. Back then, I'd believed it could. But now, having been enticed into the future, I felt I'd deceived myself. My need to believe had been too great. The reality was that the world was hopelessly violent, tossing us about by the millions, each of us, powerless, without direction.

I asked Bobbie what his brother was doing these days and he told me that he'd married Toni—surprise!—and they had one kid. He was working with an electrician but was on the firemen's list.

We drove on and Bobbie handed me another beer. We passed the corner where Corney and Spyros and Woodsie and I had waited for the church bus on Sunday mornings. Down from the corner, where there had been a large open field alongside the Dietzes', now stood two huge stucco houses with floodlights on the lawn (the "lawn" was green gravel) illuminating in bright white light a pair of plaster deer and a clutch of plaster rabbits.

"Jesus," I whispered. "This is progress. This and a few million tons of garbage in a marsh is progress. This and war."

"What?" asked Bobbie.

"It's not the same."

"Yeah. There's houses everywhere."

Impulsively, I said, "I got to get out here."

Bobbie asked, "Here?"

"Yeah. I want to say hello to someone."

The driver, who hadn't said very much, simply stopped the car and said, "There you blow."

I thanked them and got out with my stuff.

I walked along Jefferson until I came to the highway, where, like a hunted rabbit seeking a way out of the brush, I turned in all directions at once and felt trapped, doomed. There was nothing here I recognized. This was my hometown; this was where I'd grown up. I should have known the place but I could as well have been anywhere.

My house had been here. Somewhere. And my tree fort. The paths, too. And the cabin.

I wondered how the guys who had come upon the cabin had felt, bulldozing it to make room for houses and the highway. I wondered if even one of them had said, "Hey, we can't do this. I mean, look at this cabin. Ain't that just the kind of cabin you wanted when you was a kid? We just can't knock it down like this."

And wouldn't it have been great if one by one every single guy who was ordered to bulldoze it said, "Hey—go to hell. I'd rather be fired."

No one would ever consent to destroy the cabin and it would stand as a monument to the way life was when everyone got together and there was room to bust from your cocoon. When you had a buddy and the world was without sorrow.

I tried hard to get my bearings, recalling how it had seemed to happen at once, those days when the highway arrived and the woods began disappearing. I was home from NYU, November of my freshman year, and I ran into Spyros and Harry. We were having a few beers together and then suddenly Corney turned up, on leave for Thanksgiving. We started belting down beers and Spyros said, "Hey, Chun, they 'dozed your house today. Wanna go see?"

Why the hell would I want to see that? I wondered.

But Corney and Harry were up for it and said, "Yeah, let's go, Chun," as if it was a joyous event, a fuckin' joke.

I didn't want to let on how I felt, so I joined them. We climbed into Spyros's Le Mans and picked up two six-packs at the circle and tore across town.

Spyros stopped the car in front of the house. One corner of the house was still standing. The rest looked dynamited. There was nothing there but a pile of crumbled sheetrock and split and broken two-by-fours. It looked wounded and miserable, the look of an animal that had come up against something far too large and powerful, like a dog hit by a car, glassy-eyed with shock and sad in its knowledge of its pending doom.

There was still a corner of the house standing, and I could see pieces of the rooms that had been there. I recognized the living-room corner where the Christmas tree had been, and, above it, my bedroom. One end of the porch roof support was gone and the roof dropped vertically, like a broken tree limb. But the window was there, the window where I'd wandered from sleep to look for Dietz. The woods nearby where Dietz had waited were no longer to be found.

Corney clambered up the pile of debris that had been my house and took a piss. I wanted to kick his ass for it.

"Hey, Corney," I told him, "go piss somewhere else."

"In your mouth, Chun."

"Hey—I ain't kiddin'. Go piss on your own fuckin' house."

He finished pissing and then turned to me and said, "Fuck you, Chun."

"Let's go to Corney's," I told Spyros as I headed to the car. "I want to piss on his front steps."

Spyros laughed. He wanted to see that. We climbed into the car and drove to Corney's house.

"You do it, Chun, and I'll kick your fuckin' ass," Corney warned me. Apparently he'd forgotten how to say *fud'yan.*

I got out of the car and climbed the front steps of Corney's house and pissed until I was turned inside out. I watched the urine cascade down the brick steps and steam in the brisk November night.

Corney was waiting for me at the car. We had a few more nasty things to say, nose to nose, and then we started pushing and shoving each other. We flung a few punches and then rolled on the street, clawing at each other until we locked up. Spyros and Harry stood by, drinking beer and finally saying the fight had become boring.

I let go of Corney but he called me a cocksucker and still wanted to fight. I told him to go fuck himself and walked off. That was the last we saw of each other. I returned to school and he went back to Fort Benning.

I poked along the new streets. The woods were gone and I lost all sense of direction, for without the woods there were no paths, only these streets named after the children of whichever contractor had slapped together the rows and rows of houses—Mark Avenue, Roy Street, Diane Road, Sarah Lane.

The houses went on and on, as if stamped out by a tool-and-die factory. Tall fiberglass drapes were drawn across the living-room windows, and beyond the drapes I caught an occasional pulse of blue-gray television light. I was lost, the way you become lost in a dream, infinitely. I couldn't find the woods of memory and had no recognition of the present. I lost all sense of place. That deep pit that had cracked open beneath me the day we'd struck the deal to build our cabin opened again with the menacing quickness of a steel trap. It might have swallowed me for good tonight, but then, suddenly, there was something familiar, something to grab, to hang to by my fingernails. I didn't know what it was at first. But then I saw it cleanly in the light of the three-quarter moon. A patch of woods.

In front of me was a construction site with rows of houses in various stages of construction, some framed, some framed and sheathed, others no further along than a foundation or a clay-lined hole in the ground. Just beyond the row of foundations there was a darkened copse of woods, like a dear old friend sleeping beneath a cloak. I picked up my duffel and tramped across the cloddy earth, aware of the odors of construction: turned soil, concrete, sawdust, tar, diesel fuel. The bulldozers and trucks along the top of the hill took on the form of evil beasts. I gave them a wide berth and slipped into the bosom of the woods.

I thrashed around through the brush and tried desperately to find an old landmark or some secret remains of the faithful paths. But the moonlight couldn't penetrate the summer trees and I hadn't been here in years, so my formerly reliable senses were dulled. When I came to an open piece of ground where the moon managed to cast a weak pool of light I rolled out my sleeping bag and bedded down for the night. I was dog-tired but I slept fitfully, the way I would sleep after having run the woods with Dietz. I could feel my heart and I could hear my blood. *Thuk-lub-dub/thuk-dub.*

The first light of day seemed to scratch at my eyes only a moment after I'd fallen asleep. My eyelids were puffy as biscuits; I could feel the bags of tiredness there. I looked around at where I was for a moment and then suddenly sat upright.

Nearby stood an old tree stump, six inches across, and in the morning light I could see how the top of the stump formed a cone from having been worked by a hatchet. The wood was old and brown. The chopping had occurred years ago.

"Who the hell did that?" I wondered aloud.

I was angry. We'd all agreed to take the bucksaw to the stumps, cutting them flush at ground level so that there would be no evidence, no way for anyone to presume there was a cabin being built.

"Probably Spyros, that lazy bastard."

Then I was excited, thinking that by some chance, by some wild benevolent turn of luck, the cabin was still out here. And I had this outlandish idea that as long as the cabin was safe, Dietz could get home.

I kicked my way out of the sleeping bag and jumped to my feet. I explored the woods carefully. I knew this place. The houses and streets had turned me around last night, but now, surrounded by the woods, my instincts had returned, sharper than ever. I could find my way.

I started to walk fast along an old path, and then I ran. I soon came upon a wall of brambles. The thorned bushes rose high above my head, like a castle wall. The wall was impenetrable—at least so it might seem.

The only way in was the tunnel.

I got down on my hands and knees and crawled through the brambles. At the end of the tunnel I emerged in the place of the cabin, rising to my feet and feeling as if I'd slipped back in time.

I looked up. There it was, just the way we'd left it. The cabin.

Chapter 13

1

Mysteriously, inexplicably, I have a vision of Jimmy as he also has returned to the cabin. He has a dead rabbit. The rabbit dangles from his hip, cinctured there by a sisal rope that runs around his waist. His hands are bloody from having gutted the small animal. The warpaint smeared on his chest is the rabbit's blood. He reveals a switchblade knife and with a snap of his wrist he tosses it end over end. At me.

But the knife was never meant to plunge into my ribs. Instead it imbeds itself in the ground at my feet and I swear I can hear the earth groan ever so slightly. The body of the knife quivers, a seismic needle gauge, and the red eyes of the enraged dragon on the pearl handle glower.

—Therefore nothing, repeats Dietz in a mighty basso.

The walls of the cabin shudder.

—I'm Dietz, he affirms, Jimmy Dietz. —No fuckin' therefores. No whys about it.

—Regardless, I insist, squatting there on the dust of the cabin's earthen floor. —There is a therefore. It's clearly a simple syllogism.

—It's simple bullshit, says Dietz.

—To understand, you have to understand Dietz.

—It's impossible to understand Dietz.

—To understand, *therefore,* is impossible.

We are here and yet we aren't here. That's the way of things, isn't it? Never totally here, never totally there. An intersection along the continuum, of memory, imagination, and the immense unknown.

—What's there to understand, Chun? demands Dietz.

Before me lies the rabbit. Tossed there to the ground, it resembles an abused and discarded stuffed toy. Jimmy, hirsute and severe, crouches before the fire and pokes the embers with a twig. There is no roof on the cabin and the sparks dislodged by Jimmy fly off into the night sky, extinguishing themselves in their reach to be stars.

—So? asks Dietz. —What's there to understand?

—*What's there to understand?* Are you serious? Everything, Jimmy. Let's start there. Let's start with everything! Every last pinch of salt, for Christplace sake. How can it be here? And the pond? Hear the peepers? Weed Pond wasn't this close to the cabin. How did you do this? Sleight-of-hand doesn't explain it. It's impossible, I tell you, and I want an explanation. Otherwise, I just won't believe it, no matter how cleverly you dish it up to me. This just can't be, all of this—*any* of this. Everything disappeared. It was chewed up by the developers' bulldozers. The cabin was destroyed. The pond was filled in with debris. Insulation and two-by-fours and cinder blocks and all that shit. It was dumped into Weed Pond and the pond became a stinking little mudhole and the people who came out here to live in the houses were glad to see it go. I mean, what do you think, Dietz? You think you can make the world spin any way you want? This flies in the face of logic. It's nonsense. Get me a handle on it. Give me a syllogism. Give me gravity and the sky or I'm bowing out.

—To understand, *therefore,* says Dietz, is impossible. Allow me to show you, Chun, PDQ and QED.

He skewers the dead rabbit and props it over the fire. The smoke from the burning flesh rises away through the space where there is no roof, and there is no roof because Dietz forbids it. The power to do so is clearly his.

He arranges a wider demonstration and through the opening where the roof should be there appear the lights of a high-rise apartment complex, square windows and rectangular windows from which people stare out against a background of harsh light and an incessant thrum of gadgetry. There is something subliminal and yet undeniably real in the scene: as electronics are beyond perception, and visions of the Christplace, the Paymaster, Iron Jud and other shamans, black holes even, where beloved gravity is an amputee and light itself is worse off than a one-eyed Chun.

Faces press up against the supercooled liquid plate glass. They perceive us down here. With worry and suspicion they examine us, staring down into the roofless cabin, into the interior at us, the shirtless warrior and the benign inquisitive philosopher. They are confused and shocked to see tacked to the log walls the priestly vestments for mass, the skins of animals, the map of Vietnam, the map of Staten Island with infrared traces of the old paths.

While there we squat in the *thuk/lub/dub* focus, the hunter and the philosopher, two hungry bellies roasting the rabbit, all around us swirl the noises of the city: a siren, the wail of an abandoned child, a barking dog, subways and buses, shuffling feet, songs and whistles, the scritch-scratch of tiny meshing gears and the groaning crescendo of the unwieldy monstrosities of Armageddon we've devised from nuclear Erector sets. A domestic quarrel begins and soon borders on the felonious. A coffee table hurled in anger crashes through the window of a twenty-ninth-story apartment. The broken window punctures the vacuum seal of the city and now everything except for the cabin is sucked into the puncture. The window itself disappears. The city, gone.

Suddenly the trees sprout up and around us with the fortitude of good, sturdy ideas. The pond fills with pure water and the promise of life. The stars come out from hiding.

—Interesting, I tell Dietz. —Oh, not your skill at magic. I fully expected that. Interesting that you chose not to allow the cabin its roof. You never liked the whole idea when you learned how we planned to steal the plywood and shingles. But who was it eventually led us on that little foray?

—This is all impossible, right?

—You bet your sweet ass it is, Dietz. You know that as well as I do, and I don't care if I believe I'm here or not, because I rest assured in the knowledge that I can't be.

—QED.

—*QED nothing!* No conclusion, Dietz. I'm not, neither are you, here and now. It doesn't fit, and I'll be damned if I'll let you make it fit. I rescind my request for a likely syllogism.

—*Quod erat demonstrandum,* says Dietz with precise enunciation.

—Lay off the Latin. I can do without the quest, you know? *Quod erat faciendum.*

—*Ad Deum qui laetificat,* he begins, well pleased.

The God of my youth.

—Lay off the mass, Dietz. We didn't come all this way to offer the mass.

—Then let me conclude this lesson, Chun, and we can eat the rabbit while it lives.

With these strange and portentous words, the rabbit springs back to life. It had been shot through with an arrow, skinned and gutted, charred to the bone. Despite all this, it has returned to life.

—Okay, I resign. —Conclude.

The rabbit scurries about, frightened. It can find no escape. I suppose we have no choice but to eat it alive, just as Jimmy said.

—*Et tu?*

(His love of Shakespeare an elegant paradox.)

—Thou.

—I conclude:

> To understand is impossible.
> This is impossible.
> *Ergo:* This is understanding

2

The location of the cabin had remained a secret all these years. Even though many people eventually knew about it, seeing as we'd bragged about it often enough, none could find it and we never showed the way to anyone.

In the beginning, however, in the days when the cabin was new and the pure white heartwood of the chopped logs had yet to dry and brown over, we were very careful about revealing even the existence of the cabin, especially to those whom we judged to be a threat, which included of course the Purps—and the guys from Brooklyn, who, little by little, were venturing onto Staten Island.

One night we were all crouched in the brush watching a big campfire that these guys from Brooklyn had built. They always built big fires when they came out here and they always chose a spot in the woods as near a streetlight as possible. They didn't like the dark. It was never dark in Brooklyn and the dark woods out here scared them. This was wilderness to them, just as Brooklyn was the jungle to us.

There was a group of five or six of them. They'd appeared earlier that day, trooping past while we were shooting hoops in Woodsie's driveway. They had lots of unnecessary gear: tarps, lanterns, jerry cans, heavy ropes. You'd think they were on a big expedition in South America, not a mere ferry and train ride from Brooklyn.

As they went past, Corney yelled out something nasty about how they should've brought their Flintstone lunchboxes. One of the guys gave him the finger.

"What am that? Your fud'yan IQ?"

The bunch of them disappeared around the corner. We waited a few minutes and then, led by Jimmy, we slipped into the woods behind Woodsie's house and took a shortcut to the place where we knew they'd end up: the clearing near the last streetlight, just beyond Purdy's house. We sat there for a while in the woods in a concealed place and watched them, taking note of where they planned to pitch camp and make their fire. Then we returned to play basketball at Woodsie's and waited for darkness to descend.

It was ten o'clock before we crept back through the woods, guided by the bright orange-and-yellow glow of the fire at the campsite. We settled on a position about fifty yards away and whispered among ourselves about what assholes these guys were.

"What d'you want to do to them?" asked Sperm.

"Kick their fud'yan asses."

"Fat chance. Those guys from Brooklyn are tough."

"You am a fud'yan pussy. They ain't so tough."

"Yeah," agreed someone. "Jimpie beat the shit outta some Brooklyn guy at Tech."

"Jimpie's an animal."

"Let's go palaver," I suggested. "Like mountain men, y'know?"

"Go what?"

"Palaver."

"You fuckin' ass. What's palaver?"

"That am a Catholic-school word," said Corney. "It means the Chun wants to suck dick."

"Yeah," I said. "As soon as your mother's finished."

Corney dove on me and tried to kick my balls. I flipped him over and pinned him. He kicked free and blew snot at me.

"Botstein!" tittered Woodsie. "Botstein the Chun!"

"Quiet!" hissed Dietz.

We flattened ourselves. One of the guys in the campsite was pointing in our direction. He pulled out a machete.

"Can you smell it, man?" mocked Spyros. "Can you smell it? I'm just shittin' in my pants lookin' at that machete."

The guys at the campsite finally decided that it was safe. They turned up their transistor radio so they wouldn't have to hear any more sounds from the woods that they couldn't explain. They were listening to Cousin Brucie on WABC. A Beach Boys tune came on and we all lay there, quietly singing the falsetto, "Fun, fun, fun til her daddy takes her T-bird away."

We meanwhile watched the Brooklyn guys move around. They tossed logs on the fire and sharpened long shafts of saplings into spears. They practiced knife-throwing and tied a big hangman's noose and dangled it from a limb. Their shadows loomed large against the surrounding trees. The hangman's noose swayed ominously. The radio had been fading and then fell silent, the batteries dead. With the radio gone, we could hear their voices and the crackling flames of the fire. The insects of the night randomly creaked and chirred.

All of a sudden, Jimmy stood up and said, "C'mon."

We looked at him for a moment and then stood and followed. He marched us out of hiding and directly into their camp. It made them very nervous to see us appear from the darkness, and they edged nearer their spears and machetes. They were ready for trouble.

They watched us closely as we filed into their camp and formed a line. They didn't say a word and they didn't offer us a seat by the fire.

Their leader was a tough-looking guy named Rico. He wore a khaki T-shirt with the sleeves torn off. His thick jaw was dark with a day's growth of beard like a black shingle. The moment he saw us he reached for his army belt and strapped it on, his machete dangling off his hip. He looked us over menancingly.

"Whatcha want?" he demanded. "What's the idea, sneakin' up on us?"

"Maybe there's more," one of the others said, looking into the woods behind him.

Now the others tried to look out into the dark woods. They were spooked, even though they looked tough as hell. I was relieved to have run into them here and not on some street in Brooklyn.

There was no way to lessen the tension. We hadn't shown up to start trouble, but that didn't matter to these guys. They were suspicious, and that made us cautious. Eyes shifted. The light of the fire licked our faces and we felt its heat. Everyone positioned himself as if bracing for a tremor.

Jimmy said, "We saw your fire."

Rico was defensive. "Nice fire, ain't it? Don't get too close to it. You might fall in—y'know?"

"We don't want you to burn down the fud'yan woods, asshole," Corney popped off.

"Asshole, huh?" asked Rico. He turned to his buddies. "Asshole," he repeated, as if Corney had said the most ignorant thing in the world. He glared at Corney.

One of the others then tossed three or four logs on the fire just to show us that they'd make the fire as big as they pleased.

"You was the jerk with the big mouth playin' basketball, wasn't you?" Rico asked Corney.

"And you am the one suckin' my dick."

Rico straightened up and tossed back his shoulders. He looked from Corney to Jimmy and said, "I don't feel like breakin' the little shit's neck, y'know?"

"We live out here," I put in. "We just don't want the woods burned down, that's all."

Rico looked at me briefly, as if thinly amused that I could talk. He was far more interested in Jimmy.

Meanwhile, one of the others had stepped closer to me, asking, "Where d'you live? In the woods?"

"Sort of," I answered, bitterly ashamed of the meekness I felt had crept into my voice. I coughed and tried to sound cocky. "Yeah," I said. "We got a cabin."

"Shut up, Chun," demanded Spyros.

Rico's ears perked. "A cabin, huh? Yous guys got a cabin?"

"No," I said, feeling my face flush. What a jerk I was! I'd told someone about the cabin! Shit.

"Where is it?" asked Rico.

"I was bullshitin'," I said.

"The Chun am always full of shit."

But Rico wasn't about to believe this. He knew I hadn't lied. He knew there was a cabin.

The fire meanwhile began to consume the extra logs they'd tossed on it. The heat was intense. Uneven, dancing shadows made moving masks of our faces.

"Where's this cabin—Chun?" snickered Rico, moving a step closer to me.

"You want to see the cabin?" put in Jimmy, unable to stop himself from stepping between me and Rico. He gestured toward the dark woods. "We'll take you to it."

Rico cleverly avoided looking out into the darkness so we wouldn't be able to see how he felt about it.

"Hey," he told Jimmy. "If we wanted to find your fuckin' cabin, we'd find it—don't worry about that."

"Bull-fuckin'-shit," said Spyros. "Not in a million years."

With that, this guy who had been in the background stepped from the other side of the fire. He was a thick-built guy with dark hair and a forehead shaped like a horizontal brick. He was angry as hell and the veins on his neck bulged. He spluttered and thrust his face into Jimmy's. It all happened so quickly it took a moment for us to realize that the guy had a gun.

"Big fuckin' deal," he said. He repeated the words over and over, brandishing the gun. "Big fuckin' deal. Big fuckin' deal. A goddam *cabin.* Who gives a shit, y'know?"

He waved the gun back and forth, too agitated to settle just yet on a victim. Woodsie ran. The others backed away. Jimmy stood where he was. I remained with Jimmy because I found I couldn't move. My knees were weak and my mouth was dry as dust. I thought I would start to pant the way I had in the water that cold Easter Sunday: that panic and fear.

"Let's go, Jimmy," I said quietly. "He's got a gun."

The guy pointed the gun at me, and I thought I would piss my pants.

"You're a fuckin' genius," the guy told me.

He turned his attention to Jimmy and pointed the gun at Jimmy's face. "Yeah, *Jimmy,* whyn't you get your ass outta here? The man's got a gun, see? You and your fuckin' seven dwarfs here, actin' big shit just because you got a shack in the woods. Big fuckin' deal, right? Big fuckin' deal. You pricks piss me off. Get your asses outta here."

He motioned for us to scram. The guys hustled into the woods. I stepped back, reaching for Jimmy's elbow to bring him along. When I touched him, his body felt like a solid post.

"Big man," he said to the guy. "Big man with a gun."

"Jesus, Jimmy," I whispered.

The guy turned the gun on me again and warned me, "You shut your mouth."

I swallowed and nodded. I felt weak. This was it. This guy was going to kill us.

The gun barrel pivoted toward Jimmy. The guy touched the end of it to Jimmy's nose. "I'm gonna blow your fuckin' brains out."

"Yeah?" asked Jimmy, brimming with defiance. "You're going to kill me?"

He moved a step closer to the guy, who, surprisingly, backed off.

Now the guy didn't know what to do. He pointed the gun up and fired it at the black sky. The air cracked and rang my ears. My heart thumped against my chest, wanting out. My stomach twisted and my bowels were ready to dump.

Yet then there was this moment of great pause. Nothing, no one, moved. Not even to take a breath. Even the fire seemed to freeze. There it hung, this frozen pause, broken only when the echo of the gun blast was thinned to silence and Jimmy said boldly, "You missed."

Suddenly the situation was changed. I could feel the power leave them and flow to us. There was disbelief and respect in their eyes.

You missed? Who the hell was this guy? What a set of balls he had!

They told their pal to back off, take it easy. The one named Rico apologized in a way to Jimmy, saying, "Hey, he's only fuckin' with you. He gets nervous, that's all."

"Look," said Jimmy. "We didn't come lookin' for trouble. You've got to ignore Corney. He's got no brains. You guys can camp here any time you want. Just don't burn down the woods. These are our woods. We come and go everywhere."

They were in awe of him. Rico accepted him as an equal. They told us they had some beer and asked us if we wanted some. Jimmy declined. He turned from them, saying, "Let's go, Chun," and we left.

3

On the morning I had returned to find the cabin, I realized it was alive. Its heart beat in the center of a pocket of woods thus far spared the fate of hundreds of other acres.

I'd emerged into the cool light from the tunnel beneath the brambles and immediately sought out the place where I had buried the talismans. The daylight was weak and grayish but the place where I'd hidden them was still plainly marked by the wide flat stone I had always used to cover it.

I pulled the flat stone aside and removed the dozen or so fist-sized rocks I always stuffed at the top of the hole. Then I reached down for the rectangular saltine-cracker tin. I pulled it out and pried off the lid. I spilled out the talismans of Jimmy's life onto the stone where we had divided the *thuk/lub/dub* heart: the crossed-flag emblem of a Corvette (gen-u-ine, not that plastic shit), a chipmunk pelt (not a mark on it; he'd said he'd shot it through the eye with a .177 caliber pellet, and he had: there wasn't a mark on it), a busted run of rosary beads (three Hail Marys, one Our Father), the dagger speech from *Macbeth* copied in ink on a scrap of paper, a shotgun shell from the day at the rod and gun club picnic, a broken gold chain from his Miraculous Medal (—do your stuff now!), a hawk feather, a nock of arrow, the words of Matthew to resist not evil, the .22 shell from the gun that belonged to Rico-from-Brooklyn.

From then on the talismans became the focus of the morning ritual, the daily search for my soul. To begin each day properly I poured them onto the flat stone during the birdsong dimness before dawn and examined them under the light of a candle. I treated them with great reverence, for I knew that it was only in this way that I could make them powerful and seduce that power for myself.

Each day as the candle grew weak and without focus in the blossoming red and pale lavender of dawn, I put the talismans away, save for a random piece. And it was this random piece that was the seed crystal of my daylight hours. One day the separate and scattered elements of my soul coalesced around the busted run of rosary beads, another day it was the hawk feather or the shotgun shell.

After the talismans had spoken to me in the morning, the rest of the day was waiting and routine. I hauled water back to the cabin in a jerry can three times a week. I did my laundry at the laundromat once a week. I no longer used watches or clocks or mirrors. I guessed at the time. I shaved infrequently. I hadn't cut my hair now for months. I arrived at work early or late, looking some days as if I'd been pulled through a hedge. Pete was generally angry with me but I took it in stride.

I persisted in the talisman ritual. Each dawn found me at the cabin, squatting over the stone of the rabbit heart, humming the way Iron Jud had hummed, hoping to open a path from the Iron Triangle to the cabin.

When I discovered that the cabin still stood where we'd built it, that it had not yet been leveled to make way for a development, I had been filled with pride.

We'd built the cabin just the way we said we would. It was the size of a one-car garage, though two stories high. The only way in was through the triangular opening below the rear peak of the roof. No doors; no windows. That was the way we'd wanted it.

We hadn't bothered to chink the logs. We'd said we liked to be able to see outside, but I was never sure that we just didn't get lazy toward the end and say to hell with chinking.

Alone out here at night I ran my hand along the rough bark of the logs and imagined that, like a phonograph needle, I could draw my fingertips along the seemingly disordered corrugations and grooves and extract every word and every gesture, the very odors and colors of those days when we had built the cabin.

We'd worked in pairs. Two guys went out together, chose a tree, chopped it down, hauled it back, notched it, set it in place, removed it if it needed to be shaped, set it back, and then finally nailed it down with big spike nails at either end.

As I ran my fingers along a log I was convinced I could smell the freshness of the sap when the hatchet blows had first penetrated the pale heartwood. I pondered questions that could never be answered. I wondered who had gone out after this particular log when it had been a young tree. Who had cut it down, carried it back, and painstakingly dragged it through the tunnel? Who had notched it and lifted it to its position and trimmed the knobs and knuckles that would otherwise have prevented it from snugging into place? Had it been Corney and Spyros? Or Jimpie and Woodsie? Harry and Sperm? And because of the exasperatingly imponderable nature of these questions, I was convinced of their intense importance.

It was hot work, building the cabin, and we drank greedily from our canteens throughout the day. We handled the tools and lifted heavy logs, and our tender schoolboy hands blistered and turned raw. We stripped off our shirts and showed our scrawny white chests to the sun, and the sun scorched us. And meanwhile the million locusts sang on and on, chopping the air into thousands of pieces and whirling the pieces about like thin metal shims.

Jimpie cut himself one day and had to run home, his hand wrapped in a T-shirt that quickly soaked with bright red blood. But he was back out there the following morning, his hand boasting seven stitches.

We had never been together quite that way before, those few weeks in that summer when we'd built the cabin, and even though in the years that followed there were many good times and a few bad times, we would never again find the magic to be together the way the cabin had brought us together.

When we finished the walls we didn't know what to do about the roof. We went ahead and built it of logs, because this was to be a log cabin, after all, but when we saw that there were so many openings and gaps we knew that the rain wouldn't run off the roof of our cabin, and we felt we had failed.

It became our first bone of contention, the roof. It seemed that no sooner were we done with the cabin than we started arguing again.

We gathered together along the peak of the roof to decide what to do. Jimmy and I; Spyros, Corney, Woodsie, Sperm, and Harry. Jimpie was there, his hand bandaged.

Someone suggested that we raid the construction site down at Benning's hill. There was so much tar paper and shingle and plywood there, we could steal the small amount we needed and no one would ever notice it was gone.

Someone said we should vote on it, and to this day I can see the tableau we formed, lined along the peak of the roof, some of us sitting and some of us standing: Corney dangling precariously over the edge; Woodsie sitting in the center of the roof, huddling his knees to his chest; Spyros, bare-chested and tan, flexing his impressive biceps muscle; Jimpie unable to prevent himself from peeling back the layers of his bandage for a peek at his wound; Jimmy standing up and shaking his head, saying, "It's stealing."

"They won't miss it," said Corney.

"Hell, man, every guy who works there steals shit all the time," Spyros pointed out.

"That don't mean we got to," put in Woodsie.

"And it don't mean we don't got to," said Spyros.

Woodsie sniggered. "That's fuckin' dumb."

Spyros confronted him. "What the hell you mean, it's dumb?"

"It was dumb as bathtub farts, Spyros," said Jimmy.

"Fuck you, Dietz. We'll vote."

"I don't care what you do," said Jimmy. "You can't steal it."

"They're stealing the hill," I put it.

Jimmy regarded me sternly. "What's that mean?"

"It was the best sleigh-riding."

"So? We don't own the hill."

"I think it's all right to steal the stuff for the roof," I told Jimmy. "They stole the hill."

"Yeah," agreed Sperm. "The Chun's right. They stole the hill."

"The Chun ain't right," said Jimmy.

"He is too," said Corney.

"C'mon. Let's vote," said Spyros.

Jimmy knew that we would vote to steal the wood and the shingles and all. He knew that everyone except Woodsie would vote for it, but not Woodsie because then Woodsie would have to go along with the rest of us to steal the stuff and Woodsie didn't have the nerve for that.

Jimmy waved in our direction like he wanted nothing more to do with us. We watched him climb down from the roof and gather his tools and his canteen. Then, without a word passing between any of us, we watched him squirm down into the tunnel and go.

The following day he returned early in the afternoon. He saw right away that we had not gotten the plywood nor the tar paper or shingles. And he knew that we hadn't changed our minds. I could see this in his eyes. He concluded that we hadn't been able to pull off the theft, and he asked, "What happened?"

"There's a night watchman," I said, feeling that I was making an excuse. "He heard us and almost caught Sperm."

"What was Sperm doing there?"

"What d'you mean? He voted to go."

"Sperm's too slow. Of course he almost got caught."

"What's that mean?"

"You should let Sperm be a lookout. He's too slow to get close."
I said nothing.

"What time did you go?" he asked.

"I don't know. Eleven, maybe later."

"Night watchman isn't likely to be asleep that early. You should've gone at three, and you should wait till there's no moon."

I said nothing. He was right and he knew it.

"I'll make a better plan next time," I said.

"I'll show you. I'll go."

I'll go. Just like that. No explanation. I supposed he couldn't bear the idea that we hadn't been able to do it. I don't know. He just said he'd take charge and I knew he didn't want to discuss it.

4

Out at the cabin I tried to do everything the way it had been done with Dietz. Surely this would help. I had the talismans; I was Mouse-who-sees-in-all-directions; I had been apprenticed to the Paymaster. If in addition to possessing those sterling credentials I did everything in a way that Jimmy would approve, I was certain to bring him home. I'd promised never, ever, to give up on him, and yet I'd broken that promise in spirit and in deed many many times. I blamed him for becoming someone I'd not foreseen nor wanted him to become; I blamed him for ushering violence into my life that took my eye. But now I was at the cabin and I had renewed the vow and I would not give up until I brought him home.

We had always exchanged a few words over coffee, while the unstrung bows stood against the cabin and the jays and chickadees and an occasional brilliant red cardinal called out and ruffled the air in flight. The smoke of our fire rose thin. We waited for our eggs to cook and meanwhile talked casually over the steaming coffee. Jimmy examined a fishing lure in minute detail and I honed my knife until it cut smoothly, without pull. I wanted him to notice this. I wanted his approval in everything.

I could see the scene clearly, and I imagined there was a confetti snow, each piece of confetti bearing words written in Jimmy's minuscule script, not just his class notes, but all the words of his life, every sentence. And from time to time, through the good graces of the Paymaster, this entropy of confetti reversed itself and the multitudinous random pieces found themselves glued together in perfect order. Before my eyes appeared the words Jimmy savored: the Sermon on the Mount, the dagger speech from *Macbeth,* the Latin of the Pater Noster.

Then I saw Dietz. He arose from the talismans on the altar stone where we had wrenched the living heart from the rabbit's chest. The talismans were he: a button of bone, a Scout merit badge, a pearl inlay; dragon's eyes and knotted forearm veins and the lingering salt sting of seawater; a feathered flight, a wounded animal, a gold miraculous medal tight to his freckled throat; the sharp odor of a shotgun blast, then the image of Dietz: chipped-toothed brown-eyed avenger swelling with power.

Briefly he was there and then, as quickly, gone.

Fresh from sleep, I looked around. Where was he? The light that managed to find its way between the unchinked logs of the cabin was soft and diffused, not like light at all, more like the soul of the day, aroused yet sleepy, distributing itself rather lazily yet.

There was an owl nearby; the last barking chatter of a raccoon. I listened closely for the men who arrived every morning to work on the houses but heard nothing. I was satisfied that there yet was time for my rituals.

I squirmed from the cocoon folds of my flannel sleeping bag, surprised to find the morning air so chilly. I padded across the earthen floor to the plastic washbasin. I poured fresh water from the canvas water bag I'd lined with a large plastic bag into the basin and then soaked a washcloth and frothed it with hand soap. I scrubbed my face and grunted and brrr'd, shaking my head to untangle the cobwebs of sleep. I cleaned my chest and legs, standing there naked and feeling the cool air on my dampened skin. Quickly I toweled off and took down my gas-station togs from a nail hook and dressed. Today's name, stitched over the shirt pocket, was Louie.

"So, *Louie, Louie* it is," I said, singing a few bars of the old song.

I turned to the altar stone and struck a match to the plump pale yellow candle. In its wobbly flame I examined the first pieces of scrimshaw to catch my eye: chipmunk pelt, a section of rosary beads, shotgun shell, a feather, an arrow nock.

The candle burned with a pleasing fragrance, and I took this to be a good omen. Apprentice of the Pegasus. Mouse-who-sees-in-all-directions. One-eyed Shaman of the Old Paths. I was not without power.

The sun had risen quickly, and now the light stretched like a waking cat, reaching out long and luxuriantly, prowling through the bushes, climbing the trees.

There was enough light to see the maps and the newspaper articles I had tacked on the log wall above the altar stone. I'd posted the map of Staten Island with the approximate location of the cabin circled in red. A wild guess, that. New streets had been hewn through the woods faster than the mapmakers could draw them. The place of the cabin, once inviolate, was threatened. That it had survived thus far was a sign of its enormous significance.

The map of the United States was above and to the right of Staten Island. The map of Vietnam with the Iron Triangle in red was to the left.

It was up to me to hold my position along the continuum. Keep the cabin standing, keep Peggy flying.

The men who built the houses had arrived; I could hear their cars and trucks. I blew out the candle, and the smoke rose in an undulating wisp, the way the smoke had risen at the end of mass from the six tall candles on the linen-draped altar of the God of my youth. It rose past the photo of Dietz from *Time* and briefly wreathed the story from the newspaper that Frank had given me.

Silver Star Hero Missing.

By the time I left for work each day the carpenters and the electricians and plumbers and masons and the others would already have been at work for a few hours. The first morning they saw me emerge from the woods, my hair in a ponytail, wearing my workboots and a gas-station outfit they were puzzled and watched me with great curiosity.

They customarily arrived while I was still eating, and each morning when I heard their trucks and cars I judged by the nearness of these sounds how long the cabin could survive. The first morning I was able to make out their voices I felt there was cause for concern. Then, a week later, when I began to hear individual words, hearing them call each other by name, I realized a new threshold had been crossed, and I worried deeply about Dietz. I was certain that the cabin could bring him home. I was certain it had that power. And I was equally certain that without the cabin I stood no chance at all. Without the cabin there was no connection to the Iron Triangle. Without the cabin there was nothing but that voracious pit, a dark vacuum in the direction of the future.

I ate my eggs and fixed another cup of coffee. I figured the sun had been up for two hours. The men who worked on the houses were early birds. They arrived and drank coffee and spent a few minutes bullshitting and then fired up their bulldozers and aimed them at the woods. The thick plates on the metal tracks creaked ominously; the big cylinders of the engines chugged along without pain or feeling.

I'd considered spilling a few sacks of sugar into the gas tanks of the bulldozers, setting fire to the stacks of lumber and roofing materials, cutting wires and vandalizing the plumbing of houses nearest completion. But I knew these were only staying actions; I knew they would be tactical errors, drawing too much attention to me and the cabin and doing nothing to bring Jimmy home.

Now the hammers began to pound and the circular saws snarled, ripping sheets of plywood. The cement trucks arrived, turning their slushy loads, and the dump trucks jounced back and forth across the uneven ground. I could hear the men call out instructions to one another, and I was uncomfortable all over again at their nearness.

My cooking fire had burned down. I pushed the embers about and realized that the spell was broken for now. Jimmy wouldn't return today. Dawn was past, and I was sure that when he returned it would be at dawn. The day lacked magic; the night was for planning. Only the dawn promised his return.

One of these mornings soon enough, when the men arrived to work on the houses, I'd be having breakfast with Jimmy. He would have been wandering the jungle of the Iron Triangle, lost, pursued, and the jungle would fade away and become the familiar woods of home. Naturally he'd make his way to the cabin. He'd crawl through the brambles and unburden himself of his pack and his M-16 and sit down for a leisurely welcome-home breakfast, just like the ones we'd eaten together on many other mornings: bacon and eggs, coffee, a buttered roll. And when he settled back to drink his second cup of coffee he'd hear the trucks and cars and the voices of the men and the bulldozers and hammers and saws, and he'd frown and ask, "What's that, Chun?"

"Houses. They're building houses where all the woods used to be. Weed Pond's gone. The Conklin place is history. It's real sad. You wouldn't believe it."

"They're doing *what?*"

"They're bulldozing the woods. Remember how that man out there at the dump told us it would be? We thought he was full of shit, or that it would take forever. Well, he wasn't full of shit, and it ain't forever." Then I would pause and tell him. "They cut down Big Trees."

"Oh?" Dietz would ask. "Dozin' the woods? Cutting down *Big Trees?* Not while I'm here."

He'd wave his arm. That was all it would take. I mean, we're talkin' Dietz here. Just a wave of his arm and *poof!*—every last house would disappear, and the woods would return, Weed Pond would be back; Big Trees would stand tall, monuments to Dietz, and all the paths would be just as they had been.

"If that's what they got planned, I'd better not go away again, eh, Chun?"

"You got it."

"No more fuckin' wars."

"No more."

A wave of the hand. All the wars gone. *Poof!*

Yeah, he'd be back. He'd come at dawn. He'd be out there in the jungle, in the deep treacherous night of the Iron Triangle, stalking and being stalked, suddenly finding at dawn that he was walking safely along the old paths.

I knew I'd have to be watchful during those hours when the darkness started to lift. My intuition would have to be sharp and unfettered. I'd light the fat candle and study the talismans and maybe hazard a prayer to Jesus and even one to Buddha—if one prayed to the Buddha. Couldn't hurt.

I'd bring to the fore all my skills. I'd gather all the privileges and powers I'd earned as Mouse-who-sees-in-all-directions and climb to the roof of the cabin to await sunrise and Dietz. The dew on the brambles would sparkle when the light broke in the east. They would sparkle like scattered bits of impaled starlight that hadn't managed to flee the dawn. There would be great beauty all around me but I would linger only momentarily on the beauty and miracle of the new day. I would diligently practice the vigilance of a shaman. I'd be clear and sharp, awaiting Dietz, watching as the night retreated to the west behind me.

It would be as it had been when we all used to camp out, when we slept in the darkness and saw nothing but the stars until the arrival of dawn, when the surrounding trees and the other guys in their sleeping bags seemed gradually to blossom into clarity in the growing light.

When we camped out, those days before the cabin was built, we always camped at Big Trees. The three big trees formed the points of a triangle. Their branches entwined above, creating a canopy, and at night when we stoked a blazing campfire the light of the flames reflected against the underside of the branches and gave the woods the look of a place with a high, vaulted ceiling. Later, when the fire died down and was swallowed in the night, the illusion of the high ceiling succumbed to the vision of stars peeping between the branches.

The roots of the big trees coursed over and under one another, like petrified snakes, bulging the loamy soil and pushing stones to the surface. At the base of the tree trunks the roots were buttresses, forming armchairs where we sat like uncrowned kings.

Farther out from the trunks, where the roots disappeared and reappeared, dipping below the soil only to knuckle to the surface again, it was not so easy to find a place to sleep that was free of bumps and knobs. For this reason, whenever we slept out at Big Trees, we were scattered about, and when the campfire died away and darkness prevailed, you felt alone.

Yet at dawn you found out you hadn't been alone at all. The dawn returned us to one another, just as dawn would return Dietz to the cabin. It was up to me.

Feather, pelt, amulet, shotgun shell: it would work if I remained faithful and daring. I'd find the old paths. The Big Trees would stand tall. The earth that had been turned under by the bulldozers would unfold, metamorphosing into a rich topsoil decorated like a special cake with tiny twigs and bits of leaf, mouse tracks and humus, scrambling tribes of ants and scavenging beetles, wily arachnids, needles of straw and fluffy down.

When the moment was ripe, it would be easy. Dietz would stroll home and then, together, we'd bring back the rest of those poor bastards the world had so unjustly made into warriors. There would be a huge vacuum in Vietnam and it would fill with unshakable peace for a millennium. And whenever anyone tried to start a war again, the cabin would steal all the soldiers, one by one.

I tried every day to find my way along the old paths without becoming lost in the maze of new streets and muddy construction roads. There were row upon row of houses. Hundreds, easily. Thousands, probably. People had moved into them in droves. A train of realtors came and went daily. "These houses are going fast, folks. Faster'n we can build them."

And the houses did go up quickly. New foundations were carved from the earth every hour. Chain saws lopped the trees. Bulldozers scraped the carpet of the woods clean. It was all steadily advancing upon the cabin.

People eyed me suspiciously from their living-room windows as I walked along trying to find the old paths. I was a stranger here as far as they were concerned. They didn't trust me. They didn't like the way I took shortcuts through the construction sites and stood pensively for long moments before every last copse of woods, searching for clues to the old paths.

"Hey!" a man yelled angrily at me one day. "Hey, that's my brother-in-law's lot. Get out of there! Don't let me see you around here again."

NO TRESPASSING and PRIVATE PROPERTY signs became fashionable along my route. Vicious dogs prowled the yards. Stockade fences went up in a twinkling.

The people in the new houses were convinced that I was a burglar scouting the neighborhood, or a child molester, a drug dealer, a rapist. They were infuriated and called the cops, and the cops stopped me and asked me who I was and where I was going. When they asked me why I wore an eye patch I lifted it and showed them the ugliness underneath it.

But I did not tell them that I was trying to find the old paths, the paths that had been here where the houses now stood—stood at least temporarily, until Dietz returned. And then, just wait—*poof!*—they'd be gone, and things would once more be as they should: the cabin, the woods, the paths. Dietz and the Chun.

Chapter 14

1

It was bitter cold the afternoon they buried Cornelius Xavier Walsh. The air was so cold it stung my face and ears; my fingertips were thimbles, without feeling. Even breathing was difficult, my nostrils dry and frosted.

And because it was so very cold that day, the batteries in the tape recorder that the honor guard had brought along to play a cassette of "Taps" ran out of power and the recording mournfully dragged to a halt.

The frozen ground was hard as a concrete slab. I could have reasoned this even if I hadn't seen the way the earth had come from the ground in hard icy clods, the clods piled alongside the backhoe.

It would have been more decent of them to have moved the backhoe, because as far as I was concerned it wasn't right to have the machine that had dug the grave parked there for everyone to see. The callousness of this angered me throughout the burial, as had Jimmy's ramrod Marine Corps salute: his kind were to blame for Corney's death.

Dietz was on a forty-eight-hour pass from Lejeune. He had shown up the night before the funeral at the small apartment on Houston Street I shared with two other guys from NYU. My roommates were out and I was sitting at the table in the narrow kitchen, studying calculus and trying to thwart the sneaky way in which the cold walls conspired to siphon all the warmth from my body. It was then that I had this peculiar feeling, like the old radar signaling me that Jimmy was about to toss pebbles at my bedroom window. I discounted my intuition. Why would Jimmy be near?

I glanced up at the window and saw only my reflection against the frosted panes. I shifted my angle to the light, and as I did so the diagonal line of the fire escape stairs appeared where my profile had been.

Shuddering from the cold and the thought of Corney being embraced the following day by this frigid March earth, I tried to return to the welcome rationality of calculus.

But I'd been studying long and hard and the looping S-shaped integration symbols and the rambling equations began to dance and lead me on a spree that bore no relation to mathematics. I just couldn't do another problem. My attention wandered, following the dancing symbols of calculus into the wings. I looked up from my work and scratched at the layer of frost on the window. I sensed something. I sensed it strongly. That *thuk-lub-dub,* that old blood-brother vow.

I looked out the glass through the lens I'd scratched in the frost. Across the street, Jimmy appeared from a parked car, having emerged on the passenger side. He came around and said a few words to the driver before deftly crossing through the traffic. I watched him until the building itself blocked my view. When I could no longer see him I looked over at the car and surmised that Ivers and Deluxe were waiting there.

My apartment was on the fourth floor, and I could hear the elevator as it began its creaking journey up the shaft. I stood at the window and waited.

The elevator stopped at the floor below. The doors opened and then quickly closed. During that moment I thought of hiding from Dietz. Ever since his epic fight with Ralph Ivers he'd steadily become a stranger to me. He was uncomfortable to be with, even dangerous, embroiling himself in fistfights and barroom brawls and leaving a distinct trail of spilled blood and broken bone.

A moment later the elevator clunked to a stop on my floor. The door slid open and then closed. I listened closely. I heard Jimmy in the hall. His footsteps halted at my door.

When he knocked I didn't move a muscle. If it had been summer I would have taken to the fire escape and disappeared for a few hours. For the last year, even longer, it hadn't been easy to be with him. And now that I hadn't seen him since that night with the shotgun, when for some unknown reason he'd tricked me into going along with him, I plainly saw that I didn't need him in my life.

He'd written to me since then. I'd read several of the letters and had trashed the others. I'd never answered a one.

He knocked again. I restrained my impulse to go to the door.

There was a moment now that seemed incredibly long, as if the calculus equations really had come to life, snaring time in their arabesques and making off with it. The doorknob turned and I realized that it was unlocked. The chain was hooked, however, and when Jimmy carefully pushed the door the opening went only so far before the chain pulled taut.

"Unlock it, Chun," he said through the opening.

He couldn't see me. He was guessing. I waited and said nothing. It was a standoff.

"Hell, Chun. I won't beg. I just thought you'd want to drink some beer and shoot the shit. I'm on a forty-eight-hour. That's not much. Then it's the Nam." He paused. "Oughta be interesting."

So now it was to be his turn.

"I'm not here," I finally said.

"You're not here when letters come, either."

I said nothing.

I walked over and looked at him through the narrow opening. He grinned at me. He was out of uniform, tall and rock-hard. His hair was shaved above his temples and the tight skin of his skull seemed to gleam. I said, "Back up so I can get the chain off."

He stepped into the room and immediately filled it with that enormous presence of his. He asked, "What's new?"

I shrugged. "School."

"That's new?"

"Well, I haven't had the chance to fire a shotgun at anyone lately, so life's been dull. What can I say?"

He let the remark alone and looked around the room. One of my roommates was a rabid antiwar activist, and the apartment was plastered with leaflets, posters, photographs of atrocities (including one of American marines showing off Vietcong heads and strings of leathery ears)—and a large picture of Thich Quang Duc, the Buddhist monk who had immolated himself to protest the war.

Jimmy took in the material on the wall piece by piece, as if patiently touring a museum. When he came to the picture of Thich Quang Duc he examined it closely and then, pointing it out, turned to me and said, "Don't do this, Chun."

"I hadn't planned to."

He wandered over to the table where I had been studying. He looked down at the calculus text and immediately became intrigued by it. He sat in the chair and loosened his jacket and began studying. I saw him again as I had seen him those nights in his austerely neat room, when I'd spied on him from my tree house or padded so softly up the stairs—can you imagine how softly, to sneak up on Dietz?—that he didn't hear me. And although I was able then to observe him only briefly before he sensed me standing there at the head of the stairs, I managed during those moments to see him as clearly as an invisible spirit might hope to observe a mortal. I saw that he was I and I was he, though in the way of a mirror, which is not a true image but neither untrue. I saw that in him were the missing pieces of myself, the pieces I needed to make me whole. To be strong and full of courage. Steadfast. Confident. I could feel those unfilled spaces in me, and I yearned for the excess in Jimmy to pour into those spaces and remake me. I knew how it felt to lack the guts and the muscle to fight back and to be forced to turn the other cheek for lack of courage, which wasn't, really, turning the other cheek at all. The powerless and frightened must turn the other cheek by forgiving, by turning their heart away from the desire for revenge and learning therein a new and greater power. That was difficult enough; few could do it. And yet how incredibly rare and special a thing it was for the powerful on earth to truly turn the other cheek. To have Jimmy's raw strength or to be a mighty nation, to have the ability to deliver revenge and instead turn the other cheek—to do so would be to rise above the earth. When it's kill or be killed, you lay down your life for another. Impossible.

Those nights he studied at the small desk in his room, as now, his concentration was fastened to the book on the table as if by primary forces. He assimilated every word and every twist of logic; he appreciated the ironies and understood the metaphors instantly. And when something struck him as—though he would never use the word himself—beautiful, whether a theorem or a sonnet, he memorized it word for word.

He'd never graduated Cathedral. Instead he'd transferred to a public high school on Staten Island, finishing his senior year with high honors despite the fact that he roamed the island nightly with Ivers and Deluxe. He told me that compared to the demanding regimen at Cathedral, public high school was easier than beating your meat.

He went to the community college the following year but by then I was at NYU and ran into him only rarely. When I did see him in those days I didn't like what I saw. He'd become one of the tough guys, if not their leader. The bartenders and bouncers and tavern owners were forever patting him on the back and leading him to the best booth or the back room as if he were the heavyweight champion of the world.

Maybe I was envious. Maybe I wished I was the one everyone stepped aside for, everyone revered. That would have been natural enough and might have been true except that Dietz was so changed I found less envy in me than a sense of having been cheated out of a friend, my closest friend. I found a sense of loss and envied his new friends more than I envied the champ himself.

He sat there tonight in the narrow chilly kitchen on Houston Street, his hair cropped close to his pale skull, his body erect, and he seemed to me the very picture of a devout seminarian. He would have romped through philosophy and theology; he would have read Cicero in the original; he would have memorized wonderfully poetic sermons and delivered them with that intense, blinding power of his. Instead he was a fighter, a warrior. He'd grown tired of school; he'd grown tired of small-town fights. I think he wanted to prove that war was no match for him either. He'd stepped up to the counter and taken a number for Vietnam.

He abruptly closed the book and looked at me. "When's the test?" he asked.

"Day after tomorrow."

"So there's no hurry."

"I want to ace it. There's a lot to study."

"What about tomorrow?"

"What about it?"

"Corney."

I breathed deeply. "I'm going, of course."

"I was wondering," he said.

"You were wondering what?"

"I wasn't sure you'd go. You don't always face up."

It was a cheap shot. I said nothing.

He stood from the table. "Where's your coat?"

I hesitated. "Who's out in the car?" I asked.

He grinned. "The bad guys."

"Ivers?"

"Ivers and Deluxe."

"I don't know why you bother with them."

He paused before answering. "They're all right."

I paced the floor and faced Dietz from across the room. "I'll go for a beer with you, not Ivers, and not Deluxe. There's always trouble."

"That's what they told me you'd say."

"I'm glad I didn't let them down."

Dietz smiled and said, "All right, Chun. Me and you," as if nothing had come between us.

Outside, Jimmy told Ivers and Deluxe to amuse themselves for a while. The two of us then ducked into a tavern on Third Avenue. We made small talk until we'd put a few beers down, and then Jimmy wanted to know why I'd not bothered to answer his letters from Parris Island and Lejeune.

"I had nothing to say, I guess."

"Tell me the weather's fine."

I wasn't able to figure out why he had even written to me to begin with. Couldn't he see that we were worlds apart?

Yet, then again, whom else would he have written? Ivers? Deluxe? Maybe his mother, but probably not his father. His father was angry that he hadn't become a priest.

His letters were all the same, telling me about one or another training exercise or weapon, or bragging about another award he'd won. He related stories about "Charlie" that had reached Parris Island and Camp Lejeune from the jungles of Southeast Asia. It was like reading about the Green Berets, and behind it all I could sense Jimmy swelling with a conceit that annoyed me. But it annoyed me in the most paradoxical way; I found myself envious of the power of the warrior and at the same moment repelled by the barbarity and waste-fulness of war.

I was going to make a lame excuse and tell him I'd been too busy with school to write but instead I came out rather vindictively and said

I'd grown tired of hearing about whose ass he was kicking.

"Hey, whose ass am I kickin'? I'm in the Corps. If I kick anyone's butt now, it's Charlie's."

I raised my beer bottle in mock salute. "Here's to you."

It pissed him off. If I'd been anyone else he'd have folded my head up my ass and then kicked me black-and-blue. He glowered at me.

"Why'd you join up?" I asked. "You could have avoided it."

"What do you want, Chun? The world's a rough place, y'know? You've got to stand up and fight back or you get crushed."

"What the hell's got you so angry? I can't figure that out. You used to stand on the corner up here with Father Lusenkas and hand out the words of Gandhi. I just don't understand what happened, and I'd like to know what it was."

He became for a moment like a welded block of steel. Impenetrable, immovable; his own fortress of silence.

"We once promised never, ever to give up on the other guy," I reminded him, "and if I don't ask you this I'm giving up."

He said, "Things are different now. Things that make sense when you're fourteen don't make sense when you're a man."

"This makes sense? The marines?"

"I suppose what you want is for me to hide behind schoolbooks or hightail it to Canada. Tell me, Chun, what're you going to do when Uncle Sam sends you a letter? What then? What are you going to do when you get a gook in your sight who's got you in his? Are you going to preach peace to him? If you do, you'd better make it a short sermon. When it's kill or be killed—there's no choice."

"If you want me to approve of what you're doing," I said, "I can't. The hero worship ends here."

Dietz dragged on his cigarette and looked away, out the window. I could tell he wished he could find it in himself to crack my jaw. He was wondering at his own reserve, asking himself why he didn't just smack me for my arrogance. When his attention returned he said with a bit of distaste, "Well, Chun, it's probably good you've got someone to fight your fights."

"If that includes suckering me into a car when you plan to unload a shotgun at people, I'd rather you didn't fight my fights."

He crushed out his cigarette and swallowed his beer in one great gulp. He put down the empty forcefully. The table shook and a few of the empties toppled.

"We'll have to see what happens," he said.

I didn't know what he meant.

We sat for long minutes in a forced and stiff silence. Dietz restored the fallen bottles one by one, rather gently and neatly it seemed. Then he stood and dropped some money on the table and said with the bitter intonation of an actor delivering a final, farewell line, "This was on me."

2

I'd felt again the great anger in Dietz and I wasn't certain when or how this anger had been born. Though I did know that ever since he'd had that fight with Ralph Ivers, he'd not been the same. Nor had Ivers. After that fight, Ralph Ivers became strangely devoted to Dietz. In one sense it was bizarre and revealing to watch this tough guy become a toady whenever Jimmy appeared, yet Ivers revered Jimmy, which was something not unfamiliar to me.

Ivers had gained a reputation over the years as the meanest, toughest son of a bitch around. He bullied his way through dances and parties, trying to provoke fights. He smacked guys in the face and popped them in the stomach just to get some fool to take a punch at him. If guys were stupid enough or drunk enough to try to hit Ivers, they were very quickly looking up from the ground with warm blood in their mouths. At that point Ivers kicked them. He always did. He always kicked people when they were down. I'd seen him do it, and it was a mean and ugly thing. After a while, Dietz was doing it too.

Ivers was strutting around a dance one night, and it happened to be in April, when we were juniors in high school. It was just a few months after Jimmy and I had been out to the cabin on that frigid night when Iron Jud, fortunately, discovered us.

When Corney pointed out Ivers and his henchman L'il Vic at the dance I recognized them as the guys who had pushed me around out at the auction some weeks before.

Ivers, predictably, was trying to get into a fight. He blustered into the men's room while I was there with Corney and Woodsie. Without a word he reached out and smacked Woodsie across the face. Woodsie knew Ivers from high school and immediately cowered. He covered his head with his arms and was scared to peek out. He pleaded, "Leave me alone, Ralph," while Corney—the mouth—laid into Ivers, telling him he was acting like an asshole. Ivers laughed menacingly at Corney. I could tell he was drunk. "Fuckin' Walsh," he said. "Shut your mouth before I stuff it full of shit."

"Your momma," said Corney. "Your *fud'yan* momma."

Ivers lunged for Corney. Corney was quick and moved to evade Ivers, but Ivers struck like a snake and in an instant he had Corney pinned to the wall by the throat. When Corney tried to say something, Ivers choked off the words. Yet even with this punishment Corney remained feisty. He wouldn't stop giving Ivers lip.

Ivers finally let Corney go and started out of the bathroom. He saw me on his way and asked, "What're you lookin' at?"

I shrugged.

He pushed me in the chest and sent me reeling, like a bug flicked off a shelf. I fell back into the door of the toilet stall; the door crashed into the side of the stall. I stood there, shaking, and hating myself for it. Ivers pointed a finger in my face and warned me, "Stay there. Don't come out." Then he must have remembered me from the auction, for he gloated at L'il Vic, saying, "It's pig's feet." He reached into my nose with two of his fingers and quickly pulled away, tearing the inside of my nostrils with his sharp nails.

I could feel my nose begin to bleed. I stood there, feeling humiliated. I wouldn't budge. I was scared shitless. I wished I had Corney's bravado or the strength of Dietz or Spyros. But I was a hunk of raw red meat that wouldn't fight back, while Ivers, if he wished, could have gobbled me down.

"You am a fud'yan cocksucker," Corney called after Ivers as Ivers and L'il Vic kicked open the door on their way out. I reached for the toilet paper and plugged my nose, refusing to return to the dance until the blood had stopped.

"Jesus, Chun, you'll be in here all fud'yan night."

"Hey—I ain't going out there with toilet paper up my nose."

"You take too much shit from him."

"Yeah? What do you think I should do, Corney? Knock him out

cold or just smack him around a bit? If I gave him the lip you did, he'd have drowned me in the toilet."

The dance was at the church hall, and Dietz was planning to meet us there. He had stopped at the rectory to see Father Matusiak, and although he hadn't confided in me, I had pieced together things and figured he was going to tell Father that he wouldn't be returning to Cathedral in the fall. He'd given the priesthood thing a chance and it hadn't worked.

My nose soon stopped bleeding and I left the men's room. Out on the floor the band was playing a loud and fast rock song and couples were dancing wildly. Most of the girls were wearing black skirts and white blouses with suspenders, black stockings, and shoes that looked like Peter Pan boots. Their eyes were fringed with mascara and their hair was teased out and sticky with hair spray. I got a hard-on just looking at them.

The guys wore tight chino pants, pastel poncho shirts—magenta or chartreuse or tangerine—a box-pack of cigarettes in the top pocket, socks that matched the color of their shirts, and Puerto Rican fence climbers with slick leather soles that made doing the mashed potato easy as spitting.

I distinctly remember seeing Dietz enter the hall. He was so out of place, wearing a white shirt and a thin black tie, his corduroy pants fitting loosely and far too short, his plain brown shoes recently shined, his double-breasted sport jacket buttoned—all the buttons—and embarrassingly small for him. He was neat and clean, his clothes pressed and his hair parted and combed, and there was about him the awful appearance of a hayseed, a rube who had meant to go buy a Mother's Day card but had instead accidentally stumbled into this rock-and-roll dance.

I was across the floor from the entrance. The dancers were between me and Dietz. The music thumped and wailed, and Corney and Spyros were grinding close with these two hot big-chested chicks from Great Kills. Woodsie was alongside me. Sperm had gone for a soda. Jimpie was holding hands with Toni DiSogra, waiting for a slow dance. I went to take out a cigarette to light when, across the floor, I saw Ivers strut over toward Dietz, who was craning his neck to find us. Not even five seconds had passed since I'd first seen Jimmy, and I was just about to wave him over when Ivers stopped in front of him and stood there a moment and looked him up and down. I watched Jimmy glance at Ivers and then watched him glance away. Jimmy knew nothing of him or his fearsome reputation; he was of no consequence to Jimmy.

Then there was that frozen moment. It froze and stored itself in a cryogenic chamber in my mind, and whenever I desired I could withdraw it and examine it over and over again. There were few moments in life which held such power and motion, such a strange delicacy and stillness—like pressed flowers or specimens imbedded in clear plastic; few moments when the world could be spun on the merest of instruments, as on a popsicle stick or a toothpick or a threadbare unraveled stitch of the continuum, spinning the way Corney spun a basketball on his index finger or the way Spyros spun a backflip on the dance floor or Woodsie spun his wheels to run from trouble; Sperm spinning in the air while the music thumped and rolled, Jimpie spinning to Toni's whims, and everyone spinning to the electric band at the dance hall, a crescendo of *You make me want to Shout! Raise your hands up and Shout!* with Ivers across the floor sizing up Dietz and snickering to himself, and Jimmy's life, the person I'd known and admired since I'd been a dreamy boy, about to change before my eyes. At that moment I should have known how tenuous was the fate of my friends, the cabin, the woods; how our youth would run away from us as if we'd become strangers threatening our own boyhood. All things after that moment would never be the same as all things before that moment. Across the floor, the past spinning clockwise and the future counter, Ivers smiled malevolently and reached out and popped Jimmy in the stomach.

Jimmy struck back blindingly quick, smacking Ivers across the face. There was an incredible magnificence to Dietz in that moment. You could see in his face how he recognized that he was far too noble to have been treated so insultingly.

Ivers couldn't believe it. L'il Vic and Deluxe were alongside him in a flash. Deluxe, who knew both Jimmy and Ivers, made an attempt to calm things down, though that wasn't really what he wanted and he didn't try too very hard at it. He wanted to see these two come to blows.

There was scant hope Deluxe and L'il Vic could have restrained the two if Ivers and Dietz hadn't chosen on their own to take the fight outside. They left through a side door. L'il Vic Gigliotti and Deluxe followed Ivers. I was behind Dietz.

It was a wet and rather chilly spring night. There had been rain, on and off, for days, and long shallow puddles stretched here and there across the parking lot. Scattered potholes that had filled with rainwater were color-streaked by motor oil.

Word had spread quickly through the dance that there would be a fight. But since it was Ivers who would be fighting, very few people bothered to come out and watch. It would be no contest. Who wanted to watch Ivers pulverize another poor bastard?

Not a word passed among those of us who stood there in the back parking lot. The surface was cinders and mud; there was a streetlight overhead, shining down through the leafless branches of a tree. The tracks of the rapid-transit line were just beyond the rusted chain-link fence, and as we arrived a train labored around the tight curve and its headlamp illuminated us briefly in a strong sweeping light. Then it continued past and its steel wheels screeched and the third rail sparked blue and yellow and laced the air with ozone.

Dietz took off his jacket and handed it to me. I wanted to say something to him, but I didn't know what to say. Should I tell him to be careful? Should I ask him if this was really worth it? Should I break the news to him that this was Ralph Ivers?

I tried to figure out what Jimmy was thinking and feeling, but I could get no clue from his face or the way he held himself. He appeared unafraid, no more concerned than he might be if he were waiting for a bus.

Ivers was cocky, itching to get at Dietz. He could hardly stand still. He shifted his shoulders and pumped his arms and couldn't wait to knock Jimmy down and use his pummeled flesh to sop up some of the mud. He looked every bit as invincible as a mountain. I was afraid for Jimmy and began to make plans for getting him to a hospital to have his cuts stitched and his bones splinted.

Ivers marched up to Jimmy. "It's your ass," he said mockingly and hamming it up a bit. He glanced over his shoulder to grin for his buddies and then turned and pushed Jimmy hard in the chest. But Jimmy didn't budge, and for just a moment there was this look of concern in Ivers's eyes. For a moment he seemed to wish he hadn't done what he'd done.

That push in the chest was it. Jimmy needed only that provocation. He destroyed Ivers so fast that I wasn't certain what happened. He punched Ivers and Ivers went down. One punch. That was all. And when Ivers tried to get up, Jimmy hit him again and dragged him through the mud. Then Jimmy grabbed Ivers's hand and bent back and broke his thumb—*crack!*—like a dry old stick. Ivers howled like a tortured animal, crazy with pain and holding his thumb, which drooped like the thumb of a wet mitten.

One of the guys who had come out to watch the fight suddenly grabbed Jimmy and said, "You'd better get out of here," and whisked the two of us off in his car. He meant that Ivers had many friends and we weren't safe.

Jimmy had fallen into the mud when he snapped Ivers's thumb. He'd thrown all his weight into the deed and had gone down. The mud coated his shirt and pants and he began apologizing to the guy for getting mud all over his car. The guy said, "Don't worry. I'm glad someone kicked his ass."

Jimmy looked at me. His eyes were wide; he breathed excitedly. "I couldn't let him smack me, Chun. I had to break him up."

He was somewhere else, intoxicated and pumped up over what he'd done.

The guy who was driving asked, "Do you know who that was?"

"No," said Jimmy. "But I had to break him up."

We were at the circle the following afternoon, hanging out by the bench, and of course everyone wanted to hear a description of the fight. Spyros tried to discount it, saying that Ivers must have been too drunk to fight back. Corney reminded him that Ivers always fought better when he was drunk.

Jimmy had little to say. He was calmer than he'd been the night before, though he hadn't really descended from the thrill he'd found in destroying Ivers. It seemed to please him immensely that he had defeated the undefeatable, had thoroughly crushed him. He enjoyed being asked about the fight and only moments before had given the Purps a colorful accounting.

While we were gathered there at the bench a Pontiac Bonneville pulled up across the circle. Corney said, "It am Vic's brother's car."

Ivers appeared from the car. Flanked by L'il Vic and Deluxe, he marched across the circle. His right hand was in a cast.

Woodsie asked, "You think he's got a gun?"

Good question.

The three of them came over and Ivers walked up to Jimmy. He asked him, "You're Jimmy Dietz?"

Dietz stood tall and nodded. He seemed to throw his chest out as if reminding Ivers who had whipped whom. There was something different about him. Not something so different that I'd never seen it in him—he'd always been bold and without fear—but different enough in its expression that I began to feel he'd been hiding himself from me. I might have seen in this the beginning of the end of our friendship, but I wasn't perceptive enough. I was swept along by his sudden fame as much as he. The power that was to make him heady was soon to make me unimportant.

"You want to go for a ride?" asked Ivers.

"What for?"

"Get a six-pack. Bullshit. Y'know, talk."

Jimmy considered the offer. "Sure," he said.

Ivers smiled. He said, "Let's go," waving for Jimmy to follow him to the car.

Jimmy turned to me and said, "C'mon, Chun."

Ivers balked at this, asking Jimmy, "Who the fuck's this?" Then he laughed, remembering. "Pigs' feet."

"The Chun," said Dietz. "The Chun's my main man."

Ivers immediately saw that where Jimmy went, I went. He didn't like it. Not that first day, not ever.

3

Dressed in a pair of dark brown pants and wearing a shirt and tie beneath my heavy winter coat, I took a subway to the ferry early in the morning and stopped for a breakfast of eggs and sausage on the Staten Island side. Then I grabbed a bus for St. Margaret-Mary's Church.

The heater on the bus wasn't working, and when I stood up and paced the aisle to warm myself the driver gave me a ration of shit about passengers remaining in their seats. I was certain that it was my long hair that had got him on my case but I didn't want him to kick me off so I sat back down. By the time I got off the bus my hands and feet tingled sharply with the severe cold.

I walked a half block to St. Margaret-Mary's, which was a small brick church with a large eye-level crucifixion scene in a corner grotto. I presumed there was plenty of steam heat inside, which at the moment was more important to me than anything else, and I glanced only briefly at the way they'd done Jesus and then climbed the stone steps and pushed open the heavy oak door.

The light was dim. The small flames of the red votive candles fluttered noiselessly before the side altar of Mary. Apparently I was the first to arrive, though as I crept up the aisle on the Epistle side and slid into a pew I acted as if I was afraid to disturb someone or something.

The numbness quickly left my hands and feet. My ears stung briefly as they warmed and then felt hot and red. I loosened my jacket and then took it off and placed it alongside me on the pew. I sat there and waited, not knowing what to do. I could have prayed, except that I would have felt a hypocrite. I couldn't recall the last time I'd been in church or had prayed—probably at high school graduation—and by now I no longer had faith that anything that went on here could possibly make a difference. The statues were plaster-of-Paris, the relics voodoo, the communion hosts white bread, the wine was mere wine. God wasn't particularly here. No more or less than He was everywhere. Nor was Jesus. Certainly not Mary. It was just a brick building where people assembled, hoping that God and Jesus and Mary happened to come in from the cold.

I sat and waited, listening for something between the spaces of silence that never came, like a voice of God giving me the okay, informing me that the world made sense and that there really was meaning. It didn't have to be a booming voice, and I could do without bright heavenly lights. Simply a tap on the shoulder as He slipped into the pew behind me, blowing on his hands and saying, "It's friggin' cold out there, Chun, and there's a senseless war and other difficulties—starvation, disease—but everything's okay. Believe me."

I sat and waited but God and Jesus didn't arrive.

Instead, they sent Jimmy Dietz.

The door opened, the church taking a breath of frigid air. The light briefly changed: a carpet of cold sun rolled up the aisle like a heavy fog. Then the hinges of the door creaked and the door slowly closed and the light was as it had been.

I heard footsteps and turned to see who it was. It was Jimmy, wearing his dress blues. Even in the weak light of the church I could perceive the glint of brass buttons, the knife-edge crease of his trousers, the gleaming black mirror of his shoes. He didn't have an overcoat. His cap was in his hand. I'd never before seen him in dress uniform. I was impressed.

He dipped his fingers in the holy-water font, blessing himself—not quickly, but slowly and methodically—and marched up the center aisle. He didn't glance in either direction, though he knew I was there, the way he knew when there was a chipmunk just peeking from a burrow or a wily adversary creeping close. He didn't miss those things.

He continued up the aisle, past the pew where I sat, and genuflected and entered a pew on the Gospel side. He moved several spaces into the pew and placed his cap on the seat as he knelt to pray, his hand to his forehead. His lips moved. In the quiet I could hear indecipherable words. I could tell he was talking, not repeating some rote formula.

He was still angry with me for what I'd said the night before. There was no mistaking that. He hadn't allowed his eyes to flicker over my face for even a moment. To him I was a plaster-of-Paris Chun.

When he finished praying he blessed himself once again and sat back. The pew creaked ever so slightly beneath his weight. Then, except for an occasional hiss of heat and the rustle of a church mouse, there was silence.

It wasn't long before other people began to arrive, but during those few minutes while Jimmy and I sat alone in the church, him on one side, me on the other, many things ran through my head. And though I felt I understood clearly what had come between us, I had no idea how it had happened. I mean, I'd foreseen changes in him ever since that cold night out at the cabin when Iron Jud saved us. I saw that he wouldn't become a priest. He was too angry. Then that fight with Ivers and the look in his eyes afterward, when that guy appeared from nowhere and told us to get into his car. Jimmy's eyes were wide open and full of shock—like he'd turned a corner and met a monster. Until that night he hadn't known just how tough he was, but once he'd learned there was no stopping him.

As I say, I don't know how it happened. Beyond the obvious, that is. Beyond the raw facts that he was strong and quick and didn't have to put up with lip from anyone. I don't know how or why Jimmy just couldn't have avoided fights, and although I knew I detested his violent side I didn't basically understand what came between us. There was something that confused me about our inability to come close any longer.

But maybe I did understand, I thought. Maybe I just couldn't accept it.

I looked across the church at him. He'd barely moved. He was giving me a lesson on discipline. I realized just how angry I was with him. He'd destroyed the fondness with which I held my memories. He'd made the future into something I hadn't wanted and had given me no choice in the matter.

I heard people outside. I heard the handle of the door click. As the mourners slowly entered the church and shuffled heavily into the pews, all I could think was that I'd like to give Jimmy a piece of my mind and then leave his life forever.

Mr. Walsh, who was already soused, took us out for drinks after the burial service. Spyros, Woodsie, and Harry were there; Sperm was in the navy and Jimpie couldn't get off work (or so he said). Deluxe and Ivers showed up, only because they were inseparable from Dietz. I was surprised they hadn't joined the marines with him. Deluxe was slapping people on the back like he'd been one of us for years. Ivers remained aloof and dangerous, like a Doberman on a choke chain.

Outside the cemetery gates those of the guys who had been close to Corney gathered in a knot. We spoke sparingly, in short reflective phrases, and during the larger spaces between our words we stamped in place and clouded the air with our exhalations and tried to think of something more to say. We were lost in that drifting-past of the burial, when the reality of the death becomes stronger than the unreality, when even though we thought we had said enough about Corney and that no one would care to hear anything more, yet still another memory or feeling aroused someone's tongue and then we all nodded and chuckled, remembering the event, sharing the feeling. I'd planned on saying nothing but then recalled for everyone the time when Corney and I pelted some cars with eggs just for fun and then ran off through someone's backyard. It had been night, and Corney, being a head shorter than me, ran under the clothesline that I didn't see. The clothesline caught me in the throat, throwing me down on my back onto the hard ground.

"I was lucky I didn't break my neck," I said. "I had a rope burn right across here, like someone had tried to lynch me."

"What'd Corney do?" they wanted to know.

"Yeah," they asked, laughing eagerly and yet ill at ease, as if covering unfamiliar ground. "What'd Corney do?"

"You know Corney," I said, trying to recall exactly what it had been that Corney did. "He came back for me," I said. "I was lying there on the ground, holding my throat."

"He must've laughed his ass off," said Woodsie.

"Yeah," agreed someone. "Fuckin' Corney."

That was enough, it seemed. I wouldn't be called upon to make up the words Corney had said. They could see the scene and they imagined how much Corney would have delighted in it: him missing the clothesline that took me down by the throat.

"Jesus," said Spyros. "I can just see him, y'know?"

"Yeah."

"Yeah. Laughing at the Chun."

Meanwhile Mrs. Walsh had left in the black limousine with a few of her friends. Mr. Walsh was standing with Jimmy and Ivers and Deluxe. Deluxe and Ivers hadn't attended the funeral service at the church. They'd met Dietz out front afterward. The cold seemed to bother the group of them no more than it bothered the thick granite of the tombstones.

None of us were sure what to do now that the earth had taken Corney, and in a way we welcomed it when Deluxe came over and said, "Corney's old man wants to buy some drinks. Down at the Seabreeze. It's the closest place. You guys up for it?"

We all sort of nodded, looking into one another's faces. We knew that the old Seabreeze Hotel was in Midland Beach and that Midland Beach had been the place where Dietz unloaded the shotgun at that bunch of guys. And even though Spyros and Woodsie and the others who stood there with me outside the cemetery hadn't had anything to do with that, they nevertheless realized that we were fair prey in Midland Beach. Still, they didn't seem to mind going there. I figured this was because they'd not been involved with the fighting and the night of the shotgun. They'd not ventured forth in those days with me and Dietz, when the two of us had cruised up and down Hylan Boulevard with Deluxe and Ivers and L'il Vic, and so they hadn't created enemies in Midland Beach and other places. If they were guilty of anything, they were guilty of once having known Dietz.

Of course, even though I might have made enemies, I was small potatoes. I was a mere hanger-on, guilty myself of nothing more than stupidity. It was Dietz and Ivers, Deluxe, L'il Vic, and the rest of that crowd who followed Ivers and Dietz who were most unwelcome in Midland Beach. They'd made it their habit to crash parties and dances and ambush guys who had strayed too far from their own turf. They always claimed it was a fair fight whenever they pounded on someone, but that was a lie. It might start as a fair fight, one on one, but if their guy started to lose, someone would lend a hand by unleashing a stray kick or a blind-side punch, while the others, after the punch or kick had been landed, would pull this guy off and tell him that it was to be a fair fight.

Fair meant winning, nothing more, and if their guy started to lose once again, someone else would emerge from the circle of cheering onlookers to provide the vicious cheating blows.

I'd seen enough of it to want no more. I'd seen fights start over "dirty looks" or because someone had talked to someone else's girl or because someone was a stranger or acted like he thought he was cool.

Every guy from New Jersey was vulnerable. They came over to Staten Island to drink at the bars down along the south shore, because the drinking age in New Jersey was twenty-one but only eighteen over here. They were treated like invaders and they'd get beat up badly, their cars trashed, the headlights kicked out and bricks thrown through the rear window, and all for no other reason than that they were from New Jersey.

"Get them fuckin' guys," I'd hear. "They're from New Jersey."

And with that there would be a fight and it would not be a fair fight, and people were kicked while they were down.

Get them fuckin' guys—they're from New Jersey. Get them fuckin' guys—they're from Puerto Rico. Get them fuckin' guys—they're niggers. Get them fuckin' guys—they're Jews. Get them fuckin' guys—they're slopes. Get them fuckin' VC. Get them fuckin' Russians. Get them fuckin' guys.

I never was to learn if it actually had been Mr. Walsh's idea to gather at the old Seabreeze Hotel or if someone had suggested it to him. Deluxe hadn't been correct about the old Seabreeze being the closest place. There were at least a half-dozen closer places. But the Seabreeze was the sort of place Mr. Walsh would frequent. It was a cocktail lounge where middle-aged married men brought their girlfriends or hoped to find hookers. I hadn't wondered until much later—months, in fact—if it had been Ivers who had made the suggestion. I hadn't wondered until then just how carefully Ivers had plotted to set me up as the guy who had fired the shotgun.

Only one or two of the others would have suggested going to Midland Beach. Dietz might have, just to show he could go where he pleased. Deluxe would have suggested it, just hoping it would spell trouble.

Maybe it had been Ivers after all, though I still couldn't credit him with the brains for thinking far enough ahead to set me up that way. I was sure the idea to throw me to the lions came to him only once we were there, drinking at the bar. I think that Mr. Walsh, oblivious to our turf wars, suggested the Seabreeze because that's where his cronies drank, and once the suggestion had been made not a one of us was going to act spineless and refuse. And since it was afternoon we perhaps felt that the light gave us an added margin of safety. I should have known we'd be drinking until late in the evening. I should have known I was going to be the lamb.

When we arrived at the Seabreeze, Mr. Walsh tossed a wad of bills on the bar and told us all to order a shot of liquor. I ordered a Jack Daniel's and raised my glass with the others and drank to Corney. Then someone else bought shots. Then Jimmy. Then Spyros. And so it went until I was so thoroughly shitfaced that for all I knew Jesus Christ Himself was buying the rounds.

Sooner or later everyone had more stories about Corney or further embellished the ones we'd already told. At first the stories made us laugh, but then there were more stories and I grew maudlin and metaphysical, angered over the way this lousy world had been put together.

Soon enough the liquor got to me. I was ready to pass out cold. I went to the men's room and dunked my head in a sink of cold water and talked sternly to myself in the mirror, the water dripping from my nose and eyelids.

When I returned to the bar I heard Jimmy say aloud, "Corney fucked up, that's all."

This was more than I could take. I knew I was drunk and should have kept a tight lip, but this was more than I could take.

"Oh, is that it?" I asked Jimmy. "He fucked up? Corney fucked up?" I looked up into heaven and called on Corney. "Hey, Corney, Dietz says you fucked up."

Ivers was at my side instantly. He clamped his hand around my arm and told me, "Back off the man, Chun."

"The man," I said mockingly. "The *fud'yan* man. He's got a name, Ivers. Tell him your name, Jimmy."

"Let go of him," Jimmy told Ivers.

"Hey," I told Jimmy. "You oughta apologize. You can't sit there and say Corney fucked up and smack your hands clean."

"You're drunk, Chun."

"So?"

"So you'd better give it a rest."

"Oh? And what about Corney? You just sit there and say he fucked up and that's that, right? I mean, what the fuck you care? You ain't gonna fuck up, are you? I mean, you're Jimmy Dietz, and Jimmy fuckin' Dietz is the man of steel. Everyone fucks up except Jimmy Dietz. I know different," I said, poking his chest. "I know Corney ain't the only one to fuck up. He's the only one to die for it, though."

I got to him. He sprang up from the bar stool and slammed me into the nearest wall. His face was contorted. His cheeks quivered. He snorted and his nostrils pulsed. His hand was across my throat and he could have crushed my windpipe in a twinkling.

We were eyeball to eyeball when he suddenly let go and backed off a step. He raised his fist. He never raised both fists. I'd seen him fight scores of fights and he never raised both fists. He always raised his right fist at the level of his shoulders and opened wide his other hand and held it at his side. If someone threw a punch at him he didn't block it but instead caught it in his left hand and then landed his right fist in their face. He seldom needed more than one punch. There was a feeling of hot torqued metal and supercharged air. I expected to hear a sharp crack, as if something had gone beyond its physical ability to withstand tension and, irreparably, snapped in two. I felt myself turn pale. For the only time in my life I was afraid of Dietz.

"C'mon, Chun," he dared me.

"Now it's my turn, huh?"

"You want to try it?"

"Of course not," I said.

"Then keep your trap shut from now on."

"Whatever you say."

Woodsie came over and took me by the elbow and led me outside into the cold air. I'd forgotten my winter coat but didn't bother going back for it.

We walked around the block a few times and then went to the diner on Hylan Boulevard for some coffee. We were gone for almost two hours and more than once saw a number of guys who had been in fights with Dietz and Ivers. We became cautious. It obviously wasn't quite as safe for us to be in this neighborhood as we'd led ourselves to believe.

When we returned to the Seabreeze, Mr. Walsh and Ivers and Deluxe were still at the bar. Harry and Spyros were gone. I didn't see Dietz.

Ivers came over to me and said, "How're you doin', Chun? Sober up a bit?"

I said nothing to him. He grinned and rocked his head. "Listen, you dickhead, I'd like nothing more than to twist your nuts off with a pair of pliers, but I got a code of honor with the man. He said he wants to see you before he goes to Nam. He's down on the beach, waitin'. Let's go."

He told Woodsie to stay at the bar while the two of us left alone. This time I grabbed my coat.

We walked down toward the beach, crossing the parking lot where people gathered for beer parties and the blacktop was graveled with brown and green pieces of broken glass. The wind off the water came across in frigid blasts. I stuffed my hands deep into my pockets and lowered my head.

We hadn't exchanged a word, me and Ivers. We left the parking lot and walked along through the sand and crossed beneath the boardwalk. When we emerged from between the hefty poles that supported the boardwalk onto the dark and cold beach I saw a group of guys. I couldn't see their faces but I figured that they were with Dietz. Why in hell they wanted to be here, though, made no sense. It was dark and cold.

"Here he is, boys," said Ivers, chortling. "The fuckin' Chun. The man with the shotgun."

They gathered around. Someone immediately belted me with a fist. They taunted me for having no balls, using a shotgun from a moving car. One guy pushed me into another and I tried to run but they only knocked me down and kicked me in the ribs.

"It wasn't me," I told them.

"He's a fuckin' liar," Ivers assured them. "It was him."

The three guys who had caught shotgun pellets in their legs and back let me know who they were while they beat the living shit out of me.

I didn't feel much after a while. They hit me so many times in the face and head that I began to lose consciousness. Then there was a tremendous thud and a searing pain raced across my cheekbone and up into my head. I saw a cold silver fire in my eye and then I saw and heard nothing. If they hit me after that, I didn't know it.

I was lucky to be alive the following day. I was in a coma, my head cracked, my eyeball in the red-bagged hospital waste. It would be touch and go for a few days.

4

" 'The heart hath reasons which reason knows not,' " said the Paymaster, quoting Blaise Pascal.

We were sitting in a movie theater, taking in a matinee and using conversation to fill the spaces where the plot weakened. He offered me some popcorn. I declined, and he figured something was wrong.

Then he offered me sage advice. This I was more inclined to accept.

"What you really wanted was for Jimmy not to make life sound so cheap. His life would be on the line soon. Maybe he was hiding from that. I guess you wanted to tell him that he still meant something to you, and that Corney did also. What happened to you was just what corn whiskey does to the truth. It rushes it out and spills it all over the table and never gives your heart a chance to catch up with your head, or your tongue to listen to common sense."

I nodded. There was nothing I could add. The light of the movie screen flickered over us. The credits rolled.

I said, "Then and there, I hated him." I looked at the Paymaster. "He always thought I blamed him for losing my eye. He never saw me one-eyed. He wrote letters, but I never read them. I was angry with him for becoming just another tough guy, and he should never have taken me along when he blasted those guys, but I didn't really blame him for the eye. The minute that happened, down on the beach, I had this notion that it was fated, that I was pulled toward that moment the way Corney was sucked to his death in Nam; the way Dietz was raised to his heights of power.

"But I sure hated him for shrugging off Corney's life. I hated him for reminding me of how little power I had; for not seeing what was important to me."

He sighed. "Yeah," he said. "I can understand that."

The usher came down the aisle to make sure we wouldn't try to freeload another movie. The Paymaster slapped my knee and said, "Let's go, Sport. Special treat today."

We left the theater and climbed into the Country Squire. We gave Peggy her head and she glided smoothly toward her destination. She brought us to a stop at the Little League field that was to have been named after Corney. The field, however, hadn't been named after Corney because in this fold of the continuum Corney hadn't become a casualty of war. He sat in the stands today, cheering his son's team to victory. It warmed my heart.

I knew the rules of the continuum under these circumstances. I couldn't go over and talk with Corney, but I could watch all I wanted. The Paymaster apologized for this, but I said, "Hey, I read *A Christmas Carol.* It's okay. I understand."

If I'd collected the talismans of Corney's life there surely would have been an autographed baseball from one of his two no-hitters, many empty beer cans and liquor bottles, piles of condoms (boy, did he get laid a lot!), girlie magazines, illegal fireworks, a basketball, and a wheezing tape recording of *fud'yan 'fwat woo-shit, we am together, Jack!* And if I were to shake it up and toss it out, I know what would happen. It would be a particular night, a night trapped in the humid dog days of summer. . . .

We were playing basketball and the playground was crowded. Even the Purps were there, trying to play basketball among themselves. They were awkward. They wore guinea workshirts, tight chino pants, and black shoes with pointed toes. We didn't know if they were dressed for basketball or to play the Sharks in a musical. When they tried to stop to grab the basketball, they skidded on their slick soles and their horseshoe taps screeched like old brakes. Their girlfriends looked on from the alcove and giggled at them. Terry and her sister Verna were there, and Louise Hackett and Michelle Mitchell, who had huge tits. All of them looked boss in their teased hair and made-up cat's-eyes and we were certain the Purps laid them every night. We were jealous as hell about it.

A few kids were playing stickball, and some other squirts, who were riding their bicycles in and out of our basketball game, ignored us when we told them to clear out. One of these kids was a real pain in the ass and he raced his bike across the basketball court just as Corney was coming down with a rebound. Corney landed on the rear wheel of the bike and he spun aside and hit the concrete with his head. It made an awful clunk when it hit, but Corney sprang to his feet quickly and chased the kid, yelling, "Fud'yan asshole!"

The kid glanced back over his shoulder and raced off. Corney had no chance catching him. He returned to the court and was about to take up the game when we noticed that McDaniels had gone into his madman routine across the way. He had kicked aside his lawn chair and was starting over toward us.

We couldn't figure out at first who had cursed. But then we knew it had to have been Corney, though it didn't seem fair that McDaniels would be pissed over what Corney had said. After all, the kid had toppled Corney on his head.

We all stood there breathing heavily in the heat and trying our damnedest not to appear guilty.

The Purps had sensed that something was about to happen. They stood where they were and looked on. The bicycle riders chose to keep their distance and cruised out to the baseball field. Only the heat remained as it had been; we panted as it closed around us. McDaniels came through the gate. The heat had gotten to him, too. You could see it.

What followed was a scene I have never forgotten, and between the images, in the folds of what I would one day learn were the hiding places of time, there was a clear prediction of Corney's fate.

While McDaniels stomped closer we stood there motionless, as if awaiting the approach of an executioner. He was wearing those plastic-and-rubber flip-flop sandals and their sticky regular slapping sound was all that could be heard.

The Purps kept a lid on their usual round of wisecracks. They sensed trouble. They could smell the wires burning in McDaniels's brain.

Jimmy had chosen to rest on one knee, holding the basketball as if posing for a photograph. Maybe, I thought, looking at Jimmy's position, McDaniels had come to knight Jimmy but had never learned how to approach the ceremony with grace and dignity.

Corney wheezed.

Woodsie edged away, scared.

Spyros, with false confidence, said, "He's comin' to shoot hoops, that's all."

"No, man," observed someone else in a whisper. "He's pissed."

McDaniels was close enough for us to see his eyes. He hadn't said a word. He didn't look at anyone in particular, which was part of his stalking method. He didn't want to give a guy a chance to run, because strong as he was he couldn't run worth a shit. Even so, no one other than Woodsie had ever run from him.

His face was rigid and his eyes were deeply bloodshot. His hair was wet and wildly disheveled from having gone for a dip in his backyard pool. He wore his bathing suit and no shirt. "Indecent," I muttered to Jimmy, who chuckled.

Suddenly, without hesitation, forgoing his usual method of grabbing a guy and torturing him, he lunged forward with an open hand and walloped Corney across the face. Corney lost his balance, rocked back, but at the last moment was able to stay on his feet.

McDaniels pointed at Corney with a shaky hand. "You little punk!"

Corney stood there holding his jaw. He was shocked but not in the least afraid. His face had a wary look. He was being cautious, trying to determine if McDaniels had gone off the deep end.

The rest of us didn't know what to do or say. Our eyes widened, our breathing was rapid. We too wondered if McDaniels had at last lost his mind.

My mouth was dry. I was frightened for Corney. I was convinced that McDaniels would hit him again.

"I didn't curse," protested Corney. "Keep your fud'yan hands off me."

McDaniels glared at him. He reached out as if wishing to strangle Corney. "Don't you tell me—you shut your filthy mouth!"

Corney defied him. "I didn't say a fud'yan thing!"

McDaniels hadn't expected Corney to stand his ground like this. It angered him; he was insulted. He grabbed Corney's wrist and yanked him closer. As he did so, he reached out and cracked Corney's face once again.

"Shut your trap!" he demanded.

Corney wheezed. "You am a fud'yan cunt."

This made McDaniels furious. He belted Corney again. The sharp *smack!* could be heard the length of the schoolyard. It echoed in the alcove, and even the Purps, tough as they were, winced.

This was too much. We all looked at one another, wondering how much longer we could put up with this. We grew restive, shuffling. Dietz was on his feet. He let go the basketball. It rolled away.

McDaniels still had hold of Corney's wrist. Corney wriggled and pulled back like a dog resisting a collar and leash. But his wriggling was to no avail. McDaniels was too strong, too determined to lay into Corney. Nothing would stop him now.

An ugly smile crept over McDaniels's face. There was no question: he enjoyed beating the hell out of this little punk.

"Look at that!" he barked, pointing out that his wife and kids had gone into the house. "Look at what you kids do!"

Anyone with even an ounce of sense could see that his wife hadn't led the kids away because of what Corney had said. They were embarrassed by McDaniels himself. That was why they wanted to be out of sight.

McDaniels gave Corney two quick blows. *Crack!* Corney's head rocked. McDaniels yanked him back. *Crack!*

"Fud'yan pwick!" said Corney. "Cocksucker!"

Blood had suddenly appeared, erupting above Corney's eye. I wanted the beating to stop, but I was unable to move or even yell. I felt absolutely useless and angry with myself for it.

The scent of blood fired up McDaniels. His eyes glazed over and his hand curled into a fist. Up until now he had struck open blows. A fisted blow would knock Corney out cold, maybe kill him.

But as soon as the blood appeared, Jimmy was there, behind McDaniels. He must have charged over when the last blow had struck, because he was there when McDaniels cocked his fist for the knock-out punch.

McDaniels reached back to bring the big punch up from the ground, but it was then that Jimmy grabbed hold of the man's fist from behind, pulling with all his strength. Even from where I stood I could see the cords of Jimmy's arms and neck knot up and strain.

Thrown off balance, McDaniels went down hard, his feet flying forward. He didn't release his hold on Corney, however, and Corney and McDaniels and Jimmy fell together in a heap.

In a moment a dozen people were there. One of McDaniels's neighbors had come over; a cabbie who had seen everything had left his cab running in the street to run to help. Corney's face was full of blood, as if he'd been born stained, and someone yelled for ice. But Corney pushed everyone aside and said that he wanted to be left alone. He would accept no nursing from anyone; he would show no pain to McDaniels.

We all wanted to believe that Corney got revenge on McDaniels. A story circulated that Corney had sliced the tires of McDaniels's pickup truck or had poured a jar of molasses into the gas tank. Other stories held that Corney telephoned McDaniels every morning at three o'clock to call him a fud'yan pwick. None of the stories was ever verified.

One night, about a week after the incident, McDaniels had come over to say a few words, not to Corney in particular, but to all of us. He never really said he was sorry, of course. He had come over to try to establish himself as a reasonable adult and somehow explain away what he'd done.

He should have apologized to Corney. We all knew that and we all thought little of him for not doing so. He was lucky not to be in jail or to have Corney suing him. But instead of coming up to Corney and shaking his hand, apologizing for having been such a maniac, he chose instead to lecture us on misunderstanding, giving us a line of garbage about how misunderstanding was a part of growing up, but making it sound as if *we* were the ones who had misunderstood something.

He glanced at Corney only once during this lecture, and he looked away quickly. I didn't know if he was ashamed of himself or merely wanted to make sure that Corney had come out of it with nothing worse than a black eye and a few stitches.

He finished up his piece by tying it into killing Japs. "You boys'll understand better once you get a chance to fight a war," he said, and returned to his house with a cocky air, having shown us how wrong we'd been.

The heat wave never abated. It was the hottest summer on record. The lawns turned brown and the air conditioners blew fuses. The nights were miserably hot and humid. The mosquitoes danced for joy and greedily siphoned our blood. Car radiators boiled over in the middle of traffic. Everyone's temper was at the flashpoint.

We persisted in our daily schedule of basketball in the morning, the beach in the afternoon, and more basketball until dark.

One night after an exhausting game we all dropped to the pavement like damp old rags. We wanted to go for a swim but the beach was too far. Instead, we made plans to skinny-dip in Whitaker's backyard pool. We liked the way his daughters hooted at our white asses when we got caught and had to scramble naked into the woods.

We decided to raid the pool after midnight, and until then there was nothing for us to do but wait.

We wandered over to the alcove and pitched pennies. We played a desultory game of handball under the lights of the street and argued over the rules—of which there had never been any—and we grew so lethargic in the miserable heat that even the idea of skinny-dipping was beginning to appear far too complicated. We were on each other's nerves. We disputed everything, while, to the west, the sky gradually changed from rose to silver, and finally purple. There was still light when we heard this strange, unearthly sound.

What the hell was that? we all wondered, looking into one another's faces.

Corney offered his opinion. "It am two cats porkin' "

"Your ass it is."

"Then maybe it am a cat porkin' your momma."

It came again. A shriek. Then a thundering voice and the breaking of glass.

McDaniels, we realized, was having it out with his wife.

We rose to our feet and shambled from the cover of the alcove. McDaniels and his wife had come from the house. They stood under the old scaffold, enraged, hollering and swearing at each other. Mrs. McDaniels had the kids in tow. They were bawling. Mrs. McDaniels was hysterical, shrieking like something not human as she led them into the garage.

We could make out only a few words. Mrs. McDaniels said she was going to call the cops if her husband didn't get out of her way, while McDaniels was trying to drown out everything by repeating bullishly, "We'll see! We'll see, you bitch!"

Sheer madness.

We stood there snickering with delight.

"Asshole," we agreed.

"For an old bitch, she's a fine momma," said Corney.

"Well, it looks like she won't be staying home tonight," observed Jimpie. "Wouldn't it be great if you took her home and fucked her?" he asked Corney.

In the garage, Mrs. McDaniels loaded the kids into the station wagon and started the engine. McDaniels, meanwhile, was saying, "Yeah? Oh, yeah?"

"No more! Not another day!"

"Yeah? Oh, yeah?"

"I'm leaving. That's it!"

"Yeah? Oh, yeah?"

The pickup truck was parked on the road. McDaniels stumbled over and got into the truck to move it and block the driveway. He started it up and forced the transmission into drive. The truck bucked and stalled. He started it up again but by then Mrs. McDaniels had the station wagon out of the garage.

The station wagon shot past McDaniels, and he jumped from the truck and reached for the nearest object, which happened to be a rake. He heaved it at the car. It whipped through the air like a propeller and dented one of the door panels. Mrs. McDaniels floored the gas pedal and the car bounced wildly. The rear bumper hit the street and scraped clean a hunk of paving.

Mrs. McDaniels was now so frantic she couldn't get the car into drive. Her husband took the opportunity to get the pedestal of the bird bath and raise it over his head to heave at the car. He launched it just as his wife jammed the car into drive and sped off. The pedestal sailed through the air and crashed in pieces on the street. The station wagon fishtailed at the corner and then disappeared.

McDaniels jumped back into the truck as if to chase after his wife, but he drove at a bad angle across the front lawn and managed to crush the sprinkler and take out the bird bath before bringing the truck to a stop in the shrubs beneath the big plate-glass window of the living room. He then jumped out of the truck and left it running as he stomped back to the garage.

He disappeared into the garage, but we could hear him. He was actually growling as he smashed and punched and shattered things in the garage. Then he returned and spent a few minutes beating up the front lawn. He threw whatever he could lift and cursed what he couldn't. He tore up the shrubs by the roots and heaved them into the pool.

He stomped about like an rabid grizzly. Clawing. Growling. Mauling.

"He's fuckin' crazy," I said. "Truly crazy."

"What's *truly* crazy, Chun?" Spyros mocked me.

"It'd be great to see him in a straitjacket," said someone.

"Maybe we oughta call Bellevue."

"They'd better bring some strong guys."

He went into the house. He bellowed. He howled. He screamed at the "bitch" as if she were still there.

Then, unexpectedly, there was an eerie silence.

We crept closer. We were directly in front of his house, much

closer to his yard than we had ever wanted to venture. All the neighbors had come out now, like groundhogs after a thunderstorm. Everyone watched the house with great anticipation. All seats were taken.
The show could begin.

The silence grew curiously long. All the lights in the house went
out at once. The air conditioner stopped breathing.

There was crash from inside. More broken glass.

All of a sudden, the front picture window was gone. It burst into a
thousand pieces as the console television set came flying through it.
The television bounced off the roof of the pickup truck and then
bounced once or twice across the front lawn before keeling over dead.

There, at the picture window, framed by the jagged edges of broken glass, stood McDaniels, stark naked and pounding his chest like a
mountain gorilla.

"Wow! Look't him, man."

"Some fud'yan shit, Jack!"

"Hey, Woodsie, even *your* dick is bigger'n his."

McDaniels growled and snorted and beat his hairy chest.

We laughed. It was uproarious. We played monkey-see/monkey-
do with him. We pounded our chests and cheered.

A police car turned the corner. The lights were flashing but the
siren was quiet.

We had only a minute or two, but we had a plan and we all knew
what had to be done.

"On *three,* man. Ready?"

"—the cops, but—"

"Too bad, the cops."

"Yeah."

"Yeah."

"Go. C'mon, go."

"Countdown."

"Three, two, one—"

"FUCK YOUUUU, MCDANIELS!"

Chapter 15

1

Things were not going well for Pete. He was having problems with Madeleine and he was having problems at the swim club. Madeleine was demanding that they get married, and Pete turned deathly pale at the suggestion. The days of "My, my Honey Bee" had so swiftly flown to the nostalgic past. Now when Madeleine appeared in her flashy LTD, Pete swallowed dryly and muttered, "Captain Hook."

Madeleine no longer went to the track with Pete, and Pete no longer returned from afternoon visits with her dressed like a tropical tourist and smelling of suntan oil. He no longer rubbed his dick and boasted of avoiding prostate problems. He began to look longingly at the scantily clad large-breasted pin-up girl on the tire-company poster. He would point to the poster and ask me, "How'd you like to get your mitts on a pair of those?"

"What do I need tires for?" I would ask facetiously. "I don't even have a car."

Madeleine had formerly cruised right in and parked in front of the office, but ever since she'd been at odds with Pete she'd been pulling the LTD off to the side, making it clear she wasn't here for gas or oil or TBA or a brake job. She was here to talk.

Pete would shuffle over heavily, like a man approaching the gallows. He would lean down at the side of the car, his elbows resting on the window trim, and talk seriously with Madeleine. Occasionally he would return to the office for the seat covers and climb into the LTD for a ride. More often, Madeleine would drive off angrily.

Pete's problems with Madeleine began just as the dog days of summer arrived. The heat was like an oven; the air was so humid that every dollar bill I handled was damp. Waves of heat rose from the blacktop, and the gasoline streaming through the pump handles from the underground tanks felt wondrously cold to the touch. The vapors from the dump crawled below the thick air, gathered at our ankles, then slowly crept up and wrapped around us like a constrictor snake. The odor was suffocating, and I took to wearing a bandanna around my nose and mouth one day, for all the good it did. Pete forbade me to wear it anyway. He saw me just once wearing the bandanna with my eye patch and told me I looked like a highwayman. "Jesus Christ, Summerhelp, you'll give people a heart attack."

"I can't stand that smell, Pete."

"If what you want is to stop breathing, come on over here. I'll give you a hand."

Pete, of course, tried to blame the heat for Madeleine's sour, demanding moods. He was wrong, though. At least the way I saw it. The time had come to prove his devotion.

During the last week in July the temperature and humidity were making people consider suicide. It was nearly impossible to breathe the heavy air; the nights were long and sleepless, and in the morning the sheets were damp with sweat.

It was a Wednesday when Madeleine drove in, braking the LTD to an abrupt stop over at her usual spot. Pete saw her and groaned. The day's sweat had matted his thinning hair to his pate and soaked his uniform. "Here we go again," he said, and dragged himself over to the car. From his back pocket he instinctively reached for the good rag, the chrome-polishing one, and as he stood there at the car, buffing Madeleine's chrome, it looked something like apologetic foreplay as he tried to reach an agreement.

It was at that moment that he learned about the problem at the swim club. A woman with a brood of kids, her station wagon crowded with rubber tubes and water wings, pulled alongside Pete and wanted to know why, in the middle of the worst heat wave in the city's history, there was no water in the pools.

Pete told her she was crazy. "Where else would the water be?"

"Not in the pools, I'll tell you that!"

"Where's the manager?"

"Gone."

"What d'you mean, *gone?*"

"Hah! You're on the board of directors. You tell me. Listen to the kids, will you? They'll drive me crazy if they can't swim. What am I supposed to do?"

"Pete," Madeleine called, "I see you're too busy for me. I'll talk to you sometime."

He turned toward Madeleine. *"Sometime?* What the hell does that mean?"

Madeleine drove off.

Pete looked at the woman in the station wagon. "Take them to Jersey."

"That's a little far, don't you think?"

Another car pulled in, and the driver, also a woman, was looking for Pete. There were three or four kids in the backseat of her car. The kids were fighting and whining. "There's no water in the pools," this woman told Pete.

The other woman said, "See?"

"I want a refund on my dues," demanded the second woman.

"Listen," Pete told the two of them, "this is an island, right? There's beaches everywhere. And most all of them beaches have water, because that's what makes them beaches. Now that water we got at them beaches is full of hepatitis and plague and venereal disease. Whyn't you ladies take your kids for a swim at one of those places?"

The women were livid, but Pete ignored them and went to the office for the keys to the Jeep. He started it up and raced over to the swim club, where he learned that the manager he'd upbraided the month before had quit without notice. During the night the pools had been emptied.

It was to take three days to fill the pools, and during those days a wild variety of angry club members drove into the station and gave Pete a piece of their mind. Pete, never at a loss for words, told them one and all to go to hell. He knew his days as a board member were over and he had nothing to gain by politeness or diplomacy.

"You handled it poorly," I told him.

"What's this? Free lessons on bending over and kissing ass? It was that little weasel."

"What did you expect? He got even, that's all. Wasn't that the day's lesson?"

"Listen, Summerhelp, for once you're right. If you see that little prick, punch him in the nose and I'll give you fifteen cents more an hour. Cut out his tongue and bring it back, and I'll make it twenty-five cents."

"What if I bring back his balls?"

He laughed. "I'll give you the whole frickin' business." Then he pinned me with a stare. "Only joking, of course."

Between the heat and the stench of the dump, his troubles with Madeleine and the pool, he was feeling besieged and couldn't hide it. He disappeared often into the air-conditioned burrow of Hanson's Tavern. He took me along now and then, telling me I could buy a few rounds with all that top-pocket money I'd been stealing from him. He told me a few small things about Madeleine, nothing very personal, nothing I couldn't have figured out on my own, just these very general remarks couched in language that would make it appear he was giving me advice on life—older man to younger Summerhelp sort of thing. The way I figured it, he needed to tell someone his worries and was short on friends at the moment.

He'd not seen the end of his woes yet.

The day after the pools at the swim club were filled, early in the afternoon and just after Madeleine had once again driven off angrily, the hatchet fell.

The exhaust of Madeleine's LTD still hung leaden in the humid air when a Mobile Oil courier delivered a telegram from the company's marketing division. The telegram chastised Pete for having failed to score with the Paymaster. Apparently the Paymaster had stopped recently and whoever had waited on him had blown an opportunity for the Paymaster's Five Hundred.

This was a new approach by the oil company, this slap on the wrist. It used to be that if you failed to score with the Paymaster you missed the bonus and didn't get the flag to fly or a new sign to replace the Pegasus, nothing more. Now they had taken to scolding.

When Pete received the telegram—dubbed a Paymastergram—he lined us up in the office and read it word for word. Then he shook the telegram under our noses and demanded, "Who was it? Which one of you is out to screw me so bad you go and fuck up with the Paymaster?"

"When did it happen?" asked Eddie.

"How the hell do I know? If I knew when it happened I'd know which of you bums to boil in oil."

Tom had been the last to line up for Pete's roll call. He had ignored the whole thing at first and Pete had had to go into the shop and tell him to consider the visit a personal invitation to join the rest of us for a dressing-down. Even then Tom balked, saying, "I'm too busy."

There had been trouble between Pete and Tom. They'd engaged in private little arguments over the last few weeks. By "private" I mean they'd walked to the end of the blacktop to yell at each other instead of just letting loose in the shop as usual. I wasn't sure what it was all about, though Eddie took me aside one day at quitting time to explain how Tom had gambling debts and Pete always bailed him out.

"If Pete doesn't fork over the cash, Tom threatens to sell his interest in the place," said Eddie grudgingly. "Frickin' spoiled crybaby."

"What interest in the place?"

"Tom owns a fourth of this place. Didn't you know that?"

"How'd he manage that?"

"Pete's wife was like a mother to him. She owned half of the business, and when she died she split that between Pete's daughter and Tom."

When Tom remained in the shop, refusing to obey Pete and saying he was too busy, Pete warned him, "You'll be busy looking for work soon."

Tom gave him a crooked smile. He was confident that Pete would never fire him, though he finally did appear in the office with the rest of us. He didn't actually fall in line as his Uncle Pete had instructed. He just lounged against the doorjamb as if none of this had anything to do with him. Pete repeated his warning, saying, "You'll be looking for work."

"So what?"

I pieced it together that Pete had finally refused Tom a loan and Tom was itching for an opportunity to make things difficult for him.

Pete narrowed his eyes at Tom and then turned on us. He angrily reminded us of the approved procedure for dealing with the Paymaster. He pointed out the Pegasus sign he hated so much. He told us that the only reason it was still there was our laziness. He gritted his teeth and told us that not only did Bert have the new Mobil sign, but Bert's sign was on a motor and turned—"Just like this here, see?" said Pete, rotating his hand to show us. "Nice and easy. Hypnotizing those customers. You can't drive past that sign without pulling in for gas. Hell, you can't land on frickin' Staten Island without feeling that sign pull you in for gas. Then he's got you. Oil, TBA, mufflers, brakes."

He shook the telegram and glowered at us. His eyes were like a blowtorch and his head and neck were gorged with blood. He spit when he yelled, and I thought that any moment he'd make one of us eat the Paymastergram.

"I'd like to know which one of you dumb bastards screwed me this time," he growled, pacing the floor. "Is it so fuckin' hard to remember what to do?"

He counted off the steps on his fingers. "Fill 'er up? Check the oil? Is there anything else? —Let me hear you say that, George."

"Aw, Jesus, Pete. That's stupid."

"Stupid, huh? Look't fuckin' Bert. Four hundred thousand gallons a month is stupid? *Fill 'er up? Check the oil? Is there any other way I can kill your ass and take your money?* Wash the windshield and the rear window. That's all I'm askin'."

"This is fuckin' crazy," moaned Tom. He turned away into the shop.

Pete bellowed, "Get back here! Where the hell do you think you're going?" He shook the Paymastergram. "This could've been you, hotshot. I seen you out there. You act like you're doing them customers a big favor. You think you can waltz right in and run a station, don't you?"

Pete followed him into the shop.

"Hey, it wasn't me who fucked up," said Tom, picking up a brake tool. "It was probably Summerhelp."

"Yeah? Yeah? Well, I got news for you—it wasn't Summerhelp. Summerhelp's done it so many times he likes it more than sex. That little dickhead's one of the best gas jockeys I ever seen."

"Thanks for the compliment," I said.

"Shut up," Pete told me. He continued at Tom. "It wasn't Summerhelp who fucked up. No, I bet it was one of you hot shot mechanics who think pumping gas is for brainless one-ball assholes. You get your nose in an engine and you forget what pays the bills around here."

Tom was surly and nasty. "This is such bullshit."

"Bullshit?" spat Pete. He was purple. "That's cute. You fall into the business and now you think all I've done to build it up is bullshit?"

"Hey, if it wasn't for that stinking pile of garbage out there, you'd be just where Uncle Bert says you'd be."

"Oh? Oh?"

George and Eddie were in the office with me, the three of us not saying a word and wondering what to do with ourselves. Tom and Pete were at each other's throat, screaming loudly. Thankfully, a car pulled up at the pumps. I ran out and then the garbage trucks suddenly appeared, forming a long queue. I was busy pulling the nozzle from one truck and sticking it in the next when I saw Tom stomp out and jump in his red Le Mans. He started it up and screeched across the lot, chirping the gears and slicing like a knife into the four-lane.

Within a few days he was working for Bert.

2

Not too infrequently I have become terribly concerned that the Paymaster will throw up his arms and surrender to the tide of hopelessness and cynicism that has drowned so many other brave men and heroes. He will become one more victim, a member of that sad collection of lost and indecisive souls. He'll lose touch with the object of his existence. One gloomy afternoon the continuum will collapse into the quotidian and the Country Squire will appear at Pete's Friendly Service. The Paymaster will hand me the keys and walk away, looking dismally naked without Peggy. At long last even he will have grown disillusioned; even he will have ceased to believe.

"Sport," he'll tell me, "you give it a try. I've done everything I can. It's senseless. They want to go to the moon but can't make peace on earth. I can't figure it out. Wise men are outnumbered by fools; the good are crushed by the greedy; the weak are reminded every day that they're doomed.

"There's this swell vacation spot I'm interested in, a cottage under the pines tucked away in a quiet backwash of the continuum. I used to think I'd feel guilty, giving up, retiring. But I'm too tired now to feel guilty. I gave it a go. It's the world that's not ready.

"Maybe the infusion of some new blood will help. Some live blood, blood pumping through live hearts—not spilled blood.

"Good luck, Sport."

"What are you saying?" I'll ask. "This can't be so. What's the continuum without the Paymaster?"

He won't answer. He'll have said his piece. He'll simply walk off, alone.

"Hey! Hey, what's this mean? Is it up to *me?* Is that what you're saying?"

The only response will be this deep silence, this place without voice or echo. I'll be standing there at Pete's (and no doubt it will be an especially malodorous day), with the keys in my hand and the blessing of the Paymaster upon my mission. Then Pete will stomp over and demand of me, "What the hell's going on here? You posing for a Polaroid? Don't never stop moving your ass as long as you're on my payroll. There's cars need gas and tires to be fixed. The bathrooms need to be mopped and that workbench is all full of crap that's got to go."

"Pete, try to understand—"

"Understand? This is what I understand," he'll say, rubbing his fingers together.

"Pete, listen. The Paymaster was just here and he's given up. He's had it. He's just tuckered out and can't try anymore. People take his money but don't take his advice. No one asks the basic questions anymore. I don't mean that crap about fill 'er up and check the oil. I mean the *real* things we ought to be asking.

"This might come as a shock to you, Pete, but before he walked off, the Paymaster personally appointed me his successor. It seems that I'm the Paymaster now."

"You're *what?*"

"The Paymaster."

He'll guffaw so deeply the vibrations will shake the piles of garbage next door. "Yeah? And I'm Gene Autry's friggin' horse."

"I'm serious."

"You'd better get out of the sun, quit breathing them gasoline fumes."

But I'll stand my ground, what ground of permanence there might be in the ever-shifting continuum, and Pete will call out for doleful George and greasy Eddie, telling them in a mocking tone, "Hey, guess what? Summerhelp's finally flipped his lid. Do you know what he thinks? He thinks he's the Paymaster."

Pointing at me with a dirty crescent wrench, Eddie will say, "Him? Are you shittin' me or what?"

George, bags under his eyes, will advise me, "Summerhelp, your long-haired compadres slipped you some locoweed. You best stop smoking that shit or you *will* be crazy."

The only way to avoid the ridicule will be to remain silent, to refrain from telling them what I know. It will be up to me simply to get into the Country Squire and drive away. There could be no other choice. Without decisive action, the myth could die then and there. There is no guarantee that these things will go on forever.

The possibility frightens me. The Paymaster will give up and I'll be fully aware of it and, in some way, responsible. He'll leave it up to me to decide what to do.

3

There had been this medic, see? On television. I'd stopped at Hanson's last night after closing the station and there was a news special about Vietnam on TV. I watched the thing closely, figuring I'd see Jimmy and learn that he was alive and well and had simply over-stayed his tour from a sense of patriotic duty.

A medic had knelt by a dead soldier to remove his dog tags. I watched the medic place one of the dog tags in the mouth of the dead soldier just as the camera pivoted away to record some other scene. I was unable to make out clearly if the medic had jammed the tag in the dead soldier's mouth, really jammed it, the way it's supposed to be done so there aren't any lost dog tags, no unidentified corpses.

It had happened quickly, in the background, the medic performing his grisly duty in a twinkling. Yet I'd seen him place the dog tag in the dead man's mouth. I'd seen that much. The dog tag, just like holy communion, the dead body now sacred.

The ritual with the dead soldier brought to mind these dog tags that the Board of Education of the City of New York issued us in the first grade. The government was afraid of an A-bomb attack and they needed a way to identify all those dead kids. To memorialize us, I suppose. To name a Little League field after one million children—or, better yet, think of it, a million baseball fields, each named for a dead child, a million baseball fields where no one played baseball ever again. Now *there's* a memorial to war! There are few places more bereft of life than an empty ballfield. But at least the fields would have names and the dead could rest in peace knowing they had died for a damn good reason.

The dog tags they issued us in grammar school were paired, to be worn as a set around your neck, and every morning when the teacher called the roll, before it was determined if you had earned a gold star or silver star for yesterday's work, before you went over to paste a cotton puff on your weather calendar to show it was cloudy today, before you even took out your books, you were to pull out your dog tags when your name was called and jingle them for the teacher to see and hear.

No doubt there had been a rather pompous genius at the Board of Education, some Ph.D. who wrote erudite pieces for respected journals, who suggested that the teachers make a game of it. And make a game of it they did.

A game. Can you imagine? A-bombs and dog tags. A game.

"Andrew Hapanowicz?"

"Here!" *Jingle-jingle.*

God, am I a good boy!

In the military, there is a perfectly logical reason for pairing the tags. The logistics of identification of the dead require it.

On the field of battle, when a soldier is fatally wounded, one of his dog tags is removed to be turned over to his superior officer. The other tag is inserted into the dead man's mouth and, generally, lodged firmly between adjacent teeth by means of a severe upward blow to the jaw. Since the poor bastard is already dead, it doesn't matter exactly how you choose to jam his jaw, though it's reported that a solid knee kick works best.

Eventually the dog tags were no longer required as standard issue for grammar-school children. But before that day arrived it so happened that my teacher dispatched me on a journey through the long and immense corridors of the school to carry a note to the vice principal. This was an unheard-of assignment. Others in the class had been sent with notes for one or another teacher, even for the principal herself. But to the vice principal?

My classmates watched me with wide eyes as I left the room. I was about to encounter the Troll of trolls, the Ogre of ogres, the Fearsome One. For whereas the principal was a kindly, rather grandmotherly woman who always had encouraging words for us and had been known to have tears roll down her cheeks when the assembly sang "God Bless America," the vice principal was a burly man with ugly hair the color of old newsprint, a loud powerful voice, and an uneven temper. He had a small dark cave of an office on the second floor, and it was into this place that the most unruly and disrespectful students disappeared to be disciplined. Now and then when our class marched in line from the cafeteria or assembly and we passed by his office, we could hear his booming voice from the other side of the solid wood door. It sent shudders through us.

I arrived at the vice principal's office with the note, only to discover that the door was locked. I retraced my steps to the main office, which was close at hand, and a woman who worked there behind a large typewriter instructed me to take the note to such-and-such a room, writing down the room number on the back of the folded note that I felt honor-bound to deliver to the vice principal and no one else.

Arriving at the room, I knocked on the door. There was no answer. I knew there were teachers within, however, because I could hear them. They were talking, all at once it seemed, rather loudly, and laughing now and again. I didn't know what to think. I knocked on the door once again and waited, the vitally important note clutched in my small hand.

From within, once again, emerged the laughter. It was a strange sort of laughter, glazed and uneasy, and even though it was laughter it began to frighten me. Nevertheless, determined to deliver the note to the vice principal, I reached for the egg-shaped bronze doorknob. It was at eye level and it bore the seal of the Board of Education, City of

New York. I tried to turn it but found I couldn't do so with one hand. So I put the note in my back pocket and used both hands on the knob. The knob turned and I pushed on the door. The hinges creaked ever so slightly as I narrowly opened the door and poked my head into the room. When I saw what was happening, I froze. The teachers were practicing the knee-kick method of inserting dog tags between children's teeth.

A handful of teachers, under the direction of the Ogre of ogres, were taking turns practicing the technique. They were using Patty Playpal for their second-grader; she was a life-size toy doll that was the rage back then. She stood a tad taller than me and my friends', she had predominantly Anglo-Saxon features, with apple-red cheeks, a jaw that moved, and plastic teeth. Perfect.

No one had noticed me. They were that intent on their work. I watched more than one teacher step up, slide a dog tag into Patty's mouth, and give her a solid kick in the jaw. Her rubbery head bucked back and wobbled, and her poker-chip eyes spun wildly in her bashed face.

Then the vice principal noticed me. There was steam coming from his ears and fire in his eyes as he bent forward and advanced toward me. An angry scowl twisted his face and he demanded loudly, "Did you knock? Did you open that door without knocking?"

I didn't know how to answer. Did I say yes or no to such a double question?

I wanted to tell him yes, I had knocked. I'd knocked twice. But my mouth wouldn't work and my legs began to go numb. I looked past the vice principal to Patty Playpal, who had a dog tag wedged in her mouth like a small license plate. A speechless teacher held her on her feet. Her face was deformed from all the harsh treatment she'd received, and she was naked, no less.

Meanwhile, the vice principal had nothing on his mind but my lack of manners, still demanding, "Did you knock? Did you come in here without knocking?"

I felt awful about having barged in here, and as the vice principal now loomed directly over me I began to doubt I'd knocked at all.

"What's your name?" he growled, reaching for my dog tags.

I knew I was next. They were tired of the doll.

I reached into my back pocket for the note, knowing if I held this up in front of the vice principal's face he'd see that I was on a perfectly dutiful mission.

But the note wasn't there. It must have fallen to the floor.

I did the next thing that came into my mind. I squirmed from my dog tags, threw them to the floor at the vice principal's feet, and ran for my life.

4

In the morning at the cabin I awoke alone. I propped myself up and rested on my elbow. I'd slept late. I'd missed dawn and I could hear the men at the houses. They were near enough these days to be seen from the roof of the cabin. I knew what they thought about me. They thought I was crazy. Weird. Hopped up on drugs.

Drugs? Well, yes there were drugs. A little marijuana was all, though. Nothing stronger. No acid. Not even a tab of mescaline.

But it didn't matter what they thought. I was here to bring Dietz home. Wait and see. I'd make them believers. And after that there would be a long, long line of parents and girlfriends and wives and children of other missing soldiers. One by one those poor distraught souls would hand me requests written on plain paper, but paper that had been folded and unfolded and worried and clutched into a thousand creases, like the creases on the face of the aging shaman, aging before his time. The requests would be name, rank, and serial number. Bring them home. Please, bring them home.

I found no fault with the workers, and it came as no surprise that they took such joy in deriding me. They delighted in seeing me every morning as I emerged from this stand of trees. They stopped what they were doing the moment I appeared. Silence momentarily descended upon the scene while I concentrated so deeply on the path I was following that I appeared entranced. Then came catcalls and hippie jokes, shallow humor following me as I stitched my way around stacks of lumber, bales of fiberglass insulation, bundles of shingles, and buckets of black concrete sealer; along hefty planks and down into a foundation, where I ignored the masons who stood there, trowels in hand, watching; jogging through a framed house, front door to back, or back door to front, depending on how the cabin path twisted and led me, the path along which Jimmy had led the two of us the night we sacrificed the *thuk-lub-dub,* the path of the summer day the guys first assembled at the sacred place of the cabin.

The men soon learned to time their first coffee break to take advantage of my appearance. They sat like fans in a stadium, drinking coffee and eating doughnuts, their feet dangling from the second floor of a framed duplex, hooting and mocking.

"Hey! Here he comes, boys."

"Yo, Ponytail! What you been smokin'?"

Occasionally the bulldozer driver pretended not to see me and brought his machine to within an inch of me before stopping. Then he would tip his 'Cat hat in ridicule and allow me passage.

It didn't surprise me when one morning I looked up and saw Spyros at the controls of one of the 'dozers.

"You're acting crazy as shit, Chun," he told me. "I guess this is what happens when you get hit in the head with a baseball bat."

"Yeah," I said. "You go on believin' that."

I could handle Spyros, but I was easy prey for the older men, and I knew it. In their eyes I was young and untested. My skin looked tender, and my hair, though long, could not conceal the fluffy down of a college boy. On mornings when I appeared with the patch over my eye they had a whole repertoire of pirate sayings. Avast and shiver me timbers and yo-ho-ho and all that unimaginative crap.

"We seen that place where you live," one of the carpenters told me. "Don't be getting too settled back there."

"Yeah," added another. "A couple of weeks and that bunch of trees and that shitty little cabin are gone."

They said they'd been back there, but I was sure they were lying. They'd seen it from a cherry-picker bucket or from the roof of one of the houses. They hadn't been there.

They were accurate about the urgency of the situation, though. The machines dug into the earth daily, bringing up the stones and scraping away the topsoil until in every direction there appeared streaked layers of clay like scars incapable of healing. A hole was hollowed out of the earth for one after another house, until there were houses without number. The men moved the plywood forms for the concrete from foundation to foundation, while the elephantine cement trucks lumbered up, poured their slurries, and returned to do it again, day after day after day.

In the past, the advance of the developers was slow—one surveyor's stake at a time. We saw them multiply and we began to uproot them and carry them far off, convinced, perhaps, that these small acts of rebellion could delay or even prevent the inevitable. But then men appeared in pickup trucks and cars, out at the dead ends and even on the WPA roads, spreading maps and blueprints on the hoods of their vehicles, making sweeping gestures with their arms at the woods and nodding confidently. They pointed in one direction and then another. It would have taken an ass not to see their intentions. They wouldn't be content with a house here, a house there, leaving the woods and the paths between them. No, it all had to go. Every last tree. The woods, the paths, the sacred places of boyhood.

From the hidden location in the woods where we had chosen to spy on the men we could see how happy all of this was making them. We could smell how rich they were going to grow.

Like Robin and his Merry Men, we did what we could. We waited for them to get into their cars and then scampered off to our ambush. From a rise of thick woods we pelted their windshields with rotten eggs and bad tomatoes. We tossed down plastic bags filled with orange and green paint, the bags bursting open in splashes of color across the hoods of their cars and trucks. They screeched to a stop and jumped from their cars hopping mad, and one day they even fired a shotgun in the air. But they didn't come into the woods after us, because they knew they'd never catch us. Not even the cops would chase us into the woods. They might park on the road and venture a few feet into the brush and thickets, and at night scan the woods with a spotlight, demanding, "All right, you kids, come out of there!" while we lay low, skillfully hiding the glow of our cigarettes, snickering, the telltale evidence of ugly paint splotched on our T-shirts as we repeated mockingly, "All right, you kids, be stupid shits and surrender."

When finally the trees that had formed the trusty redoubt of the deep woods were felled, it seemed so sudden that I suspected the treachery was far more widespread than any of us had dared imagine. The bulldozers dragged away the trees, which then, along with the construction debris of plywood, scrap lumber, tar paper and shingles, twisted wires, and old sheetrock, filled Weed Pond. It was all part of

this unthinking, unfeeling, monstrously hungry machine greased by
money and fueled by men who lacked vision. Nothing could stand in its
way. It had tasted vast profits and didn't care now what had to be
destroyed. Acre after acre of our precious woods was taken without a
second thought. The men who did it had never learned the magic of
the place, had never cared to try. Not the carpenters, not the plumbers
or electricians, not the bulldozer driver, the architects, contractors,
lawyers, bankers, politicians—not a one of them really knew what was
being destroyed. How could they? They'd never been here. They'd
never run the woods on the full-moon nights. They'd never taken to
the paths.

Those who would come to live here would arrive at a place far
different from the place it had been. They would never understand its
myths; they would never know its wisdom and its joy.

They were blameless, though. They wanted a house, that was all.
A house with a narrow plot of lawn, a driveway, a small maple tree.
They had worked hard to buy these things and they would work even
harder to keep them. They couldn't be faulted for wanting a better life,
for wanting to get out of a tenement in Brooklyn.

Yet even though they were blameless, in the way that humans are
often blameless, it was nevertheless sad that the woods would yield to
crowded duplexes and the paths to streets without sidewalks; that the
secrets of Weed Pond, the Big Trees, Iron Jud, the Conklin place, and
the endless thrills of midnight runs and bushwhacking cars and camping out beneath the stars would disappear forever into a place where
only the Paymaster or a true shaman of the paths could ever again find
them.

Chapter 16

1

The Paymaster's casualness could fool you. He was generally at ease, not terribly excitable, yet I'd learned that there was little he did that was without meaning or consequence.

We'd been up north in mountain country, putting a few gas jockeys to the test, and I was concerned that any day now the cabin would be gone, and with it the paths. So I asked him how I'd be able to find Jimmy. He was eating pistachio nuts when I posed that question of questions. He smacked his lips and wiped the salt of the nuts from his red-tipped fingers.

"That's a tough one, Sport. What do you mean?"

He was a stickler for detail when it came to posing a question. The more sensitive or mysterious the information I sought, the more delicate or complex the maneuver I expected of the continuum, the more precise I had to be in framing my question. The Paymaster had said that the continuum was like a trampoline. It responded in kind. "You press here, the continuum gives; you let go, it returns to what it was before you pressed it." Since it responded to every question, he explained, the need for clarity was paramount.

"Sometimes you get an answer that confuses you," he pointed out, "because you asked a different question than you thought you had."

"I guess what I mean," I said, "is that I'd like to know where Jimmy is."

"Oh, is that it? That's no problem."

"It's not?"

"No. No problem at all. He's in the continuum."

"That's no answer. The continuum's everywhere. It's all places and times."

"Sure. That's a fact. The basic continuum: here and now, there and then. Wonderfully handy device. And the real beauty of it is that there's just one." He raised his index finger, the finger with the missing distal joint. "Just one continuum. So you can take book that Jimmy's out there."

His mind was the ultimate Zen koan. A puzzle not meant to be solved, as life is not meant to be solved, only experienced.

I was dissatisfied with his answer about Jimmy. I couldn't accept his remark as anything other than a glib evasion. Perhaps this was unfair of me, to judge him that way. But I was confused and my need to see Jimmy was strong.

"Are you hungry?" asked the Paymaster, seeking, as does a parent, the simplest solution first. "Whyn't you eat that sandwich?"

"Later," I said.

We continued along. Nothing fancy. Night had fallen and Peggy casually wound her way around the mountain roads. The headlights of other cars appeared, blinked at us, and were gone. The stars came out at eye level above a ridge to the east and a fist-sized meteorite melted down from the purple darkness o'erhead.

Eventually we came upon a gas station. The Paymaster said, "Here we go. Get me a fifty from the box. We'll see if this guy's on his toes tonight."

He turned the Country Squire into the station. *Last Gas For Miles*, the sign read, scrawled there in orange paint by an amateur sign-painter. "Another chili factory," quipped the Paymaster. I grimaced. It was an old joke.

The tires of the Country Squire rolled over the bell hose and the bell clanged loudly within the station. I had meanwhile taken a fifty-dollar bill from the Dutch Masters box. We came to a stop at the pumps and waited, but no one appeared.

"Put the stopwatch on him," I suggested critically.

"Not yet. It's night. The rules have to bend a little."

"The rules never bent for me," I responded.

"That's because sometimes you're too busy feeling sorry for yourself to see it."

He was right.

We sat in the car and waited. The gas jockey was nowhere to be seen. I finally said, "I think he lost out." I opened the cigar box to replace the fifty, but just then a tall rubbery man sauntered from the dim recess of the shop. He was tightening his belt and muttering aloud as he made his way over to us.

"Hold your horses," he said, trying to sound apologetic. "I was on the john."

He came to the driver's side, touching his forehead as if there were a cap there. "Howdy."

Okay, I thought, that's *one.*

"Fill it with high test?" he asked.

Two.

"Last gas for miles," said the Paymaster. "Guess I'd better."

"Yessir. Yes, indeedy."

While the gas flowed into the tank, the man cleaned the windshield and the rear window. He even hummed a light tune and tapped the beat on the fender with his fingers.

Three. Two more points and he'd have the bonus.

The gas nozzle clicked off automatically. The man removed it, hanging it back on the pump. He returned to the window. He wiped his hands on a paper towel. "How's the oil?" he asked. "Whyn't I give it a look-see?" He grinned knowingly. "Last oil for miles, too."

Don't say it, I thought.

"That's a slick remark," quipped the Paymaster.

The man laughed lightly. "Slick," he mused.

"Thanks anyway," said the Paymaster. "But the oil's fine. She hasn't burned or leaked a drop since she came off the line in Detroit."

The man stepped back to take in the lines of the car. He nodded approvingly and said, "A 'fifty-three, isn't she?"

"Every inch."

"They sure don't make 'em like they used to. This here's a class piece of machine."

The Paymaster motioned for me to pass him the fifty.

"He didn't get the five points," I whispered.

"Close enough."

"Close don't cut it. You've told me yourself: *There's certain rules to this game.*"

The gas jockey leaned close to the window and said, "That's six dollars and seventy cents."

The Paymaster handed him a ten. The man took the bill and went inside to make change.

"He got four out of five," the Paymaster said. "That's good enough for me."

"I don't believe this. How can you arbitrarily lower the standards like this?"

He shrugged. "Simple. I'm the Paymaster."

The man returned with the change. As he counted it out I held firm to the fifty. The Paymaster meanwhile insisted that I pass it to him.

"Well," said the man. "Thanks. And if you're needin' any TBA., come back soon."

Five.

I slid the fifty across.

"TBA?" asked the Paymaster. I could tell without looking that he was grinning from ear to ear. He just loved it when someone earned the bonus.

"What's TBA?" he asked, pretending to be new at this.

"Hell," replied the man. "I screwed up on that again. I should've come right out and told you what it means. Jesus, if you was him—the Payman—why, I guess I'd have dug my own grave and well deserved it. My boss drives me crazy about all this, saying how we got to push TBA and screaming about how the company's quota for TBA gets higher and higher. And he never shuts up about how the Payman won't give you a second look if you forget TBA. It's a silly game of theirs. Who knows if it's even true? They say if you do everything the way you're supposed to—well, you'll get your bonus from the Payman."

The man chuckled and lounged easily against the pump. It was as if some element in his relation with us had changed and now he was permitted to relax. "You never know when the Payman might show up, they say. Why—you might not believe it—but it could be you. Imagine that. Imagine if you was him? The Payman?"

"Imagine."

2

My back was propped against the wall of a new foundation being built on land that had been the Murtaghs'. I sat looking across their pool at the window above the sunporch where the night framed a lonely rectangle of yellow incandescent light. I watched for movement there, in Eileen Murtagh's room, but when movement came it came as shadows and the shadows seemed desperately alone and thin, as if the ashen remains of a brilliant spirit.

Every August there had been a big party for Mrs. Murtagh's birthday. I think it had been the favorite day of the year for Mr. Murtagh. He'd always hired a band and a caterer and set off fireworks. I'd liked him for that, for being so happy his wife had been born.

There was no party this year, however, nor was it likely that there would ever again be one resembling the others. Like everything else around me, this too had changed, and this too had taken me by surprise.

I'd learned that morning that Mr. Murtagh had been struck by a car the night before on the Belt Parkway. He was returning from the airport, where he'd just placed Mrs. Murtagh on a flight for Maryland. Mrs. Murtagh had gone to Maryland to participate in a prayer vigil for Father Lusenkas, who was being arraigned with a group of other people for having destroyed Selective Service records. By the time Eileen Murtagh had received the news of her husband's accident and was able to return to New York, Mr. Murtagh was dead.

I'd been at Art's Diner for breakfast, eating a short stack of pancakes, when this man at the end of the counter who always read aloud pieces of news to Art while Art worked the grill read the piece about Mr. Murtagh's death. According to the paper, Mr. Murtagh had gotten a flat tire, and when he stepped from his car to change it he was struck by a passing motorist.

No matter how I tried, nothing changed the fact. I first refused to believe my ears, and then, having read the news myself, I refused also to believe my eyes. But even when I knew it had happened, I didn't know what it meant that it had happened, other than it meant that he was gone.

I crept along through the day like a man who wishes to slough off reality but continually grows new layers of skin, finding that the skin he grows is, strangely, both highly sensitive and hopelessly numbed. Images of the living Ed Murtagh raced through my mind; his voice echoed in my head. *Hello, boys. Bag any game?*

If I'd known Ed Murtagh better, I suppose I would have wept a bit, which no doubt would have helped. But I'd not known him that closely, and so his passing, rather than filling me with grief and sorrow, left me keenly aware of the thin thread by which we hang to life. I felt the unfairness of his death—its timing, its manner—and felt how angry I'd be if fate ever dealt with me in the same fashion.

My thoughts and sympathies quickly turned to Eileen Murtagh. I wondered what would be proper to do or say, and I wondered if I even had the strength to speak to her without choking on my words. I felt far more sorrow for her than for Mr. Murtagh. He was gone, after all, and whatever that meant was beyond my comprehension. But Eileen remained, and I knew I would have to say or do something to show her I recognized her pain.

Toward the middle of the day I became so busy at work that I eventually stopped wondering about Mr. Murtagh and grieving for Eileen Murtagh. Yet I had decided to send her a card, and at the end of the day I grabbed a ride with Eddie to a gift shop.

While I looked through the sympathy cards I could feel my stomach turn solid, the way curing cement turns solid and heavy. I could find nothing in the cards that said what I thought should be said. They all sounded the same, and so I plucked one from the rack at random and borrowed a pen from the clerk at the desk to sign the card and fill out the address on the envelope. There was a stamp machine at my elbow, so I bought a stamp and pasted it on the envelope and mailed the card at the corner.

Having mailed the card I walked pensively through the new neighborhoods and then tramped through the construction sites toward the cabin. The men had left for the day, and a feeling of isolation and desertion seemed to have crept up from some burrow to gnaw at the buildings and mark its territory with a heavy sour odor.

There was no longer any need to crawl through the brambles to get to the cabin. When the trees nearby had been taken down they'd fallen on the brambles and flattened them. I scrambled along the dead trees as if crossing a log bridge over a stream, and when I arrived at the cabin I washed myself down from head to toe and put on fresh clothing.

When night arrived I took to the old paths, having found them wide open and beckoning me with the sweet and transient fragrances I customarily associated with spring. They were fragrances leading me into different spaces and times, the continuum of the paths.

I raced back to Big Trees and then to Weed Pond, where I watched the moonless night encircle the water and make of its surface a dark smooth stone. I ran to the old Conklin place and thought I saw Jimmy disappear between the fruit trees. It was spring out there and the peach and cherry blossoms were bursting with nectar.

I ran the path to mass, the early-morning mass at the chapel, and on the way I ran past Ed Murtagh and he waved. But then the sad light in the window stopped me cold and the paths dwindled and were gone. I looked up at the room where I knew Eileen was alone with her great sadness and I sat down and waited, unconvinced that her sorrow would ever pass.

3

We parked the Country Squire beneath the tall pines of—appropriately—the Tall Pines Cottages, and booked a small place for the night. The stream we'd followed up the mountain road rumbled through a narrow cut of granite out back. The air was fresh, despite the musky odor of a skunk on its nightly rounds.

We carried our few belongings inside, where there were two enameled frame beds with linens and blankets and folded comforters. The mattresses were thick and raised high off the floor. Seeing that I wouldn't need my sleeping bag, I took the opportunity to hang it out for an airing, maybe give it a touch of skunk too.

A friendly sort of mustiness pervaded the place, the way your grandmother's house might occasionally be musty, and it seemed that in some strange way this place had been awaiting us.

All I had with me was a change of underwear and socks, my toothbrush, and a number-two Chez Joey hero: capicola, ham, provolone, shredded lettuce and sliced tomato, vinegar and oil with basil and oregano.

The Paymaster, as usual, had his belted leather suitcase, his small tool kit, and a few of those mysterious newspapers that came from the future and the past. He put down his suitcase and asked, "Want to see the birth announcement of your first child?"

"Pink or blue?"

"Blue."

I was tempted but turned down the peek into my future.

"I'll wait."

"Most do."

He hummed a tune and tempted me further. He was feeling a bit devilish. "How about the mother? Like to know that?"

"Only a hint."

"Such as?"

"Have we met?"

"Not quite yet," he said.

"Good. There's something to look forward to."

He opened his suitcase but didn't unpack it quite yet. He went back to the car and then returned with an old steam iron, a Philco radio, and a Kodak Brownie 127 camera, all of which he put on the table in the kitchenette. These were tonight's projects. He'd said he wanted some rest up here in the mountains, and tinkering with wires and bolts and knobs was his rest.

The Rembrandt, filled with fifty-dollar bills, remained in Peggy. The doors, of course, were unlocked. This was part of the trust demanded by the continuum, as he'd first told me back in that diner in DIXON, wherever and whenever that had been.

"Before something new and unexpected can happen," he'd told me one other day, "you have to believe that it *can* happen. That's faith, and you don't get faith without trust."

"I wish I could be sure," I'd said.

"Hey," he said, grinning wryly. "Trust me."

I unwrapped the butcher paper from my Chez Joey and started to eat. I asked the Paymaster if he'd care for a piece. "Good stuff, this capicola," I assured him.

He declined. He sat at the small kitchen table and cracked open his copy of *The Way Things Work,* Volume II. He bent his head over the book and mumbled about the Brownie camera.

The overhead bulb was missing from the socket that dropped from the ceiling by twisted wires and a brass chain. The Paymaster instead used a small table lamp to see his work.

There was old easy chair in the corner, the fabric on the arms worn and shiny, darkened by the oil of many hands. Alongside the chair stood an ashtray, one of those that had a knob for opening a trap door to dump the ashes into the bowl below.

The wooden kitchen table had two mismatched chairs that were held together at strategic joints by twisted coat hangers and angle braces. On the walls were a framed (without glass) photograph of a politician, circa 1920, making a speech before a big microphone, and a notice, tacked to the opposite wall, announcing a Grange meeting.

In the far corner stood the real treasure of the place. A large radio that stood on its own, with Bakelite knobs and a circular dial the size of a saucer. It took forever to warm up when I turned it on, but once it had done so the music emerged clearly. Big Band Night. Tommy Dorsey and Glenn Miller and Duke Ellington and all the rest of those WWII jitterbug people.

By chance there was a can of beer in the Kelvinator. I took it and popped it open and poured some into a glass for the Paymaster.

"Pilsner," I told him.

"Ah—mead."

I returned to the bed and sat up, eating the remains of my Chez Joey and washing it down with the beer.

"Hold it right there," said the Paymaster.

He was pointing the Brownie 127 in my direction. He pressed the shutter. The camera clicked but there was no flash.

"Hmmm . . ." he wondered aloud. "I thought I had this one ready for market."

In the next moment, *flash!*—the bulb went nova.

"Back to the drawing board," he chuckled.

A while later I realized I was drifting into sleep. The music had grown fuzzy and distant. I heard the Paymaster say, " 'Night."

" 'Night."

He shuffled into the bathroom, saying, "My lease on that beer is up."

I laughed. Same old jokes.

I didn't recall that he returned from the bathroom. I was dreaming. Dreams come softly to me. I dreamed wings and lovely young women, the cabin and Jimmy and things that crush us. I dreamed finding this scrapbook that was filled with photos of me and Jimmy, Corney, Woodsie and Harry, Sperm, Spyros and Jimpie.

I slept a wondering sleep. I slept deeply and sweetly, drooling all over the pillowcase. I dreamt I saw myself, some years younger, climbing out my bedroom window onto the backporch roof, late at night in the spring when the buds were just out and not all the snow was melted and so the air was chilled. Jimmy had tossed pebbles at the window and I wanted to find him. I dropped lightly to the ground alongside the wisteria. Champ barked. I hushed him and looked for Jimmy. I padded along cautiously, terribly alone, deeper and deeper into the woods. I called Jimmy's name but he was silent and wore garments of darkness.

I awoke once and I saw the Paymaster at the kitchen table. His shirtsleeves were rolled up and he held a soldering iron in his hand. The sharp odor of vaporized tin and lead twitched in my nostrils. I heard the flux go *pffft* as he manipulated the soldering iron and set about fixing or readjusting whatever it was he'd arrived here to correct.

He turned to me and said, "It's been a rough time for you, Sport. The cabin and all. The old buddies grown. I've got one last trick up my sleeve before I retire for a while. Maybe it'll work, maybe it won't." He flexed and unflexed his hand, the one with the missing joint at the index finger, saying, "The old legerdemain's come down with a bit of arthritis. Even the Paymaster has his day, it seems."

I didn't like the tone of goodbye that had crept into his voice, but I'd learned how to take a deep sigh and accept the passing of friendships and times whose time had come.

"I'll miss you," I told him.

"Yeah, Sport. Me too."

4

During the night there had been a thunder-and-lightning storm unlike any other I could remember. A bolt of lightning had torn the earth from beneath my feet; the heat singed my nose hairs and temporarily blinded my good eye. It had nearly melted the glass eye into a clinker of abstract sculpture—the bolt had been that close.

Later, when morning arrived, the ground shook again. I could feel it beneath me, the earth rising and falling, thrusts like a woman's hips, but not quite so accommodating. This was a more purposeful shaking. The earth insisted on handling me roughly. Given the opportunity, it would fling me off into deepest space.

A muffled explosion followed this rude treatment. The bones of my spine closed like an accordion. I sat up abruptly, opened my eyes—if you will.

The men were using dynamite to clear outcroppings of rock. I'd seen them at it just a few days ago. They had stopped for a while. Now they were at it again. They drilled into the formation with long carbide-steel bits and then set the charge with just enough dynamite to fracture the rock but not blow it to bits. They followed with their machines and iron bars, their muscle and sinew, hefting heavy chains, splitting the rock and dragging off the pieces.

Well, that might change the face of the earth, but it wouldn't hide the paths. The paths rested on far more than geology. The earth was a mere three or five billion years old. The paths and the continuum were eternal.

The morning hung gray overhead. The storm had abated only temporarily; it lay in waiting. The small raindrops swirled like a wet fog, lost and directionless droplets of last night's monster thunderstorm.

For hours the lightning had illuminated the woods in wild random flashes. The rain fell hard and ran on the ground under the bottom logs of the cabin. There had been a blinding light, a fierce crash. I heard a tremendous splintering and suddenly everything seemed ozone and electric, like the interior of a large overtaxed magneto.

Now another charge of dynamite was detonated. The ground shuddered once again. My stomach rolled uneasily.

There was a missing piece of information about the previous night, a vital element left unaccounted for. I might as well have awoke with a misplaced limb or inside someone else's identity. What was it?

I found myself wondering where I should be. Was it early or late?

Was this really morning, or perhaps gray and dismal afternoon? Should I be at school? At work? In the army? With Dietz? With Corney?

The rain had arrived the night before in one sudden downpour, dropping straight from the sky as though from a precipice. Later came the wild gusts of wind and the cracking bolts of lightning, whipping and twisting in the sky like torn and frayed power cables. The thunder wobbled the large plate-glass windows in the office at Pete's and finally one of them cracked, top to bottom. Then the power went out and the gas station was dark.

I closed the place a half hour early and left in the driving rain. I was soaking wet in an instant.

Out on the main road the cars crept along blindly, their headlights blurred by the thick sheets of rain. I stuck out my thumb for a ride and the first car that crawled past stopped for me.

"What the hell are you doin' out there?" asked the man.

"Swimming," I told him.

He smiled briefly.

"Man alive," he said. "You're soaked to the skin."

He was correct; my work clothes were stuck to my skin. The water dripped from my long hair and I was getting his seat wet. He didn't seem to mind, or was so intent on finding the road ahead that he didn't notice. He hunched over his steering wheel and peered into the shifting gray wall of water. Finally he stopped along the shoulder of the road, saying, "I can't see a thing."

I sat there for a moment while he fiddled with the radio dial to try to get a weather report, which I found more than a trifle ridiculous. Knowing I'd be called upon to make small talk with him, now that we were stuck, I simply said, "Thanks," and left.

The rain came at me horizontally and pelted my face so hard it actually stung. The wind was unruly and strong, flapping the edges of my wet clothing like a flag in a gale. The lightning sizzled across the sky; the thunder rumbled over me like a passing locomotive.

It was wonderful.

The more fierce the storm grew, the more I loved it. I turned my face into the rain and wind until the drops hurt too much to bear or the wind clasped my mouth and nose and tried to suffocate me. Then I turned away, gathered my senses, and faced the wind and rain once again. I laughed gleefully, crazily, like a man made drunk by adversity. I bellowed, "Is this the best you can do? Come on—kick my ass. *Kick my ass."*

I slogged along and eventually came upon a small piece of the old marsh, where only the tallest reeds and cattails were above the water level. The cabin, I felt certain, would be lifted on the waters, and I would soon see it float past.

At the intersection where the five roads had formerly come together, that junction where Al Deppe's and the miniature golf course had stood, the traffic was snarled. A truck had careened off the road, striking a utility pole. The pole had snapped like an overburdened tree trunk, crashing down onto the road. There were live wires dancing and hissing on the wet surface. The traffic lights and the streetlight were extinguished. A row of headlights stretched in one direction; red taillights gradually faded in the other. At the center of the intersection, illuminated by the pulsing emergency lights of the power-company trucks, stood a man in a yellow slicker, directing traffic. He looked to me like a cod fisherman on the deck of a boat in a fierce nor'easter.

I walked through the intersection like a man from another era who was wholly unconcerned with the failing mechanisms of this time. It appeared to me that the entire world was busting at the seams. There were leaks and cracks; there were short circuits and confusion.

I suddenly realized that this was no ordinary storm. It wasn't, really, a storm at all. It was the Iron Triangle come to meet the cabin; it was the jungle of the Dragon Valley entwined by the paths. It was Dietz trying to get home.

I hurried through the rain, my booted feet splashing the deep puddles. The runoff was wide and strong, flooding the road like a burst hydrant. I hurried along the middle of the road, continuing past those places where I could have slipped onto the paths. I'd temporarily fooled myself into believing I'd make better time on the road. But then I realized that only the paths had power tonight. There was a special and rare energy there. The Paymaster's parting gift.

The houses were without power. Bereft of light, the inhabitants lighted candles. My feet slipping on the wet grass and slickened clay, I ducked between the houses and bestowed a blessing on those houses where candles were lit. Then I felt myself momentarily loom large and powerful. I picked up the houses and the bulldozers and highways and tossed them like talismans.

Along the construction roads I sank ankle-deep into the mud. My boots were nearly sucked off my feet, and more than once I had to get down on my knees to yank loose my foot. The flashes of lightning illuminated the darkness only briefly before they were themselves doused by the rain. Then the wind flailed and another streak of lightning raced along the ground like silent white fire.

Suddenly, it stopped. Like a runner who unexpectedly reached exhaustion, the storm was suddenly becalmed. A raindrop or two fell, squeezed from the gray; the wind dissipated in small puffs and curls. The lightning had been neutralized; the thunder made mute. The ground was still wet and the air was very warm. The rainwater began to evaporate as thickly as it had fallen. The houses around me faded like poor photocopies, leaving only the pinpoint lights of candles. The woods began to grow, thickly, and with a new character. It was the path through the Dragon Valley! I was sure of it!

A stray bolt of lightning crashed from the sky into the earth, cracking wide the path and leaving the earth smoking. In its flash I spied Dietz. He was running for his life through the steamy thickness.

I gave chase through the darkness, unsure if I should call out his name. It seemed the storm had started as quickly and mysteriously as it had abated. Lightning bolts showered from the sky; thunder shook the ground.

But then I realized that it wasn't lightning and thunder, but flares of some sort and mortar shells, tongues of napalm burning through the jungle, claymore mines detonating, the sharp staccato of automatic weapons. There was fear here and no forgiveness. There was life or death.

In the fleeting light of the charged electric air, I saw Dietz again. More rapid than the blink of an eye he was there and gone. But in that strobic moment he was eerily frozen, vulnerable to minute examination, and I could see that his face was tired and worn, his youth permanently camouflaged by the strain of survival. He carried his M-16 at the ready. He was prepared to stop the heart of the enemy before it beat even one more beat, and he was prepared to do it again and again, through war after war, until the heart of the world and men no longer beat and all our blood soaked the earth.

He was tired but he was still sharp; sharp as they come. He was quick and sharp and strong, though no longer holy. The war burst around him and all inside him, a pestilence and a parasite, a firestorm Apocalypse and the inherited disease of the ages of man.

He fought relentlessly. He fought war and he fought the enemy. He fought to survive and he fought to die. I could see this and much more in that brief and solitary flash of light, that focused strobic frame: he was no longer holy, yet his very breathing had become the most meaningful of prayers. He was strong; he was sharp; he was brave, and, I believed, still agile enough to sidestep mortality.

I raced along and the war had fled. I came upon the playground: Dietz taking a jump shot, a graceful form against the waning autumn light; then Dietz on the altar in his altar-boy garb—red for passion and blood; Dietz, stalwart, Rico's gun to his head; Dietz with the dragon-eye knife, cutting the living heart from the rabbit and slicing it for us to eat as we swore the blood-brother oath: never, ever, to give up on the other guy. Never.

I followed him in the scattered and blurred light of the candles of the houses without power, in the lonely framed light of Mrs. Murtagh's grief, in the phosphorescent flares of war and the strange friction of electric blasts from the sky. I didn't know where in all of this I might find the cabin. I didn't know if I could lead Dietz there and keep him until dawn. And I doubted I could survive out here—unarmed, naive, trusting.

5

Eileen—Mrs. Murtagh—sat in her station wagon at the far end of the blacktop. She had her children with her. She'd come in for gas, and when I waited on her I saw how sad and tired she looked. There were dark circles beneath her eyes and her voice sounded weary. The kids were quiet, more quiet than kids are supposed to be. While I stood there pumping gas, looking through the side window into the sad and quiet car, I thought I'd cry.

I didn't know what to say to her but I knew I should say something. I'd said hello, of course, and asked how much gas she wanted, but I'd not said anything about Mr. Murtagh's death, and I knew I had to do that.

She'd asked for five dollars' worth of gas and given me the exact amount, so there was no time left to run inside and make change and screw up my courage. I had to speak up then and there.

"I'm sorry about Mr. Murtagh," I said.

She smiled weakly and then said, "Thank you, Andrew."

"I liked him," I added.

"He liked you boys too," she said.

I wanted to say goodbye and walk away but I couldn't move from the spot where I stood. I glanced at the two kids, the older boy and his small sister. The boy was coloring with crayons in a coloring book; the girl was just sitting there alongside her mother.

"I used to think I'd like to grow up to be like him," I said. "I mean, you were a nice family and all."

I suddenly thought that it had been a stupid thing to say, to remind her of how things had been.

She said nothing. She swallowed and tears welled in her eyes. She barely managed to say "Thank you" before the words were choked. She put the car in gear and drove away from the pump.

It wasn't until I'd pumped gas into a few garbage trucks and returned to the office that I noticed she had driven no farther than the end of the blacktop.

"What'd you do, Summerhelp?" asked Pete, noticing the car. "Screw up the change?"

"No."

"Where's her priest friend? Still in jail?"

"I think so," I said.

"Can you imagine her husband getting killed like that?" Pete mused. He seemed to have some sympathy for the situation, but then he smacked his lips and added, "Imagine kicking off and leaving something that sweet behind." He snickered lecherously. "If that damn priest was smart he'd make bail. He's got it all to himself now."

"How the hell can you talk like that?"

"Shit, Summerhelp, take it easy. You and that friggin' thin skin of yours."

I hustled out of the office, running to Mrs. Murtagh's car. She was sitting behind the wheel, crying, wiping her eyes with a tissue. Her little girl was curled into her. She was crying too. The boy was lying facedown across the backseat, talking to himself.

"Can I do something?" I asked.

She took a deep breath and smiled weakly. "No. Thank you, Andrew. I'll be all right." She bit her lower lip; her chin quivered and she looked away through the windshield. "Thank you," she repeated, and I somehow knew that she was thanking me for having said what I had about her and Mr. Murtagh having such a nice family. Maybe she really meant it, or maybe she'd said it so I wouldn't think it had been a stupid remark after all. Either way, it was thoughtful.

Pete was bellowing for me. The cars were backed up at the pumps.

"If I can help with anything," I said, "I'm here almost every day. I could come over and do yard work."

She touched my hand and nodded.

When I returned to the pumps I was too busy to notice that Mrs. Murtagh still hadn't left. It wasn't until I was standing at the cash register, making change, that I finally realized she was still sitting there in her car.

Pete stood behind me, breathing down my neck because I was taking too long at the register. I was trying to figure out why Mrs. Murtagh hadn't left, and I was also trying to hide from Pete the fact that I was breaking his cardinal rule and making change for more than one customer at a time.

"C'mon, Summerhelp. What's the hangup here?"

"Give me a second, Pete, okay?"

"In case you ain't noticed, Summerhelp, there's cars and trucks out there waiting. You want to guess what they're waiting for?"

"Gas, Pete. They're waiting for gas. If you'd quit interrupting me—"

"A thousand fuckin' pardons. And it ain't just gas they're here for. They're here to make me rich—and you're slowing down the process."

I held a ten-dollar bill in my hand above the open drawer of the cash register. I'd already put a twenty on the sill above the drawer. Pete was scrutinizing my moves. He was suspicious now.

Two more cars pulled in across the bell hose and the bell

clanged—*clang-clang! clang-clang!* From the shop there erupted the banging ring of a pneumatic wrench in action.

I was trying to put one past Pete, which now that he stood looking over my shoulder would be next to impossible. He was up on his tiptoes, looking down over my shoulder into the money drawer. His skin had become horned scale and his fuming breath hot acid.

"What the fuck are you doing there, Summerhelp?"

Clang-clang! Clang-clang!

Just about every car and truck in the western world had crowded in now, eager to make Pete a billionaire. I stood stock still at the register. I knew Pete had caught me making change for a ten and a twenty at the same time, and now, having been unable to get Mrs. Murtagh off my mind, I suddenly couldn't recall which customer had given me the ten and which one had given me the twenty.

"Where the fuck's Summerhelp?" demanded tall George. "I got to bleed these brakes. Where's that kid?"

Pete poked me in the back.

"What's your problem? Make change for that ten and get out there and pump gas. Let's go."

It was bad enough that I was standing there breaking Pete's cardinal rule, but there would be hell to pay if, besides, I short-changed a customer. I knew I would have been able to do this—make change for two customers at once—because I wasn't an idiot and in the past I'd made change for as many as three customers at once, but that damned pneumatic drill and the clanging bell and tall George wanting me to help bleed brakes, Frank looking over my shoulder, and Eileen Murtagh still sitting there in her car, probably crying—with all of that going on I couldn't handle this elementary transaction. I was confused, unable to remember if the lady in the Chevy had given me a twenty and the man in the blue sedan a ten, or if it was the other way around.

Now, finally, Pete had caught me.

"Jesus Christ, Summerhelp! What's the sense of trying to tell you a thing! You don't listen, do you?"

"I listen—"

"Yeah, and the queen's got herself a pair of hairy balls."

He took a step into the shop and called for Eddie to pump gas. As Eddie went past, Pete turned back to me, saying, "Me and Summerhelp are having ourselves here what the frogs call a tet-to-tet."

He stood akimbo, his one hand grasping a sheaf of money. "Ain't I told you never to ring up two sales at once? Ain't I told you a million times that you'll end up giving someone the wrong change or go home with money in your top pocket?"

"Listen, Pete, if you were allowed to *think* around here, without all this noise. I mean, this is a noisy place, Pete."

"It's a fuckin' service station. We fix cars, if you recall. Maybe it's makin' you deaf. Maybe you oughta be working in some real quiet place. Like underwater."

"All I'm saying is that if you'd just back off my ass once in a while—"

"Back off? You listen to me. You make change for one customer at a time, or hit the sidewalk."

"It doesn't make sense to run back and forth."

"Don't you tell me what makes sense. I'll decide what makes sense for both of us."

I had change for five dollars' worth of gas from a ten in one hand, and change for five dollars' worth from a twenty in the other hand. Who got what?

I wasn't going to allow Pete to turn me on the spit. My head ached besides. I fumbled with the money in my hands and managed to pop out my eye. Pete said, "Ugh—cut that shit."

I covered the socket with my pirate patch.

"Don't expect sympathy because of that. I felt bad for you once— it won't happen again."

"I got customers," I said, leaving.

Pete followed hard on my heels. There was no way out of this jam. I couldn't be sure that one of these customers was more honest than the other, so I couldn't come out and ask either if they'd given me a ten or a twenty.

I could hear Pete behind me, stalking like a bad dream. It had not been a good day; it was getting worse.

I formulated a strategy for dealing with this problem. The woman in the Chevy came here regularly for gas. She chitchatted with Pete from time to time and allowed herself to be suckered into Pete's "sales." I'd be foolish to shortchange her. On the other hand, the man in the blue sedan was a stranger. I'd never seen him here before today. He was a tradesman on the road and he'd probably never again stop for gas, whether I shortchanged him or not. And he had a poker face. He'd be able to lie successfully if I asked him if he'd given me a ten or a twenty. So there was no sense asking him if he'd given me a ten or a twenty, and since he wasn't a regular customer it wouldn't hurt the business too badly to shortchange him.

That was the solution, all right. Pragmatism over fairness. A good slogan for the oil-company flag.

I gave the woman the change for the twenty, carefully watching her face. But she saw Pete behind me and wanted to say something to him and so she blindly grabbed the money and stuffed it into her pocketbook. Meanwhile Pete took a moment to tip his cap and start small talk with her, polish the chrome trim, make a sale.

"Excuse the boy for his slowness," he told her. "He's new at this."

On my way to give the man in the blue sedan his change I feared I'd made the wrong decision. I don't know how it came to me, but as I looked back and watched the Chevy pull away from the pumps I knew I'd made a mistake.

Now I'd have to shortchange this man and lie to his face. Shit.

The only way out would be to reach into my own meager store of cash and give the man the money he had coming. But even if I had the ten bucks I would be unwilling to do that. Had I known that this man in the blue sedan was no ordinary customer, I'd no doubt have acted differently.

"There you go, sir," I said brightly, handing him the five. "Thank you and come back soon."

The sun was up behind my shoulder and thus the man was obliged to squint as he looked at me.

"Isn't there a mistake?" he asked.

"A mistake?"

He chuckled, annoyed. He glanced back at the gas pump and said, "I know I didn't get fifteen dollars' worth of gasoline. This car wouldn't take fifteen dollars' worth of gas unless there was a hole in the tank."

I shrugged and said weakly, "Well—"

"Or else you're pulling a fast one, young man."

I swallowed. I wished I had ten dollars. I couldn't go ask Pete, either. There would be hell to pay. I'd just have to lie, that's all.

"No, sir—"

He held up the five and said, "I gave you a twenty, right? I got five dollars' worth of gas. You owe me ten dollars."

"No, I don't think so," I said, unsure of my footing in this no-man's-land of deception.

Pete chose this moment to step up and chat with the man. From the corner of my eye I saw Mrs. Murtagh drive across the blacktop and enter the stream of traffic.

"Is everything okay, sir?" asked Pete, polishing the trim.

"No, everything is not okay," said the man sternly. "Are you the proprietor of this business?"

"Proprietor?" asked Pete expansively. "You might say that. Proprietor, chairman of the board, manager, owner, taxpayer."

"Well, then," said the man, "I think we need to have a little discussion."

The man shoved the car into gear and told Pete, "Over there, so we don't interfere with business."

"A man after my own heart," said Pete, who, I could see, was already concerned over the man's tone of authority.

The man drove to a spot beyond the air pump and braked to a stop roughly. The car lurched in response. He jammed the transmission into park and jumped from the car. He was angry, to say the least.

"What the hell did you do to get him so pissed off, Summerhelp?" Pete whispered to me as we walked over. "Did you ask for a blowjob or something?"

"I shortchanged him."

"You *what?*" He looked at me and then at the man, who stood there impatiently awaiting us. "And you admitted it?"

"Not yet," I said lowly.

"How much?"

"Ten dollars."

"Oh—the big time, eh? You can't swipe a dollar. No, that would be beneath a smooth operator like you."

The moment we came to where the man stood he pulled out his wallet and flashed it open like a cop, showing us an ID card. He said, "The Paymaster."

Pete's face fell all the way to China. "Shit," he said. He glared at me and made to reach for my throat. "I don't believe this."

"Your ace jock here shortchanged me ten bucks." Looking at me, the man added, "Up until then you had it made, kid. Look't here."

From the inside pocket of his lightweight suit jacket he withdrew an envelope. Inside were five crisp one-hundred-dollar bills. The man spread them out like a royal flush for us to see.

Pete salivated over the money. He asked me, "Don't it make you sick to your stomach, Summerhelp? For a lousy ten bucks?"

"Let's get something straight," I said. "I wasn't *stealing* anything. I had a ten and a twenty—" I stopped. "Never mind."

I looked from the man to Pete and said, "This guy's full of shit anyway. He's not the Paymaster."

"The boy's been out in the sun too long again," Pete said. "It's the long hair. When his hair gets long and thick it heats his brain and fucks him up."

"Listen, son," said the man, holding the money at eye level. "I'm the Paymaster."

"If you're the Paymaster, we'll all know you next time you come in, right? We'll all do what we're supposed to do. It doesn't make sense."

The man shook his head and looked at Pete. Pete also shook his head. They were lording their experience and so-called wisdom over me.

"Wake up," said Pete. "The oil company's got more Paymasters than Macy's got Santa Clauses. What's with you? Don't you think?"

Pete turned to the man. "Listen, he did everything right except for this little problem of ten bucks, right?"

The man nodded tentatively.

"There's something here you ought to know. Our Summerhelp got whomped in the head some years back and every once in a while he has a bit of a blackout, know what I mean?"

"I didn't have no fuckin' blackout. I screwed it up, that's all."

There was no way out of it. Pete paid the man the ten dollars and the man drove away. Then Pete asked me if it was the woman in the Chevy who had made out on the deal.

"Yes," I said.

"Well, we'll have to get that back on her next brake job."

He was leaving something unsaid. We stood side by side and the wind shifted. The odor of the dump smacked us square in the face. A car pulled in for gas. *Clang! Clang!* I started toward the pumps, but Pete told me, "Wait a minute." He hollered for Eddie and then turned to me and said, "This is it. That stunt was more than I can handle."

"I see," I said.

"You can come back tomorrow to get paid. Minus that ten bucks, of course."

He didn't look at me. He pulled a folded paper towel from his top pocket and ambled over to one of the cars at the pumps. He wiped the door handle and started jabbering with the customer. The eternal salesman, the quintessential conniver. He was right. He had to fire me.

I went back to the compressor room and snatched up my extra boots and the two or three paperback books I had there. Then I left and walked back to the cabin.

6

The summer was disappearing over my shoulder like salt superstitiously tossed to the wind. Jimmy was no closer than an extinct species and the Paymaster was nowhere to be found. The bulldozers encircled the cabin like vultures awaiting death.

I would never have thought there could be all these alternatives, all these choices. The Paymaster had taken great pains to advise me that if he and I weren't careful, proceeding meticulously, "according to Hoyle and all that," we might only make things worse for Dietz. I didn't see how that was possible, but the Paymaster assured me it was so and I took him at his word. He'd already shown me a great deal, and I had no reason not to believe him.

He told me to follow the paths whenever they appeared. He told me that to succeed I would have to see beyond the backyard patios, the freshly seeded lawns, the bulldozed earth and tree stumps, the driveways, the foundation pits, the surveyors' stakes, the utility poles, and the sewer trenches. I had to see the paths, nothing else; see them as they had been and follow them.

I studied the talismans under the light of the fat candle. I waited for night, for darkness or the moon.

The cabin path went from here to the Big Trees path. And from the Big Trees was a path to the auction and two paths back home: one to the

*circle and the playground, the other through Murtagh's yard to the place
where Jimmy would challenge the beast. . . .*

*A path to the golf course, where we went at dawn to caddy—only to
lose our hard-earned money to the colored kids from the Sandy Grounds
in a poker game; the path to Deppe's, a path to Whitaker's backyard pool
for a midnight skinny-dip; a path to Weed Pond; a path—*feather, button, bowstring, talisman of the reigning gods—*a path to Iron Jud's, a
path to the* thuk-lub-dub.

One of these, I reflected. *Just take one of these. They all connect.
Then find Jimmy and bring him home.*

The Silver Star Hero. The Silver Star Hero had been swallowed by
the pathless jungle of the Iron Triangle. I'd last seen him when I'd last
had both eyes. The night of Corney's funeral. Bone-chill night.

There were paths beyond measure. Paths in excess. Supernumer-
ary paths. A path to the baseball field and a path to the cemetery
where the soldiers had buried Corney to the tune of "Taps" on a tape
recorder.

There had to be a path to Dietz and a way to bring him home.
There had to be a path from the schoolyard to Vietnam. A path from
the cabin to that nameless and faceless pit of war. There had to be a
path—how else had they gone?

*Find that one. It has to be there. They followed it to war. Find it,
bring them home, then close it, seal it, disallow it forever.*

—Chun, he would say, what we'll do is hunt our way to church.
We'll take the path, the long way. You know the one. The rabbits are
slow in the morning. We'll bring our bows and hunt. When we get to
the place behind the church where the old spring is, we'll hide the
bows. But you got to know your Latin. Do you know it?

Ad Deum qui laetificat, I began, unsure of the rest.

—*juventutem meam,* Chun. Don't forget.

That's the way tonight. The hunting path to church.

Squatting there on the dirt floor of the cabin, I arranged the pieces
of the spell: the arrow nock, the Impala emblem, the chipmunk pelt
(I'd used it as a bookmark all through high school and it had sat on the
bookcase in my apartment at college), the rabbit's skull. I did it the
way Iron Jud had done it, pattering self-made prayers and drifting into
a trance.

—Rabbit!

Dietz had whispered it and then, up ahead, drawn his bow and let fly an arrow.

—Miss!

I took my green fiberglass bow from where it stood in the corner of the cabin. I grabbed two field-tip arrows and climbed through the open hatch to the second floor, then up and out the triangular opening at the roof. Perched there, I lowered the bow and arrows to the ground and then climbed down, using the logs as ladder rungs.

This was the path. . . .

I left the bow unstrung until I had crawled out beneath the brambles. Then I rose to my feet and looked around. It had worked. The rows of development housing had disappeared. The woods had returned. The hunting path opened wide.

—Chun. Hey, Chun!

There's Jimmy, just up ahead. He was setting the pace once again. *Keep up with him. Just keep up for now. Don't try to catch him. Just keep him in sight.*

—Listen, Chun, over in the brush—

The song of a redwing blackbird, the squeak of a chipmunk . . . a doe breaks from cover, she bounds effortlessly through the woods. Jimmy straightens, draws back the bowstring.

Along the paths I raced. The woods had remained standing here; the bulldozers had never arrived. Yet down another way the houses were crowded like people standing shoulder to shoulder; and there was Woodsie, older, a veteran cop, in the middle of a shootout; a turn at the outcrop of rock beyond Weed Pond and suddenly I'm in Corney's living room and Corney's alive but he's an alcoholic and he beats his wife and goes over to the playground to yell at the guys who curse when they get fouled in basketball, and he tells them boastfully how he killed Vietcong—"Me. Yeah, that's right. I killed them VC"; Deluxe has a son who steals cars and a daughter who walks the streets; Ivers is a hit man for the mob who really enjoys his work.

The Big Trees campsite becomes a parking lot for a convenience store right before my eyes, the blacktop stained by oil from leaking engines, the dumpster overflowing with trash, and there stand these guys with nothing to do (there's no cabin to build, see? no *thuk-lub-dub,* no paths to run)—nothing to do but hang out and act tough. They huddle, laugh maliciously, and then one of them goes inside the store and sets off a smoke bomb while his buddies swipe a few cases of beer.

There was no way to know where a path would lead. It was all a gamble. The choices gave me vertigo. Which future did I make real? What if only Corney or Dietz could live? What if that was one of the unavoidable alternatives?

I would sacrifice Corney then. If I couldn't find a way both to bring Jimmy home and raise Corney from the dead, then I would allow Corney to die. I wanted the future where Dietz came home, alive and in one piece. Yes, it was important that he be in one piece so that we could do things together, like shoot hoops and take canoe trips, build a cabin in the woods in the Adirondacks or out in Oregon, someplace where no one would ever put a development. And if Jimmy became a priest after all (there was a path leading there, rest assured) he would be Father Jim to many people, saying mass, speaking at communion breakfasts, coaching CYO basketball, teaching religion, drilling altar boys in their Latin. A radical priest. A priest who lived for peace and found a way to make it work. There was that path, too. Overgrown, concealed, not for the fainthearted or the lazy, not for the vindictive or greedy, but it was there.

As far as I could figure it all depended on the cabin. The cabin was the way home for Jimmy, perhaps the way to peace for the world.

I ran the paths day and night. I'd discovered that the spell worked whether the moon was full or new; it didn't matter that the sun was up or down, or that all the people in town could see me as I ran past as if in a trance, humming to myself, my ponytail slapping up and down. They heard me call out the names of that dead boy Walsh and the missing hero Dietz. They figured I was on drugs—though that failed to explain how it was that I passed effortlessly through walls and windows on the run and followed unerring routes that no one else could even see. "Leave him alone," the cops said of me. "He'll settle down." But that was not true. I only grew more intense. At the supermarket, seeing me run down an aisle and leap the conveyor belt at the register (—the creek across the path to the golf course—), the shoppers whispered behind their hands, "There he is. They say he's crazy. Too bad. He was such a nice boy." Then, in a flash, I would appear in the hallway of a model home being shown to a couple from Brooklyn, and the agent, unable to use some real-estate double-talk to dismiss my instantaneous presence in the downstairs powder room, would finally mention, "His best friend was that hero in Vietnam. He was killed over there or something."

The cabin was the central ganglion. It pulsed with energy; it was the font of deep knowledge. After all, it was the place we'd all touched, each of the guys, and in the remnants of that touching, that devotion of ours, there dwelled tremendous power. Without the cabin, all was lost.

I sat one night beneath the stars and scratched out my plan in the dirt. I hummed and rocked and consulted the talismans. There was no other way that I could see. The cabin *must* remain. What could be done?

"I need some time," I explained to the foreman the following morning.

He looked at me quizzically. "What for? What are you talking about?"

"I need some time to save the cabin."

The workers had ceased their hammering and sawing to watch. They treated me to the usual catcalls about my hair, my eye patch, the supposed unbalanced state of my mind.

"Hey, kid," said the foreman, "if you want to live in the woods, that's fine by me. But this ain't the place to do it. The days of the woods out here are gone for good. In case no one's told you—this is New fuckin' York."

"Just a little time. Not forever."

"What's the story? You bring girls back here and you stick it to them? Whyn't you take them someplace else, someplace nice? Take them where they ain't goin' to get full of spider bites and ticks."

"It's nothing to do with girls. There's a friend of mine. Jimmy Dietz. He's coming home from Vietnam soon. He's a hero. It's been in all the papers. *Time* magazine, too. Jimmy Dietz."

"Hey, kid, I don't care if Jesus H. Christ is on his way."

I felt frustrated. I felt embarrassed for having pleaded.

"When?" I asked.

The man failed to understand my question. "When? When what?"

I pointed to the bulldozer where it sat idling. The driver had stopped to watch the negotiations. He found it amusing, as did the others.

"When will you be at the cabin?" I asked.

"Tomorrow. Better pack up and leave."

I stood there. The foreman had said his piece. He waved his hands and shouted for the men to get back to work. The hammers and saws jumped to life; the bulldozer lurched forward on mindless steel treads.

Meanwhile I accelerated my exploration of the paths. I hurdled the backyard fences and barbecue grills and plastic pools and doghouses, my muscles in perfect coordination, my breathing smoothly controlled.

As the duplexes succumbed to a vision of Weed Pond, I searched diligently for Dietz. The waters of the pond glinted in the sun, while— Dietz!—*"Hey, Jimmy!"*—stood out there in his pram casting a line for sunnies and perch.

I should have been on shore, starting a small cooking fire for the catch, but I couldn't stop, for if I slowed down at all the pond would fade and the debris of construction would choke the waters.

I realized that someone with a scientific bent would say it all had to do with mathematical manipulations and relativistic physics. The continuum and the paths, that is. Yet I thought differently. I thought that it was what Iron Jud had said, that what you see now is the small part of the world. Much more than that exists, however. The world is everything that can be, at all possible places, all possible moments. The unknown will always outmeasure the known. There were secret paths galore and always would be. Paths for a shaman and a dreamer, paths that others, who never saw them or who needed numbers or equations to believe them, discounted.

I found myself up at dawn one day running the paths to weekday mass, distributing communion to my old friends: the roofer who wore Old Spice, the two old women, the cop, Mr. McGarrity, the pious girl. They wished me luck in my quest for Dietz and clapped me on the back as I whisked past. They said too bad about the sad news. Too bad about Mr. Murtagh.

I ran the paths and the Big Fire swallowed me. Everyone in town had thought that Iron Jud died in the Big Fire. Jimmy and I had raced through the flames all day, watching houses become kindling and trees flare up like torches. Fireballs crisscrossed the air. The thick smoke burned our eyes and throats. Everywhere there was fire, and Jud's dry old shack was devoured in an instant, gone to charcoal and ash like something in a crucible.

We were the first to arrive, Jimmy and me. We'd arrived from the charred, smoking woods that still cast heat upon our faces. (The paths were so obvious, unburned.) We were stopped in our tracks to see the pile of blackened wood which had been Jud's place. We knew immediately the lump which had been Jud, which had been a living man. The sight shivered along my backbone, and I wondered what of the world was real and what was not.

We went close to the burned man and when we felt certain it was Iron Jud we hurried off to tell the police. They finally followed us there but they found nothing. They lectured us about pulling a prank.

I found him years later, in a YMCA in Iowa where I'd retreated while hitchhiking through a blizzard. He had a small room on the second floor and he didn't remember me at all. His talismans were laid out on one of those TV snack trays alongside his chair. He sat there looking out the window at the thinning snow of the end of the blizzard. I returned in the morning to say goodbye. I found him dead, sitting up with open eyes. I told him, "Fool me once, shame on you; fool me twice, shaman me."

Iron Jud's, then, out this way (across the driveway and over the car—like bushwacking, ha!—right through the shrubs without leaving a mark), along the path that would take me to the Conklin place except for the quick turn—there, the way it should be (right through the front door of the house, across the living-room shag carpet: Vietnam on the news, then sitcom, then buy-this and buy-that, and you ought to look like this and you ought to look like that and you ought to laugh like laughter in a can), exhorting myself to pick up the pace—C'mon, Chun, I demanded, lean into that uphill run (bolting through the kitchen of the house, unseen, unheard) if you intend to keep up with Dietz. C'mon, Chun, do it! Keep up with Dietz. There he is. You can catch him. You did it once, remember? When the wasps were on your tail? Never before, never since, but that day you sure did keep up with him.

He was just up ahead now. I raced through the half-built house, down the stairs to the basement, out through the door, around the piles of bulldozed soil and the loads of sand, past the steel box where they locked the dynamite and blasting caps at night, Jimmy just out of reach, his passage marked by bobbing branches, a print in the soft earth, a startled rabbit, the thrumming *thuk-lub-dub*.

Faster, Chun. Faster. Burn for it. Faster.

My muscles ached and my heart thukked. My lungs strained. I ran leaping over the beds of sleeping, snoring, weeping, fucking, talking, TV-watching-by-remote-control people, and out the window and down the newly blacktopped street past Rico-from-Brooklyn who wondered why the hell he wasn't happy out here with his Chevy Impala and his two point three children; he watered a scrawny sapling out front that wouldn't grow, wondering where the fuck all the woods had gone. That's why he'd moved here after all, for the woods.

I took a turn along the path toward the rod and gun club, across the field where Jimmy first fired the shotgun I'd won for him, the field where Jimmy hadn't allowed anyone to step up and show him how to use it, saying aside to me, "You point a shotgun, you don't aim it. It's not a rifle. It's a shotgun," while the men set up a target and every last person at the picnic—all the beer-drinkers and plump women and pretty girls, all the never-to-be-satiated hot-dog eaters, the old VFW men in their caps, the little kids and the greasers with their leather-jacket black-stockinged girls—everyone gathered down at the field to watch this kid ("They said it was a kid who won. Looks almost like a man, though") level the new shotgun—"And you don't squeeze off a round, like you do with a rifle, Chun. You pull the trigger. It's a shotgun, remember that" (no need, I figured, I'll never fire it. I don't like rifles—sorry, shotguns), to watch this strong kid point the shotgun at the target: a big pumpkin on a plank—his form absolutely perfect, like a figure on a trophy, perfect on a summer afternoon before anyone knew that there was a place called Chu Lai and that a person could die horribly there, perfect on that blue-sky day, both Jimmy and I victorious in our separate ways (my ticket had won) as he pointed the shotgun and pulled the trigger: ker-blam! and when fire snorted from the mouth of the barrel, Jimmy absorbed the recoil, and in a flash (quick, like the paths and Peggy with the pedal down) the pumpkin exploded and the orangy pieces shot out in all directions across the blue-sky day, the crowd cheering, while I raced on, watching it over my shoulder, unable to stop, racing—feather, amulet, shotgun shell, chipmunk pelt, Shakespeare and basketball, shreds of Latin—outracing the shards of the exploding pumpkin, the racing form of the ponytail shaman, gathering together the pieces of Dietz.